ARCADIA

Di MORRISSEY

ARCADIA

MACMILLAN
Pan Macmillan Australia

First published 2018 in Macmillan by Pan Macmillan Australia Pty Ltd
1 Market Street, Sydney, New South Wales, Australia, 2000

A catalogue record for this book is available from the National Library of Australia

Typeset in 12.5/16 pt Sabon by Post Pre-press Group
Printed by McPherson's Printing Group
Endpapers designed by Alissa Dinallo

Pictures in endpapers: 'Masked Owl', oil mixed charcoal on paper, by Jahne Meyer.
Images in Prologue and Chapters 2, 4, 6, 8, 10 by Margaret Hope, courtesy of Allport Library and Museum of Fine Arts, Tasmania.
Images in Chapters 1, 3, 5, 7, 9 and Epilogue by Patricia Negus from *The Magical World of Fungi*, courtesy of Cape to Cape Publishing.

The paper in this book is FSC® certified. FSC® promotes environmentally responsible, socially beneficial and economically viable management of the world's forests.

To all environmental warriors, who do their best . . . who stand up, speak up, and do what they can, big and small, to protect the most precious thing in the universe – planet earth.

Acknowledgements

For my grandchildren, Sonoma, Everton, Bodhi and Ulani . . . who bring me joy and inspire me to make our world a better place – for them.

Dearest Boris, loving, loyal and patient. And always there for me.

My beloved children, Dr Gabrielle Hansen and Dr Nicolas Morrissey.

To all the Revitt and Janjic families.

Dear friend Bernadette Foley, thank you for once again doing a brilliant editing job.

The loyal team at Pan Macmillan Australia – Ross Gibb, Tracey Cheetham, all the publishing, printing, and sales teams.

Thanks Brianne Collins for your sharp-eyed copy editing and lovely notes, and to Super Editor Georgia Douglas.

Thank you Ian Robertson AO and Holding Redlich.

In Tasmania . . . old friends Robert Dessaix, Peter Timms, and the many new friends Boris and I made in our travels.

Also ... Assoc/Prof Alastair Richardson, Honorary Associate, School of Biological Sciences, Discipline of Zoology, University of Tasmania and Academic Director, The Bookend Trust.

The staff at the Royal Tasmanian Botanical Gardens.

In the USA – thank you for your help, Dr Reese Halter, passionate environmentalist (*DrReese.com*).

And special thanks to Paul Stamets, inspiring mycologist, author and advocate of bioremediation and medicinal fungi.

In the Manning Valley, thank you Dr John Stockard, DDS OAM.

Prologue

South-east Tasmania, 1993

LOOKING DOWN FROM THE dark green peaks, the specks of colour on the ledge above the stream could have been two small creatures, one blue, one red, inching their way above the rushing water. With careful, deliberate movements they seemed to be heading towards a gaping hole in the cliff face, a burrow, perhaps a cave?

As the sub-zero wind swirled down from the mountains, ruffling treetops, the red speck suddenly staggered, before rolling off the ledge, through the last line of trees towards the narrow river that foamed around rocks as it rushed to the sea.

The blue speck reacted immediately, and, if we were to zoom in on it, we'd find a small girl in a blue raincoat with its hood blowing off her chestnut hair. We'd see her slide down on her bottom, heedless of thorns and branches, and then force her way through the tangle of weeds, roots and long grass along the bank of the wild stream.

The girl in the red raincoat was now slumped among the reeds, dazed and seemingly lifeless, her legs in the icy frothing water and mud oozing around her hair.

'Sally! Sal . . . I'm here . . . get up!' cried the other young girl as she splashed towards the white-faced figure. The force of the river flow was pulling her legs and dragging her into deeper water.

The girl in blue pushed through the murky weeds, stumbling over submerged branches and rocks, shouting, 'I'm coming, Sal . . .'

When she reached the motionless red figure that was sliding further into the current, she grabbed an arm in a tug of war against the flow.

'Sally! Wake up . . . help me.' She tugged and struggled, feeling her feet slip as they sank into the mud. She felt panic loom as she began to sense that she wasn't big enough, strong enough.

The limp figure in red suddenly jerked, slipping out of the other girl's hands, then rolled and gagged as the girl in blue frantically lunged, grabbing at the red raincoat. Coughing, the prone figure lifted her head, and then instinctively began scrabbling and clawing at the reeds.

'Quick, Sally, take my hand.'

Squelching and slipping, half crawling, the spluttering, sodden girl collapsed on the edge of the bank, spitting out muddy water and heaving for breath.

'Sal . . . are you all right? What happened?'

'I don't know. I feel sick.' She spat and coughed again. 'Ugh.'

'You fell off the ledge. You scared me.'

'I didn't mean to fall!'

'Are you hurt?'

Tears rolled down Sally's frightened face as she nodded. 'I want to go home, Jess.'

'C'mon.' Pulling Sally to her feet, all of a sudden Jessica saw not her brave, fearless friend but a small, hurt eight-year-old girl who winced and gasped with pain as she leaned against her.

'Is anything broken?'

'I don't know!' Sally was at the edge of angry tears once more.

'We have to get home, Sal. Come on. I'll double you on my bike.'

'Jess, they won't let us come back to the cave,' Sally mumbled miserably.

'They don't know about the cave. We'll just say we were exploring.'

Arms linked, one leaning against the other, the two girls slowly picked their way back up the bank from the river.

Behind them, the winter mist slid down from the brooding hills, quickly obscuring the dank trees and surging water.

I

Hobart, 1999

SALLY SAT CLOSE TO Jessica in the crowded airport; both girls were swinging their legs and their eyes were downcast.

'I hate this. It's not fair. Why has your dad got to move?' Sally twisted her hair, fiddling with the ends.

'Sal, stop splitting the ends. It's his job, you know that,' Jessica said. 'We'll always be friends. You'll come and visit, and Mum says we'll come back here sometime to see the family. What about me?' she added angrily. 'I have to start over! A new school, no friends. It stinks. I'll never have a best friend there like you. I'm closer to you than anyone. We're better than *sisters*.'

'Yeah, well, at least you have a brother, even if he is only seven. I don't have anyone, except Mum and Dad. We're teenagers, Jess, everyone says it's the hardest time for us, in all our lives, and you're moving away.' Sally's tone was accusing.

'I know, but what can I do? It's horrible. Don't blame me, Sal.'

The two girlhood friends glanced over at the group at a nearby table: Jessica's parents, her brother, Anthony, and Sally's mother, Mollie.

'You promised, remember. To phone me, and write and stuff.'

'Of course. You too.'

'It's worse for me, 'cause I'm stuck here,' Sally said. 'You'll be having adventures, doing new things, at least.'

'Oh, sure. Like I'll be having fun in the big smoke! I miss our farm already.'

'Sydney will be more interesting than here . . . oh, here comes your mum,' Sally said.

'Sorry, girls, it's time to say *au revoir*. Not goodbye. We'll be back at Christmas, I'm sure. And I've spoken to your mum about you coming and staying with us next year for the Olympics, Sal. Won't that be exciting?' Mrs Foster leaned down to kiss Sally, and then she looked at the two of them. 'You girls will always be friends. You've grown up together, and that creates a special bond. Now come over here, both of you, we want to take a photo.'

The girls dutifully stood together, arms around each other's shoulders, smiling rigidly at the camera. Then as the two mothers embraced, and Jessica's father and brother waved goodbye and started to head through the departure gate, the girls hugged each other tightly, tears now spilling down their cheeks. At fourteen, each felt they'd never have such a good friend, ever, ever again. It just wasn't fair.

Sally stood beside her mother as they watched the plane begin to taxi away from the gate.

'I'm going to be so lonely,' Sally said.

'Sal, you have lots of friends,' said her mother. 'Jess will have a much harder time; she doesn't know anyone in Sydney. But no one will be as close as you two. Believe me. C'mon, we have to get home to Dad.'

*

Sally's mother was right. As time passed, the girls remained 'besties' even though they followed different paths and only saw each other every couple of years. They knew their friendship would always be there. Rock solid.

Jessica's mother had been right too: their shared childhood had created a special bond between them, perhaps partly because of the isolation of the small Tasmanian township in which they'd grown up. At the time they hadn't considered their home on the south-east coast of the island state to be out of the ordinary, but looking at it through adult eyes they saw they had been raised in a magical adventureland, with horses to ride, bikes to race through woods and lanes, fruit to pick and dogs to chase, creeks and cliffs to explore, rivers to row and fish, bays to sail, and wild deserted beaches and coves to picnic and sometimes swim.

They'd shared secrets and dangers and dreams. And yet each was as different from the other as could be.

Sally Adamson was a dreamer, with curly blonde hair and grey–blue eyes. She was seemingly the quiet one, but her droll sense of humour was appreciated by the extroverted Jessica, with her dark brown curls, blue eyes, and ready laugh.

Their parents thought of them as chalk and cheese and often laughed about how they were the perfect example of opposites attracting. They had come to regard them as a pair who were only separated by sleeping at home during the school week; they had sleepovers on weekends and camped with one family or the other during the holidays.

So when Jessica's father was transferred to Sydney to take up an appointment at Sydney University, managing one of the science laboratories, it was a huge wrench. But the girls' friendship survived. And flourished. They saw each other as often as they could, and both wrote copious outpourings in letters to the other, as phone calls were considered too expensive for idle gossip during their schooldays.

In their early twenties they went overseas together for a year. And although they'd sworn they'd remain single, free and adventurous for as long as possible, Sally fell head over heels in love and brought home a fiancé – Toby Sandford, a Tasmanian country lad who was backpacking before heading home to help on his parents' farm.

They had so much in common. Sally, who'd grown up on her grandfather's property, Arcadia, in the south-east of the island state, was keen to settle down to a rural life-style. They held their wedding in the gardens of Arcadia, which Sally's mother had inherited, and that was where the couple decided they would live and farm. Jessica was bridesmaid and then returned to Sydney, where she was building her career at the university, following in her father's footsteps.

Not long after Sally's wedding, Jessica was swept off her feet by advertising executive Harden Blake. They moved into a smart apartment in Mosman with glimpses of Sydney Harbour, and eighteen months later they married in a small, trendy ceremony in the garden of an exclusive Bellevue Hill home belonging to a friend of Hardy's.

Toby moved off his parents' farm and he and Sally settled into farm life at Arcadia. They lived for several happy years in a small cottage on the property, but when Sally's father tragically died of a heart attack, and not long afterwards Sally became pregnant, Mollie insisted the young couple take over the big house, and she moved into the cottage.

While Sally was pregnant, she and Mollie went to Sydney to visit Jessica, and Sally said to her friend, 'I'm barefoot, pregnant and happy. We're shopping for baby stuff for the nursery and I'm being spoiled.' She grinned. 'When are you going to have a baby and settle down too?'

'I am settled down!' exclaimed Jessica. 'I'm married, we have good jobs and an amazing apartment. What else could I want? We're not ready for babies yet. Hardy wants the big house, garden, pool and the directorship at the agency first.'

Sally looked at her oldest and best friend. It seemed their lives had become worlds apart. 'But what do *you* want, Jess? I guess you've moved on from rural Tassie but, I don't know, I just thought, well, that we wanted the same things.'

'Of course we do!' Jessica hugged her. 'Nothing has really changed. I'm not ready to be a mum, that's all.'

Sally hugged her back, but she suspected there was more to the story.

Their busy lives absorbed them and their visits with each other were sporadic. Toby, the quiet, calm farmer, and Hardy, the slick, ambitious ad executive, couldn't have been more different, so the girls tended to see each other without their partners. On one trip Sally brought baby Katie to Sydney, and they all had lunch at Jessica's parents' home. Sally told them how she and Toby were developing new products, turning Arcadia's old paddocks and land into a producing farm. Meanwhile Jessica finished her PhD and was stepping up the career ladder, taking on more responsibility managing one of the research labs in the university where she'd studied.

A year or two later, Sally called Jessica via Skype for a catch-up on her birthday and they paused to consider when they'd last seen each other, been together, just the two of them. They were surprised and saddened to discover how long it'd been.

Well, this is life, this is how it goes, Sally thought. Busy, fulfilled, happy, successful enough, but knowing one could always call upon the other.

Then one day, the call came.

'Sal, it's me. I need to see you. I'm coming back home. Just me.'

A myriad of fears and questions leapt to Sally's mind, but she simply answered, 'Of course, Jess. When, where? I'll meet you.'

For the moment every tree was still. The sun was sliding behind the mountain peaks, haloed in spun-gold light. But the beauty of the land around her took second place in her mind as Sally put her phone back in her pocket and thought about her friend.

South-east coast of Tasmania, 1935

Stella Holland lowered her field glasses, which Stephen had bought on a trip to Sydney, as his wedding present to her. She was thrilled with them. They were so much sharper than the old opera glasses she'd been using for years, and were especially made for the outdoors. They hung on a stiff leather strap around her neck, nestling against her paisley silk blouse. Bringing them to her eyes again, she swivelled to focus as she scanned the canopy of the old eucalypt forest.

She studied a thick branch where it joined the solid trunk. In the sinking light, she concentrated on a shape that was visible behind a gently moving curtain of leaves.

She caught her breath. Yes, there it was, the bulky body sheathed in patterned feathers like a padded cape or coat flung movie-star–style over the shoulders, baring its creamy white breast. There was no mistaking the dramatic white-masked face, a kohl-black outline framing the dark eyes and its curved beak as the bird sat motionless, observing the minutiae of the forest floor and the clearing between them.

Her hands remained steady, but she breathed softly to herself, 'White masked owl.' It was the creature she had most wanted to observe. It had taken her a while to identify the screech she'd heard, after trying to mimic it to several other birdwatchers she'd met. It was not the gentle *hoo-hoo* she'd expected from the secretive night owl. When she'd invited the small birdwatching group to visit their woodland, the more experienced leader had pointed out the strange furry regurgitated pellet and white droppings at the base of a tree where the owl had been feeding. Since then, she'd made sure to watch the big old tree. She knew that although masked owls could be found all over the state, it was unusual to see one in the area around Burridge, the closest town to the Hollands' property. They were much more common up in the north of the island.

As if hearing her, the bird lifted its gaze and stared directly at her with an unwavering, fearless, slightly curious expression that caused Stella to pull her face away from the binoculars, half expecting to find the owl directly in front of her.

Stella glanced through the undergrowth to the grassy clearing that bordered the stands of old eucalyptus trees they called the Far Forest. The massive, ancient swamp gums towered above the thick understorey, their buttress roots covered in rough grey bark while the trunks trailed streamers of bark, revealing a faint blush of pale wood like a peeling sunburn. Between their outstretched branches were hidden hollows.

Looking back up at the tree she'd been studying, Stella could discern the faint blurry shape of the owl clinging to one of its branches. She knew she was far too obvious, so she shrank back between the trees, gathering her composure as each waited for the other's next move.

The sun was setting and it felt almost as if the remaining daylight was being sucked from the sky above the trees. Already it was becoming too dim to make out details, however Stella was reluctant to move. She knew she should return to the house as it would be dark by the time she trudged back.

But then came the reward for her patience.

In a swift move, the owl took off from its branch, spearing into the clearing with its magnificent wingspan of bronzed, cream and tawny feathers edged in black. It swooped low to the ground before delicately grabbing its prey, a small rodent, and rising triumphantly above Stella to disappear silently into the treetops.

She quickly lifted her glasses but could see little in the gloaming light. The owl had left to feast on its supper in some private space. And all was still and quiet once more.

Or was it?

Stella kept the glasses pressed to her eyes as a flicker of movement caught her attention. Ah, yes, there was something further along at the edge of the clearing. Two figures, dark shapes in thick jackets, were dragging something. Why would they be trespassing? Were they hunters? What sport could be out here? she wondered. Deer perhaps? A large paddymelon?

At that moment there was a rush and a blur streaked past her field of vision. She dropped her binoculars, lifting her arms to shield her face, and felt a rush of wind from large wings. The owl had swooped so close to her, she'd stumbled a few steps backwards into the foliage. She glanced up and saw the owl sitting in a nearby tree, watching her, its head tilted slightly to one side.

Aware again of movement, she looked back at the clearing where a man, deerstalker hat pulled low, carrying a branch in his hand as a walking stick, passed by her.

She went to step out and greet him, as one did when crossing the path of another walker in the woods, but the young man's rapid stride, downcast eyes and grim expression stilled her, and, at the same time, she realised he was unaware of her presence among the trees.

She glanced up at the owl, which was close enough now to make out its dramatic markings without her field glasses. Its bright eyes blinked as if bored, but as Stella moved, the owl's gaze darted to her, then its head swivelled, body remaining in position as it looked behind and all around from its perch on the leafy branch.

Slowly, Stella reached into the pocket of her woollen skirt and pulled out her notebook with its pencil attached on a cord. Keeping her movements slow and deliberate, she opened the book to a blank page and glanced at the owl, the passer-by now forgotten.

As she swiftly and delicately moved the pencil over the page, glancing from notebook to bird and back again, the owl haughtily ignored her. But she had the sense the bird knew it was being sketched and, by the angle of its head, was posing, giving her its best profile.

A smile hovered at Stella's lips as she traced the pattern of gold and black feathers, the arch of its beak, the bright eyes, its gnarled claws gripping the branch. She worked swiftly, capturing the highlights, the body of her drawing to be filled in later where the feather pattern was perfectly repeated. She closely studied the bird's expression, hoping it wouldn't take flight.

It was now too dim to see well, and the sudden realisation that she was a fair way from home made her close the notebook and slip it into her pocket. Stella smiled at the silhouette of the bird.

'Thank you, beautiful creature.'

She walked across the clearing to where she'd left her bicycle leaning up against a low stone wall below the road. She looked for the track among the trees that would take her to the creek, and then to the fields below the house on the hill – sometimes she rode, other times she hiked directly down from the house.

A light mist drifted through the valley as she walked briskly by the stream and headed up the hill, pushing her bicycle to the dirt road home.

Then she saw the outline of the man she'd glimpsed across the clearing. She recognised his deerstalker hat, rubber waders and the long walking stick as he rapidly made his way towards the old road. Where had he sprung from, she wondered. And where was the other man who'd been with him? Perhaps they'd been fishing in the creek.

She was some distance behind him so he was oblivious to her presence as he disappeared over the rise.

As she settled herself on the bicycle, adjusting her skirt and cramming her beret in place on her head, Stella heard her husband's car approach along the road, giving a large blast on the horn. The new 1935 Buick was the doctor's pride and joy.

She hoped some animal hadn't crossed in the path of her impatient husband. Dr Holland was a busy man with a quick temper and he didn't suffer fools or malingerers. The local townsfolk respected him, however, as he was a skilled medical man and dedicated to helping his patients.

He was often away attending meetings and medical events, so Stella, and Dr Holland himself, were pleased that she kept herself busy with her 'art hobby', as he called it. Her painstakingly delicate paintings of the birds, and sometimes flowers and other wildlife she observed around their home, were considered 'very pretty' by her husband. Had he known the hours and hours she devoted to each one, Dr Stephen Holland might have considered it something of a lavish expenditure of her time. But with the help of Mrs James, the housekeeper, their home was always neat and clean, meals were served on time, and although he rarely ventured into the domestic area to see it, the kitchen, pantry and laundry were always spotless.

It sometimes occurred to Stella that this was not the life she had imagined before meeting the charming and urbane Dr Holland while she was attending art classes at the Hobart Technical College. She had taken a short, basic course in anatomy for artistic purposes rather than medical ones. She and the doctor had been introduced at a small reception at the college, where Dr Holland was a guest lecturer for several nights. He'd been intrigued that she had taken her art so seriously as to take this course.

'If it was good enough for Leonardo da Vinci, I thought it might help me,' she'd said, and smiled.

Then, on a visit to the historic buildings of the Tasmanian Museum and Art Gallery, Stella had felt a light tap on her shoulder. Dr Holland had explained he was there to pass the time on a pleasant Saturday afternoon, so together they wandered through the galleries and exhibitions. He'd then suggested he take her for a cup of tea.

Over the following weeks and months, their paths crossed several times until one day he asked her to join him for lunch.

She'd learned he was a widower and that he hadn't been 'out and about in the world' for quite some time. Her sense of humour made him chuckle and he declared she was the best medicine he knew. He asked if he could see her again.

Their courtship, that of the serious medical man and the pretty young art student, had given her the impression that she was rescuing a mature and mourning man and showing him new ideas and a rather different world. She had shared with Stephen her bubbling enthusiasm, her adventurous spirit and a carefree, happy demeanour and chatter, which had long been absent from his life. There had been many dark years of tiptoeing around a bedridden wife and whispered, painful exchanges, she discovered.

For his part, Stephen had told Stella he found her independence and energy, her passion for art and her great interest in birdwatching somewhat refreshing.

They had seen each other several times when, one day, Stella mentioned that she was planning to go on a sketching trip with another woman artist. Stephen suggested his local township and recommended a good, affordable boarding house, then offered to drive them to the many attractive places where they could sketch and paint in the south-east.

Stella fell in love with the Huon River area, and indeed, eventually, also with Stephen Holland.

After he proposed, Stella had made it clear that her art, while not a career, fulfilled and cheered her and that it would always be a part of her lifestyle. She had assured Stephen that it would not get in the way of her duties in the home. But her husband-to-be had waved a hand airily and told her, 'You are fortunate, my dear girl. The home part is established. You will have little to do to occupy yourself, as Mrs James has it all under control and knows how I like things to be. So, by all means, dabble away in your free time.'

Stella had still had doubts about her decision to marry the doctor, because she'd read enough and heard enough from other women artists about the challenge of keeping up with one's domestic life while also pursuing your art. Although she'd known she wasn't marrying into a life of drudgery, she was more than aware that domestic toil could take a toll on her creativity and weigh on her artistic freedom. She reasoned, however, that if Mrs James and her husband, who was the property's caretaker and farm manager, came with the marriage, plus the ready-made home, she should be grateful, even if she wouldn't have the opportunity to create her personal space with her own stamp on it.

The wedding was small but elegant. The candlelit reception was held at Dr Holland's club, and the magnificent floral arrangements, the expensive table settings, fine food and smartly attired guests indicated that this group was sailing through the Depression in style.

Stella had chosen a wedding dress, made by a well-known Melbourne seamstress, of melting cream satin that flowed around her body like a second skin, discreetly edged with seed pearls and lace on the bodice. From a beaded cap a long veil floated, with tiny flower buds along the border. Her huge bouquet was of white roses, orchids and lily-of-the-valley nestled among trailing ferns and ivy.

Stephen Holland could barely keep his eyes from his dainty and beautiful young wife.

And so Stella moved to Arcadia, Dr Holland's farm, and dwelled in the shell of a previous woman's life, releasing her own taste, flair and fun in the studio Stephen had set aside for her personal use.

On a rare visit to Stella's space, the doctor and Mrs James had noted the chamber pot planted with brilliant nasturtiums on the windowsill; bunches of grasses and twigs and shells and rocks on a ledge; a jug and fruit and dried loaves of bread – rock hard, protected by a coat of lacquer; all amid the drifting odour of turpentine and candle wax.

The doctor had given a tight, indulgent smile and commented, 'Very bohemian, my dear.'

The only time her husband relinquished his formality was in their bedroom, where, on occasion, he was robust, rough almost, in his lovemaking, to which she submitted meekly, being unschooled in the matters of sex.

Once one of the models in her life class had commented, 'The fancier and more proper men seem to be, the raunchier they are with their fine jackets and clobber gone.' And she'd given a raucous laugh and made a rude gesture, causing the other students at their easels to laugh.

Mrs James occasionally gossiped about people in the village and their dire episodes of hardship and tragedy, remarking how lucky Stella was to have a lovely home, no financial worries, and a good husband.

Stella had nodded and agreed that she was a very

fortunate woman. Married life might not have been quite what she'd expected, but she felt lucky indeed.

But now, a couple of years on, the good doctor was settling into middle age and seemed less interested in sharing her passions. Although he rarely spoke about it, Stella was well aware that he hoped she would soon settle down. Perhaps she'd soon have a baby, which would anchor her and focus her attention. But so far, a child had not been conceived. He also found that women had become rather too independent in general in the years since the flapper era, as he would declare to her while he read the newspaper. It wasn't that Hobart had exploded with jazz music and permissive women drinking and smoking. But even in this quiet village women were becoming more adventuresome and taking matters into their own hands more often. While their husbands might have found it admirable, they also felt the ground shifting somewhat beneath their feet.

*

The doctor's car slowed beside her bicycle.

'You're out late, my dear. This is dangerous, you have no lights on your machine. I nearly ran into some fool walking across the road back there. Why are you out in the dark? Shall I wait for you?'

'No, thank you, dear. Go ahead. I've been observing the most beautiful owl, and time got away from me.'

'Well, it's far too dark to see much at all. Please hurry yourself. Mrs James has supper prepared, I take it?'

It was a small admonishment; all good husbands had a right to expect a pleasant wife, a glass of sherry and a light supper to welcome their return at the end of the day. Too frequently of late, Stella knew, Stephen would frown

19

and disappear into his study when he arrived home to find that she was still completely lost in a painting or some project in her studio, unaware that six o'clock had ticked by long ago. The doctor was a man of order and routine. Tidy and meticulous. But, nonetheless, he was always prepared to go forth when needed in the dead of night or at other inconvenient moments, if his medical expertise was required.

Mrs James had left their supper ready to be served. She had Mr James and a brood of her own to look after at home, so she rarely stayed unless the Hollands ate on the dot of six, in which case she would wait and clear the dishes afterwards. The Jameses lived in a cottage on the Hollands' land so it was a short walk through the fields for her.

Stepping into her studio, once a conservatory attached to the kitchen where the first Mrs Holland had stitched and sewed in the good light from the tall windows, Stella took off her jacket and scarf, removed her sturdy shoes and smoothed her silk blouse. She breathed deeply in the tranquillity of her personal retreat.

'Stella . . .? Is that you?'

'Coming, dear, just cleaning up a little.'

As they ate, Stella only half listened while her husband recounted the small triumphs of his day.

Obviously aware that he didn't have her full attention, he paused, took a sip of his claret and asked, 'So, you found a few birds of interest that kept you out late. An owl, you said?'

'Not any owl. The masked owl. Endemic to our island state, I believe. Wonderfully marked and it seemed so . . . smart. We watched each other. I had the feeling he allowed himself to be seen.' She smiled. 'I did a preliminary sketch. I'm hoping to find it again to get more observations of its movements, habits and so on. It's very similar to the barn owl.'

'Hmm. Well, be careful. Owls are night creatures, and I don't want you out in the dark. Especially when there are odd bods wandering around the place like that chap on the road. Surely you must have seen him. Fishing, I assume; it looked like he was carrying a rod.'

'It looked to be a rather large walking stick. I think I saw him earlier as well, with another fellow heading towards the stream. They appeared to be carrying something. Maybe they were planning to camp and fish, or maybe hunt something? I didn't see them well. I just knew it was the same chap on the road by his hat. And that very solid branch he was using to walk with.'

'That's a bit odd. I don't like strangers in our neck of the woods. Fishing people always ask permission. And there's no hunting here, even in these straitened times.' He gave a tight smile. 'Could you not restrain your birding to closer to the garden? Seems to be enough twittering out there for you to observe.'

Stella lowered her gaze to her unfinished soup. 'Perhaps, dear.' She doubted the owl would venture so close to the house. 'Would you care for some cheese now, or by the fire? Edna Browne made it from the Holmeses' cows' milk. It's rather delicious and creamy.'

Dr Holland demurred and soon after retired, so Stella returned to her studio and, by the warm yellow glow of her desk lamp, began to transfer the sketch of the owl from the notebook to the thick art paper at her easel.

It was as if the creature were coming to life as the delicate hues of watercolour paint slid across the surface of the cotton-rag paper. But the intricate details of feathers and the depth and expression in the dark eyes eluded her. She knew she needed to see the owl more closely again. And again.

*

It was two weeks later that Stephen announced he had to go to Hobart for a seminar.

'Would you like to accompany me? Maybe go to the theatre, and you always enjoy the art gallery while I'm occupied at work. Visit the stores . . .?'

Stella shook her head. 'You'll be busy. And we were there not long ago. I am quite happy to be here with Mrs James, but thank you for thinking of me, Stephen.'

He smiled and shrugged. 'Please yourself, my dear. It can be very lonely down here; I just thought you might like to see the bright lights a little more frequently. Of course, we shall be going to the mainland in a month or two. You will be coming to Sydney, I hope?'

'Of course. A week or more, isn't it? I am looking forward to seeing my sister. And, well, the usual things we do.'

'Shopping, teas, visit the zoo and ride on the ferry perhaps?' He smiled. 'We'll plan something together. You choose. And, of course, there will be the Medical Association Dinner.'

Stella tried to look enthusiastic, but she found Stephen's formal Medical Association functions a strain. The other wives were older and seemed to know each other and Stella had little to contribute to their chatter. They were polite and made cursory conversation, but what with the age gap, their differing spheres of interest and the fact that they rarely saw each other, they had little in common.

Stella had her own plans for the Sydney trip, though, including visits to the Mitchell Library, where she would do some research to collect botanical and ornithological information, and to the Art Gallery of New South Wales. She also liked to accompany her sister to quaint tearooms, the cinema and for walks in the Botanic Gardens and around the city foreshores.

While Dr Holland was financially secure, they led a quiet life on their land close to the south-east coast, so Stella did enjoy a change of scene sometimes, and was glad to stock up on the art materials that were hard to come by in their small village.

Now, in the mid-1930s, with the Great Depression forcing everyone to become more resourceful, Stella had embraced self-sufficiency by growing vegetables and keeping hens and bartering eggs for other commodities between neighbours. Indeed, the island state was pulling together and faring better than the mainland, which had led to one local group raising the notion of Tasmania pushing for independence from the rest of Australia.

At occasional get-togethers with his cronies, Stella would hear Stephen comment that Tasmania, with its shared resources, had a good economic future. That economic sensibility extended to his own home. Stephen gave Stella a modest stipend to spend on 'fripperies' for herself or their house and garden. He seemed pleased that, even though she was still a young woman, she had little taste for jewellery, fashionable clothes, or other 'wasteful' expenses. He knew she preferred to spend her money on books and art supplies for her hobby. She had once heard his gentleman friends congratulate Stephen on choosing such a pretty young wife with such moderate demands.

*

Once her husband had left for two days in Hobart, Stella gave Mrs James the days off, assuring her that she was quite capable of fending for herself. 'Besides, I rather like keeping my own hours while Dr Holland is away,' she admitted with a smile.

The first evening, Stella set off before darkness fell, gathering up her Everready pocket light torch, her binoculars (even though it might soon be too dark to use them), a candle and a box of matches just in case, her sketchbook and pencil and one of Stephen's walking sticks, which he used when venturing out on one of his infrequent walks. The doctor walked with a purpose: a barn to inspect, a visit to check on the cows Mr James supervised for them, or to look for noxious weeds or unwanted plants, such as blackberries, encroaching through their hedgerows and the dry-stone walls the original English settlers had built using Ticket of Leave men as labourers.

Stella, however, loved to simply ramble. She walked for the sheer pleasure of fresh air and sunlight, the beauty of her surroundings, and the views from the top of the hill, towards the apple orchards in the adjoining properties in one direction and across the river in the other.

Sometimes she persuaded her husband to drive to the windswept clifftops overlooking the rugged coastline, where sheer cliff faces rose from the churning sea. Between some of the sharply angled cliffs were caves and blowholes. And at their base, on the exposed rocks, washed by waves, the fur seals sunned themselves, dived, played and slept, their sleek brown bodies gleaming in the sunlight.

Stella loved to watch the shrieking seabirds as they angled across the sky before spearing into the sea, sometimes emerging with a silver fish, as well as the shaking glittering spray from the wet bodies of sleek cormorants, and the gliding compact shearwaters with their huge wingspan.

'Just think, Stephen, those birds have flown all the way from the Arctic to here. What a journey for them.'

'Hmm, yes indeed.'

Stella had never imagined she would end up in such a wildly beautiful, if remote setting, where, she presumed, she would spend the rest of her life.

It was damply chilly that evening, so she buttoned her jacket and tied a woollen scarf over her head. Thankfully there was no wind, and still some daylight. She made her way on foot, staying close to the home paddock where there was a stand of English oaks planted by the first white settlers. She walked along the small creek to a gully that was always full of birdsong, then ventured into the Far Forest, where the old eucalyptus trees with deep hollows in their trunks offered the perfect spots for owls to roost.

Several of the Hollands' paddocks had been fenced for cows and cultivation, and the remainder of their property ran into the boundaries of Crown Land, identified on old government maps in some musty council storeroom. The first owners of the farm had experimented with various crops, hops being one of the last efforts, but a glut had seen them give up. These days, Stephen was content to grow feed for their four cows, and he allowed Mrs James and Stella to maintain their kitchen garden with some flowers and vegetables. Running repairs were made courtesy of Mr James. The apple orchard had been let go wild, though Stella sometimes ventured there to pick apples when they were ripe and free of disease. Mrs James then made apple sauce and apple pies for a week or more to exchange with their neighbours. The Depression had taught the locals to gather and share whatever they could.

A new jetty had been built at Fish Head Point, and fishing was becoming a profitable enterprise. Indeed, with the new ice trucks, the fish emptied from nets and crays from the crabpots were packed in ice in the morning, transported to Hobart and sold for supper before the day was out.

Stella paused as she heard the call of a parrot settling for the night. She ventured closer into the forest and put her binoculars to her eyes, scanning the tall eucalypts in the shadowy twilight. She felt a shiver of excitement as she saw the bulk of an owl perched quietly on a branch. In the trunk of the tree she noticed the dark hollow of its nesting place. She couldn't believe her luck at finding one so quickly. She strained forward, studying the large bird. If it wasn't the same owl she'd seen before, it was none-theless a masked owl. Such reticent, rare creatures.

And then, to her amazement, the bird gave a call, a not very musical screech, and a moment later there was an answering call. Whether it was a mate or a courting call, the fact that it had been so swiftly answered meant there was another owl in close proximity.

Stella wished she could discern between the male and female calls, but just knowing they were out there was thrilling. Were they a pair? Were there babies in their roost? Or was this a courtship ritual? Oh, how she wished she could turn on her torch to see them better, but she didn't want to frighten them away.

Her eyes began to adjust to the gloom and she strained to identify the rustlings, mumblings and twitterings she could hear.

Then she saw the owl suddenly crane forward. It remained motionless but she knew its attention was focused on something below.

Stella moved quietly to get a better view, then stopped as she heard the loud snapping of branches and what sounded like heavy footsteps. What animal could be so clumsy, so heedless of where it was plunging? The answer came to her all too quickly.

Suddenly she shrank back, her husband's warnings about going alone to the forest at night ringing in her ears.

'Who's there?' It was a gruff male voice.

Stella froze for a moment. Then she decided to brazen it out.

'Hello! I'm just observing the owls. Did you see them?' She marched out from the trees so as to be seen more clearly.

'Owls? Didn't see any. Is that what you're doing out here? Bit late for a lady to be out alone, isn't it?' The man gave a mean smile. He was possibly the same age as her, although that was where the similarity ended. He was dishevelled and had a shaggy moustache. As he moved towards her, Stella noticed the heavy stick in his hand and recognised the deerstalker hat.

'Are you a birder too?' She could see him more clearly now. She kept her face calm, but her mind was racing. Which would be the best way to run from him? She knew she'd slip on the mossy rocks near the creek, so best to run through the trees, was all she could think.

'I'm not after your birds, lady. I have bigger fish to fry.' He gave a cackle, lifting his stick and shaking it.

'Oh.' Stella turned to run. But from the corner of her eye, she suddenly saw the silent spreading wings and a spearing movement down towards the man. She heard him stumble backwards and shout an expletive as he fell. Stella didn't glance back but darted away through the trees, holding her small satchel and clutching at her scarf.

She found the path and swung around towards the road, gasping for breath, hoping someone would be driving past as she ran towards her home. She wondered fleetingly if she should detour down to the Jameses' cottage, but her house was closer and she could lock the doors.

She did not see a second man appear and help the angry man to his feet.

Panting, she flung open the unlocked kitchen door, slamming it behind her and sliding the bolt across. Catching her breath, she checked the other doors and windows. Should she telephone the Jameses? she wondered. Stephen had agreed to put the telephone line through to their cottage, which Mrs James had thought an unnecessary new-fangled indulgence, but Stella was glad of it now.

All was quiet. Stella turned on the light in her studio, dropped her satchel and reached into the slit pocket of her skirt. Her sketchbook had gone. She must have lost it in her mad dash from the stranger. She glanced out the tall windows that overlooked the garden, windows that had no curtains as she had never had any need to draw them. Stella clicked off the light and hurried from her special place, closing the door and retreating to the sitting room with its heavy drawn drapes. She turned on the lamps.

Then the telephone jangled, making her jump. She glanced at the mantle clock. It was probably her husband, checking in as he always did when he was away.

Lifting the bulky handpiece, she chatted briefly with Stephen, realising from his tone that he was tired. She kept her voice light and said nothing about disobeying his orders not to leave the house of an evening.

The following morning, in the sunlight, her fears of the previous evening evaporated. Perhaps the scruffy fellow was just a tramp, or one of the many poor men who were looking for work and sleeping rough during these hard times?

And when she stepped outside the front door, she was surprised to find her sketchbook resting on the front step. Oh, how nice of Mr James, she thought. He must have found it.

Then she remembered that Mr James was going into town this morning and wasn't due back at Arcadia until midday. Had some neighbour known it was her note-book? She hadn't written her name in it. She bent down and picked it up, glancing across the garden to the front gate. Their neighbours were some distance away and there were few passers-by on the lonely road. Shaking her head in bafflement, she went back inside and got on with her day.

It wasn't until later that morning that she began to sift through the memory of the encounter with the stranger who had seemingly been attacked by the owl. Settled in her studio, Stella had opened the little book to her rough sketches of the owl when a turned-down page caught her attention. Turning to it, she froze in shock.

It was a coarsely drawn sketch, obviously done in haste, but there was no mistaking that it was a drawing of Stella in her skirt and jacket and the scarf over her head, hanging by the neck from the branch of a tree like a broken doll, holding in her hand an owl by its feet. Drips, presumably blood, oozed from the bird's dead body.

Stella dropped the book, gasping. Her hand flew to her mouth in horror.

She turned and ran from the room, almost bumping into Mr James, who was returning from his errands and carrying the mail.

'Mrs H, are you all right? What is it?' he called in alarm as Stella turned and rushed down the hallway.

When he heard Stella gagging behind a closed door, Mr James smiled slightly to himself, recalling his wife's many pregnancies. Perhaps, he thought, there was a baby on the way to this quiet house at last.

2

Hobart, 2018

JESSICA WALKED THROUGH THE doors of the baggage claim area, surrounded by a swirl of colour, noise and movement as people jostled for luggage, trolleys, friends, and relatives. It was all a blur for a moment, until she saw, a little to the left of centre, an island of stillness.

Sally was standing there, smiling, one hand in the pocket of her jeans and the other holding the strap of her shoulder bag. She had that familiar expression of self-contained calm, a somewhat quizzical lift of her lip, as if to say, *So we haven't seen each other for years. It's no big deal.* And it wasn't, Jessica reflected. When you've shared a childhood, you're linked forever by memories, shared adventures, secrets and dreams.

As Jessica walked towards her friend, it was as if she

were suddenly in a silent tunnel: everything around her stopped, like a freeze frame. Then they were hugging in the midst of airport noise, laughter and shouts, and the clanging of the baggage carousel.

'How much stuff have you brought?'

'Not much. No idea, I can't remember!'

'So you're not moving in then?'

'Maybe.'

They shared easy laughter, both talking a mile a minute about nothing important. Silly, simple stuff. They were together again, and that was enough for now. They both sensed the heart-to-heart would come when the time was right.

They threw Jessica's bags in the car and hit the road. But the closer they got to the coast, the quieter Jessica became, and the longer the pauses in their conversation. Sally seemed to understand, and only occasionally made a comment.

'Remember the old jetty at Fish Head Point? Where we used to sail? Whole thing got damaged in a storm and it's been pulled down. A few people rescued some of the timber, though. Some of it's being used for vegie beds the way they use old railway sleepers.'

'I loved your grandad's old boat. The Huon pine clinker. What would that cost now? What happened to it?' said Jessica.

'It's in the boatshed! Dad had it fixed up a bit . . . not long before he died,' Sally said quietly. 'I always feel close to him when I'm sailing her. Those old Huon pine boats are collector's items. There's a wooden boat club at the shed where the jetty used to be; there's just a small landing there now. People store their boats and some fellows build sailboats in the old style.'

32

'We had some fun times in that boat,' mused Jessica.

'Yeah. If only our folks knew what we got up to, eh?' Sally chuckled.

'Hmm.' Jessica was thoughtful. She stared out the window for a bit. 'Can't remember when I was last here . . .'

'We saw you in Sydney three years ago when Katie was one. You said then it had been more than a year since you'd come back home.'

'Home . . .' Jessica said slowly, looking out her window.

Sally glanced at her friend, wincing at her pinched expression. While Jess hadn't said much in their phone calls, Sally knew this was all to do with Jessica's disintegrating marriage.

She remembered the time, about nine years ago, when she had first met Jessica's new boyfriend. She had never really warmed to Harden Blake, but Jessica had seemed so in love that Sally had never been anything but supportive of her choice. After Hardy proposed, Jessica had asked Sally what she thought about him. 'I am doing the right thing, aren't I, Sal?'

Sally hadn't known what to say. Do you rain on your best friend's parade when she's deliriously in love and risk wrecking a friendship, or do you lie brightly that you think he's terrific? Sally had known Jessica would see through her if she'd lied, so instead she had suggested to Jessica that she and Hardy live together a bit longer and delay the legal stuff.

'But I don't want to wait any more. I want to make a commitment. I'm tired of being led on, thinking this or that guy is the one, and then finding out they're cheating, or restless, or don't want to do anything that could smack of permanence. Hardy proposed. I said yes. That's all.'

33

Sally had let it drop, but she had always felt uneasy about the conversation and wondered if she should have handled things differently.

As they drove, Sally decided to plunge in. 'So what's going on, exactly?'

Jessica didn't answer straight away, but finally said, 'I'm divorced. It's over. Done. Been a nightmare.'

So here it was, the event that seemed inevitable in retrospect. The break-up. At least Jess didn't have kids.

'Why didn't you tell me more about this before? From the little you did say, I knew things weren't good, but I could've helped you, Jess.'

'How? Change his personality? Tell me you knew this would happen, that you never liked him?' Jessica's voice softened. 'I knew you'd be here for me when I needed you.'

Sally reached over and touched Jessica's arm. 'Of course. I could tell from your phone calls that you were stressed and maybe even a bit depressed, but I didn't realise how bad it was. I didn't want to make matters worse.'

'I knew you always thought I never should have married him.' Jessica's tone was sad rather than accusing.

Sally sighed. 'Friends also know when to shut up rather than spoil a friendship.' She waited a minute. 'So, what next?'

'No idea. I just knew it was time to get out of that poisonous atmosphere.'

'What brought it all to a head? Another woman?'

'Been several of them, I suspect. One I am sure about. But you turn a blind eye, or do the same thing to pay him back. I never did, though. Only because I didn't find anyone remotely attractive and I knew I'd just whine and blubber on their shoulder if I did.'

'Big turn-off.'

'Yeah. I wasn't ready for another rejection.'

'Do you think it was an age thing, you getting married?' mused Sally. When Jessica didn't answer, she went on. 'Y'know what I mean? Biological clock ticking, you don't want to waste time on guys 'cause you start to realise that they all want the same things and they never really grow up until they do marry and settle down. And here was a guy asking you to marry him, so you grabbed the opportunity.'

'I don't know what I thought.' Jessica sighed.

'I wanted you to be happy more than anything,' said Sally.

Jessica turned to her and smiled. 'Like you and Toby?'

'Yes. And yes, I know you and I lead different lives, but our dreams and hopes used to be so similar. Different in some ways but fundamentally the same.'

Jessica looked away again. 'Yeah. Nice husband, sweet kids, interesting careers, family acceptance.'

Sally's heart ached for Jessica. Eight years of marriage and now this had happened. Separation. Divorce. Although she didn't know the details, Sally could feel the pain and sadness, anger too, radiating from her dearest friend.

'Has this been coming for a while, or did you just wake up one morning and decide to leave?' she asked tentatively.

'Bit of both. I knew we were in trouble, but I pushed it to one side. I could've walked out, but I buried it, ignored it. Hoped things'd get better. Blamed myself.'

'Don't ever do that. It always takes two. Maybe you should have stood up to him. Called him out. Suggested counselling, all that kind of thing.'

'Easy to say. Easier to shut up and just keep on keeping on. I didn't want my parents saying, "We knew this'd happen." Maybe I'd have got round to a decision quicker if you'd been there in person to talk to. I've really missed that.'

'I'm sorry, Jess. I know it's not the same on the phone –' began Sally, but Jessica waved a hand.

'It's okay. It's hard. I'm hurt, he was being a bastard and my work was suffering.' She gave a small smile. 'Now, I wake up in the morning and I'm alone. I had to fight him for a fair share of all our stuff. But you know what? I feel good now that it's over. Calm. Scared, but the black cloud has gone. God knows what I'm going to do with my life, though.'

'You have a great job at the lab. I'm sure the uni will support you taking leave and stuff.'

'Probably. But I quit.'

'What! Jess, you didn't quit your bloody job? That's stupid! Why?' Sally hit the brakes and pulled onto the shoulder. 'What the hell for?'

For the first time, Jessica looked slightly cheerful. She smiled at Sally's shocked face. 'That got you going, hey?'

Sally dropped her head onto the steering wheel. 'God, Jess. Don't say stuff like that, you really shocked me. That's not funny.' She sat up, looked in the wing mirror and pulled back onto the empty road.

'It's true though, Sal, just the same.'

Sally glanced at Jessica's face, calmer now, her shoulders and body seemingly relaxed. 'I don't get it. Have you got money? You're divorced, on your own. Will you be able to manage?'

'I'm not sure. But I needed time out. I needed you, Sal. Us. I want to go back to you and me against the world, babe.'

Sally paused. 'Oh, Jess. You can't go back. We can't be kids again – we have . . . responsibilities . . .'

She broke off and they drove for a while in silence. 'Hey, do you remember when we played hooky one sports day and climbed almost up to the peak through those massive trees? God, some of them might have been a thousand years old . . .'

Jessica nodded. 'Hell, yes. And we found that man with the axe . . .'

'Yes! I don't know who was more shocked and scared . . . him or us! Man, did we start running. Must've been an illegal logger.'

'I remember feeling like I was running underwater, nothing was working properly, and everything was kinda green, and those massive tree buttress roots. You wanted to hide in them.'

'Each one was the size of a room or a hut. I jumped in one and there was a paddymelon sitting there dozing. It bounded off like a crazy thing.' Sally started to laugh. 'You just kept zigzagging, flying like a maniac down the hill through the trees.'

'You were squealing like some crazy creature. Remember the birds taking off in the canopy? We shook that mountain, girl!'

'And then we came to the ledge, the stream . . .'

'And the cave!' they shouted in unison.

Both fell silent for a moment.

'Have you been back there at all?' Jessica asked.

Sally shook her head. 'No way. And I wouldn't want my child exploring up there.'

'We did some mad and fun things, didn't we?' said Jessica quietly.

'Stupid. Crazy, wild. Like a lot of kids, I s'pose.'

'No. No, Sal. We did some *really* crazy things. I miss that.'

'We're s'posed to be grown-ups now,' Sally said, chuckling. 'That's all behind us. I don't know that I want my daughter finding out about some of the silly things we got up to!'

'Why?'

'Why do you think? I don't want Katie sneaking off and doing stupid stuff.'

'No. Not that. Why should it be behind us?' Jessica leaned over and grabbed Sally's arm. 'Why don't we get out there? Have a crazy adventure, live a little, go wild, just the two of us! Like we used to!'

'You're nuts. You've been stuck in a lab in a white coat for too long.'

'Yes, I have! I want to go and see the cave again. See if it's still . . . as special as I remember. I've never told anyone about it, have you?'

Sally shook her head. 'No. No, I haven't. I wonder if anyone else has been there? It wasn't easy to find. Anything could have happened, a rock fall or something. Maybe we can't get in there now, anyway.'

'Well, let's go and have a look. Could you play hooky, Sal, and let Toby run the farm for a day?'

'Of course,' she said quickly, defensively.

'You're not afraid of the cave? After the last time we were there?' Jessica paused. 'Don't tell me you don't remember? Have you blocked it out?' Her voice was light, teasing.

'Oh, you mean the time you saved my life? That mere bagatelle? I'm struggling to recall . . .' Sally frowned, and then they both burst out laughing.

But Jessica's laughter stopped, and she dropped her face in her hands.

Sally reached over and touched her, trying to keep her

eyes on the road ahead. 'Oh, Jess . . . Wait, let me find a place to stop.'

Jessica leaned her head back against the seat, her eyes closed, a tear slipping from beneath her eyelashes.

'Oh, damn, there's never anywhere to pull over when you need to,' muttered Sally, and then noticed an empty farm stall and drove up in front of it. She turned off the engine and reached over to Jessica. 'What is it? You can tell me. Please. C'mon, let's get out.'

Sally put her hazard lights on and by the time she'd hurried around the car, Jessica had tumbled from her seat and was sitting on the verge, her head resting on her knees as she wrapped her arms around her legs.

Sally sat down on the grass beside her. She put her arms around Jessica's shoulders as they shook with muffled sobs, and she waited.

Eventually Jessica drew a long breath and straightened up. 'Sorry. This has nothing to do with you. Us. The cave . . . It's just . . . I'm thirty-three, with no partner, no job, no home. What have I got? I feel like an old knitted jumper that's unravelling.'

'Everyone has unravelling days, when you think even one more small tug will send your whole life spiralling out of control. When you don't think you can hold it together a minute longer, Jess. I do too.'

'You? Don't tell me that. It's difficult enough with my mother being worried and looking wounded because I didn't "confide" in her. Like, what could she have done? And now my perfect friend with the perfect life tells me she unravels too. About what? Tell me about something horrible in your life and make me feel better.'

Sally gave a bit of a smile. 'It's all relative, isn't it? I was glad you seemed to be leading such a stimulating, interesting life, even if it was with the obnoxious Hardy,' she said. 'I sometimes feel I'm trapped in a backwater, albeit a beautiful one, with the perfect family. But something's missing. Look, we don't have to wade through all this right now. Let's get home to Arcadia, enjoy the view, play with Katie and the dog, share war stories, have a glass of our neighbour's vino.' She leaned over and gave Jessica a quick hug. 'I'm so glad you came. It's always been you and me, against the world, babe. Right?'

'Yeah. Right.' But Jessica's response was flat, a rote reply.

As Sally helped her friend to her feet , her heart ached for her.

*

As they cruised through the landscape surrounding Burridge township, where Jessica had spent her childhood, she was struck by the familiar and the memories she'd thought were buried, which now resurfaced. She noted the new additions to the town where, under other circumstances, she would have loved to stop a while, linger and explore. For the moment, she just wanted to curl up in a safe haven and let the world pass her by.

The original 1880s hotel, which she recalled as seedy and faded, had been revamped, no doubt with a trendy website to promote it to the tourists. Along the waterfront were smart cafés, a wine and oyster bar, a maritime museum, and the marketplace, set up for weekend markets of local produce, handicrafts, knick-knacks and antiques, it seemed.

The old cattle yards and apple storage sheds were still there, if, apparently, leading a different life these days. The sheds had become a co-op, and a sign at the yards advertised a coming rodeo.

'Oh, my gosh, even here! Look at that.' She clapped her hand to her forehead in mock shock.

A group of Chinese tourists, selfie sticks angling their phones at their eager smiles, posed before the town's symbolic old apple tree, a relic from and reminder of the town's glory days. An enterprising stall was selling every kind of food made from apples, while baskets of fresh apples were being picked over by the visitors, who were taking more selfies of themselves pretending to bite into real fruit with stalk and leaves attached.

'Yes, Chinese tourists are mad for Tassie. Real food and all that. You see them stopping whenever they see a live animal or fruit on a tree, and they take a zillion selfies. They've never seen food on the hoof, or not wrapped in plastic in a supermarket,' said Sally. 'If they can afford the best meat, milk, produce and fruit at exorbitant prices in Chinese stores, you can bet it comes from here – clean and green and safe. That's us.'

Jessica was looking forward to spending time at Arcadia now that the farm belonged to Sally and Toby. She knew it so well from the days when Sally's parents had run it, mainly as an apple orchard. Sally and Toby had embraced the new gourmet food products that Tasmania was becoming well known for, and were experimenting with boutique crops including truffles and saffron.

'Is that how you label your products? "Clean, green and safe"? Surely you need more exciting brand names? Sun Gold, Dawn Sun Saffron. And for the truffles, Black Gold, White Passion? That sort of thing? They're a valuable and exotic crop, right?'

Sally smiled. 'Sure they are, and rare, and hard to protect from thieves! Marketing them is the easier part. My mother has grand ideas of add-on products like oil and salt and dried truffles, but we have enough trouble just meeting the demand from restaurants and chefs.'

'Is there any competition?'

'It's on the way. We're lucky we had an eight-year head start. It's a contentious subject. There're a lot of food producers doing well all over Tasmania who've moved from the mainland. And it's pushing up prices for the locals. You know, land, property. Talk to Toby, but be warned, he gets a bit riled about it all. Even though it will hopefully benefit us in the long term.'

'I can't imagine Toby "riled".' Jessica managed a smile.

'Oh, he's a calm, gentle sort of soul, I agree. But he's poured a lot into this new enterprise. In fact, there's a TV mob interested in coming to film what we're doing.'

'Gosh, from what I've heard, the island is crawling with film crews and foodie experts,' said Jessica. 'Flavour of the month, eh?'

'Sadly, most of it is due to climate change.' Sally sighed. 'The mainland vignerons have moved here in a big way. Getting too warm in some states to grow cool-climate wines and, by mainland standards, housing, land and businesses are ripe for the picking here. Sleepy ol' Tasmania, wake up, we're being sold off to the highest bidder! And it's not just Aussies . . .'

'Not a lot of other countries let foreigners, especially government-owned corporations, buy your land, water and birthright,' said Jessica bitterly.

'The world's changing, Jess. But not all for the better. It's not like when we grew up. Jeez, I sound like my mother.'

'Aha! But look where we grew up, Sal! Here! How lucky is your Katie? I see kids in the city who have hardly any idea of farming and live animals. A petting zoo, something at school one morning, maybe a community garden on the verge if it's that kind of neighbourhood. But really, for most kids, food comes from a supermarket, end of story.'

'There're a lot of people and groups working to change that, although it's a hard yard to hoe,' said Sally.

'You guys are farmers who get your hands dirty. I was married to someone who wouldn't dream of doing physical work; who wanted to be George Clooney and Roger Federer rolled into one . . . the fancy coffee, the watch that can navigate to the moon, the trendy stubble and Armani suit, all the trappings but none of the talent and certainly none of the social conscience.'

Sally burst out laughing. 'And none of the humour. Hardy-the-try-hard. Honestly, Jess, you're better off out of it.'

'Yeah, well, I'm just pleased the divorce is done. He kept trying to dredge up stuff over the property settlement. He was trying to wear me down.'

'So he could walk off with everything.'

'That's right, but somehow I summoned up the strength to fight for what was mine,' Jessica said. 'And really, the most important thing for me now is that I'm free, Sal.'

Sally glanced at Jessica and could see the pain in her face. 'You're free as a bird! No mortgage, no bonds. A lot of people would envy you, Jess. Clean slate, the world's your oyster.'

Jessica shrugged. 'I don't know about that. But, hey . . . speaking of oysters, there's an oyster bar. Let's stop and have oysters and champagne.'

'Hold on just a bit longer,' Sally laughed. 'Toby has

a bottle chilling, and we mightn't have any oysters, but Mum will want you to try some of her cheese.'

They drove down the road and pulled up at the old wooden gate with a sign announcing *Arcadia* swinging off it. Jessica jumped out and opened the gate for Sally to drive through, then closed it and got back in the car. They headed up to the house, which sat comfortably atop the hill like an elegant old lady, her skirt of roses spread around her. As the car slowed they saw Toby marching through the front garden with Katie on his shoulders, waving excitedly, and Jasper the dog running around his legs.

As they got out of the car, Katie ran towards them, shouting joyfully, 'Aunty Jess, Aunty Jess!'

'Hi, gorgeous girl! Look at you!' Jessica swept up the little girl with her bobbing blonde curls into a bear hug. 'Gosh, you are so grown up. I haven't seen you for ages and ages.' Jessica smiled as Toby leaned over to give her a kiss. She could tell that Toby and Sally had been talking about her to Katie, reminding the girl of the 'aunty' she hadn't seen in years. Jessica gazed around the cottage garden and rose beds she remembered so well. Down the hill was the tangle of dark trees of the Far Forest, which looked as secretive and mysterious as ever. But where there'd been empty fields there were now orderly culti-vated rows of trees and long beds covered with a pale purple haze.

'Goodness, you've done heaps of planting,' said Jessica. 'But so much of the Old Farm still looks the same.'

'We call that area up there where we have most of the crops the New Farm. Come and see what we've done to the house. We have a great new entertaining area,' said Sally.

'And I have a treehouse,' exclaimed Katie, taking Jessica's hand and skipping beside her.

Jessica paused at the front door with its leadlight glass panels. The house presented a formal welcome; had it a thatched roof it would have looked at home in the English countryside. As she reached for the handle the door was flung wide and a beaming Mollie stepped out to embrace her.

'Jess, dearest, how wonderful you're here at last. It's been far too long. Come in, let's sit on the terrace. Tea, coffee? Is it too early for a G & T?'

Arcadia, 1935

Stella sat at her painting table, staring from her window at the grove of trees at the bottom of the hill. She'd put the finished sketch of the masked owl to one side, and she was at a loss as to what to start next. She hated to admit it, but she was still rattled by the horrible drawing in her notebook, which she had put in a bottom drawer of the big desk. Before she'd done so, however, she'd added a sketch of her own.

Carefully, including as much detail as she could recall, Stella had drawn the face of the man who wore the deerstalker hat and carried a staff. As she thought of other details – his clothing, or the scar on the side of his face next to the straggly moustache, she added it, before putting the sketchbook away with a shaking hand.

Maybe she should show it to her husband? Or Mrs James? Someone . . . but something held her back. Stephen would be appalled if she called the police. People such as the Hollands didn't get into situations where the plump old sergeant had to be called and the townsfolk would know and gossip.

She had stayed in her studio all the next day, but on this morning, seeing the sun shining outside, she jumped to her feet and announced to the room, '*Carpe diem*! So here I come.' She picked up her field glasses and camera and called to Mrs James that she was going out for the morning.

'So you're feeling better, Mrs H?'

'Oh, it was nothing. I just felt like a quiet day yesterday,' said Stella.

Mrs James just smiled, thinking about what her husband had told her.

Stella strode across the field with her chin lifted, jauntily swinging her bag, just in case she was being observed. *Look at me – defiant, strong, fearless.* Well, she hoped that was what her demeanour portrayed to any onlooker. If her husband was to be believed, women were not generally considered to be brave. And if she was honest with herself, she *was* still a little spooked; the thought that maybe she was being watched, that someone knew where she lived and had threatened her by drawing her death and that of her little owl saviour, still deeply disturbed her.

Stella had no set agenda, but soon the fresh, crisp air, the clear sky and calm surroundings soothed her. What harm could befall her on such a peaceful morning? It was market day in the village, and Mr and Mrs James were heading off to buy, sell and bargain. Dr Holland had arrived home from his conference but was already doing his rounds, seeing patients.

She took a different track towards the township, which led down to where their stream flowed into the river beside their landing and small boatshed. A few years before they married, Stephen had developed an interest in sailing and had commissioned a compact little sailing dinghy of the

46

lovely local Huon pine, named the *Charlotte-Ann*, after Stephen's mother.

Stella loved the river and its busy activity. With the coastal steamers, the ferry to Solitary Island, the work boats and the barges carrying wood from the sawmill, there was always something to watch. Sometimes she took bread to throw to the seabirds and swans. Occasionally she fished from one of the jetties dotted around the shore-line, accompanied by Mr James. Dr Holland had made it clear that he was not pleased about this unladylike activity, but he had realised his young wife was bored and had asked Mr James to keep an eye on her to make sure she was safe.

Stella enjoyed Blackett James's company, even though he was relatively taciturn. Known as Blackie due to his name and swarthy colouring, he was a gentle soul. She'd been surprised to learn how fond he was of animals, and saw how gently he spoke to them, soothing cows and horses; and the depth of his knowledge about the local birds, as well as the other wildlife and their habitats, was quite remarkable. He was a kindly, considerate man, too. Sometimes, when Mrs James took her fortnightly after-noon off work, Mr James would take Stella and Mrs James for a short sail in the *Charlotte-Ann* around the bay to the channel entrance.

Stella loved the different perspective of the small township as seen from the water. The moored boats bobbed in the swell around the busy government pier, and watercraft came and went from the private jetties in front of the few houses that were scattered around the curve of the bay. Tucked further along was Jarrard's sawmill, beyond which rows and rows of apple orchards stretched into the distance.

Towering above, the hills rose from rainforests with spreading tree ferns and sassafras trees, to the tall, ancient eucalypt forests and, on the other side, the stands of Huon pine.

This was a world of their own, best accessed by water, the road to Hobart being still a challenge for some, but which her husband enjoyed in his motorcar. Here she felt safe and protected.

Stella walked to their landing, pulling her short jacket around her as a fresh breeze blew up.

The sound of hammering came from the slips, and she stopped where a boatman was working on the *Charlotte-Ann*. She watched him for a few moments until he paused and saw her. He gave a short wave of acknowledgement.

'Is there a problem?' she called.

'Not really, ma'am. Just her annual check-up. Clean the hull of growth, touch up the anti-fouling paint. She's in fine fettle. Were you wanting to take her out, ma'am?'

'Oh no, thank you, not at the moment. She is such a lovely little thing, isn't she?' Stella jumped down and picked her way to the slips where the sailing dinghy was resting, tethered by strong ropes.

'She certainly is a nice little rig. She'll be around a long time provided she has some care. The Huon hull will outlive the lot of us,' he said, and chuckled.

'It's beautiful wood. Do you work with the boats? Are you a boatbuilder?'

'I'm from the mill, Mrs Holland. This is a little extra job for the doctor. Mind you, I do some part-time work with the scallops when there's a big season. There's still plenty of work round these parts. Plenty of fine wood. Dr Holland would know all about that.'

'My husband is a medical man, not so much a businessman.' Her husband never discussed business matters with her, or anything about his practice, as he took doctor–patient confidentiality very seriously. Although, when she thought about it, neither did she discuss her art with Stephen.

The man smiled at her. 'Now, I'd best get back to my work and we'll have her shipshape and afloat again in a day or so.'

'Thank you,' Stella murmured, and walked back to the path that wound around the waterfront. To one side were lawns and a picnic area where locals had once sat to watch the sailing races. The ferry race from Hobart had ceased years before, but she'd seen photographs of it in her husband's office.

At the main wharf there was a lot of activity as the steamer readied to pull away with passengers bound for Hobart. She stood and watched while a crewman hauled in the fat ropes and the passengers settled themselves on board, several standing at the railing.

And then she saw him. He was staring towards the mill, where the tramway was piled with logs and planks. His eyes were shaded beneath his hat, but even at that distance she recognised the crumpled coat and scraggly moustache. Slung over his shoulder was a leather bag and he was gripping the handrail. Stella shrank back, even though she doubted he would see her. Did he know her? But then her notebook had been left at her door, so he knew where she lived. Who was he? Standing beside him was a well-dressed man with fair hair. Stella wondered if he could be the other man she'd glimpsed in the forest.

The gap between the steamer and the wharf was widening, and she felt some relief that the vessel was leaving with him aboard. But for how long? Who was this man whom she'd seen hurry away from the creek that evening, and would he return? And why did he presumably wish her dead, which was the only interpretation she could imagine from the ghastly sketch?

Again she thought perhaps she might show the drawing to her husband, but then she thought better of it and decided to mention it to Mr James instead.

*

When Stella looked out and saw Mr James working in the garden close to her studio she took her notebook from the desk drawer and brought it out to him.

Blackie James, though he appeared big and tough, recoiled as he looked at the shocking sketch Stella opened before him, and his face blanched. 'Good God, Mrs H, that's you? Why would anyone draw such a picture? How did you come by this thing?'

As Stella explained what had happened, he shook his head. 'Well, you shouldn't be out alone in the evening. Please, promise me you won't go out at dusk or later. If you want to study them birds, I'll come with you, lass.' He paused, thinking, before continuing, 'And while I'd never encourage a wife to deceive her husband, perhaps in this case some things are better left unsaid.' He raised an eyebrow, studying her face.

'It's all right, Mr James, I won't trouble my husband with this drawing. He would only fret. And Dr Holland has already cautioned me about going out in the evening.' She gave a small smile. 'You have to see the owl, though. He's beautiful. He attacked the fellow, so I ran, and that's when I dropped my sketchbook.'

Mr James looked dubious. 'Take care, Mrs H. I think

this man means you harm. Doing something like this.' He slapped the cover closed. 'That's a threat, that is.'

'Well, he's gone on the Hobart steamer, with a fair-haired man.' She hesitated, frowning. 'He was carrying a large stick when he was in the forest. Like for hiking. There was another man with him when I first saw him. I wonder if that was the fair-haired man I saw today?'

'Hmm. They've been on your property. Don't sound like poachers or fishermen. I just wonder why he'd bother returning your book. He's sending some sort of message. If the doctor is away, be sure to lock the doors. You give the missus or me a call if you're concerned. Anytime. The cottage is a skip and a jump from the big house.'

'You're both too kind.'

'Put it out of your mind, Mrs H. So . . . when are we going out t'see this owl friend of yours?'

*

After dinner that night, Stella sat turning the pages of a magazine as Stephen Holland read his newspaper, puffing on his pipe. He lowered the paper and looked at Stella.

'You're not dabbling in your studio this evening?'

'I will shortly. I thought I'd keep you company while you had your port.'

'I'll put the radio on, shall I? Maybe some nice music?'

As he fiddled with the dial on the radio console, Stella commented, 'I went down to the waterfront for a walk this morning. I saw that the *Charlotte-Ann* is getting a health check.'

'Yes, I asked one of the workmen to clean her up. She's a grand little boat, pays to keep her in good nick. I might take her out when she's done. Haven't been sailing for a bit. Too busy, I'm afraid. All these new poliomyelitis cases are taking up such a lot of time. It's very concerning.'

'Dr Fraser is a good locum, isn't he?'

'Yes, thank goodness. I'm hoping he'll stick around, as he seems to have taken a fancy to one of the girls in town. But at the moment we are both being kept busy. I just hope this terrible illness can be contained before it turns into something bigger and more serious. Ah, there we are.' He found a station broadcasting classical music and sat back down, tapping out his pipe.

Stella flicked through the magazine, but she wasn't really looking at the pictures or articles, nor was she paying attention to the music. Her mind was full of thoughts and images: the masked owl; the strange, almost luminous green light in the old forest; the rich, dank smell of fungi, and the delight she felt at the sudden appearance of the tiny, delicately hued mushrooms and toadstools.

The concert on the radio came to an end and as the audience applauded, Stella put her magazine to one side.

'It's been a long day so I might turn in,' she said. 'Good night, dear. Sleep well.' And she slipped from the room. But instead of turning down the hallway to the bedrooms, she changed her mind and went into her studio.

She was deeply immersed in a drawing when her husband's footsteps paused at the door and he peered in.

'I'm retiring now, Stella. Please finish what you're doing and join me. I have locked up the doors.'

It was a summons. Sighing, she put down her charcoal, resenting what was to come. Did all wives feel like this? If she was honest with herself, she recognised that, while she still loved him, the attraction and sophistication of Dr Stephen Holland had worn off within a year of their marriage, and having never had sex, or 'relations' as Stephen called it, with anyone else, she had nothing to compare her experiences to or with. She wished she had a close female friend she could talk to about such things. Certainly not her mother, and with her sister living in Sydney they rarely had a chance to catch up. She'd come close once to an intimate conversation with Mrs James, who had such a large family, when the housekeeper had once made a passing reference, with a wink and a smile, to Mr James being playful beneath his reserved exterior, 'If you know what I mean, Mrs H.'

Stella had smiled and nodded, but she hadn't really understood, thinking that 'playful' was not the word she'd apply to Stephen's demands in the bedroom.

Sighing, she turned out the light and moved reluctantly down the hallway.

Arcadia, 2018

After a late night chatting and reminiscing with Sally and Toby once she'd read Katie a bedtime story, Jessica woke early and crept quietly out of the house before breakfast. She was finding it difficult being back on home territory, even though none of her relatives had stayed in the area after her family had moved to Sydney. And, even though this wasn't her own farm, which had been sold long ago, this was the place that held her first memories.

Her mother had given Jessica a list of old friends and neighbours to visit, but Jessica wasn't ready for that. For the questions, the curiosity, the family news. Every time some friend or acquaintance kindly asked how she was doing, it felt like pinpricks jabbing at her, as if they were piercing her confidence with their well-meaning concern.

She felt as though her hurt and worries were leaking through the tiny holes.

Sally was exactly the person she needed to be with, as was the quiet and stoic Toby. The ease of being with old friends, where she could be herself, was calming. She loved little Katie, who simply treated this new person in her home as family. Like most four-year-olds, she was already demanding Jessica's attention, wanting to play or snuggle quietly together with a book whenever she got the chance.

Now, in the mornings, Jessica had taken to walking in the Old Farm, where solid oak trees had begun to join together, linked in a shady embrace, sheltering, everyone hoped, the strange tubers and fungi around their roots. It was a moody oasis of shadows and damp soil that encouraged occasional wild truffles – 'black diamonds'.

On the New Farm, stocky little hazel trees inoculated with truffle stock marched over the low hills in orchestrated rows, which made for easy harvesting and care but not the same atmospheric romance of the old woods. On the hilltops the crocus blooms opened their petals to the sunlight in neat rows of purple and gold, like a floral marching band.

The homestead, on the crest of the hill, looked like it had been there forever. Its tall windows on the ground floor overlooked the rose garden and framed a lovely vista of fields and woods and a glimpse of the creek. The cottage close by was surrounded by a glorious English flower garden at the front, and a large kitchen garden at the rear, which Jess knew had been planted by the old housekeeper in Sally's grandparents' time, Mrs James.

Sally had told Jess how much she loved living in her grandmother's and mother's house. She treasured the sense of continuity and belonging. Two of Stella

Holland's delicate paintings still hung on the wall in Stella's old studio. Sally's grandfather's den, with its old framed medical certificates, was largely untouched; walking sticks and everyday items that had been used for three generations were still kept in the kitchen and the delicate Minton china in the dining room, and many old tools and gardening things were still in the shed and the garden nursery. Sally's mother had modernised the house so it was easier to live in and bought some new appliances over the years, but essentially it had remained as Jessica remembered it from her childhood.

When Sally and Toby had moved into the big house and Mollie decamped to the smaller cottage, Sally had added a few touches of her own, including a sheltered entertaining area with a pizza oven, which she called her 'outdoor dining room'. However, she hardly touched the conservatory, Stella's old studio, other than some slight changes to the furniture so that it could be used as a comfortable sitting room. She would escape there whenever she could grab a free half-hour to have time out and read. Mollie explained to Jessica that she was now the business manager of the farm, keeping track of accounts, staff, orders, and the myriad details of an expanding family business.

Within days of being at Arcadia, a place of such happy memories, and in the warmth of a friendship that never changed, Jessica felt the tension melting from her body. For the first time in a long time, she had a sense of tranquillity, and a faint hope that her life would change for the better.

*

With Katie tugging at her, Jessica followed Toby and Sally as they walked slowly across the fields, crouching every few yards to inspect the rows of low purple flowers, petals still furled around their precious hearts. The well-trained Jasper trotted behind.

Jessica squatted beside Toby as he pointed to the little rust-red rocket heads jutting from the centre of each crocus.

'See the stigmas peeping out? As the sun comes out they'll push up and open, and there will be all the powdery stigmas. Three threads to a flower.'

'That's why they're called the "flower of the sun",' said Sally quietly, almost reverentially. 'We harvest every crocus by hand, thousands of them, and process them the same day. Takes thousands of threads to make just a gram of saffron.'

'So their life span is sunrise to sunset?' asked Jessica.

'Not really, only once the stigmas are ripe. We pack them in black glass to protect them from the light and they stay fresh quite a long time. Some chefs make a bit of a thing about them . . . like hearing your tea leaves were picked on a Sri Lankan plantation at dawn, or telling a customer in Perth their salmon was swimming in the Tasmanian wilderness that morning. They don't mention that the poor thing was swimming in a smelly fish pen with hundreds of others.'

Toby straightened, cupping one of the crocus blooms in his hands. 'Precious cargo. Sally and Mollie make a fabulous paella. The saffron makes all the difference.'

'Turns any dish gold,' Sally said and smiled. 'Curries, spicy dishes, desserts, and even gin. We'll give you one of our special saffron-infused G & Ts tonight.'

'Good idea,' said Toby. 'So, have you decided yet if there is anything special you'd like to do while you're here, Jess, or anywhere you'd like to go?'

'No plans,' said Jess quietly. 'Just hanging out. Right, Sally?'

Sally glanced at her. The tone of her voice didn't sound like the Jessica she knew. It reminded Sally that her friend was still trying to deal with her world falling apart, even though she mostly put on a brave face.

They returned to the glasshouse carrying baskets of the delicate crocuses, handing them over to the team of workers sitting at the long tables ready to trim the red stigmas to be dried and packed.

*

At the end of Jessica's first week, Mollie had a party, 'just a few friends round to dinner', some of whom Jessica knew, while others were recent arrivals in the district.

Everybody brought something they'd made or grown: sourdough bread, jams, pickles, fresh produce, a basket of mushrooms, local wine, a delicious dessert. Mollie made a curry and saffron rice, Sally made tangy chutney and naan bread, and Jessica did a salad, throwing in flowers from the chives, and petals and leaves from the nasturtiums.

The long table was set in Sally's outdoor dining room overlooking the rose garden. Candles flickered in the slight breeze and kerosene lanterns cast a warm glow on the comfortable old cane lounge and chairs with their colourful cushions.

Katie and another little friend were kept occupied with a dollhouse and blocks in a room just inside the house, where they could be seen from the long table. Conversation ranged from world events to local politics, the issue of forest logging rearing its head again, the import–export market, the influx of mainlanders with money, increased traffic, the rising cost of land and houses and the threat of high-rises around Hobart harbour, although they all talked about water and weather before any other subject.

Toby carried the steaming bowl of curry to the table, helped serve and pass dishes, topped up wine and was attentive in his quiet, easy way. He'd rolled the sleeves of his good blue shirt tightly above his elbows, its colour reflecting the blue of his eyes in his tanned face. His sandy hair dropped over his forehead as he tilted his head, listening intently to a fellow farmer opposite. His arm rested on the back of Sally's chair as she leaned her head on his shoulder, her hand on his knee. Sally's blonde hair shone in the candlelight, her pretty face barely touched with make-up, and, seeing them together, Jessica was happy for Sally. Toby's gentle strength and modest wisdom continued to surprise and cheer her. Feeling mellow, Jessica leaned back in her chair with her glass of red wine.

*

Sally caught the movement and glanced at her, trying to read her mood. She saw that Jessica looked relaxed and calm, her attentive curiosity and intelligence tuned to the quiet conversations around her. She knew Jess could be fiercely passionate at times, and debate her way out of any argument, be it friendly or heated. She was so beautiful in her dark and exotic way; she always attracted attention when she entered any room. Sally remembered that Jessica could also be shy, and no doubt Hardy had wounded her self-esteem, but the Jessica she knew so well would bounce back. Sally sent a silent curse down on Hardy.

A few hours later, two sleepy little girls and a dog were curled up on the lounge. The conversation level had dropped to the intimate, guests putting off leaving, contemplating the last of the wine. Mollie and Sally were in the kitchen serving up Mollie's special cheese and liqueurs as two helpers stacked the dishwasher.

Bec, one of Sally and Jess's old schoolfriends, came into the kitchen for a fresh bottle of white wine. 'It's so nice to have Jessica back here again,' she said to Mollie and Sal. 'Will she stay, do you think?'

'Hard to say,' said Sally. 'She needed a break. Time out. And we enjoy having her here so she can stay as long as she likes while she works out what to do next.'

*

Jessica and Sally had fallen into the habit of meeting at sunset in the conservatory for a quiet drink before dinner, each having filled in the day in their own way. Katie often brought her tea set and quietly played 'ladies', handing them tiny cups of imaginary 'magic tea'. Sometimes Mollie joined them.

'How are you doing?' Sally asked one evening as she dropped ice cubes in her wineglass.

'Sal, you still do that! Why ruin such good Tassie wine?' said Jessica.

'When I was in Spain and Italy, the locals put ice in red wine. Good enough for them, good enough for me,' she said easily. 'How was your day? I saw you head down to the creek.'

'Yes. Made me think I'd like to go out fishing. Just throw a line in off your landing. Or better still, go out on your boat.' Jessica stretched out and sipped her wine. 'I've decided I'm over feeling tetchy and wasting time feeling mad at Harden. I bet he's not gnashing his teeth over me.'

'Of course not.' Sally gave an inward cheer that Jess

might finally be letting the awful Hardy go. 'Nor should you over him. You rock, girl.'

'Hello, girls. How has your day been?' Mollie pulled off her glasses and sank into a chair. 'Pour your mother a drink, please, Sal. I've been number-crunching.' She turned to Jessica. 'What are you two planning for tomorrow? I think we should take you out, Jess, and have a fun day. All work and no play is damned boring.'

'I told you I didn't need to be entertained, Mollie. I'm happy to just hang out.'

'I thought we might head over to CoCo's café for lunch on Sunday and wander around a bit. The markets are on and they're fun.' Mollie smiled up at her daughter, who handed her a drink.

Sally nodded. 'You should see it all, Jess. Amazing food, lovely things to buy. Katie loves it.'

'I want to go to CoCo's,' cried Katie, her ears pricking up.

'Sure,' said Jessica.

'We were thinking of taking the boat out tomorrow,' Sally said.

Mollie looked from Jessica to Sally. 'Well, you two plan a nice day and take a picnic. Do you good to get away from the farm for a bit. I'll do something special with Katie.'

*

The girls were lying in the sun on the end of the small jetty in front of the boatshed. Sally was glad that Jessica was starting to relax. The tightness had gone from her face and body and she seemed also to be allowing herself to feel sad. And hurt. She'd talked about her family, the differences between their parents, and how she just couldn't share anything with her brother. Anthony had graduated from university and was living in India with his own family, researching a project for his PhD, so Jessica rarely saw him.

For her own part, Sally was grateful and happy that she had Toby and their adored daughter, plus a loving mother. Yet, a sense of something missing in her life niggled at her. Sally realised that having Jessica blow in with storm clouds raging around her, seeking the safe harbour of a close friendship, had ruffled the smooth waters of Sally's own life.

'All right, so are you ready to take the *Charlotte-Ann* out for a spin?' suggested Jessica.

Without opening her eyes, Sally sucked her finger and held it up to the faint breeze.

'Easterly. That's good. Pretty mild. She hasn't been out for a while.' She sat up and smiled at Jessica. 'You always loved this, didn't you? Sailing up the river, mooring somewhere quiet to chip oysters off the rocks, explore, light a campfire, collect seaweed for Mum's vegie patch . . .'

'Yeah. Then we moved to Sydney and it was heading to the drive-through hamburger joint, hanging out at the beach waiting for the surf-club boys to notice us. Blue light discos, first time getting drunk, wandering the shopping mall, always looking for someone with a car to take us places . . . away from parental supervision. Another world from here.'

'Yeah, I didn't do much of that at fifteen,' said Sally. 'Pretty boring and quiet even in the bright lights of Launceston and Hobart.'

'Well, we did live a little when we took that overseas trip,' Jessica said with a grin. 'And then you met Toby. Who else would find a Tassie boy in Marrakesh! Lucky you.'

'Yes, Toby was going to work in that village in Africa and I was going to conquer the world. And here we are.' Sally jumped up. 'Right. Let's take the boat out.'

She pulled the key off its hook under a flap of loose plank and unlocked the rusty padlock, and the two girls went into the shadowy, salty, oily-smelling boatshed, where shafts of sunlight glinted between loose boards and slanted under the edge of the old tin roof.

With the double doors open, they pulled the tarpaulin off the boat and slowly winched the polished curved wooden hull down the slipway into the water. She was sixteen feet in the old measurement, gaff rigged, and her sleek Huon pine hull and half-deck gleamed. Her sails were cotton, batten seamed, and it was family lore that when she'd first glided into the water in 1928 at Muir's boatyard, Sally's grandfather Stephen had fallen in love.

'All set for you to come on board,' said Sally as the little craft bobbed into the water.

Jessica undid the mooring rope and swung into the boat while Sally stowed the oars and began unfurling the rigging. Then Jessica pushed them off from the jetty.

'Bit like riding a bike, isn't it?' Jessica laughed. 'How it comes back to you.'

With the mainsail billowing, their feet propped against the gunwale, Sally at the tiller and Jessica holding the mainsail rope, the *Charlotte-Ann* gathered speed as they headed into the main channel of the river and skimmed parallel to the riverbank.

'She's like a horse let out of the stable,' said Sally.

'Wow, I've missed this,' called Jessica. 'Remember the time we got stranded when we went to the falls?'

'Oh, yes. Had to wait for the tide. That was a bit of a hike. So beautiful up there.'

'Spooky, though. Everything was covered in lichen and moss. Thought we'd have to camp overnight. Tourists haven't found that spot yet, have they?'

'Doubt it. Too steep to build a cabin or anything up there, thank goodness. Hikers tend to stick to the trails. You don't see many tourists that far upriver.'

'Nice that this area hasn't changed all that much,' said Jessica. 'Apart from the trendy cafés and paddock-to-plate farms around the town.'

'The locals want to keep it this way, not get too touristy or developed by mainlanders.'

'Must have seemed isolated in your grandmother's time,' said Jessica.

'I wish I'd known her. She died before I was born,' said Sally. 'I just love her paintings in the conservatory. That was her studio, remember.'

'Are those the only paintings of hers you have? Where are the others? I thought your mother said she was a dedicated artist?'

'Her obituary describes her as a keen amateur artist, so read "Sunday painter". Mum says there's more of her work stashed away somewhere – there's still lots of stuff from my grandfather's era about the place. One of the joys of living in a house that's been in the family for a few generations, I suppose. I think that's why Mum likes living in the little cottage now though. It's all her own space, not filled with too many memories.'

'I love your house with all that family memorabilia.'

Sally nodded. 'Me too. I love that I can wear my grandmother's gumboots in the garden. Use the same garden tools, read books that belonged to my grandfather.'

'Once we left here and went to Sydney we moved so often that heaps of stuff got thrown away and a lot of sentimental things went to charities,' Jessica said. 'It didn't mean much to Anthony and me at the time, but when I set up house with the wretched Hardy I found I had very few meaningful possessions. I'm not really materialistic, but I didn't appreciate sentimental stuff till I started to make my own home.'

'Go about!' Sally swung the tiller and the boat changed direction as Jessica ducked beneath the boom and changed sides, leaning out over the water, letting the mainsail re-adjust as they tacked across the wide river.

The girls watched a double-decker cruiser of tourists glide past, the well-heeled ensconced on the top deck while backpackers and grey nomads snapped photos from the railing of the lower deck or sat waving to them from inside.

'Are they just sightseeing along the river or do they stop and go ashore?' asked Jessica.

'They go down to the Channel and along the coast to Solitary Island, if the sea is safe enough.'

'Oh, I remember that, we had a school excursion there once, didn't we? Was that the place where escaped convicts set up a community until they were found by the authorities?'

'That's the one. Then they built a prison there, which was pretty gruesome from what I recall. There was even some cannibalism. Though a few convicts did get away, didn't they?'

'That's right, to New Zealand, and someone even got to Jamaica! And they say you don't learn anything at school!'

The two friends chuckled.

'Do we have time to sail down to the mouth, to Rocky Point? See if the seals or sea lions are there?' Jessica asked, her eyes bright. 'I remember going there once with you and your dad.'

'Yeah, we nearly drowned! The sea is so unpredictable around the Channel,' said Sally.

'Do you remember how we always said we'd try to take a boat through the Channel on our own? Why don't we, Sal?' said Jessica.

'Well, not now! I have no idea what the sea is like down there. I think we'd need a motor launch; this'd never get through the passage between the cliffs. And why do it? It's a totally mad idea.' Sally laughed. Then she stopped, seeing Jessica's expression.

Jessica flung out an arm, her eyes bright. 'Because I feel like being mad and reckless. I feel like I've been in a box, under Hardy's thumb, my life on hold. I want to live a little!'

'A little is right,' said Sally tartly. 'It's a crazy idea and we'd probably get killed.'

'Then something else, Sal! Let's take off, you and me, and do something crazy. Just for a week or so. Toby and your mum can look after Katie and the farm. Please. C'mon, when are you ever going to do this again in your life?' demanded Jessica with a big smile and dancing eyes. 'You always play it safe, Sal,' she added.

A memory suddenly surfaced that Sally hadn't thought of in years.

'Remember when you dared me to climb over the fence into old Mr Lambert's place and steal his fruit? I just couldn't do it. That bothered me for years. I always felt I'd failed in your eyes,' said Sally. 'Failed myself somehow, too.'

'No way! It was lousy fruit anyway. And didn't he turn out to be some nutter?' said Jessica cheerfully.

'I was so torn. I wanted to please you, and be brave and crazy like you, even though it was stealing and that was wrong.'

'Oh good lord, did you tell your mother and say I was naughty and a bad influence?'

'Of course not. I've never told you, but I went back later and pinched some of his plums and gave them to Mum. When she found out where they came from, I got into trouble.'

'You didn't! Well, there you go, you are wild and foolish and naughty after all. Just like me! So now we have to go and take off, do something just for us!'

Sally shook her head. 'I have a family, Jess. Half a day off here and there is fine, but I have responsibilities, I'm needed at the farm . . .'

'Then I'll go alone. Something tells me I have to do this,' said Jessica.

'Jess, let's talk about it later. The wind is getting up, I'm going about.'

As the small boat changed direction and the girls changed position, the wind stiffened and the *Charlotte-Ann* scudded across the water. Their hair whipped about their faces, and they were lashed with stinging spray. The two friends were silent, concentrating on keeping the boat from keeling too far over, but both were glad of the distraction, deep as they were in thought and memories.

*

Sally poured the gin as Mollie put her feet on the needlepoint footstool and turned to Jessica. 'You went sailing this afternoon? How lovely. I remember you girls messing about in that boat when you were around eleven or twelve.'

'*Charlotte-Ann* is travelling well for an old girl,' said Jessica.

Toby poked his head into the conservatory. 'Hi there. Can Katie and I join you guys?' He had a cold beer in one hand and Katie was carefully balancing a tray with her plastic tea set on it. 'So, how was the sailing trip?' he asked as he sat down.

'We didn't go far. Tough Jess wanted to take *Charlotte-Ann* down to the Channel,' said Sally, handing her mother and Jessica their drinks.

'Oh, dear me, no,' said Mollie quickly. 'Not in a sailboat. The sea is far too unpredictable down there. Beautiful place, though. I wonder if the seals are still there?'

'I remember it being very rugged,' said Jessica. 'Sometimes you couldn't get out of the harbour. I loved the times we went up the coast, and went rafting in those magnificent wild rivers. Have you been, Toby?'

'I'm a landlubber, not a happy camper in a small sailboat,' said Toby with a shudder.

'What's a landlubber, Daddy?' Katie asked.

'That's someone who likes staying on dry land. Though we like swimming, don't we, sweet pea? But not in the river. Or the creek, right?'

'Can we go to the beach, Daddy?'

'When it gets a bit warmer,' said Toby. 'It must have been cold out there on the river.'

'We were rugged up. There's a lot of tourist cruises here now,' Sally said to Jess. 'Everybody wants to see the last great wilderness, but in comfort and safety.'

'Yes, the mountain walks have huts and rest stops these days, even five-star pit stops in some places,' Toby said.

'The trail bike rides are the big thing up north. There is stunning scenery up there, but I don't think whizzing as fast as you can and throwing your bike over rocks and logs is really appreciating the place,' said Mollie. 'Oh dear. Am I sounding like an ageing mother?'

The others laughed. 'Yes!'

'But I do agree with you,' said Jessica. 'Sal, let's go for a hike, get out in the bush for a bit. Can we take off for a couple of hours early in the morning, Mollie?'

'Of course you can. Katie's little legs won't keep up with you two fit gals, though. We'll find something to do here. I think there're new ducklings on the dam. I'll make brunch or lunch for us all when you get back.'

'Thanks, Mum. We should all do something together. Maybe a picnic or something,' suggested Sally. 'We used to do that a lot, but we haven't had a picnic for ages.'

'Yes. We used to go up to the big rock with Dad and watch the sunset, light a campfire and cook sausages on sticks. Remember, Jess? You used to come along too, sometimes with Anthony. Hard to believe how long ago that was; everyone is all grown up now . . .' said Mollie.

'All grown up and getting on with things,' said Jessica. 'I'm the one who's a bit adrift.'

'Was quitting your job the right thing to do?' asked Mollie gently.

'Mum, let Jess be,' said Sally.

'It's okay. Actually, Professor Lang said I'd be welcome back any time if I changed my mind. Though the uni admin people might not be so accommodating,' said Jessica. 'But I'm not going back.'

'Something will turn up,' said Mollie cheerfully. 'Be sure and wear sturdy boots tomorrow morning.'

Jessica sipped her drink, looking at Toby, Sally and her mother: Mollie so practical, Sally so careful, and Toby so reliable. Is this how she and Sally had imagined their lives would turn out when they young? She wondered if Sally remembered their whispers in the dark when they had sleepovers. All the talk about the things they'd do, the people they'd be, the adventures they'd share. It had all been so very different from the way they saw the lives of the grown-ups. Yet here they were, Sally being safe and she being reckless. Well, feeling reckless. And why not? What had she to lose? But then there came the small voice at her shoulder. She needed Sally. She always sought her sensible, safe, but comforting friendship. She was closer to Sally than she was to her brother.

Jessica glanced at Sally's gentle, calm expression. And suddenly wanted to shake her.

3

Arcadia, 2018

TOBY CARRIED A PLATTER aloft and, with a bow, deposited it on the breakfast table in front of Sally, Jessica, Mollie and Katie, who clapped her hands.

'Bravo, darling. You make the best scrambled eggs. Thank you,' said Sally.

'These are not for the faint-hearted,' said Mollie. 'You should see the butter and cream he throws in,' she added to Jessica.

'There's greenery on top, parsley, very healthy,' said Toby. 'And, of course, a grating of truffle.' He walked back to the bench and returned with two more platters. 'Here're some tomatoes in garlic olive oil from a neighbour, and some bacon, also from friends.'

'A few slivers of truffle and truffle salt goes a long

way in the local swap meets,' Sally said.

Jessica ladled the eggs onto her sourdough toast, cut from a loaf Mollie had baked. 'Gosh, this could be the next big thing in the café world. Smashed avocado is so passé.'

'I want the truffle salt, Mummy.'

'Say "please",' Sally said, as Jessica broke into laughter.

'I'd like to see what goes into her lunchbox,' said Jessica. 'Yum, thanks, Toby. This is delicious.'

After breakfast, Toby pushed back his chair and stood up. 'I'm heading out. Honeybee, when you finish, brush your teeth and come down to the barn and help Daddy, okay?'

Katie nodded, her mouth full as she slowly ate the last of the toast.

'So, are you girls still planning a walk today?' asked Mollie. 'I thought Katie and I might go into town later and see Mrs Hamilton, do a few errands, have a milk-shake, right?'

'Yes, please,' Katie said eagerly.

Jessica smiled, grateful to Mollie for giving them both a ticket-of-leave. 'You bet we are. A nice long walk to relax and breathe in the fresh air.'

'Sounds good,' said Mollie.

'Are you sure, Mum? You don't need us to do anything?' asked Sally. 'Katie, have you finished? Go and do your teeth like Daddy said.'

'Of course I'm sure,' Mollie said, as Katie skipped out of the room. 'I love stealing Katie away for some time together, just the two of us. And I'm happy for you to have some time to yourself, darling. Doesn't happen often enough round here.'

'Rubbish, Mum, I'm so lucky to have you here. You're a huge help, not just in the business, and it's special for Katie.'

'Speaking of the angel . . .' Mollie waved as Katie passed the door. 'Put your boots on, sweetie, if you're going down to the barn.'

Sally smiled. 'Once a mum . . .'

Mollie laughed. 'Yep, it's true. But being a grand-mother is special. Quite different from being the mother.'

'Oh, you mean you hand them back when they get cranky,' said Jessica. 'That's what Mum says about Anthony's kids.'

'Yes! Gosh, your brother has two now, doesn't he? Your parents must enjoy that.'

'Yes, although they live overseas as he's still in India, so they only see the kids when the family comes back for Christmas holidays. Sometimes I feel as if I've let the side down a bit, especially with Anthony living so far away.'

'Don't say that, Jess!' exclaimed Sally. 'Just think, if you'd had a child with Harden you'd be tied to him. It's much better to start over.'

'Value your freedom to choose, Jess,' said Mollie quietly. 'I was so fortunate I had the right man in my life.'

Jessica looked at Mollie. Her eyes were downcast as she sipped her tea, so Jess couldn't read her expression, but she realised that Mollie had been widowed for a few years now and there must be times when she was lonely, even though her family were living on the farm with her.

'You and Dad always seemed to be a true partner-ship,' said Sally, who also sensed her mother's mood had changed.

'Yes, Sally, we were, but even in my generation that was unusual for many couples. You girls, well, I mean young women today, say they still have a long way to go for equality and fair treatment in so many ways.' Mollie sighed. 'But it takes a generation or more to shift attitudes.

When I think back to my mother's time, how men still ran everything even after women proved themselves in the war years . . . Attitudes have changed so much. You girls have a lot more choices and freedom.'

'A bad marriage is a bad marriage, and I still felt like the underdog,' said Jessica.

'It's called bullying, Jess,' said Sally.

'I think my mother was, well, not *bullied*, but perhaps dominated,' said Mollie. 'My father was a doctor – serious, older, expected to be a protector, the provider. I suspect Mother sometimes felt a little suffocated. Women who'd lived through the Depression and the war looked for stability, maturity. In that era they were told that men had superior intelligence.'

'You and Dad seemed to be happy,' said Sally. 'I thought you were a very modern couple.'

'We thought so too,' Mollie laughed. 'We came out of the hippy, free-love age and all that.'

'Like my parents,' said Jessica. 'When I married Harden I thought we had it right – both of us independent, good jobs, supposedly sharing the housework, money, lifestyle equally. In reality, though, he was deceitful and selfish. What upsets me most is that I didn't see it for so long.'

'Maybe because your lifestyle seemed to be so hectic,' Mollie said gently. 'You have to stop and smell the roses, as they say. Or as Toby says, the fresh dung and warm goat's milk.' Mollie smiled.

'That's my man,' said Sally, smiling. 'Earthed.'

'There's a lot to be said for living in nature,' said Mollie. 'You know I was reading there are now scientists and researchers studying the effects of nature, especially forests, on humans. A simple walk among trees, connecting with the earth's healing energy, can revitalise physical and mental health. And we have it all on our doorstep!'

'Yes, you guys have it all around you! You could open a forest spa!' said Jessica.

'I know being here helped my Graham enormously after his first heart attack,' said Mollie softly. 'It always amazed his doctors how well he did. I had a wonderful husband. It was a hard time after the second attack took him from me; he was still young . . .'

Sally reached out and squeezed her mother's hand. 'I treasure living here with you, Mum, and Toby does too.'

'I don't want you and Toby to ever feel obliged, you know, to stay here because of me,' began Mollie, but Jessica held up her hand.

'Enough. Sal, Toby and Katie adore you and this place, and wouldn't want to be anywhere else. Right, Sal? You guys have your own lives, own space, yet you share every-thing you love most. Family and this amazing property.'

'Yes, I am lucky.' Mollie sighed. 'There're a lot of memories here. And from the families before us, too, I'm sure.'

For a moment Jessica felt a shiver, as if a draught had swept into the room, but she shook herself and straight-ened up. 'Hey, Sal, we have a sunny day awaiting us. Let's get out there. I have an idea.'

*

'Bloody hell!' Sally pulled a thorny tangle of branches away from her shirt. 'I'm getting scratched to pieces.'

'It's so overgrown. I don't think anyone has been up this way since we were last here, and that must've been about twenty years ago!'

'Just animals, see the tunnel in the undergrowth – something has been crawling through there. We might be better off on our hands and knees.'

'I don't remember it being this rugged,' muttered Jessica. 'But of course, we were a lot smaller then too.'

They were scrambling through thick, scrubby undergrowth on the hillside above the narrow tributary of the river. Jessica looked down at the clear water rushing over the sharp rocks and had a sudden flashback, seeing the small shape of Sally crumpled in her red raincoat against the jutting boulders at the edge of the stream. She shuddered, and called out, 'You okay, Sal?'

'Yes. I'm okay,' Sally said firmly.

Jessica felt a sudden rush of affection for her friend. Few might guess at her strength and determination, her stubbornness and loyalty. She seemed a dedicated and settled mother, partner, and farmer, living where she was born, nurtured by a loving family. People would be forgiven for thinking that there had never been harsh edges in her life, but Jessica knew better. The delicate frame, the gentle voice, soft blonde hair and fine features disguised a tough young woman with a big heart and a determined will.

'Stand back, Jess.' Sally pulled a small machete from her backpack and, wielding it like a Japanese master, she slashed at the undergrowth.

Jessica yanked at the severed vines and bushes. 'That did it. Oh, look, Sal, there's the crevice!'

'Can we still squeeze through? It looks so much narrower than I remember.'

'Of course we can, c'mon. It just looks narrower because we're bigger.'

On their hands and knees they crawled behind the

rock, through the hidden tunnel, to emerge, a little further in, at the mouth of the cave. They stood, brushing themselves down.

'Phew. Well, there it is,' said Jess.

Instinctively they lowered their voices at the opening of the cave, where a chink of light shone in from what they knew to be a side opening overlooking the valley and river. An earthy, warm, musty smell hit them, but a breeze drifting in from the outside brought some fresh air.

'We could have camped in here for days, if we'd been allowed. Why didn't we, Sal?'

'Because we were little kids who had to be home before dark!'

'Yeah.' Jessica closed her eyes and sighed.

They moved through the tunnel entrance into the opening of the compact cave, and found it dry and protected.

'Good grief. Those old pieces of furniture are all still here,' whispered Sally.

'Well, what's left of them.' Jessica looked around. 'Amazing there's no dampness in here. I'd kinda forgotten what it was like. Seems smaller than I remember.'

The two girls stared around them in the slanting light, then walked in further.

'It's like we left twenty years ago and no one's been here since,' said Sally softly. 'I don't even think any animals have been in here . . . remember the birds that used to fly in?'

'We never really thought about who all this stuff belonged to,' Jessica said, staring at a rusting metal chair, storage drums and rotting hessian bags, a dusty blanket and pillow – the detritus of a temporary life. Bird droppings covering it all had dried to powdery dust.

Sally joined her. 'Whoever camped up here tried to make it nice, at least. It didn't look so decrepit when we were kids.'

'Well, at least they didn't die here. It feels creepy, though. Why hide out all the way up here, dragging stuff up the hillside?' Jessica said.

'Yeah, you don't realise this is so high up, because the climb feels short, but it's steep,' said Sally. 'Funny, we never thought twice about that climb when we were kids. How many times did we come here and play, bring picnics and stuff?'

'Dozens. Remember the time we brought the dog and he ran away?' Jessica said.

'Poor boy. You dragged him in here and he took off with his tail between his legs. Strange, thinking about it now. He was such a feisty little dog. I thought he'd take on anything. Y'know what Jack Russells are like.'

'Remember when we lit a fire in the ring of stones at the front there, and embers blew into the grass and started a fire? We were so stupid.'

'And lucky. You ran for the blanket and I tipped the water out of the old can and jumped on the flames. Mum never understood how the bottoms of my sneakers had melted!' Sally said.

Jessica laughed and walked over to the old bed made from rough-hewn branches and a log. She wondered who had put it together, and then recognised an old blanket of her mother's that she'd once brought up to the cave. She yanked its frayed remains, removing one of the planks in the process. 'This old thing . . .'

'Careful! Could be a snake in there,' warned Sally quickly.

Jessica jumped, dropping the rug. Then leaned forward.

'Hey, what's this? Here, help me shove the bed aside.' Together, they shunted the wooden frame far enough from the wall that a small hole in the wall behind it became fully visible.

'What is it?' Sally asked, peering into the cavity in the stone.

'It's a tin box. One of those old bank locker things.' Jessica banged the rusty metal. 'Stand back.'

Making sure there wasn't a snake hibernating nearby, she lifted up the old cash tin. 'A bank robber? Do you suppose it's full of money?'

'Is it locked? Quick, open it. Do you think it's been there all this time?' said Sally.

'Maybe, but I definitely didn't see this here when we were kids, I would have remembered. We wouldn't have been strong enough to move the bed, anyway. This tin isn't locked, just rusty.' Jessica wrenched it and the rusted latch fell apart. She yanked the old tin lid and it fell open.

Inside was a canvas bag with the remains of a large envelope.

'They're papers, and other things. Look, there's a grey feather and, oh gosh, an eggcup. Seems to be engraved, but I can't read it.' Sally looked over at Jessica. 'What are the documents?'

'Letters, envelopes, all sorts of stuff,' said Jessica as she carefully unfolded them.

'Can we read them, is the ink still legible?' Sally leaned over Jessica's shoulder.

'No, not on most of them. Hang on, here's a high school certificate of merit, made out to "Thomas William Broadbent". Heard of him?'

Sally shook her head. 'They look fragile. Let's take them home and go through them gently there. We can check the registry. Births, deaths, marriages. You can do it all online now.'

'Gosh, this is someone's personal stuff. I wonder what happened to him? Whoa, look at this newspaper cutting. It's your grandmother!'

'What? Let me see . . .' Sally tilted the paper into the light. 'So it is,' she said wonderingly. The quality of the image was poor but the caption was clear: *Talented Lady Artist Wins First Prize*. 'I think it's the painting that's hanging up at home! Why would someone want to keep this?' Sally looked at Jessica with a puzzled expression.

'I've no idea. Do you suppose he died up here in the bush somewhere? Poor old bloke,' mused Jessica. 'Maybe he had a secret crush on her.'

'C'mon, let's get out of here,' Sally said with a sudden shiver.

Jessica glanced around. 'There's nothing else, is there? No personal belongings or anything? Funny there are no clothes anywhere. Do you think he could have lived here?'

'It would be quite cosy up here, cool in summer. I guess you'd need a fire in the winter. And it has a fabulous view.'

Jessica rattled among the old boxes, pulling out a tin mug and a spoon. 'Bit sad if this is all you have left in the world,' said Jessica, picking up a dusty enamel plate sitting on a short piece of wood that acted as a shelf.

Sally sighed. 'Let's go, this feels uncomfortable now.' She looked at the tin cash container in Jessica's hands. 'Should we leave it, or give it to the police or something? He might have been a missing person when he was alive.'

'I'm interested in these papers.' Jessica shuffled through them, pausing to pull out a faded violet envelope dated 1949. 'What's this?' She slid a note out and passed it to Sally, who peered at the document.

'It's hard to read, pretty faded and smudged. Oh, listen to this: *My darling . . . my heart is breaking. I am leaving this, knowing you will be here soon, but I will not . . . It is time. I have to stop seeing you. I am fearful and I don't want you to be hurt, it is too dangerous. Know I will always love you . . . you are the love of my life . . .* I can't make out the signature.'

'The cave must have been a trysting place!' exclaimed Jessica. 'They probably met here secretly . . . no motels around here in those days. But who is it? What else is in that pile?' She delved into the box and took out a folder holding a few stained negatives and small black-and-white photographs. 'Oh, look at these little old photos.'

She rifled through them quickly. 'Scenes from around here. Some birds. Oh, look, an owl. It's caught something. And . . . oh gosh . . .' She gave a low whistle. 'It's a naked man!'

'What? Show me, you're joking!' Sally reached for the photograph.

'He's asleep. Well, I assume so,' said Jessica.

They peered at the apparently naked man, a blanket draped over his hips. His arm stretched out in sleep, one bare leg exposed.

'It's in *here*,' exclaimed Sally. 'Look, there's the shelf behind him. It's taken in here!'

Heads close, they studied the photo. 'Gosh, he's good-looking. Like a Greek god,' said Jessica. 'Looks posed, doesn't it? Who would have taken it?'

'Jeepers, what else is there?' Carefully Sally flipped through the photos, then stopped with a gasp and peered closely at a small photograph.

'There's more?'

Her eyes wide in disbelief, Sally handed the photo to Jessica.

It was an idyllic setting of a stream, shaded by an old tree, rushes and wildflowers studded along the banks, and in the sparkling water a pretty woman was laughing up at the photographer as she lay beneath the surface of the water, her naked body gleaming silvery white.

'It's our creek, the spot where we swim, near the big hole,' said Sally, almost breathless.

'Yeah, it could be. Who is this?'

Sally peered closely at the photo, then looked at Jessica. 'I'm sure of it. She has such a distinctive face, so pretty. I recognise her from Mum's album. It's Stella.'

'Your *grandmother*! Holy cow! She's gorgeous. I mean, that could be today. So . . . who took the photo?' Jessica stopped, staring at Sally as the reality dawned on her. 'Your grandmother was swimming naked with the Greek god! And this was their love nest!'

'Don't say that!' snapped Sally, still in shock.

'Oh, I'm sorry, Sal.' Jessica reached over and put her arm around Sally's shoulders. 'It's nothing to be ashamed of, is it? I mean, she married an older man. Wow, do you think your mum knows?'

'Of course not!' Sally exclaimed. 'Well, I wouldn't think so,' she went on in a faltering voice. 'My grandfather was . . . well, I never met him, but my mother respected him. He was the driving force here. I hope he never knew about this. If it did happen . . .'

'It happened! Look around. Doesn't it all make sense now? More to the point, do you think your grandfather, the stuffy old doctor, found out? We'd better go through the documents.'

'We can't let my mother know about this. She adored her mother, and her father,' Sally wiped her face. 'I can't believe this. But I just can't think how to bring this up with Mum.' Sally shook her head and paused to re-read the letter.

Jessica looked around with fresh eyes. 'Sal, you have to find this guy, or his descendants.'

'Why? He'll be long dead. And what's the point?'

Jessica hesitated, then shrugged. 'Okay. It's your family. We should take these papers and photos, though. In case you do want to pursue this.'

Sally didn't answer as she held on to the fragile note.

Jessica put all the papers back in the box with the old eggcup, and glanced around.

Sally stood up. 'Say goodbye, Jess. A small door in our childhood just closed. No way I'm coming back here.'

'Maybe a window opened? No, you're right. This seems too creepy now.' Jessica looked down at the metal locker. 'We'll keep this between us, if that's what you want. Just for now. But this isn't the last of it. You'll have to find out more or it will haunt you.'

Sally recognised the look on Jessica's face. She'd always been intuitive, and Sally had learned that when Jessica made decisions or comments out of left field there was always a reason for them, even if Jessica didn't know it herself. They'd both learned to listen to Jessica's 'inner voice'.

Silently, they left the cave and, with Jessica carrying the tin box, they scrambled down through the rough scrubby undergrowth and rocks to the river.

Without saying anything to the other, each knew a bridge had been crossed. But there would be a journey ahead of them.

South-east Tasmania, 1938

Mrs James mopped her forehead. 'I swear I'm going to melt. You'll come in and find just a puddle on the kitchen floor.'

'Yes, it's dreadful. Please don't think you have to bake or cook hot meals. We can eat cold roast pork, and cold soups and sliced apples and cold custard. I'm sure there are other things too,' said Stella, feeling rather at a loss as she was not a dab hand in the culinary arts.

'Don't you fret, Mrs H. The men need their victuals. Especially Dr Holland. He's been working long hours.'

'Yes, he has,' agreed Stella. 'Surely this heatwave can't go on much longer.'

Mrs James grimaced. 'Some of the old bushmen are saying it's going to be bad. It's already broken records.'

'Dr Holland mentioned something about that too. He seems quite concerned about people's health in this heat,' said Stella. 'How is your family?'

'My kids are spending time at the creek or down at the bay; young Terry is with my mother. Some of their friends seem to be wagging school, although, I suppose, what with Christmas coming, school is winding down anyway.'

That night, Stella and Stephen sat in the sitting room after dinner with the French doors wide open, hoping a breeze might spring up.

'The heat is terrible, and they say it could go on for months!' Stella said. 'Everything is so dry.'

'It's very worrying for my patients. People are not coping well, and there's a very real chance our state could be facing an epidemic. There's been an outbreak of polio-myelitis on the mainland and in New Zealand, and if it takes hold here in these conditions, the humidity . . .' He shook his head and sighed.

'Is there nothing that can be done, some method of prevention?'

'There's no cure, though I'm sure scientists are trying their best to find one. There are different treatments, and we can quarantine the patients, of course. But I can't say I agree with Sister Kenny's methods.'

'Who is Sister Kenny, dear?'

'Oh, she's a nurse from Queensland who's working on the mainland, no official nursing credentials, although she did her bit in the Great War. She's developed an unorthodox technique she's been using on patients with the poliomyelitis. Exercising their muscles and such. Quite the opposite of the official thinking, which is to keep patients immobilised.'

'You mean in the iron lung and restrained in their beds?'

'Indeed. She seems to have built up quite a following all over the place. She's a rather controversial character,' said Stephen.

'Surely one must try everything. Let's hope the epidemic doesn't reach us in our valley,' said Stella. 'Perhaps we should curtail any trips away for the time being.'

'I have to agree. Leaving here would not be wise.'

Unfortunately, Stephen's fears were soon realised. Within weeks, Tasmania was gripped by a severe polio epidemic that would prove to be one of the worst in the world. It stretched services and treatments and tried tempers as restrictions on travel were enforced, and care centres were quarantined. Fear of catching the infection led to families isolating themselves or being kept in their homes by doctors and the government, and children stopped going to school and stayed away from friends. There was whispered gossip of families smuggling children in the boot of their cars to far-flung valleys, farms, the seaside or even to the mainland to try to escape the infection, not considering that they might be carriers themselves.

Fathers were isolated from families for fear of bringing germs home from work, or they lost their jobs when their bosses were afraid they might spread the disease if someone in their household had become infected. Neighbours retreated from old friends, engagements and marriages broke up when someone contracted the disease, homes were fumigated and sufferers were ostracised. Stephen told Stella that some nursing staff in Hobart's hospital and treatment centres underwent extreme bathing and cleaning procedures, sometimes having to soak in foul phenol baths before travelling or visiting friends and family.

It pained Stella to see the tiredness and concern on her husband's face as the weeks dragged into months and the death toll and number of infected children rose. He explained that there were few medical staff who knew how to use the newly introduced respirator machines, which terrified the young patients.

After one particularly trying day, Stephen sat slumped in his chair, rubbing his brow. 'It's draining on the families, and now the children know that they could die or be crippled for life. When I go into the hospital in town, I see the young trainee nurses outside scrubbing the linen in the yard in giant tubs of strong disinfectant, as no laundry will take linen from the infected patients. And today I found one of the senior nurses on a meal break so exhausted she was asleep at the table with her veil in her soup.'

Stella's heart went out to him. 'My dear, you are doing more than your share. You're called out in the night so often; you're not getting adequate rest. And I can't forget that story you told me of having to treat children on the doorstep of the hospital, holding them upside down to clear their throats so they could breathe. You are so patient and reassuring to worried parents.'

Stella wanted to do whatever she could to help, so she threw herself into projects in the community to support 'the crippled children'. She heard terrible stories, such as mothers being hospitalised and their children distributed among other families, sometimes for years. Some children, after lengthy stays in hospital and rehabilitation, even forgot they had brothers and sisters. For some parents the trauma of seeing their children undergoing painful treatments became too hard to watch and they stayed away. For other parents it meant a three-hour bicycle ride each way on a Sunday to visit a sick child.

But with schools closed for months at a time, the lucky children who escaped the scourge were able to spend long days swimming, blackberrying, rabbiting and picnicking, running wild while attention was focused on the sick and the needy. There was a silver lining to everything, if you looked hard enough, Stella supposed.

*

Stella had snatched a rare morning to spend in her studio to take her mind off the endless rounds of worry and work.

As she quietly got on with the rough sketch of old forest trees that she'd started, she felt herself sinking into the peaceful quiet greenery and mysterious shadows of the place. The room was silent save for the ticking of the mantelpiece clock and the swishing of her brush as she changed colour.

Suddenly the door opened and Mrs James hurried in, looking stricken. Before Stella could speak she burst out,

'I have to go. It's Terry . . . my youngest. He's sick, he's got the polio, we think . . .'

Stella jumped to her feet. 'Oh no! Has Dr Holland seen him?'

'No, we've got to take him now. Maybe get him up to Hobart. Would you mind keeping an eye on my other kids, please, till, well, I dunno when?'

Stella dropped her brush, 'Of course! You and Mr James take Terry. I'll take care of the family. Please don't worry, Mrs James.'

Mrs James was already hurrying down the hall, untying her apron.

For the next six weeks Stella cared for the brood of James children, ranging from Matty, aged eight, to Flora, who was nearly fourteen. She kept them away from school in case another of them had been infected, and moved the four of them into the big house, as Blackie James was intermittently travelling between the hospital and Arcadia and trying to keep on top of his work. Stephen was also keeping long hours, and so Stella engaged Winsome, a young woman from the village, to help her with meals and cleaning.

In the mornings, Stella supervised schoolwork with Flora's help, and each afternoon she took the children on nature walks around Arcadia to observe, draw, collect specimens, look for platypuses in the river or find wombat holes; indeed, anything that caught their attention.

One balmy evening Stella gathered them together and, as a special treat, and with strict instructions as to what to do and how to behave, they followed her through the field and down to the wild Far Forest in the late afternoon light.

She had not seen any strangers in the forest since the episode of the man in the deerstalker hat a few years ago, but thinking about his drawing still deeply unsettled her. Stella refused to have her greatest pleasure – walking amongst the tall eucalypts – tarnished or taken from her, no matter how disturbing the experience had been.

The children had never ventured there before. When glimpsed from the house on the hill, it was a place of deep green mystery and secrets. The ancient trees clung together, linked by vines and an understorey of layers of mossy logs, fungi, ferns, and dripping spores and springs. In one part, through a storm-torn break in the canopy, the sun filtered down, illuminating a clearing of grasses, patchy shrubs and brightly coloured plants, which Stella whispered to the children was the 'animals' playground'.

She knew this spot well, and she told them to sit in the shadows at the edge of the clearing where they were not to make a sound, fidget or fuss.

'If you sit quietly, settle down and wait and watch, we may see a surprise. Something special. Don't speak and don't move. Just watch. All right? Understood?'

'I'm scared,' whispered Gladys.

'No, this is a secret, it's special,' said Flora, patting her younger sister's hand.

'I don't see nothing,' Matty said.

'Anything,' corrected Stella.

'What's in the bag?' asked Donald, seeing Stella pull a little cloth bag from her satchel.

Stella put a finger to her lips and smiled. Once the children had calmed and were waiting expectantly, she moved quietly out into the clearing, looking up into the trees on the other side. Softly she began calling, '*Dododo, doodoo.*'

Suddenly there was a *whoosh* and a soft shadow speared

from a tree across the clearing. The children caught their breath as the magnificent owl glided to the ground, folding its wings, and stood several feet in front of Stella, its beautiful white face watching her, its head tilted expectantly.

Stella reached into the cloth bag and grasped something wriggling. The owl swiftly opened its wings, soared above her, then turned and arrowed across the clearing to where the small creature Stella had released was making a dash for shelter.

Talons forward, wings spread, in a swift pounce the owl angled to the ground, scooped up the mouse and returned to its tree across the clearing.

'Wow!'

'What was that?'

'Ooh, poor little mouse,' squealed Gladys.

'It's so big! Make it come back again,' cried Matty.

'He'll be eating his dinner. Sometimes the mouse escapes,' said Stella, though it had only happened once. She'd developed quite a knack for trapping the mice from the barn.

'That's the most beautiful bird I've ever seen,' said Flora, close to tears.

'He's my friend,' said Stella softly. 'He watches out for me, so I bring him a mouse occasionally.'

They took turns birdwatching with her field glasses, all hoping to spot the masked owl as it sat quietly camouflaged on its branch.

Back in the big house after supper the children spread themselves around the long kitchen table with paper, pencils and paints to record what they'd seen. Everyone drew a picture of the owl. They had also started a scrapbook of plant samples and took turns to describe the habitat they each came from.

Watching them, Stella realised that while the children played games around the house and garden near the cottage, pedalled a billycart and had a swing in a tree, helped with the cows and did their chores, they hadn't developed skills to observe the world around them.

But now they were all enthused. Even Matty, who was usually hard to settle, seemed to enjoy his task of helping to sort a selection of feathers, grasses and seeds they'd collected, putting them in little boxes and envelopes.

As they finished their pictures and were packing away the materials, Stella saw that Flora held a blue flower in front of her and stopped in surprise. The small bloom and unusually shaped leaves were unlike anything she'd seen before.

'Flora, where did you pick this? It's lovely,' said Stella.

'Oh.' Flora looked a little flustered. 'Um . . .'

Stella waited expectantly.

'I sort of found them.'

'Goodness. Where might that have been?'

'She took it out of the old shed,' blurted Gladys. 'There were some bags of yucky looking mushrooms there too.'

'What shed? Whose shed? You mean you stole it?' asked Stella in a puzzled tone.

The children were all silent, staring accusingly at Gladys.

'We told 'im we wouldn't go back there,' said Matty.

Stella sat down and said calmly, 'It's all right, you can tell me. I promise I won't say a word. I just thought it's a rather unusual little flower.'

'It was growing next to the mushrooms in a special place. And you can't get any more,' said Matty in a swift prattle.

'That's a shame. I rather like it,' said Stella. 'So tell me, where is this shed?'

The children were quiet a moment.

'We're not supposed to tell,' said Matty.

'It's up the river,' began Flora.

'Who told you not to talk about this?' asked Stella gently.

In a rush the story tumbled out, with all of them talking at once.

'The man who comes here. He has a boat.'

'He brings things. Sacks and bottles and stuff.'

'He has plants and seeds.'

'You mean like vegetables? To grow?' asked Stella. 'Where does he live?'

Flora shook her head. 'Don't think he lives here. He doesn't grow things. He keeps a boat at the shed.'

'Just a little one. He goes down to the Channel.'

'He's scary.'

'How did you meet this man? Does your father know him?'

'Nooo.'

'We were fishing and we just went in to have a look around.'

'He yelled at us.'

'But then he was all right. We promised not to go inside his shed again.'

'When was this?'

'Yesterday.'

'I thought you were milking? And Mr Fowler was popping in to pick up the afternoon milk?' Stella began to fret. It was the one time she had agreed to let the children go and do chores without her.

'We did that. We just went down to the river to play before supper.'

'Children, you are not to go anywhere, especially the

river, without me, or Winsome, or your father when he's here,' said Stella sternly. 'I am responsible for you all.'

Winsome turned away from the stove, where she'd been preparing the evening cocoa. 'Cocoa is ready, children.'

'All right. Have your cocoa and get ready for bed,' said Stella firmly as everyone scurried over to collect their cups. She had the sense they were all relieved at Winsome's timing.

Stella picked up the small flower and held it up to the light, noticing how the colour seemed to shift from purple to blue. She wondered how she could capture the rich hue in a painting.

Arcadia, 2018

The sun was setting and pillows of mist rested softly in the dip below the hill, undulating slowly to some rhythm of the earth beneath.

The air was fresh and Jessica felt more alive than she had in, well, she couldn't remember how long. Maybe it was because of her happy childhood memories of the farm, which she hadn't really appreciated at the time. Perhaps it was the contrast between her city life, her marriage, her intense work in the lab, and the simplicity of her life growing up in a rural town at the bottom of an island state.

Now, seeing her childhood companion's lifestyle gave her pause. The familiar hit her with the intensity of its difference. Had she forgotten what it had been like to grow up in what her Sydney friends considered a backwater?

The practicalities of working the land for a living had changed but, thankfully, swathes of natural landscape, by dint of being left to its own devices, had survived.

It seemed to Jessica that her grandfather, and his father before him, had treated their land as a blank canvas, to be wiped clean of undergrowth, trees, grasses. Where sheep and cattle and machines had stomped the delicate environment into submission, the river courses had dried up, the droughts and dry seasons had been longer and more intense, and production had decreased each year. Her father had inherited their old farm but, being an academic, he had brought in a manager, and eventually, it had been run into the ground. Jessica sensed that her father had been quite relieved to pull up stumps and move to the mainland, to a city. He'd felt defeated by the bastardry of this apparently English countryside, which refused to behave in expected ways, instead turning all the rules of farming – as they knew them – upside down.

Yet here at Arcadia, almost twenty years later, Jessica found herself in a gentle land. She admired with fresh eyes the way this family seemed embedded in their home, making a living and a life on their farm by apparently changing as little as possible. The ancient trees, especially the thick forest, the wild grasses and creek, where few if any introduced animals had ventured, was untouched and untroubled. The crops were planted in rows across the hills, but within their contours and around the original stands of trees, following paths dictated by the earth rather than the wounds imposed on its surface. When she'd commented on this, Toby had explained to her that he was experimenting, living *with* their land not *on* it, 'in a partnership with nature'.

As she watched the sunset, and the dappled shade cast by the green hills and old trees, Jessica recognised a softness here, like Stella's gentle watercolours, that was so different from the images she was used to seeing: concrete highways, steel and glass high-rises, the anonymity of cookie-cutter, cheek-by-jowl homes with no backyards.

Over the past couple of years, as her marriage had started to crumble, Jessica had occasionally escaped to the beach to try to relax on her own, but parking was a nightmare, people were often surly, and rips and sharks lurked. What should have been enjoyable times had only increased her feelings of stress and being trapped. No matter what she did she could find no respite from an atmosphere that was always frenetic, angry almost, and where life was dictated by a screen. People literally walked into her, looking down at their phones rather than where they were going.

So one long weekend only a few weeks ago she'd flown out west, to the edge of the outback. But the dust, the heat, the flies, the seared surrounds had defeated and depressed her.

And that was when she'd called Sally. 'Sal, it's me. I need to see you. I'm coming back home. Just me.'

*

In the fading light Jessica walked into Stella's old studio, next to the kitchen. The long windows sliced the expansive view into quadruple vignettes, each a narrow portrait of a section of the garden, fields and forest. The last of the sunlight warmed the beautiful wooden walls, the comfortable chairs and wide bookshelves. Two of Stella Holland's paintings were hanging above the oak desk where Jessica had put the old metal cashbox from the cave.

She studied the paintings while she waited for Sally. She wasn't an expert, but she thought them exceptionally good, and wondered again why there weren't more of them on display around the house.

The owl was her favourite. The dark eyes in the white mask stared directly at her with penetrating concentration and a hint of quizzical amusement. The feathers looked so real she felt she could reach out and touch their softness, each one perfectly groomed in its place in the dramatic pattern. There was a small plaque on the frame stating that this was the painting that had won first prize in 1939 from the Art Society of Tasmania.

The other painting was of the delicate leafy fronds from a shrub or tree, with some tiny flowers in the corner, growing among some oddly shaped mushrooms. At the bottom of the picture Stella had written in a small flowing cursive script, *Untitled Species. Arcadia, Tasmania.*

'Okay. I'm ready. I brought you that G & T I promised.' Sally came in and handed Jessica a crystal glass containing a faintly golden liquid and a slice of lime.

'Thank you. This is fast becoming my favourite tipple.'

They clinked glasses.

'It's special, isn't it? It's all in the saffron and a few other local ingredients. The boys have done a great job. Did I tell you we won a medal at the Food and Beverage Show? There's heaps of competition now, though, which is good. Toby wants to brew his own beer. The water here is so crystal clear I think we should produce a whisky.'

'Everybody in Tassie claims their water comes from the pure snow melting off Cradle Mountain!' Jessica laughed.

'Maybe it does. I'm all for diversifying, but you can go a bit mad. I guess you settle down and specialise when you find your niche. We've got the perfect soil for the crocus flowers, so we're doing well with the saffron. The truffles are a bit more hit and miss, but we're persevering. Now, let's get into the box while everyone is out.'

The girls put down their drinks and Jessica eased open the rusted lid of the old box as Sally peered over her shoulder.

Carefully they laid out the contents on the desk, before going through the documents again.

Some papers were loose while some were in tattered envelopes, almost all of them too damaged to read. There was also a small diary, the blackened eggcup, the photos, the newspaper cutting and the violet note of farewell.

Jessica gently spread out several documents. 'Okay, this certificate for Thomas William Broadbent. You're sure you've never heard of him?' she asked.

Sally shook her head. 'What else is there?'

Jessica picked up the diary and flipped through it. 'Doesn't seem to be much detail in here. Oh, what's this?' She showed Sally a pressed flower, some crumbling leaves and seeds pressed between the pages. 'What do you suppose these are?' Gently she touched the plant. 'Do you recognise it?'

'No. Careful, it's really brittle. Wait, let me take a photo before we handle it.' Sally took out her phone and photographed the dried plants. She looked at the pressed flower. 'Something about it looks familiar. Where have I seen that?'

Jessica suddenly felt goosebumps and looked up. 'It's your grandmother, Stella, her painting . . .' She pointed to the wall above them. 'See, in the corner of the picture of the fronds!'

'Oh, wow!' Sally stared at the old flower and then at the intricate depiction of a single purple–blue flower that was almost hidden by a cluster of mushrooms and the larger leaves that filled the picture. 'It's the same, but it's not a plant I recognise. Do you?'

Jessica was leaning forward, studying the picture more closely. 'It's like a tiny orchid.'

Sally looked to where Jess was pointing. 'I've never really looked at this one carefully before because the owl painting has always been my favourite. We should find out what this plant is. I've never seen any of them anywhere, but they must have grown here if they're in Stella's paintings.'

'We can look it up. What's the diary say?'

The two women leaned, heads together, poring over the pages.

'*Unidentified plant being used by TWB to investigate potential properties . . .*' read Sally.

'TWB. Thomas William Broadbent! He *must* be the secret lover,' said Jessica.

'I still can't quite believe it,' said Sally softly, as she fingered the pale violet note.

'Do you want to raise the topic of your grandmother having a lover in the back paddock?' Jessica raised her eyebrows.

'I'm curious to say the least, but I don't want to say anything to Mum just yet, until we find out more.'

*

When Mollie joined them in the conservatory before dinner, Sally glanced at Jessica and ventured, 'Mum, we were looking at Grandma Stella's paintings earlier. Was anyone else in her family artistic?'

'No idea. I hardly knew them, really. Some of the cousins turned up for our wedding in Melbourne. No one came here to visit that I recall – too remote, probably. But my mother loved it here.'

'I think her art is stunning,' said Jessica. 'I'm surprised

there isn't more of it exhibited. Did she sell her work or only paint occasionally? There's so few of her paintings around.'

'She was quite prolific, actually; if she wasn't gardening she was painting. Or the other way around. After she was widowed she got very involved in various art projects at the Art Society.'

'I didn't know that,' said Sally.

'She left some of her paintings to them,' said Mollie.

'You didn't share the same interests? It seems a shame such amazing work went out of the family,' said Jessica.

Mollie waved an arm. 'Look around you. This house is crammed with memorabilia. And there're more boxes somewhere. In the attic, I think.'

Jessica glanced at Sally, who quickly picked up the cue. 'Mum, would there be old family stuff up there? Like going back to Grandad's time?'

'Good grief, I can't remember. My father put a lot of stuff up there before he married my mother. Your grandmother was a young woman, remember, barely twenty-three when they married. He was an older widower, so I suppose he packed away his previous life. Like I said, this house has been in the one family for several generations. I don't know much about my father's first wife's family. I wasn't born till Mother was forty and Father died when I was still quite young.' She uncrossed her legs and stood up. 'I'm getting peckish, I might go in and start dinner. Toby and Katie must be back from feeding the chickens by now.'

Jessica looked at Sally. 'The attic. After dinner. With chocolates and wine.'

*

98

The candle was sputtering, so Sally and Jessica had propped up two torches to shine a light on the papers spread around them. The attic had no power and smelled musty and faintly of mice. Sally wondered what else might be stored in the suitcases and cartons stacked up here, and in what condition their contents might be.

In the small pool of light, Jessica picked up her glass of red wine. 'The more I read, the more confused I get. The papers from the tin in the cave don't seem to have anything to do with Dr Holland's old stuff.'

'There have to be more of Stella's things somewhere. Mum told me once she remembers her mother keeping a sketchbook even when she was an older lady.'

'Why would the guy in the cave have kept that newspaper article about her winning first prize in the art competition?' said Jessica.

'He was proud of her? Or she gave it to him? Maybe she was proud of the painting.'

'We need to look further. What's in those wooden boxes? And there's a steamer trunk over there.'

'Jess, we'll be up all night at this rate.'

'Okay. So what do we have? This man, Broadbent, was seeing your grandmother secretly. But why would he leave some of his personal papers up there in the cave?'

Sally frowned. 'There could be lots of reasons. Maybe this was his special place. Maybe he was homeless. Maybe he was hiding from someone. Like the police.'

'Oh, maybe he was a criminal! A murderer! Or just a loner. I wonder where his family is?' Jessica said. 'That's it, I'm googling him.' She sat on the floor and began tapping her phone. Sally continued to rifle through the tin box, pulling out a heavy sheet of folded paper.

'This looks like some sort of drawing . . . it's a map. Oh, where's the buried treasure?' Sally said, laughing, then was suddenly serious again as she looked at it for a moment longer. 'It's of some property, see, there's a river marked and there's an X up here. And it's marked *Forest*.' She turned the paper around. 'Jess, this looks like here. Our place. Arcadia!' Jessica looked up from her phone as Sally continued. 'Why would he have done this? Maybe he had a bad sense of direction? The X must be the cave!'

'If Stella was meeting some man in the cave, he wouldn't want to be spotted on her property,' said Jessica. 'Though there is that swimming-in-the-creek photo.'

'I remember Mum telling me that my grandfather used to go to Hobart and stay at his club. She said Dad stayed there once but said it was too pokey. So my grandfather must have left Stella alone some of the time.'

'Wasn't the housekeeper still working here?'

'I doubt she would have prowled around the forest. Though Mr James might have.' Sally was about to fold the map when she saw lines of spidery handwriting on the bottom.

'What's this, an address? *Seawinds, Shelter Bay.*'

Jess returned her attention to her phone. 'There's nothing coming up on Google about him – unless he's a thirty-year-old accountant in Cairns. Hm, there's also a guy who was some sort of scientist, but he lived in England, so that can't be him. Hang on, let me add in this Shelter Bay place.'

Sally yawned while Jess tapped her phone.

'Hm, still nothing. Must be too long ago. But we need to keep looking. C'mon, let's open one more thing.' Jessica started to pull the leather trunk away from the back wall, dragging it across the floor to the light.

Sally jumped up and together they undid the old buckles.

Sally sniffed. 'Ooh, smell the camphor. At least someone thought of storing things properly.'

Jessica leaned into the box. 'There's a shelf that lifts out. Oh, gosh, this might be . . .'

Sally held up a torch as Jessica untied and unfurled a bundle of large paintings and smoothed them out, spreading them across the floor, where they curled up again. Jessica smoothed one out and sat there staring at it. Sally picked up another. And another.

'Stella's stash,' she said.

'These are . . . stunning. Beautiful.'

'I can't believe this. Look at this one, it seems to be all wildflowers. With their botanical names. I love these! Oh, wow, they should be framed, or in a book! And look at these watercolours of mushrooms,' exclaimed Sally.

'And they're in perfect condition. Let's see what else there is.' Jessica dived into the depths of the trunk. 'Oh, look! Oil paintings. Here, take the other end.'

Gingerly they unrolled a large oil canvas. It was a painting of a romantic and mysterious glade in a woodland setting of tall trees, filtered shafts of sunlight, thick ferns among roots and fungi. The little mushrooms and strange-shaped fungi were clustered over logs and lichen.

'It's like fairyland,' said Jessica. 'Magical. Ooh, look in the dark branches up there – the owl!'

Sally squinted as she studied the painting. 'I recognise it. It's down in the Far Forest. Near the creek.'

'That remnant rainforest land you've never touched?' said Jessica.

'Yes. It's not heritage listed or anything, but my

grandfather had in his will that it should remain as it is. I've forgotten why now . . .'

'This should be framed, it's significant to the house,' said Jessica.

'Mum says we have no more room, and I think she's right! That's probably why these have been left here and forgotten. Stella really had a talent, didn't she?'

'What else is there?'

Eagerly but gently, they continued exploring the contents of the old trunk. By the time it was empty, they were surrounded by paintings, watercolours mainly, save for a few large oil canvases. There were also several botanical reference books, sketchbooks, and bundles of letters, which seemed to be correspondence between Stella and her family on the mainland. There were several packets of photographs and negatives. Her paint palette, still smudged with dried paint, brushes, boxes of chalky pastels, tubes of oil paints and tins of watercolours, all smelling faintly of linseed and turpentine, lined the bottom of the trunk.

'She was well prepared,' Jessica said, thumbing through blank sketchbooks and several notebooks. 'What's this? Here's another one.'

From the bottom of the pile she pulled out a pad of paper labelled 'The Artist's Sketchbook' and flicked through it.

'Looks like she did rough pencil sketches and took photos as well, and brought them back to her studio,' said Sally. She paused, seeing Jessica's expression. 'What is it?'

Jessica handed her the open sketchbook. 'Get a load of this!'

'Ooh, ugh! Horrible!' exclaimed Sally in shock.

Jessica leaned over and stared at the rough pencil sketch. 'It's Stella, isn't it?'

'It looks like it . . . But why? What does this mean? She didn't die like this! Who would draw such a thing?'

'And the owl . . . poor dead thing,' added Jessica in a small voice. 'What do you think it means, Sal?'

'I've got no idea. It's sick.' Sally flipped through the sketchbook. 'Look at these sketches. Some man with a moustache and a scar on his face, who's he? Why'd she draw him? It's not the Greek god.'

'It's pretty rough, maybe she didn't draw it,' suggested Jessica, forcing herself to look at the drawing again.

'Well, that makes no sense.'

They stared at the face with the straggly moustache, wearing a deerstalker hat over long wispy hair.

Sally closed the sketchbook. 'That gives me the creeps. 'Specially the poor owl.'

'Where do you think your grandmother saw this man?' asked Jessica.

'Do you think she *knew* him?'

'Who's to say? From what I've heard, your grand-mother led a pretty sheltered life, and now we find out all this about her!'

'I suppose so . . . I remember Mum saying she didn't like the social hoopla in Hobart. My grandfather usually went off to those things on his own. If she went to the city it was for Art Society things, exhibitions and talks.'

'So she probably saw him here . . . maybe he tried to shoot the owl?' wondered Jessica. 'And what's with the flower and the seeds and the other stuff?'

'I have no idea. Come on, it's late. Let's pack this all away or start again in the morning,' Sally said. 'I promised Katie I'd take her down to the Hendersons' farm to see their new lambs first thing. This can wait. Katie will not.'

'You take her and after breakfast I'll tidy up here. Your mum might want to come and go through some of it.'

'Maybe. Mum doesn't tend to linger over the past even though she's surrounded by it. And if she wanted to tell me about this, she would have.' Sally picked up one of the torches and turned towards the attic doorway.

Jessica straightened up. 'Sal, we're going to do it.'

'What's that? Do what?'

'Take off. A road trip. Chase a mystery to Shelter Bay,' Jessica said.

Sally stared at her. 'I'm not convinced that's such a good idea.'

'Come on, Sal, we've got a whole collection of documents from some strange man in the cave. He had a newspaper clipping about your grandmother's painting, *and* a pressing of the flower she painted. And those photos and the farewell letter! They must have been lovers. Plus there's that creepy drawing in her notebook. What if they're all connected?'

'We can't just rock up. Anyway, they're probably all dead and gone.'

'I don't know, there might be some descendants of Broadbent's still living there,' Jess said. 'How far away is it?'

Sally got out her own phone and looked up Shelter Bay on the map. She looked thoughtful. 'It's north-west. Remember Chrissie from school? She lives up in the north now with her husband. It might be nice to visit them and then drive on to Shelter Bay, I guess . . .'

'Great. I reckon we should swing through Hobart on the way and go to the Botanical Gardens with the pressed flower and ask someone there to check it out. Then, who knows?' The excitement in Jessica's voice was growing.

'Sal, there's something strange about all this. We've stumbled on it for a reason, I reckon. You know my intuition. There's more to this. I just know it.' Jessica spread her arms, suddenly looking elated. 'Please, Sally. Come with me. See where we end up!'

Sally looked at Jessica standing there with arms outstretched, ready for anything. 'Oh, Jess. You're nuts.'

'So? We're going. *From the mountains to the sea . . . Just you and me . . .*' she sang.

'Well,' said Sally, giving in with a laugh. 'I suppose I can't let you go alone.'

4

Arcadia, 2018

WHERE THE DUSTY ATTIC had seemed mysterious, secret and alluring the previous night, in the bold morning light it looked forlorn, a place of forgotten lives and abandoned dreams.

Jessica tidied the boxes and carefully placed Stella's art back in the trunk with the letters and other items. But on an impulse she put the sketchbook with the drawings of Stella and the man in the hat to one side. She wondered if Mollie knew about it and if Stella had ever hinted about a rendezvous or a 'friend', or if indeed Mollie knew of the cave's existence.

Mollie was brewing coffee and she turned to Jessica with a smile as she came into the kitchen.

'Just in time. Would you like a cup?' she asked, then

her eyes fell on the items Jessica was carrying. 'What have you got there? Sal said you two found a few intriguing things last night. No one has ever been interested in all that old stuff, and I've run out of room in my little cottage to fit in anything more.'

'You might want to build another room, maybe a gallery and tearoom, to display it all,' Jessica said, sitting at the kitchen table. 'Did you know there's a collection of your mother's art in a trunk? Truly stunning work. It should be on show. Sally suggested maybe publishing it in a book.'

'Yes, Mother did some pretty flower paintings. I thought they were all given to the Art Society. We kept the ones she hung in her studio – they seemed to mean a lot to her.'

'Yes, the one with the blue flower and fungi and the painting of the owl. What was with the owl? It's a theme in several of the paintings we found.'

'Mother loved that owl. It was wild and lived down in the woods. She used to say it was her special friend. Not exactly a pet, though I believe it sometimes flew into the garden. I was afraid of it when I was very young, but when I grew older I would look forward to seeing it.'

'Did anything . . . bad ever happen to it?' asked Jessica cautiously.

'Not that I know of. There were a few years when I wasn't living here, before I moved back with Graham, but, my mother would have said something if it had; she'd have been heartbroken.'

While Mollie poured the coffee, Jessica put the sketch-book and the tin box from the cave on the table and took a deep breath. 'Sally suggested I show you these while she's out with Katie.' She'd managed to convince Sally to let her ask Mollie some questions without giving too much away.

Mollie glanced at Jessica's serious expression and sat down opposite her. 'Goodness, what dark secrets have you girls found in the attic?'

'Actually, we found this cashbox on the edge of your property, in the bush. It has some man's personal papers stashed inside, as well as a newspaper cutting that mentions Stella winning first prize for the owl painting. When we saw that, Sally thought we should see what Stella had packed away that you mightn't have gone through, and that's when we found this sketchbook in the attic.'

'I can't say that I've ever looked through every little thing up there. My mother had rolls and rolls of pictures, some unfinished, and a lot of paperwork. It's a project waiting to be taken on and I confess I had quite forgotten about it.' She looked at Jessica. 'So what have you found?'

'There's a drawing in the sketchbook that's rather shocking.'

'Shocking as in lewd for its time, or . . . what?'

'Well, it's horrific, actually.' Jess turned to the page and put it in front of Mollie, who gagged on her coffee, spilling some as she put the cup down in the saucer.

'Good lord, that's my mother! *Hanging*! Oh, sweet mercy, the owl . . . who drew this? Not her . . .'

'It's not very good art but there's no mistaking who it is,' said Jessica quietly. 'We wondered if you'd ever heard about this . . .'

'God! No! Close it up, I can't bear to look at it. My poor mother, why would she keep such a terrible thing?'

'Well, there are also sketches of a man . . .' Jess flipped through to the drawings of the man in the deerstalker hat. 'Do you recognise him?'

Mollie studied the pencil portrait and shook her head slowly. 'I don't think so. I doubt Mother would have known strange men outside the Holland circle of friends.' She took a moment, sipping her coffee, then turned to the cashbox. 'What's in the tin?'

Jessica opened it and showed Mollie some of the contents, carefully avoiding the violet letter. 'Personal documents belonging to some bloke who might have been a bit of a loner, considering where we found it. Perhaps your father knew him, treated him, maybe?'

'It would be very hard to know,' said Mollie, shaking her head slowly. 'Could have been from the Depression years when a lot of people were homeless or roughing it. Just someone passing through,' she added. 'My father never talked about his work, whereas my mother used to let me draw beside her when she was painting. When I was older I preferred to curl up and read. She was a great reader, too. Looking back I've come to realise that my mother was a very talented person.'

Jessica nodded and put the sketchbook to one side. Obviously Stella had never mentioned anything to her daughter and, apart from her shock at seeing the drawing, Mollie didn't seem particularly interested in the papers.

'Sally said she wishes she'd known her. I think it might be a good idea for her to do something with Stella's paintings, even just to protect them from ageing and fading,' said Jessica. 'We also found some pressed flowers and seeds in an old diary. We thought we might take them to the Botanical Gardens in Hobart to see if they can be identified.'

'Good idea, if you're really that interested! Goodness, I can't get over that dreadful drawing in Mother's sketchbook. It's like a threat or a premonition of some kind.

But she lived a long and happy life, and so, I presume, did Nyx.'

'Who?'

'The owl. In Greek mythology Nyx was night. She lived in a cave somewhere at the edge of the cosmos. My mother read a lot of Homer and Hesiod.'

'Oh, I see. Well if she befriended the owl, someone must have known it meant a lot to her. Surely your mother didn't have any enemies who would wish her such a terrible fate?'

Mollie refilled their cups. 'I can't imagine. She was a sweet and gentle person. Dreamy, like artists tend to be. Not that she was an artist as we know them today. It was her private passion. Though you just never know what goes on inside someone's head, do you,' said Mollie with a shrug. 'In a small village you think you know people pretty well, then it turns out the kind old lady down the road killed her husband and buried him under the cowshed.'

'Hit him over the head with a leg of lamb and cooked and served the lamb to the detectives looking for her missing husband,' Jessica said, and laughed.

'So they never found the murder weapon,' added Mollie with a smile. 'I read those old British crime novels too!'

'Maybe he was a wife basher and deserved it. Though Miss Marple would never say so!' said Jessica.

'Anyway, I do know that my mother was highly intelligent, artistic, and rather adventurous. She was also a devoted birder. Birdwatcher,' she added when she saw Jessica's puzzled expression.

'I wish I'd known her. There's something mysterious about her,' said Jessica.

'Why are you girls so absorbed with my mother's art?'

'It's so under-appreciated publicly, under-acknowledged,' said Jessica. 'So, Sally and I thought we'd do a bit of research, and have a kind of break at the same time, seeing as you and Toby offered. I want to reconnect with my home island again.'

'Oh, of course, of course, Sal mentioned it this morning. I think it's a great idea that the two of you head off on a bit of an adventure for a few days. Be good for Sal to get away. Have you worked out an itinerary? There's bad mobile reception in the most remote places, and sometimes none at all. Just where are you headed?' Mollie walked over to the sink and rinsed out her cup.

'A place called Seawinds, Shelter Bay. It was mentioned in one of the documents we found. We looked it up, it's in the middle of nowhere on the north-west coast.'

'Why on earth do you want to go there? Who lives there? That area is very rugged and remote.'

'Hopefully someone who knew the person who owned all this stuff lives there. I'm really curious to find out more.'

'What makes you think you'll find someone still in the area who knew that fellow? That place doesn't ring a bell with me. It's not somewhere we've ever had any connection with.'

'Where's your sense of adventure, Mollie?' Jess teased. 'Actually, it's kinda near where Chrissie and her husband are farming now. Remember Chrissie? I'd love to see their place.'

'Chrissie and Paul! Of course, I remember her well from when you were all at school. Don't they have something to do with TV? I saw an ad for a new cooking show and Sally said it was being filmed there,' Mollie said.

'Look, as far as I'm concerned, if you girls want to take off on some wild-goose chase, go ahead. It will give you both a chance to have a little time out together.' She smiled. 'Been a long while since it was just the two of you. Sally would never go away on her own, but she deserves a break. I'm glad you've convinced her to go.'

'Sal did say she wanted to see what Chrissie and Paul were doing. Game birds and things?'

Mollie sighed. 'Truffles I can live with, but spare me screechy birds. We had peacocks and guinea hens here, briefly – never again.'

'And geese! I remember my dad had geese when we lived here. They were scary. Good watchdogs, though.' Jessica laughed. 'Anyway, we'll go and check out the pheasants, do a bit of a loop up north then west and back here. Go where the mood takes us.'

'Good idea.' Mollie cocked her head as a car door slammed outside. 'Ah, that must be Sal and Katie coming back.'

Jessica packed away the papers and Stella's sketch-book as Katie came hurtling towards the kitchen squealing, 'Granny! Granny . . . I fed the lambs with a bottle!'

Arcadia, 1939

Stella sat in her studio in the fading light, staring into the twilight roses but seeing another scene entirely. She couldn't help but linger over the details of the unexpected encounter that morning.

Once the James family had settled back at Arcadia with their youngest son, Terry, who was still receiving treatment but was recovering from his exposure to polio, life had fallen into a routine. Winsome was retained

112

part-time to help Mrs James, and Stella resumed her birdwatching and painting. She returned to her habit of wandering along the riverfront, which was coming back to life after stagnating during the Depression and the years that followed it. Sometimes she took photographs, idly considering painting a river scene, but as always, she was drawn to the strange and compelling beauty of nature around her home, so little observed by the outside world.

Even though it had happened years ago now, thinking about her run-in with the strange man in the Far Forest still rattled her, especially as she was so sure she'd seen *two* men the first time.

Now, however, she felt emboldened whenever she was in the forest because of the presence of Nyx, the masked owl, who felt like a protector, a guardian who mysteriously appeared when she wanted or needed him. Stella was glad that the James children had kept his existence to themselves, and she thought the novelty of their day in the woods had been forgotten probably in the daily kaleidoscope of their lives.

Dr Holland had repeated his request that she not wander alone in the forest, providing no specific reason and assuming that his mere command was enough. So Stella had not challenged him even in the mildest manner. She had learned that the less said the better; a small smile and the matter was closed.

Or so Stephen may have believed.

Stella had adopted a compliant manner, and, while she wasn't meek, she certainly didn't challenge her husband. Mrs James once mentioned to her that she saw an occasional spark in Stella's eyes, a certain set of her mouth as she turned away following a flat edict from the doctor.

Both Stella and Mrs James clearly understood that the doctor assumed his words were never disobeyed, and that suited everyone.

On her walk that morning, Stella had paused near the jetty with the shed that the James children had explored when they were in her care. She had often thought about coming here to see for herself what the children had been talking about but had never found the time, until now. She noticed a boat, some stacked boxes, and a man standing in the entryway to the shed.

He was slim and fair, fit looking, dressed in hiking clothes and with a faint air of the mountaineer about him. Unlike most men he wasn't wearing a cap or hat, instead his thick fair hair flopped over his forehead. Stella thought he seemed familiar, but she couldn't seem to place him.

He smiled at her. 'G'day, miss. Lovely afternoon. Take care on the path there.' He pointed at the protruding roots from a nearby tree and a small pothole. He was well spoken, his voice roundly modulated.

'Thank you. Are you waiting for a boat?' Stella replied.

'I'm shipping out some items on the ferry,' he said.

'I'm afraid it's not always on time. The captains are friendly fellows and they do like to chat at each stop, or help people, which slows them down,' she said.

'So I've noticed. It's one of the nice things about a river. It seems a bit of a backwater but it's a connected community, if rather strung out between stops.'

Stella smiled. 'We like it that way. It's our highway, our link to each other, yet we have our own special piece of the river.'

'You live here then? It's a rather secret world tucked up away from the wild sea.' He returned her smile and she noticed his intense blue eyes.

'Yes. I'm not a local, though. Your family has to have been here a generation or two before you can actually say you come from this area.' She laughed. 'My husband is the local doctor; he's been here quite some time.'

The man's face clouded for an instant, but then he quickly smiled and said, 'Well, you're lucky, I wish I lived here. I live up north-west.'

They both gazed at the calm, silent river as the old ferry boat chugged towards them, slicing through the glassy surface, ripples radiating in sharp lines towards the bank.

Then he straightened. 'Good morning to you, Mrs Holland. I had better see to my cargo.'

She watched him walk away, feeling faintly disturbed: how did he know her name?

Hobart, 2018

Hobart was chilly, and an icy wind whipped around Constitution Dock as Sally and Jess headed to Salamanca Place.

'It's a bit touristy now, but you can always find something to take home for pressies,' said Sally. 'Mum loves the local lavender products and leatherwood honey. Katie wants a backpack . . .'

'This is day one, Sal, we can't start stocking up on gifts already! We didn't come to Hobart to shop.'

'Salamanca is fun even if you don't buy anything. We can still check out the shops, and there are some good places to eat. If we were here on a Saturday we could go to the markets.'

'Hey, look at that ketch, she's so beautiful!' Jessica paused to admire a classic boat berthed at the dock. 'Wow, it's the *May Queen*. She's been restored. Amazing.'

'She's 150 years old.' Sally read the small plaque. 'The oldest trading ketch in Tasmania. Restored by the Maritime Museum. She was built down our way.'

'Huon pine . . . wouldn't it be great to sail in her?' Jessica sighed. 'There's something about the classic old boats, they're so graceful. Wish your *Charlotte-Ann* was bigger, then maybe I'd rent her off you to live on.'

'You're not serious?' Sally stared at Jessica as they walked across the cobblestones towards the old waterfront buildings.

'A girl can dream, can't she? In fact, you and I could go on a voyage . . . an adventure.' Jessica grinned.

'We're already on an adventure, remember?' said Sally with a chuckle. 'Anyway, where would we go, and why do you think we could suddenly live on a boat and sail away somewhere?'

'Well, why not? Couldn't we share a tiny cabin and face the dangers of the southern seas?' Jess asked teasingly, knowing Sally was the better sailor.

Sally shrugged. 'The explorers Bass and Flinders did. Two young Englishmen in their twenties, best friends, sailed a tiny wooden sailboat around most of Van Diemen's Land to discover if it really was an island. Could we cope with months at sea, cooped up in a boat like the *Norfolk*? The *Tom Thumb*?'

'Were they gay?'

'I don't think so. Matthew Flinders wrote letters to his sweetheart, later his wife. I've read them. Such a beautiful love story. All those long years apart, and then he died the day after he finished his book on the journey to Terra Australis. There's a fictionalised version of his life, *My Love Must Wait*, written yonks ago by Ernestine Hill. Mum has it.'

'He died young, didn't he?'

'Yeah. Forty. He was imprisoned for years on Mauritius. He never tried to escape. Silly man. Duty and discipline and all that.'

'Different breed of men then. Well, Hardy could never have been called the principled type. Toby is a good and decent man, though. You're lucky. It's been nice getting to know him better.'

'Do you think it's luck, Jess? Finding someone to team up with forever, have kids with, trust to look after you, all that sort of old-fashioned stuff?' wondered Sally as they headed towards the row of galleries and boutiques. 'He thinks he's pretty lucky finding me,' she added.

'He is! You're both lucky. Maybe that's the knack, knowing it's a two-way street. Then you tend to look out for each other. A shared life.' Jessica paused, then walked into a leatherwork shop.

'Hey, look at these bags!' said Sally. 'Let's find Toby a present!'

*

Later, after what they agreed was an excellent Italian meal at a café beside the parade of shoppers along Salamanca Place, they put the locally made leather satchel-cum-briefcase Sally had bought for Toby in the back of the car. They also loaded other gifts and treats, 'necessities' as Jessica called them, which they'd bought for their trip – wine, handmade chocolates, spiced salt, grissini sticks and lavender soap.

'What's this?' Jessica lifted up an envelope with *Jess and Sal* scrawled on it.

'That's from Mum. She said she left something for us in the car. What is it?'

'A CD.' Jessica turned it over and burst out laughing as she read the sticker on it. '*Mum's fave road music.* Oh, no! Did she make this for us?'

'Eeek, no way! It'll be all 80s and 90s stuff. What a riot.'

'Let's wait until we're out of radio range and desperate,' suggested Jessica as she put it in the glove box. 'Okay. Let's go to the Botanical Gardens and find someone who can help us.'

*

They parked outside the large wrought-iron gates of the beautiful old gardens overlooking the wide Derwent River. The young man in the small information booth just inside the entry was busy handing out brochures and answering questions.

Standing by the information board that showed a large map of the gardens was an older gentleman. He had a lanyard around his neck that read *Guide*, and was giving directions to a couple. As they moved off, he turned to the two women with a smile and said, 'Can I help you with something, ladies?'

'Yes, please. We want to see if a plant we have can be identified. It's a rather old specimen,' said Sally.

'Fragile, she means. We found it in an old diary,' explained Jessica.

'Really? How exciting. You've looked it up on the internet, have you?'

'We tried, but it was hard to search for as we don't know its name. We've brought it in for someone here to look at. Isn't there a plant identification and collection unit here?' asked Jessica.

He nodded. 'It's in the nursery section on the other

side of the gardens. C'mon, there's a bit of a lull, I'll take you over. Hop in.' He pointed to the golf buggy parked nearby and turned back to the man in the information booth. 'Roly, I'm taking these girls over to the seed collection lab. Back shortly.'

Sally nudged Jessica as the older man reached for a walking cane and walked awkwardly on hobbled feet supported by bulky shoes.

They walked slowly beside him to the buggy.

'Put your seatbelts on please, ladies. It's required by law.'

'I'll sit in the front with you,' Jessica said. And seeing his name on the lanyard around his neck added, 'Hi, Terry. I'm Jessica and that's Sally in the back.'

As they drove, Terry rattled off the Latin botanical names of various plants, giving them a bit of history of the beautiful gardens.

'Second oldest in Australia, originally land was occupied by the Muwinina people. When the governor later claimed it from an ex-convict, it became known as the Colonial Gardens.'

'I can imagine strolling around on a Sunday in my crinoline,' said Sally.

'Driving in a carriage,' decided Jessica.

'Oh, wow, look at the fernery!' exclaimed Sally as they passed the lush misty miniature rainforest with its cascading waterfalls. 'It's fairyland.'

Terry braked. 'Hop out and have a look, take a photo.' He began to list the names of the giant ferns and pointed out the tiny delicate plants the size of a finger.

Sally laughed. 'Terry, you seem to know the Latin name of every plant in the gardens!'

'How long have you been here?' asked Jessica as

they got back into the buggy after taking photos on their phones.

'Oh, I've had a bit of an interest for a long time.' He smiled. 'I've only been a guide for the past six years. When I turned eighty I thought I'd better get a proper job!'

'What! You're eighty-six?' said Sally. 'How did you learn so much about plants? Was that your work?'

'I was an amateur botanist, I guess. Now, over here is the Tasmanian Seed Conservation Centre. We're a partner in the International Millennium Seed Bank Project, which holds our island state's collection of seeds and rare and threatened plants. They're also conserved in the nursery garden. The Subantarctic Plant House is here too. I collected some specimens myself on a field trip to Macquarie Island one year,' he added proudly. 'Here we are. If you want a ride back, ask someone inside to give me a call. But you should walk back, take your time. I can recommend the restaurant.'

'Thanks, Terry, you've been very kind.'

'Where are you girls visiting from, anyway?' he asked as they got out of the buggy.

'We're locals. Well, from down south a bit,' Sally replied.

'Good luck with your plant. I'd be quite keen to know if you've found something of interest.'

'We'll let you know,' said Jessica. 'What's your phone number?'

'Would you? That's kind of you. Hang on.' He fished in his pocket for his mobile phone. 'I have to look up my number, never remember it.'

Jessica punched the numbers into her phone as he read them off.

'Good luck, girls.'

'Thanks, Terry,' Sally said. They watched as he whipped the buggy into a U-turn and zipped away along the wide path. 'Can you believe him? How fantastic at that age!'

'What's wrong with his feet, do you think? Doesn't seem to have slowed him down, if he was able to trek around Macquarie Island,' commented Jessica. 'You have the diary in your bag?'

Sally patted her shoulder bag. 'Yep. Let's hope someone is around to help us. Maybe we should've made an appointment.'

'How long could it take to check out one flower?' said Jessica.

*

'So how did you find us?' asked Denyse Briggs, the botanist, after she had introduced herself. 'Not everyone ventures this far into the gardens.'

'Oh, Terry, the guide. He drove us here after a bit of a tour,' said Jessica.

'He seems very knowledgeable,' added Sally.

Denyse smiled. 'Ah, yes. Good man, Terry. Amazing bloke, and how he gets around, not only at his age but with his legs and feet the way they are. Nothing slows him down.'

'Yes, he mentioned he'd hiked around Macquarie Island,' said Jessica. 'Do you know what happened to him?'

Sally winced at Jessica's blunt question, but the botanist gave a small, philosophical shrug.

'He was one of thousands of children who contracted polio during the big epidemic here in the late 1930s. The world's second-largest polio outbreak, he told me. Way before the Salk vaccine came along. He hasn't let it stop him, though. Now, let's see this plant of yours.'

Sally carefully took the diary and the small plastic bag of seed samples from her bag. She opened the diary and handed it to Denyse. 'It's probably been in that book for years. We've only just found it,' said Sally. 'My grandmother did a painting of the plant's setting too.'

'Interesting. I doubt it would have been growing in a domestic garden,' mused the botanist as she examined it closely. 'Oh, and seeds too. Hmm, may I take this out?'

She took a pair of tweezers and delicately lifted the faded bloom and rested it on a clear sheet of glass, adjusted her glasses and studied it for a few seconds.

'The family genus could be known; the leaves are unusual, and it has a large bulb. The flowers will help to identify it. Pressed plants are the mainstay of herbaria, and the history of plant identification is tied to herbarium specimens – that's when a species is designated a type specimen when it is described scientifically. Our Tasmanian Herbarium has some of the original specimens collected by Joseph Banks when he and Captain Cook first explored Australia, or the Great Southern Land as it was then.'

'Wow, really? And what about these seeds?' asked Sally.

'It's not always possible to identify something from seed. It would be interesting to have a soil sample, that's where all the action happens. One option would be to grow the seed, but a lot of native plants have complex dormancies so even though they germinate readily in the wild, it may take a lot of different treatments and sometimes years before we can germinate a species in the lab.'

'We do have pictures, well, a painting, of this plant growing in a small remnant forest on our farm. Would that help?' said Sally.

'Indeed it might. Can you email a photo of it to me, please?'

Sally nodded and made a mental note to ask Toby or her mother to take one.

'So what do you do to identify this? Trawl through the internet or old books? Sit and look at images of plant samples?' asked Jessica.

'The time taken to ID something varies – often I'm familiar with the plant or know what genus it belongs to, so it doesn't take long. Sometimes I know the family and work back that way to the genus and then the species. I use various websites and books and keys where appropriate. I find that there's often a run on a plant, so when it is first brought in it may take me about half an hour to ID it and then someone else will bring it in a few days later and will be really impressed that I can immediately say what it is.' She laughed. 'But it's time-consuming,' she admitted. 'I'll need to keep this specimen for a few days while I work out what it is. It will be well looked after. Is that okay with you? I'll give you a receipt.'

'Yes, of course,' said Sally. 'We'll be interested to hear what you discover about it. Thank you.'

They stood at the front desk as Sally gave Denyse her details, address and phone numbers.

'We'll be in touch as soon as we find out anything. Oh, hi, Dan.' The botanist smiled as a casually dressed but very handsome man walked in. 'These ladies have brought in a mystery plant. You might want to have a look if you have time. Dan is one of our top botanical specialists,' she explained.

He grinned at Sally and Jessica. 'We like mystery plants, surprising how often they turn up. Where's it from?'

'The old forest on our farm in the south-east,' said Sally.

'Always interested in anything from old-growth

forests. Did you happen to bring some of its soil or material where it was growing?'

'Oh, we didn't collect it, it's years old. It's from my grandmother's time,' said Sally.

'Sounds interesting, especially if Denyse couldn't recognise it straight away! Are you staying in Hobart?'

'No, we're on a short holiday,' said Sally. 'Taking some time out.'

'Road trip. A girls' adventure,' Jessica said, grinning.

'How cool! Have fun,' said Denyse, handing a receipt to Sally. 'We'll let you know if we have any luck and we can mail your specimen back to you by registered post.'

'That makes it sound like some nasty disease!' said Sally with a laugh.

The girls walked back to the grand entry gates and Sally stopped. 'Let's take a selfie – to mark the start of our big adventure.'

They stood close together and smiled. 'I'll put it on Facebook with the line, "Our very own road trip to reveal long-lost plants, visit Chrissie and Paul, and see what we can discover at Shelter Bay." Toby can show it to Katie. She'll love it,' Sally said.

'Okay, let's hit the road,' Jessica said as they got back in the car. 'Right, so what're we playing first?'

'Not Mum's music!'

'What, you don't like *Graceland*, Paul Simon, or Shania Twain?' Jessica laughed. 'Let's go with Mia Dyson.'

'Fool!' they both called in unison, as Jess hit play and Sally pulled out onto the road, heading for the Brooker Highway.

Later they traded places to share the driving, but after a while they decided it was time for a coffee break. In the main street of a small town they saw a sign outside an old house advertising that it was a bookshop and café, so they pulled over.

Opening the front door, they were amazed to find that every room of the stone house was filled with bookcases, except for the kitchen and the lounge, which had been converted into an informal tea and coffee room. A pot of soup simmered on the stove and next to it was an appetising row of freshly baked scones. There were extra tables and chairs in the lounge room plus a long sofa in front of the fireplace. The owner sat behind a counter that was smothered in books save for an antiquated computer and credit card machine. He looked up over his glasses.

'Looking for anything in particular, ladies?'

'Not really, but I'm sure we'll find something,' said Jessica. 'Do you have new books too?'

'More or less. What are you after?'

'Actually, do you have any books about native Tasmanian plants?' said Sally suddenly.

'Hey, smart thinking,' said Jessica. 'Like old botanical books?'

He gestured to the hallway. 'Third room on the right. But it's mostly early local history. Maritime is in the second room, there's a heck of a lot of that.'

'Gosh, I could spend all day in here,' said Jessica.

'Me too. I'm going to look for some children's books for Katie as well. Where are they?' Sally asked the owner.

'There's collectibles in here, first editions of Enid Blyton and even some Australiana . . . Mary Grant Bruce's *Billabong* series, for example.'

Over an hour later, the girls sat down to coffee and buttered banana bread as they examined the pile of books they'd collected.

'I reckon we've got a haul and a half. Fascinating.

I could have gone crazy over those original May Gibbs *Snugglepot and Cuddlepie* books. But I've got Katie *Marmaduke the Possum*. She's just the right age for it.'

'Pixie O'Harris! I loved that. I have my mother's copy,' said Jessica.

As they sipped their coffee, Sally pointed at the framed photographs for sale on the wall.

'Look at these amazing photos by Peter Dombrovskis. That's the Tarkine wilderness area. Even though it's near us I've never ventured far into it.'

The owner collected their empty plates. 'See it while you can. Logging is raising its ugly head again. They want to clear some parts of the ancient forests for woodchips for Asia.'

'I thought they'd restricted that to commercial wood plantations,' said Sally. 'Though they're destructive, too.'

'Let's go see,' said Jessica. 'We can take the route over the mountains, can't we?'

'I don't want to see cleared rainforest,' said Sally. 'It's too depressing.'

'Just take the route through the hills, it's spectacular but rugged,' suggested the shop owner. 'Are you taking all these books?'

*

They put most of their final selection of books in the car, and Jessica settled herself behind the wheel. Sally kept several books on her lap.

'I'm going to thumb through the botanical ones. And this one of Margaret Hope's art. She was around in my grandmother's time.'

'Do you think Stella was influenced by her?' Jess asked, glancing over.

126

'My grandmother's work is not as dainty, or quite so detailed in the botanical sense. She had a more romantic, poetic approach. You feel there's a story within it, not just the reproduction of a plant,' mused Sally.

'And don't forget Nyx, the owl.'

'Yes. I hope we find out about the flower from the Botanical Gardens people.'

'Do you think there're still some growing on your property? In your woods, perhaps?' asked Jessica. 'The Far Forest.'

'Yes. Mum says my grandfather was very English, even though he was born here. He always referred to that land as "the woods".'

'It's a bit wilder than English woods, I imagine. Remember the late afternoon we were out there once and got scared by the bats swooshing around us and we ran for our lives?' said Jessica.

'Yes! Thousands of bats chasing those swarming insects. I had a bat tangled in my hair and I couldn't stop screeching!' Sally laughed. 'Funny, though, they never came back in the same numbers. And the insects disappeared. We hardly ever went to those woods again.'

'Well, we grew up and moved on, didn't we?' Jessica sighed.

'Katie has only ever been down there once or twice. I guess we have plenty of other walks, trees and fields for her to explore. I wonder if she'll be as adventurous as we were,' mused Sally.

'You should hope not. But give her a couple more years! C'mon, more music.'

Sally searched for a track, announcing, 'Missy Higgins. Love her stuff.'

The road rose in twists as if it were lost and had to

127

keep looking over its shoulder to find a way up the mountainside. On one side the trees stretched to the sky like a sheer green cliff above thick undergrowth, while from the other edge the hillside disappeared behind intermittent trees and giant clumps of ferns and saplings. A distant range of mountains, thickly forested, coiffed by wispy clouds, rose on the far side of nothingness, the valley too far below to be seen.

Once they finally levelled out they saw a faded signpost reading *Valley View Township*.

'Another coffee?' said Jessica. 'That drive was stressful.'

'You bet.' Sally looked at her phone to find directions. 'Damn. No reception.'

Jessica turned down the old road, barely wide enough for two cars. 'Where the heck is this township?'

'Was there another turn-off? Oh look, there's a building.'

'Looks like a café. Well, that's a start.'

They turned into the scruffy, overgrown car park beside the old wooden building where a thin trail of smoke floated into the sky. The girls shivered and glanced up at the thickening clouds.

'Is it going to rain or is it because we're up so high?'

'Either way, I need a hot coffee to warm up and I want to stretch my legs,' said Sally. 'We have time, we're not in any rush.'

They climbed out of the car and crunched over gravel to the front of the building, where the café offered a view across the high hill. They stopped and stared at a row of cottages with neglected gardens lining a street, along with a church and a sort of fellowship hall.

'Is this the township? No shops, no nothing? Looks deserted.'

'There's a park,' said Jessica, pointing to the broken swings, rusting see-saw and leaning basketball hoop.

'This place is sort of creepy.'

'Someone's in the café, though. Let's go. It's getting cold.'

*

A pot-bellied stove and delicious baked-muffin aroma gave the place an inviting warmth.

It was simply decorated with wooden tables, bunches of flowers, a counter with takeaway food choices, and a small gift shop, with displays of woollen items and jars of homemade pickles and chutneys.

A woman appeared, not much older than themselves, wiping her hands on her apron. 'Hi, are you eating, or just having tea? Coffee?'

'Coffee, please, and I think I'd like to eat something,' said Jessica. 'This is so cosy.'

'Something smells good. Let's call this a late lunch,' Sally suggested.

'There's a fresh pot of pumpkin soup and homemade bread rolls.'

'We'll have that,' Sally and Jessica answered in unison.

Sally sat at a table overlooking the vast valley as Jessica went to the gift shop.

'Hey, Sal, come over and look at these great hand-spun woollen socks and the soft pashminas. There're some cute knitted animals too. I'll get one for Katie.'

'They're lovely. I'll buy Mum one of these shawls.'

'Who makes these?' Jessica asked the woman as they were served their food.

'A friend of mine. She gets the wool from a local farmer and spins and dyes it and knits them.'

'Fantastic. Tell me, what's with the cottages down the

road; are they for rent or empty? Do people live here?' asked Sally. 'It seems pretty quiet.'

The woman gave a small laugh. 'You might say that. This was once a busy little township, but it closed up when the hydro workers left. Some holidaymakers rent the cottages occasionally. But there's not much to do up here.'

'You mean for tourists?' asked Jessica.

'When they built the hydroelectricity facility, this was the workers' township. You can see the pipes, pumps and powerhouse further down the hill there. The government is looking at the whole power situation at the moment.' She shrugged. 'Plans seem to change, though. Renewables and others are against the power station mob, and vice versa; the usual. I just think it a shame that this little town is empty. There's a schoolhouse, a general store, a small roadhouse, a church, a hall. They used to have great dance nights, and a good library. It's closed too. All the books are still in there. Such a waste.'

'What? You're joking,' exclaimed Sally.

'So there's no work here now?' Jess asked.

'No. People have had to move away to look for work. We have a small farm and rely on passing trade. No one stays. I'll just bring your bread.' She hurried back into the kitchen.

'What a shame. Think what a bunch of refugees could do up here,' said Jessica as they ate their soup. 'Turn it into a thriving community.'

'It seems a sad sort of place,' said Sally. She shivered. 'I think we should move on before dark and get settled somewhere else. Maybe we should have booked a hotel.'

'Flying by the seat of our pants, living in the moment, as the mood takes us, no commitments, remember?'

Sally sighed and drained the last of her coffee. 'Let's

see if there's any phone reception. I want to check in with Toby.' She took out her phone and pressed his number.

Jessica paid for the food and gifts. 'How far to the next petrol station?' she asked the café owner.

'Not far, over the next hill, where the road divides at the junction. That way they get everybody before people take a different direction at the roundabout.'

'Let's take a photo before the sun goes,' said Sally, re-joining them.

'Would you like me to take one of you both?' The woman took a shot with Sally's phone then said, 'There's a good picture from the front too, and if you walk a hundred metres down that way, you can see the hydro station pump house and the pipes. The water is pumped up from the river below. It's quite spectacular. There's lots of great things to see around here.' She paused. 'Have you seen the Mountain Gallery?'

'Ah, no, what's that?' asked Jessica.

The woman chuckled. 'Surprise yourself. Here, I'll draw you a map.' She pulled the notepad and pencil she used to write down orders from her pocket and drew a quick sketch. 'Take this back road round behind here rather than going straight back down the mountain. It'll take you cross country until you get back on the road to Livingstone, that's the highway crossroads.'

'What's there?' asked Sally.

'It's quaint. Scenic. Bit of a testimony to man's ingenuity and appreciation of his surroundings,' she said enigmatically.

'Okay then. We'll go and look at the pump station first. Thanks a lot.'

'Are we really going to take that back road? And what's she mean by a "testimony to man's ingenuity"?'

131

asked Sally after they'd taken in the pump house and massive pipes and were walking back to the car.

'One way to find out,' said Jessica cheerfully.

'This is so interesting. I'm going to put these photos of the pumping station up on Facebook as soon as we get in range,' Sally said as she took her turn in the driver's seat.

*

The afternoon sun was being swallowed by clouds and spearing trees as the gravel road wound through the quiet light.

'This is primordial; are we going to return to civilisation?' wondered Sally.

The CD had come to an end and putting on more belting pop music didn't seem appropriate.

'I think we should keep going,' said Jessica. 'We need to get to a town and find a bed for the night. And a large glass of something.'

'This probably wasn't a smart idea – it's getting dark and it feels like a large glass of something could be a long way off . . . hey!'

'What the hell . . .?'

Sally slowed the car.

'Was that a man . . .?'

'Whoa. Stop. Pull over.'

'There's nowhere to stop, it's a one-way road.'

'Well, there's no one else up here . . . except . . . them . . .' said Jess.

Both girls craned forward, peering into the green gloom.

The figure of a man was silhouetted between the trees. And as they looked into the forest on either side of the car, a dozen or more people stoically observed them.

'Are they . . . oh, God, look at the trees . . .' whispered Sally.

When they stared at the thick, towering trees they saw the writhing figures of sprites and animals, nymphs and children cleverly carved into the trunks, growing with the trees. Among them, standing, as if pausing to watch their car pass, were life-size figures. A woman's bonnet strings, an apron, a man's shirt, a kerchief, fluttered slightly.

'They look so . . . life-like,' whispered Jessica.

'Are they carved? They look like they're real people who've just been frozen. Like someone from space zapped them!'

'Let's go see.'

'Jess . . . are you sure? I'll wait in case I have to move the car off the road.'

'Sally! We haven't seen one car all the way up here! C'mon. Bring your phone, we definitely need photos of this!'

The girls stepped out of the car in the middle of the road and turned in a slow circle, feeling dozens of eyes on them.

Jessica strode over to the nearest wooden figure – and realised the stockman was actually larger than life-size. He had a coiled stockwhip on his shoulder, a plaited leather belt, moleskin pants and worn riding boots, and he peered at her from under his battered Akubra hat.

'G'day, mate. We're just cruising through,' she said aloud. 'Where's your mob of cattle?'

'Over here!'

She jumped and spun around to see Sally standing on the other side of the road. Flinging her arms open, Sally called, 'There's cattle here! Cows and calves and even some sheep! Jess . . . look, they seem so real, but they're all made of wood!'

'So're these guys! Has to be Huon pine. They'll last hundreds of years out here!'

'Ooh, come and see, there's a pioneer woman, and kids with a milk pail,' called Sally. 'The detail is stunning. Who would've done this?'

Jessica plunged into the forest past the carved trees and stopped in front of a World War One digger carrying a wounded mate, a masterful piece of realistic carving. Something about it brought a lump to her throat and she paused, tears springing to her eyes as she gently reached out to touch the young soldier.

'Easy does it, girlie.'

'Yikes!' Jessica started, leaping backwards.

Spinning around, she caught her breath at the sight of a stocky, thick-shouldered man standing before her, a small axe held loosely in one hand, various picks and chisels strung from his belt.

'Hi, sorry. You startled me. Did you carve these?' she stammered in a rush.

'I did.'

'They're amazing. So life-like.' She looked over her shoulder towards Sally but couldn't see her.

The man stared at her impassively, waiting, his hand on his axe handle.

'Why did you make them? I mean, why isn't this a museum? They're all . . . incredible,' said Jessica.

'I consider it my own tribute; some might call it an outdoor museum. I did them for myself.' He took a breath. 'I wanted to tell our story . . . it's a living story. The land, the people of the land . . . that is why I tell it in the wood of our land, so that it will not die for a thousand centuries . . .'

'The Huon pine?' asked Jessica gently, unsure about this strange man as she edged to one side, trying to see where Sally was across the road.

'If we lose our stories, we lose who we are.'

'How many people come here? I mean, who knows about this? Your work is unbelievable,' said Jessica.

'It's here.' He shrugged. 'How'd you find me?'

'The lady in the café in town drew a map for us but didn't tell us what was here,' Jessica replied.

He nodded. 'She doesn't tell everybody.'

'I'm glad I've seen this,' Jessica said quietly. She was about to say more when Sally walked over to join them.

'Are you the artist? This is really amazing. I've just been looking at the group of Indigenous people over the other side.' She looked at the enigmatic man. 'Thank you. This is so . . . special. A museum, an art gallery, it's like a . . . living history of these parts . . . where all these people and animals might have lived.'

'Yes. There's a lot of history here, good and bad. Some people don't want to know, or care.' He shrugged and hefted the axe lightly in his hand.

Jessica leaned close to Sally, radiating caution, but Sally was starstruck and she nodded enthusiastically. 'That's right.'

He stared at them intensely. 'I feel we're losing our stories, and the trees have always observed our history. I've just incorporated a bit from more recent times, as well. Taken me years to do this. Don't want to harm the trees. I only carve individual pieces from fallen trees. I watch out for the forest. This can't, shouldn't, ever be logged. Got to keep our stories alive.' He gave them a piercing stare. 'When we ignore our past, we condemn our future.' He paused, then turned away. 'Travel safe, ladies.' And he walked into the forest, disappearing among the shadows.

Jessica and Sally watched him go, too stunned to say anything. A bird shrieked and they jumped.

'I'll take some photos too, no one will believe this,' Jessica murmured.

'If you weren't here, I might have thought I'd imagined it. What a strange man.'

'I was nervous about that axe, and the tools. Perfect murder weapons. We could've ended up carved into trees,' said Jessica.

'Jess! Stop that! Why do you always think the worst of people?'

'Because I'm not as trusting as you. C'mon, it's time to find that large glass of something.'

*

Settled in a modest motel at the edge of the river, the girls looked at their photographs of the tree carvings.

'Like you said, people aren't going to believe these. Makes the ones I posted on Facebook from the hydro station look a bit boring,' said Sally.

'Y'know what, Sal?' said Jessica suddenly. 'I wouldn't mention the axeman to our families. And my instinct is not to put these pictures up online. You don't know who might take it into their heads to, well, go up there and trash them or something.'

'Why would someone do that?'

Jessica shrugged. 'Don't know. Why do people do mad, crazy, cruel things? Even when they're not on drugs. Let's save the photos till we get back and show our families then. You've talked to Toby and Katie. I've rung my parents. Let's leave it at that for now. In fact, I vote that we go down the road to the pub. I bet they've got good food.'

They stepped outside their room, shivering slightly in the evening breeze that wafted up from the broad expanse of the river. The lights from the motel restaurant glimmered on the water. Jessica flung out an arm.

'Pretty setting for the restaurant, but it looks a bit boring. Have you noticed something?'

'About what?'

'This is a stunning view: huge river, fishing boats, leisure craft moored along the water's edge, pretty park and pathway winding by the river into the picturesque township . . . Great setting for a motel at the water's edge. But look, except for the cabin staying *Staff*, every room faces the parking lot in the middle. Why wouldn't you turn our rooms around to face the view? Who wants to look at a bunch of cars?'

'Yep. You're right. The builder probably worked it out to do with parking, or access, or something non-aesthetic.'

'You'd fit the same number of cars in if you turned the rooms outwards. After all, the guestrooms are just boxes with a bathroom.'

'Didn't you once think about doing architecture?' Sally asked.

'Yes. Thank goodness I stuck to science and nature. The natural environment designs things so much better than people do.'

*

The Buona Vista Hotel was crowded, warm, noisy and friendly. Two attractive men bought them drinks and told them they worked on one of the cruise boats that went upriver into the gorge and rainforest.

'You should do the trip. It's stunning scenery. Can get rough sometimes but tomorrow will be good.

Come along,' said one of the men, who was out from Canada on a working holiday.

'We'll think about it,' said Jessica.

They'd politely refused the offer of dinner, and had enjoyed the crayfish stew and crusty bread in the pub's dining room and were now back in their motel room. Sally sat on her bed poring over the map of the area, while Jessica was browsing through one of the books they'd bought.

'This book is about early settlers on an island off the north-west coast. Talk about getting away from it all. Imagine farming, raising a family, the only people on the whole island. Reliant on a boat or rickety plane to come in from the mainland, while in the other direction there's nothing between your farmhouse and South America,' said Jessica.

'I couldn't live somewhere so remote.' Sally studied Jessica. 'How come you didn't want to have dinner with the nice Canadian guy? We could have gone on that cruise. He was pretty cute.'

'I don't need a cute Canadian. He's going to go home. I don't want to live in Canada. Nice place to visit. I bet he doesn't want to settle down in Tasmania.'

'I was only suggesting dinner,' said Sally mildly, 'not planning the rest of your life.' She was relieved when her phone rang.

'Hello?' There was silence on the other end. 'Hello? Anyone there?' She glanced at the phone, but no number was displayed. 'Hello . . .?' She shrugged. 'They hung up. Funny, someone was definitely there, I'm sure.'

'Wrong number. So, we're pushing on to the north tomorrow?'

'Yep. That'll bring us to Paul and Chrissie's, and

138

they're near Shelter Bay. We can go to Seawinds after visiting them . . .' said Sally.

'But? You sound hesitant. I'm dying to find out anything we can about the two lovers in the cave.'

'I don't know, Jess, do you really think going to Shelter Bay will help us discover anything about the guy in the cave? All we really have is a name and some old photos.'

'It's a start. I just have a feeling. What's the harm in checking it out?'

Sally refolded the map. 'Okay. After all, it's what precipitated this trip,' she said. 'And hopefully we'll hear something from the Seed Conservation people at the Botanical Gardens soon, too.'

Jessica got out her phone. 'Well, now that we finally have reception I'm going to try the Births, Deaths and Marriages site,' she said, typing the words onto her screen. '*Researching family trees,*' she read out, 'maybe I can start there.' She read silently for a while then yawned and said, 'I give up. We'll have to do this when we're back at your place and can use the computer in your office instead of trying to do it on my phone. Even then it will take a minimum of ten days to get any information.'

'Okay, leave it and we'll work on it at home,' said Sally. 'Now, I don't know about you but I'm exhausted. I'm just going to finish putting the pictures from dinner up online so Katie can see them in the morning, then I'm going to sleep.'

''Night, Sal.' Jessica turned off her phone and then her light as Sally expertly uploaded the photos of them laughing and waving a crayfish claw at the camera.

''Night, Jess.'

*

The next morning they headed down a lane between hedgerows, with glimpses of paddocks and hills and an occasional headland in the distance, and beyond them, a strip of blue sea.

'Gosh, what beautiful land,' said Jessica.

'Red basalt around here; makes the sheep turn russet brown,' said Sally. 'But Chrissie and Paul run mainly dairy cattle and grow fabulous heirloom vegetables. Their friends in the neighbouring farms also grow some amazing stuff.'

'I thought your truffles and saffron endeavours were pretty amazing. Adventurous,' said Jessica.

'Risky too. But even a small crop is worth it,' said Sally. She turned off the lane onto a driveway and they rattled over a cattle grid. 'Look how beautiful their house is. There's three houses on the property.'

'Oh, wow,' said Jess as the homestead came into view. 'Hey, what's going on over there?'

They saw a small group of people standing beside some trees, next to a long table where a man was holding a fat black and white jersey cow and a small lamb. 'Oh, I see the lights set up, they're filming.'

'Must be the TV crew Chrissie mentioned when we talked on the phone.'

As Sally drove up to the restored historic house, Chrissie appeared at the front steps and gave a welcoming wave. 'Oh, there goes my phone.' Sally pulled up by the house and looked at her mobile as she answered.

'Hello.' She glanced at Jessica. 'Hello?'

She handed Jessica the phone, putting her finger to her lip.

Jessica listened, and although there was silence, she had the distinct impression someone was on the line.

'Hey, who is this?' There was a faint sniff, or breath, and the line clicked off. 'No number registered. Hmm. Odd.'

'Hi, girls!' Chrissie was opening the car door. 'Come in, come in. Man, you've come when it's all happening.' She hugged Sally. 'Jessica! Gosh, I remember you from school. How fabulous to see you. C'mon, let's get the tour out of the way and have a stickybeak at the TV people. Drives Paul nuts; they spend such a long time over the smallest detail.'

'Hey, I recognise him, from *MasterChef* on TV,' said Jessica, looking at one of the men in the group.

'He was a contestant a few years ago. He's from around here, didn't win, but he was very popular. He does this for our local Gourmet Tourism Trails,' Chrissie said as they walked over to the stand of trees. 'I tell you, the interest in food is amazing. Groups come from the cruise ships, bus tours, all kinds of garden clubs. They call them Farmgate Tours. And some people just drive in. Incredible.'

'How do you get any work done?' asked Sally.

'All the local farms and producers have banded together, so we take it in turns and do it seasonally, rotating which farm is open when. People here are growing wonderful things, black garlic, wasabi, pepper berry, sea urchin roe, and smoking is big – not just meat, but the salmon and oysters. Friends of ours are raising Wessex saddleback pigs, lots of heritage breed ducks, poultry, not to mention the ice-creams, berries, feijoas, olives, ciders, beers and wine,' she added.

'What're feijoas?' asked Jessica.

'Myrtle family, a fruit, like guavas but they're incredibly sweet. I'd describe the taste as a mix between strawberries, pineapple and guavas, with undertones of quince, lemon and mint.'

141

'Sounds divine as a drink! Sal, you should plant some trees.'

'I brought up some saffron and I hope to do a swap and go back with some feijoa cordial,' Sally said.

'We have a concentrate that goes well with your gin,' said Chrissie. 'Come and meet our friend, Carmen. She's into medicinal herbs and edible weeds. She came over to be in the filming.'

Jessica looked at Sally. 'She might know about your plant,' she suggested.

'What plant is that?' asked Chrissie as she led them down towards the TV crew.

'Oh, long story,' said Sally. 'In a nutshell . . . we found a pressed flower in an old diary and we couldn't identify it, so we took it to the Seed Conservation Centre at the Botanical Gardens in Hobart.'

'Ooh, how fascinating, have you heard back from them?'

'Not yet.'

'So why are you so interested? Is it unusual? Do you think it might be rare or valuable?'

'Oh, it's a modest-looking little thing,' said Jessica. 'But Sal's grandmother Stella did a stunning painting with it in one corner, so it would be nice to know what it is. Hopefully the botanists at the Gardens will work it out.'

They stood and watched the filming for a moment as the chef sprinkled crushed seeds on top of the elaborate salad he'd prepared from local ingredients. The table was laden with a cornucopia of dishes made from local produce.

'I'm hungry,' whispered Jessica.

'Stunning-looking food,' said Sally. 'But I just couldn't go to all that trouble.'

A woman in her fifties, dressed in a long, faded cotton dress, a tasselled shawl and sturdy sandals, her wild brown hair streaked with strands of grey, leaned over. 'I'm with you. Throw it all in one bowl, raw, sprinkle lemon juice and oil on it. Eat. Done.'

Chrissie motioned that they should move away as the camera crew prepared to do another take.

'Sally, Jessica, this is Carmen Vandemeer. Queen of Lone Island, I call her. Out there.' Chrissie waved an arm out to sea.

'You live out there? On an island? How exotic,' said Jessica.

'Not really. It's a sparse old landscape. Wild. Windswept. But I love it. Lot of history. Lot of shipwrecks. Lot of ghosts.' She gave a cheerful laugh.

'Let's head back to the house via the dairy and say hello to Paul,' said Chrissie. 'Then we can eat. Want to come along, Carmen?'

'Love to. I enjoy someone else doing the entertaining.'

As they walked, Sally and Jessica listened to the chatter between Carmen and Chrissie. While the older woman seemed rather rough around the edges, there was something else about her that neither could pin down. Sally decided she was a second-generation, late-blooming hippy. She had broken fingernails, tangled hair that had barely a nodding acquaintance with a brush, and had obviously dressed for practicality and comfort. Jessica sensed more of the overexcited kid let out of school; someone who lived an isolated existence but who was happy to be around people sometimes too.

'So who else lives on your island?' asked Sally.

'Just me, darlin'. And two helpers. The boatman comes regularly, that's if the damn weather isn't against us.

Plane comes in when needed. Between them we make things happen.'

'What do you farm over there? Do you raise cattle or anything?' asked Jessica.

'I raise tourists, love.' And she roared with laughter, seeing their faces. 'Actually, we do have a cow. And some goats, not wild; if they took off we'd all be shot. The island would be overrun before you could turn around. We have the basics in the garden. We feed the visitors pretty darn well, though. The boatie puts down traps, so we always have some seafood.'

'You look after people very well, Carmen,' said Chrissie. 'You've fixed the old farmhouse up a treat, and your little huts for the guests are gorgeous.'

'Well, thank heavens we don't get gourmet fuss-pots coming over, who expect hand-turned sculptures from cucumber skins and the like on top of their dishes. Most people are so knackered at the end of a day, they're happy with whatever they get on their plates.' And she laughed again.

'What do visitors do on Lone Island?' asked Jessica.

'You'd be surprised. We have some of the most dramatic scenery in the world. Wild and woolly on one side, tropical-looking paradise on the other. Except for the water temperature. Why don't you two girls come and see for yourselves? From the headland you can see straight to South America. Deserted beaches, interesting wildlife, some pretty amazing plants, forests, even a romantic lagoon.'

'You should go, it's a magical place,' enthused Chrissie.

'That it is.' Carmen chuckled heartily, then added, in a suddenly calm and normal-sounding tone, to Chrissie, 'Your friend Dan is coming over again. They've found petroglyphs that haven't been identified previously. And a

144

possible new species of fern, or something or other. So he's investigating the botanics at the site.'

'I look forward to hearing about it. Oh, here's Paul. He wants to show you the new milking set-up. He's very proud of it and the cows love it. Follow me.' Chrissie headed to the bails with Carmen.

The girls hung back.

'Carmen is a bit of a character,' said Sally. 'There's something . . . unusual about her.'

'Yeah, living alone on an island will do that, I suppose. But the place sounds pretty fantastic. Could be interesting. My instinct says we should pop over,' said Jessica.

'What! Why?' asked Sally in surprise.

'Because she invited us. And you're never going to come here for a holiday with Katie and Toby. The plants, the history . . . I don't know. Why not?'

'I'm not sure I could spend long evenings with Carmen,' said Sally.

'From what Chrissie said, it sounds like there's separate accommodation for visitors. And there's that friend of Chrissie and Paul's researching something over there that sounds interesting.'

'C'mon, you two,' called Chrissie.

'Let me think about it. I'll talk to Toby,' said Sally uncertainly. But she could tell by the glint in Jessica's eye and the set of her head that her friend's mind was made up. They were going to Lone Island.

*

An hour later, Sally sat on Chrissie's back verandah looking across the fields as she talked to Toby on her mobile.

'You know what Jess is like. Once she's made a decision about something, that's it.'

Jessica would go to the island, Sally knew, and as always, she'd follow. Mollie had once asked her why she always did whatever Jessica suggested, and Sally had laughed. 'Mum, I'm not being led by the nose, nor am I in Jess's shadow. But I do feel responsible for her. She can be a bit crazy-wild as well as crazy-fun. I'm the sensible one. Jess always thinks she knows best and she's the leader. So I let her be. But I'm actually always watching out for *her*.'

Toby's comforting voice brought Sally back to the present.

'That doesn't mean you have to go. You can stay there with Chrissie and Paul. You don't have to do what Jess says all the time. But you decide what you think is best and what *you* want to do. That was the idea of the trip, wasn't it? When you're back you can tell me all about how Paul and Chrissie are going, what they're doing.'

'I took photos and have some material Paul gave me. Anyway you can see it on TV, they had a cooking show filming here today.'

'No, I want the nitty-gritty, behind-the-scenes stuff. Paul said they had a new system of soil enrichment, microbes or something. His goats and cows had increased their milk production because of it.'

'Yes, he says he's keen to talk to you about it. You guys could Skype each other. Anyhow, I'll be home in a couple of days, probably. I don't think Jess will want to stay out on that island much longer than a day and a night.'

'No worries. Whatever you decide, take as long as you want, have fun. We're fine here. Hang on, Katie wants to say something.'

'Hi, Mummy ... I'm baking with Granny. We're making cupcakes!'

Sally smiled as Katie bubbled on about the coloured cupcakes, but felt a pang. 'I miss you, darling girl. Give Daddy a kiss for me.'

Toby came back on. 'She's raced off again. Your mum made her a new apron and she loves it. Oh, before I forget, some lady rang for you. Denyse Briggs? Said she couldn't raise your mobile.'

'Briggs . . .?' said Sally. 'Oh yes, from the Botanical Gardens, the seed people. We've been out of mobile reception quite a bit. And I had a couple of strange calls with no one there. No one who said anything, anyway.'

'Well, this lady remembered you were heading off somewhere that might be out of range so she rang here. Don't think she would have rung your mobile more than once, though.'

'What did she say? Have they found out about Stella's plant?'

'Apparently not. Only that it's pretty rare. She'd shown it to some guy who wanted to see any other samples or pictures of your grandmother's art.'

'Oh, that's right, I meant to ask you guys to email them a photo of her painting. Would you mind asking Mum to look after it please, darling? Just ask her to take some close-up photos of the blue flower at the bottom of the painting hanging above the desk. She'll need to call the Seed Conservation Centre at the Gardens to get their email address.'

'Of course, no worries, we'll get it done.'

'You're a darling. I'll give you a ring again tomorrow while we still have reception. Love you.'

'We miss you, and love you. But all's good, you and Jess have fun.'

As Sally got up to join the others inside, her mobile

rang again and she quickly answered, thinking Toby must have forgotten something. 'Hi . . . Toby?' She glanced at the phone, but there was no number displayed.

She listened for a moment and knew it was the same mysterious caller as before.

'Listen, stop calling me. You have the wrong number.'

She paused, sensing the breathing at the other end of the line, but then, to her shock, a low male voice said, 'I know where you are.'

And then the line went dead.

5

North-west Tasmania, 2018

THE WIPERS CLICKED MONOTONOUSLY to and fro, leaving a wet fan shape on the windscreen. After the warmth and familiarity of being with Chrissie and Paul, driving along a deserted road with the cold and mizzling wind blowing outside was a shock to the system.

Sally and Jessica had set out after lunch, leaving Chrissie and Paul to catch up on their work around the farm now that the television crew had left. The weather had closed in and the girls were glad they'd thrown their padded jackets into the car. They'd said their goodbyes, had Carmen's directions, and were heading out to meet her at the small harbour to go over to the island.

Jessica drove and Sally checked her phone and Facebook. 'I just can't stop thinking about that creepy call,' she said, sighing.

'Well, Carmen said there's no reception on the island, so you won't get any strange calls there,' said Jessica.

'Do you really think somebody is following us? Knows where we're going and where we've been?' asked Sally in a hesitant voice. 'Of course, anyone could see where we are by looking at the photos I've put up on Facebook. From now on I'm going to message them to Toby instead.'

'Maybe someone could work out where we are,' said Jessica, 'but why would they bother? No one apart from your family knows about the papers and stuff we found, or that we're planning to go to Seawinds. And even if they did, there's nothing sinister in that.'

'Well, there're the plant people we spoke to at the Gardens . . .' began Sally.

'We didn't say much to them, and anyway, it would be very unlikely that they'd be making the calls, don't you think?'

'Yes, but . . .'

'But what?' persisted Jessica.

'I just feel there's something that's not quite right about all this . . . like finding the name of a house, Seawinds, at Shelter Bay. Who lives there now? Is there any connection with my family? It's unnerving that the tin was in the cave on Arcadia's land. It's not like we were out bushwalking just anywhere and stumbled over it.'

'True,' said Jessica slowly. 'As kids we just figured it was a swaggie's hangout from the old days. The tin box must have been there all along but we weren't strong enough to move the bed. Also, I suppose we were so busy playing and making up our own games there that it's no wonder we didn't find it. You know, I never thought I'd go back to that cave.'

'How innocent we were as kids,' Sally mused. 'What would have happened if we'd found the old tin box and taken it to our parents back then? What can of worms might we have opened?'

'Who knows? But you're right, maybe it's lucky we didn't come across it then. Now we can try to find out something about the things that were in it without telling anyone just yet,' said Jessica.

'I suppose so. And now here we are, trekking halfway across the state because of some man's connection with my grandmother. It was a good excuse to get away together, have a bit of a road trip, investigate a mystery and have fun,' said Sally. 'But the phone calls. They've freaked me out. I just have the scary feeling there's something more to it. That someone's monitoring us and taking notice of where we're going, what we're doing.'

'I have to agree,' said Jessica slowly. She glanced in the rear-view mirror. 'Well, there are no other cars on the road.'

Sally began fiddling with her phone and snapped a photo of the drizzling rain from the car window. 'I'm texting this so Toby can see this awful weather. Apparently it's sunny at home. Katie loves seeing what we're seeing.'

At that moment Sally's phone rang. 'It's Carmen,' she said to Jess as she answered. 'Hi Carmen, I hope there's going to be better weather than this on the island. We've just left Chrissie and Paul's . . .' Sally listened. 'Oh, that's a shame. All right. Let us know as soon as you know anything.' She hung up. 'Damn. Carmen says we can't get to the island in this weather. The sea is up, it's too rough.'

'Oh crap. So what now?'

Sally turned and looked at Jessica, knowing they both shared the same thought. Jessica pulled over.

'Right, I'll see how we get there,' said Sally, who already had Google Maps open on her phone.

'Just put in Shelter Bay. We don't have an address for Seawinds so we'll need to go to the town, if there is one, and ask around,' Jess said.

'Okay. I'll just try Google Maps in case something comes up for Seawinds,' Sally said, tapping the screen. 'You know, even though I was reluctant at first, now I think I'd be disappointed if we can't get over to the island with Carmen.'

'The island won't go anywhere, and I'm sure Carmen will call us when the boat can safely pick us up,' said Jessica.

Sally studied her phone. 'The town's a bit off the beaten track. Google Maps isn't coming up with anything for Seawinds. I think we need a proper street address or house number.'

'Let's ask someone when we get into town. In such a small place, hopefully someone will know where it is and maybe even who owns it,' said Jessica.

'So when we find it, what do we say to the people who live there? Should we ask them if they know of this fellow, Broadbent? And what should we tell them about the stuff in the tin?'

'We could say we were bushwalking, sheltering from the rain in a cave and golly, gee, we found all this stuff. And saw the name of their house on the old map. Sounds reasonable, don't you think?'

'Hmm, I guess so. Then what?'

'Sal, let's wait and see what happens. We can't script the whole thing.'

*

It was late afternoon and the rain had eased somewhat by the time they drove into the small and seemingly deserted township of Shelter Bay. They were silent as Jessica drove slowly past the shuttered garage with its broken-down pump out the front, near a peeling, lopsided *Closed* sign. The Royal Lion Hotel was empty, shutters barring the door, and the chicken takeaway shop had boards on its windows, while the charity shop had a large sign out the front, *Do Not Leave Goods. Out of Business.* Nevertheless, a few rubbish bags with old clothes leaching through tears in the plastic were bunched on the front step. The post office was bolted and abandoned with a sign reading *Moved to New Premises*, and a map hung lopsidedly on the front door.

'Good grief, the whole place has closed down. Everybody has left town,' said Sally as they passed the dusty, unused laundrette.

'Should I just put my foot down and head for the city lights?' said Jessica.

'Well, we're here now,' Sally replied uncertainly.

'Here? Where? There's nothing here. Shelter Bay is kaput.'

'Are we in the right place, do you think?'

'We passed that sign that said *Shelter Bay 5 km* just back there.'

'Perhaps they should take it down.'

'There's no one here to take down the sign and turn off the lights.' Jessica stopped the car. 'Let's see the map. Where's the next sighting of civilisation? I don't feel like sleeping in the car.'

'It'll be getting dark soon. I couldn't face the drive back over that mountain range at night. It's too scary. No lights, no rails around those bends, and a huge drop below.' Sally sighed.

'We can take the coast road. See here, we're only a kilometre or so from the coast. Maybe they moved the town,' said Jessica. 'Look, there's a bay marked here.'

'*Yikes!*' screeched Sally suddenly, flinging herself against Jessica as she shrank away from her door, where a young man's head and shoulders had appeared in her window.

He tapped with hands in fingerless gloves. His sleeves were rolled up, showing elaborate tattoos. He was saying something.

Jessica hit the button for the passenger window and rolled it down an inch or so. Sally recoiled, moving close to Jess again.

'G'day. Where's everybody gone?' said Jessica, leaning over to Sally's window.

'Town's closed. All gone from here. What're you looking for?'

'We're looking for Shelter Bay.'

He gave a stretched smile showing bad teeth. 'Nothing here any more. There's a few places down at the waterfront. On the bay. You looking for a feed, or something? Where youse headed?'

'Just kind of touring,' said Jessica. 'Is there a pub or somewhere to eat on the waterfront? Has the town moved?'

'Moved on, more like it. Once the tin mine closed.' He tilted his head over his shoulder. 'Too many blokes died.'

'Oh, how tragic,' said Sally. 'Well, thanks for your help.'

Jessica put the car in gear but held her foot on the brake. 'You lived around here a long time?'

'Long enough. No one comes here much.' He straightened up. 'Kilometre or so down that way, turn into the waterfront at the old jetty. Restaurant should be open.'

'Thanks very much, we'll grab a bite and be moving

on,' said Jessica cheerfully, and slid the window closed. He stepped back and they drove away.

'Moving on to where?' asked Sally. 'There's nothing for miles. We'll have to stay here.'

'Well, I'm not telling him that. Who knows? We might've interrupted some drug deal.'

'Jess, you can be so judgemental sometimes. He was actually quite helpful!' Sally said. 'Let's find somewhere to stay tonight. With your wild imagination, you're making me feel nervous now.'

But when they wound down the road into the small community they were surprised.

'Hey, this looks all right,' Jessica exclaimed.

'Who would ever have guessed? It's very quaint. Do you think it's old, or mocked up to look that way?' said Sally as they turned into the main street lined with refurbished shops, small businesses, a milk bar and a restaurant.

'Oh, look, that guy was right, the restaurant's open. Let's stop,' said Jessica. 'It looks very 1960s.'

Beyond the glass counter with a display case of fresh ingredients – salads, meats, cheeses, as well as sausage rolls, pies and cakes – was a line of booths, each set with tomato sauce, mustard, pepper and salt, and paper napkins twirled in a glass beside plastic menus and a small posy of fresh flowers.

'I bet they serve milkshakes in metal containers,' said Jessica.

Sally was looking at the menu. 'Maybe, but they also have fresh scallops, oyster pies, and kedgeree, yum.'

As they settled themselves in a booth, a young woman came over, brushing her hands on her apron. 'Sorry, I was just getting a cheese damper out of the oven. What can I get you?'

'It smells wonderful. Maybe we could have an early dinner?' said Sally.

'All our seafood is caught here,' the woman said. 'Would you like to start with a drink? Coffee? Tea? We also have some good local wines. I'm Petal, by the way.'

'What a cute name. Unusual.' Jessica smiled.

'My mother, grandmother, aunties and cousins are all named after flowers. I think they'd run out by the time I was born.' She glanced over her shoulder as a man came through from the kitchen. 'Oh, here's Roger. He'll fix you up. I'd better get back in there; I've got something on the stove.'

Roger gave them a smile. 'Have you decided? Our seafood is popular.'

'If we're staying the night here, we'll have a glass of wine,' said Jessica. 'Could you recommend somewhere to stay? We've just driven in so we haven't had a chance to look around.'

'We were a bit shocked at the state of the main township when we came through,' said Sally. 'Closed up completely.'

'Yes. Nowadays most people drive straight through it then find their way down here. As for accommodation, there's only one option really, Rose Lawn. It's a guesthouse that is rather, er, quirky. But comfortable and clean.'

'Sounds good,' said Sally.

'What do you mean by *quirky*?' asked Jessica.

Roger shrugged. 'Hamish Holroyd, the owner, is a bit . . . eccentric. Odd sort of bloke. I've only met him once or twice. I can ring and book you in.'

'Well, beggars can't be choosers! It would be great if you could call him, thank you,' said Sally.

'Will do. Now, we have a local red wine, or would you prefer white?'

'If we're having seafood, I might go for the white,' said Jessica.

After Roger had taken their orders and walked away, Sally tapped a quick text into her phone. 'Toby will be relieved to know we've found civilisation,' she said.

'Yes, and he's not the only one,' said Jess.

*

Petal persuaded them to try her fresh fig custard pie for dessert and Roger brought them small glasses of sticky wine on the house to go with it.

'You're booked in at Rose Lawn. It's only ten minutes down the road. There's really not much else here since the big pub closed. A room in the old boarding house, but that's a bit basic. After the mine closed, there wasn't much call for the boarding house.'

'What happened at the mine?' asked Jessica.

'There was an accident. Few years back now. They never got to the bottom of what really happened.'

'Thank you so much,' Sally said to Petal as she paid the bill. 'Everything was delicious. I'll have to bring my husband and our daughter here one day. By the way, do you know of a house near here somewhere called Seawinds?'

'Oh yes, the big old place. I can draw a map of how to find it from here, if you like,' said Petal.

After drawing the map and showing them where to go, she handed it to Sally. 'You should be able to find it easily enough. I don't know if anyone is still living out there. Take care and enjoy your time up here in the north,' said Petal.

'If you come by for coffee in the morning, you can let us know what you thought of Rose Lawn,' Roger said, smiling. 'I'm sure it will be fine. Have a good night.'

'Nice couple. The place was a bit kitsch but the food was great,' said Jessica as she pulled on her seatbelt and started the car. 'Okay, so time to find this Rose place. I have to say Roger didn't fill me with confidence about it, though!'

*

As they swung into the driveway, their headlights lit up clumps of rosebushes on the front lawn and creeping roses covering the portico. A light shone above the door, which opened and a man waved at them, indicating the large carport and cleared area. 'Park over there,' he called out.

Hamish Holroyd fussed over them, lifting their bags from the boot and attempting to carry both before Jessica took hers from him. He paused to point out a large shape near the house that was shrouded in green plastic.

'Hot tub. It's turned on. In case you girls want to have a nice soak.' He gave a bit of a giggle and Jessica looked at Sally, rolling her eyes at his 'nudge nudge, wink wink' tone as they were ushered inside.

As soon as she'd set foot in the door she recoiled with a stagger at the intense odour of old-fashioned roses.

Sally coughed to smother a giggle, or possibly a gag, as they headed down the hallway, with Jessica waving her hand in front of her face.

They barely took in the striped wallpaper in multiple shades of pink, the bunches of dried roses tied with pink bows, the jugs and bowls bearing fresh roses and potpourri mixtures, and the rose-scented candles. The smell of roses was overpowering.

'This is Room One, here you are, dear,' Mr Holroyd said in a broad Cockney accent, as he put Sally's bag on the stand inside. 'We call this our Old Rose Romantic

Room, and across the hallway here is Room Two, our English Rose Room. See if you can spot the difference . . .'

He gave a cackle that turned into a wheezy cough. Sally and Jess stood in the doorway, frozen, as they eyeballed the child-sized figures of storybook characters that were posed around the bed.

'Cinderella, Snow White, those naughty dwarfs, Goldilocks . . .' he said, introducing them.

'We know who they are,' managed Jessica.

'Mrs Holroyd made them. We do so enjoy them . . .'

'They're looking at me,' said Sally in a slightly strangled tone.

Jessica jumped across the hall, sticking her head into her room.

'Oh my God.' She didn't know whether to laugh or scream.

Sally was at her side clutching Jessica's arm. 'Holy moly . . .'

'You know them, of course,' exclaimed Mr Holroyd with a delighted smirk, scratching his thin grey moustache.

The Cheshire Cat with a huge, evil grin was curled up on the centre of the bed. Ranged around it were the White Rabbit, a mean-looking wolf in a red cape and a grotesquely plump pig. 'Clever, isn't she? All made from scraps, you know.'

'Are there sound effects?' whispered Sally, but Jessica jabbed her in the ribs.

'Right, do we share the bathroom with . . . people?' asked Jessica, closing the door of Room Two.

'Room Two has a small ensuite, Room One has the big bathroom.' Mr Holroyd flung open the door. 'But of course, as I said, the hot tub awaits you young ladies. And then . . .' He put a finger to his nose and grinned, moving back into the hallway and opening bevelled-glass double doors to reveal a small sitting room with a sofa for a cosy twosome, two armchairs and a small table next to a drinks trolley with decanter and glasses.

'Nice,' said Sally, noting the dust on the decanter.

Facing the chairs, a cumbersome television set crouched, seemingly embarrassed by its antiquity.

'Now, for breakfast . . .' Mr Holroyd led them to the end of the hall where there was a tiny dining area, with a tea setting on the sideboard and a little table set for two. He pointed to a small hatch, sliding back the cover to reveal a dark hole.

'The old dumb waiter! Your breakfast will come down in the morning. Do leave your selection sheet outside your doors. Now there are towels for the hot tub in your rooms. Shall I take the cover off for you?'

'No! Thank you,' the girls said in unison.

'It's been a long drive . . .'

'Yes, terribly tired . . .'

'Early start . . .'

'Thank you for your help . . .'

As Mr Holroyd stood beaming, drinking them in, it seemed, and making no move to leave, both girls darted to their respective rooms and hurriedly closed their doors. Jessica sat on her pink ruffled polyester bedspread, staring around her once she was able to wrench her eyes from the odd cast peopling the room. The towels, sheets and doilies were all rose-hued, and the walls were covered in pink-framed pictures of formal rose gardens. Bunches of rosebuds beside the bed were cloyingly fresh. She pulled down the blind, then listened at the door and slowly opened it before dashing across the hall into Sally's room, where she burst into giggles.

Sally had hung towels, clothes and anything she could find over the heads of the homemade toys. 'Their eyes follow you,' she declared. 'And there's no phone reception! I think we should leave. Look at the toilet . . . even the water is pink! I'm going to throw up with this smell. And I *loved* roses!'

'What I want to know is, where's Mrs Rose Garden?' Jessica said in a whisper. 'There's a lot of dust about, so she's been gone some time, I reckon.'

'Jess . . . this place is really weird! I don't know whether to laugh or cry. Thank goodness we had dinner before we came and don't have to eat anything that was cooked here.'

'I need a drink.'

'Don't touch that sherry in there!'

'We have wine and nibbles from Salamanca. See, I told you'd they'd come in handy.'

'Of course! Do you suppose the telly works?'

'Yep. Probably only black and white though.'

Wrapped in pink hand-knitted rugs, the girls watched an old French movie – filmed in black and white – glad they'd brought a bottle of good wine with them from Hobart.

'Well, let's get some sleep.' Jessica turned off the TV when the movie finished and went to open the door to the hallway. She leapt back with a gasp.

Mr Holroyd was standing there in striped pyjamas buttoned to his throat, the top tucked into matching bottoms, the cord tied in a bow high around his midriff.

'Are you girls comfy? Anything you need?' he asked, looking past them into the room. 'So you watched a foreign film, eh?' He raised an eyebrow, waiting for details.

'We're fine, thank you. Just heading to bed. G'night, Sal.' Jess ran across the hall and closed her door firmly.

Mr Holroyd squeezed through the doorway and Sally jumped into the hall. 'I'll just take these glasses. Or are you having a nightcap?' he asked as he walked out.

'No. Thanks.' Sally fled back into her room.

'See you at breakfast,' he called.

Behind their respective doors the girls waited, listening until they heard his shuffling footsteps retreating down the hallway. Jessica opened her door and ran into Sally's room.

'I can't sleep with these creepy things watching me,' Sally said. 'Even with the towels on their heads.'

'I have a better idea. Grab them.' Jessica took two of the toys and marched into her room, where she flung them on the bed, then picked up her bag and went back to Sally's room. 'It's a Disney horror story! I'm moving in. The creepy toys are moving out.'

Together they piled all the toys on Jessica's bed, closed the door, and Jess returned to Sally's room.

'Lock the door,' whispered Sally.

'There's no lock!'

'Push a chair against it,' Sally said. 'I so want to get out of here.'

'He's already got your credit card details, right?'

'Yes. No need to see him in the morning.'

'And we're not doing breakfast. Get some sleep. We're outta here at dawn.'

*

There was a heavy dew as they drove into the curtain of rising mist, the precursor to the sunrise. The lush green fields were damp and appeared cushion-soft.

'What a place. Now we need to look for the sign and turn-off to Seawinds,' said Sally, studying Petal's map.

'Do you suppose the old boy knows we've gone? Maybe he's busy getting breakfast ready.'

'No, we didn't turn in our breakfast sheets. And he must've heard our car pull out, the way we skidded on the gravel.'

'I couldn't help it. I just wanted to get away from there,' said Jessica.

Sally looked at the mountains rising along one side of the road. 'There's such a lonely feeling out here,' she said. 'Nothing around but forests and those pine plantations. I hate it when they're logged and the whole hillside is denuded. It looks like some awful wound.' She sighed. 'It never grows back to how it was.'

'All the more reason not to whack into the old-growth forests,' said Jessica.

'I always feel small living here. I mean, even though we live on the crest of a rise, wherever you are in Tasmania you feel small. The mountains are always there . . . brooding,' said Sally thoughtfully.

'Yes, true. You can feel protected, like they're watching over you. But you can also feel a bit intimidated; this is an island, so there's no escape from them. We are separated from the mainland so we have to rely on ourselves, a bit like being shipwrecked. Fortunately this island has a lot more than a coconut palm going for it,' said Jessica. 'I always feel happier here when I'm facing the sea or a river.'

'What? So you can swim for it?' Sally laughed. 'Ooh, look, there it is.'

The sign was somewhat dilapidated, pointing towards the ground, and the letters spelling the name *Seawinds* were faded and peeling.

'Do you suppose someone still lives there?' wondered Sally.

'Let's find out. Invite ourselves in for breakfast.'

'Yes, but it's super early. We can check it out and if it's deserted, well, we can find some coffee somewhere.'

The narrow gravel road curled alongside thick eucalypt trees, but then as they passed the crest of the hill they saw below them lush green paddocks and, surprisingly close, the cliffs of the rocky coastline. Behind them rose the mountain range they'd driven down, and directly ahead was a rocky knoll surrounded by a thicket of old trees.

'The house must be behind those tall trees,' said Jessica. 'And it looks like there's somebody home, I can see some smoke.'

'Yes, I wonder if they're up, though. Why don't we drive to the end of this road, see where it goes. That'll fill in some time,' suggested Sally.

As they descended the mountain they came to a lake and both caught their breath. The water was inky dark, the pale early light gilding its unruffled silky surface, which mirrored the majestic mountains sheltering it. Seemingly impenetrable trees walled in the lake's perimeter.

'Photo op!' they chorused together.

'What is this gorgeous place?' said Sally as Jessica posed them against the stunning backdrop for a selfie. 'There's no sign anywhere.'

'It's probably marked on Google Maps. Let's keep going and see where we end up.'

*

Several kilometres on they came to a fork in the road. An old post-and-rail fence had a padlocked gate and a sign reading *Private Property*, while the public road veered to the right.

'Oh. We're locked out,' said Sally.

Jessica stopped the car in front of the gate. 'That's where we want to go. This is Seawinds. C'mon.'

'The gate's locked.'

'So we walk.'

'Hang on, Jess. There must be another entrance. Or else they don't want visitors. We'll be trespassing,' said Sally.

'This has to be an entrance to Seawinds, there's nothing else down here. You saw the sign. Listen, we're here. We can say we're lost. And we sort of are a bit lost. It's now or never, Sal.'

'Okay. Let's just take a bit of a peek. It's too early to bang on the front door. Give it another hour. Get the lay of the land first.'

They grabbed their shoulder bags and looked at the locked gate.

'Just make sure it's not electrified,' said Sally.

Jessica studied the fence for wires and checked the gate. 'Nope. Easy enough to climb over.' She swung herself onto the old-fashioned wooden gate and jumped down. 'Piece of cake.'

The sun was rising fast as they walked along the track, which wound its way down towards the shield of pine trees. Sally suddenly pointed. 'What's that through the trees over there? It's not a house.'

'It's hard to tell. Let's go a bit closer,' said Jessica.

They walked into the sunrise and saw the first rays glinting on the tin roof of a large shed. It looked to be quite old, and initially appeared abandoned. But then Jessica noticed the satellite dish on the roof, the security doors and some sophisticated-looking drainage pipes and equipment.

'I've seen this kind of gear before. It's very high tech,'

said Sally. 'The new glasshouses and growing sheds use this computer-controlled temperature gauge to regulate carbon dioxide and humidity and stuff.'

'Must have a few cars or trucks coming and going,' said Jessica, pointing to a side road and large turning circle.

'Everything is locked and bolted,' said Sally as they got closer. 'High security. What could they have in there that's so valuable?'

'Drugs?' suggested Jessica.

'You mean like a laboratory or a still or something? Maybe,' said Sally. 'There's probably CCTV around here, let's not go too close. We're not *that* interested.'

'Have you guys ever thought of growing your truffles like this?' asked Jessica suddenly.

'Nope. Truffles need nature; it's a symbiotic relation-ship with the roots of trees. Now we can inoculate the host trees with the fungus and grow them in orchards, like fruit.'

'Except your crop is underground.'

'And we'd have trouble finding them if it wasn't for Jasper! Even so it's like a marriage or falling in love, Toby says. You can't force it.'

They edged around the shed, keeping their distance.

'It seems like an old property. But the gear and a set-up like this are pretty modern. I wonder if any of the Broadbent family are still here,' said Jessica.

'We really haven't thought about how to handle this,' said Sally. 'I mean, just rocking up and knocking on the door seems a bit, well, strange.'

They could now see the back of the house, its gabled roof, casement windows and rust-red bricks, surrounded by dark shrubbery that gave it an olde-worlde air. A wisp of smoke rose from one of the chimneys. It seemed decades old, a home whose family had moved on, leaving perhaps one elderly resident or caretaker.

'The coast is quite close, but with those cliffs there's probably no beach, just rocks,' said Sally.

'Let's do a circuit, see if we can get to the front of the house,' said Jessica. 'If we go through that stand of old trees, no one will see us.'

'Just like the old days.' Sally giggled. 'Look, there's a path,' she added as they headed into the trees.

'It goes back towards the hill, and I don't fancy climbing. We could walk down along the coast over that way,' said Jessica.

'But this is such a worn track, it must be used a lot, so it has to lead somewhere,' said Sally, walking further along the trail.

In a few minutes she called back over her shoulder, 'Jess, come see,' and Jessica hurried to catch up with her. 'Look, it must be an old mine tunnel or something,' Sally said, pointing.

They stopped and stared at the stone wall almost covered with creepers, and a doorway in the middle. The girls were dwarfed by the arched stone entranceway with its metal door, large handle and elaborate rusty old lock.

'Wow, that's one serious door. Why would the place be sealed off like this? It has to be abandoned now by the look of things.'

'Wonder why it's locked?'

'Could be a council thing, for safety reasons,' said Sally.

Jessica tried the lock and, to their surprise, managed to open it.

'Shall we have a look? I can use the torch on my phone,' said Jessica, pulling the door.

'Let's not go too far inside . . .' started Sally.

Jessica peered in. 'No, let's go in one at a time. I'd hate that door to swing shut and lock us in there!'

Sally waited as the thin beam of light from Jessica's phone disappeared into the gloom. And then a minute or two later Jessica reappeared, heading back towards the entrance.

'How far back does it go?' Sally asked.

'Quite a way. There are two smaller tunnels going off it. I didn't want to get lost, it's disorienting in there.'

Sally stepped through the entrance, peering into the darkness. 'What's that smell? Wet earth or something?' She sniffed.

'Mushrooms. It's a mushroom farm of some kind.'

'Magic mushrooms?'

'Who knows? There're different sorts and shapes growing on the walls and on wooden posts. They've got quite an elaborate watering misting system in there. I couldn't see that well. Are you going in?'

'No, I'll take your word –' Sally stopped and they both turned, listening.

'It's a car. Shut the door, we don't want to be up for trespassing.'

Once the sound of the engine had faded, they walked back through the trees.

'I wonder if that's what they're propagating in there,' said Jessica, pointing to the occasional clump of fungi growing around the old tree trunks.

'When we looked into growing truffles, we heard of a fellow growing mushrooms near us. He made quite a lot of money with them,' said Sally as they made their way back up the hill. 'Certainly more predictable than truffles.'

'But you win the lottery if you produce truffles,' said Jessica. 'Do you ever worry about someone just walking in and stealing them?' she asked.

'That is a concern, but they're hard enough to find even when we know where they are. They pop up where they want, really. That's where Jasper comes in.'

Jessica laughed then stopped still. 'I hope whoever is driving out doesn't see our car,' she said. 'Maybe they'll go out the front entrance and head the other way. It's past seven o'clock. Let's go back to the car and wait till it's a bit later. Then we can walk over to the house and see who we find there.'

*

The house looked bigger close up, but careworn, showing its age as they walked down the driveway.

'You can hear the sea,' Sally said, making her way up to the front verandah. 'The upstairs rooms must have a great view.'

Jessica rang the old-fashioned buzzer by the nameplate, *Seawinds*, next to the front door, and heard it echo through the house. They waited, exchanging a glance.

'Guess they've gone out. It's still early; just gone eight o'clock. They might not be up.'

'No, wait, I hear footsteps.' Jessica leaned close to the door. 'Old person,' she whispered.

It was a slow shuffle, then they heard the lock turn and the door opened enough for an elderly woman, dressed in her bathrobe, to peer out at them.

'You girls lost? What are you looking for?'

'Hello, we were wondering if any of the Broadbent family are still here. I'm Sally Sandford, and this is my friend Jessica Foster.'

'Why? Who wants to know?' The woman frowned suspiciously.

'I was Sally Adamson. I live at a property called Arcadia, down south near Burridge, and we believe a Mr Broadbent used to stay near there, years ago.'

'Thomas William Broadbent,' added Jessica.

'What'd he do?'

'Nothing, nothing at all, that we know of. So you knew of him? We just have some questions . . .' said Sally. 'Family search, you know.'

'And we have some of his belongings,' added Jessica.

The woman pressed her lips into a thin line. 'Nothing to do with us here.'

'Could we come in?' pressed Jessica, smiling. 'We just have a few questions. We had a terrible night at a B&B and we sort of ran away early.'

'We paid the bill, it was just that we were . . . uncomfortable,' said Sally.

'I don't run no boarding house here.'

'Oh, we understand that. We were just curious about Mr Broadbent. He left some things in a box on my property,' said Sally.

'What's that to you? Why you sniffing round here? What you say your name was? What's your family?'

'My grandfather was Dr Stephen Holland.'

The woman's mouth tightened. 'My son don't like strangers here.'

'Does your son run the mushroom farm? We're farmers too,' said Sally.

The woman's eyes narrowed. 'You girls got no right t'be here. You'd better skit before he comes back. Like I said, he don't like strangers here. You get going.' She sounded agitated.

'Well, thanks, Mrs . . .?' said Jessica, with a querying raised eyebrow. But when the woman ignored her, she added, 'We don't want to make trouble. We'll post you Thomas's things.'

'Don't you bother. Just stay away from here. Gordon knows what he's doing and it's nobody else's business.' She slammed the door and they heard the latch lock.

'What the heck was all that about?' said Jessica, glancing at Sally with raised eyebrows. 'Who's Gordon?'

'I don't know and I don't care. She gives me the heebie-jeebies. Let's get out of here.' Sally turned away.

Jessica paused, looking up, and saw the curtain in an upstairs window drop back into place.

North-west Tasmania, 1942

Stella's silk scarf fluttered around her in the breeze from the open car window. With a leather-gloved hand she tugged at her French beret, sitting it more firmly on her head.

'Too windy for you, my dear? Roll up your window,' said her husband.

'I'm enjoying the fresh air. I think I can smell the sea.'

'Yes, we'll be heading down towards the coast any minute.'

They drove in silence for a short while.

'I see smoke,' said Stella as a wraith of white smoke dissipated into the grey-blue sky.

'Probably the stamp battery from the old tin mine. It had closed up but in these difficult times a few hardy souls are having a go again.'

'I can see the tiny miners' cottages. What a harsh life,' Stella said. 'And how barren the hillsides look.'

171

'The water is probably contaminated too,' said Stephen. 'I fear these old mines are leaving a bad legacy for the future. But people have to make a living. The coalmines are far worse for the men's health, I'm afraid.'

'There's the sea. How refreshing. I'm so glad we're near the coast.'

'It's not very accessible here and there's no beach, but there is a dramatic coastline view from the clifftops if you wish to take a walk.'

'It sounds like a Miss Brontë novel,' said Stella with a smile.

'Hmm. Perhaps.'

'And who is the man you have come so far to see?' she asked, having received only vague responses from her husband when she'd asked him earlier that day.

'Old family connection. I promised I would maintain contact and keep an eye on the family. They seem to have fallen on hard times.'

Stella had noticed the exchange of letters but had said little, as Stephen kept his correspondence to himself, and she'd learned not to ask in case it concerned his patients. He also insisted on handling all business and household mail and bills, telling Stella 'not to worry her pretty head'.

'I feel rather badly leaving the Jameses to manage everything for a few days, with their boy not long back from the rehabilitation home. He was there for so long and it's been such a difficult time for them.' Stella knew how Mrs James adored her youngest son, Terry, and how concerned she'd been when they'd seen and heard such terrible stories of other children suffering from polio, and some dying. But Terry had pulled through, and for such a young child was showing great resilience and learning to adjust to the impairment the polio had left him with.

'The lad will be moving around all over the place before they know it. He's lucky only his feet were affected.'

'Oh, is that where we're going?' Stella pointed to a sign reading *Seawinds* and with an arrow indicating the way.

'Yes.'

'And are we staying there this evening? Or at a hotel?'

'We'll go to the local guesthouse in the township. I don't wish to put them to any trouble. I will need to have a private conversation with the man who lives here and perhaps with his son too. I haven't seen the young fellow since he was a boy.'

'Of course. I understand,' said Stella.

'They have a pleasant garden you might enjoy.'

*

Stella strolled around the grounds, admiring the newly planted rose beds and the large house, thinking that if it had a thatched roof it would look like a very traditional English home. She was intrigued by the glasshouse and popped her head inside, where she was surprised at the difference in temperature. Assorted orchids and ferns covered the shelves and long boxes of soil were stacked in the corners. There was a faintly pungent smell that somehow seemed familiar.

She turned away and saw a side door that went into the house, so she decided to see if it led to the kitchen. She was thirsty, and while she'd been invited to take tea with Stephen and his friend, she knew it was merely a polite gesture and they wouldn't talk business or discuss anything personal while she was there. The man of the house was widowed, and she hadn't liked to ask if there was a housemaid. She could help herself to a glass of water.

A dim electric light bulb showed a doorway to the right and to the left a flight of stairs leading downwards, probably to a cellar. She went to the right, only to find that the door she'd thought would open into the kitchen was locked. The door to the stairs was ajar, and a pocket flashlight was hanging on a hook next to it. Impulsively she took the torch, turned it on and headed down the stairs.

It smelled dank. When she reached the bottom she saw a dangling string in the middle of the room, which she pulled, and a light came on. She saw she was in some sort of storeroom. There were shelves with bottles, cleaning items, boxes with seemingly seldom-used tools and on the far side, stacks of wooden crates and hessian bags. Again she caught that same pungent smell from the glasshouse. Tantalisingly, at the far end of the room was another narrow doorway. She looked around for tubs or a tap but there was nothing. Suddenly Stella was overcome with the sense that she was trespassing and shouldn't be here. But as she walked towards the stairs she heard footsteps at the top coming down. In a swift move she pulled the string, clicking off the light. Shading the beam of torchlight with her hand, she hurried to the small far doorway and slipped through, leaving the door ajar and turning off the torch.

In the darkness behind the door she pressed herself against the wall. From the short glimpse she'd had, she thought she was in some sort of brick-walled tunnel. She felt embarrassed at being there, and more than a little afraid.

The light in the cellar came on.

Someone was looking for something. Boxes were being dragged. She peeped around the door, wondering if she should announce herself but not wanting to startle whoever it was.

But as Stella watched from the dark doorway, she saw the figure of a slim man lifting one of the crates, and she couldn't stifle a gasp.

He turned, and she flattened herself behind the door again, holding her breath. She heard footsteps coming towards the entry of the tunnel and she closed her eyes in fear.

Then the door was pulled shut with a jerk and she heard the latch turn. She leaned against the wall, trying to clear her head and catch her breath, rubbing her eyes in the darkness. Why? How? Surely it couldn't be?

The man with the wispy hair, the narrow face, the straggly moustache. This time he wore a leather jerkin, not his deerstalker hat. But it was him, there was no doubt. Then it hit her. Did Stephen know this was the man she'd caught trespassing in their woods?

The door handle rattled and Stella jumped. Should she run, wait, or confront him? She now regretted the impulsive and, as Stephen would see it, incredibly rude and peculiar behaviour that had led her into the cellar in the first place. Her desire for a simple glass of water now seemed very far-fetched.

Stella waited, her eyes closed, taking deep, slow breaths to steady her nerves. When she could no longer hear any movement in the room beyond, she drew one more long breath, then found the handle and pulled the door.

But it was latched and locked. With mounting panic she rattled and then pulled and pushed and finally shouted for someone to come and help her, but nothing stirred on the other side. She turned on the torch and fumbled with the lock, but the door was firmly secured.

Her breathing started to come in short, anxious gasps. As she waved the torch around, all Stella could see was a narrow tunnel, initially lined with bricks and then with walls of packed earth, leading into darkness. There seemed to be no choice but to hope the battery in the little light would hold out as she hunched over and made her way along the narrow tunnel.

It could have been minutes or hours as she groped her way behind the thin beam of light along the earthen tunnel, longing for fresh air and daylight. What time was it, how long had she been down here, trapped like a blind animal?

Should she turn out the light to save the battery and just feel her way? she wondered. This tunnel could go on for miles. And it suddenly occurred to her: why was it here?

She tried to hurry, stumbling on the rough earth, telling herself all the while to keep calm, to keep her senses alert. She couldn't hear anything, but her hopes lifted when the smell of rich earth, of clay, and something else she didn't recognise, began to change. Was the air cleaner, easier to breathe, or was she just getting used to fumbling along like a wombat in its burrow? Stella paused, cocking her head. Every sense, every hair on her body seemed to strain and quiver. Was that a sound in the distance?

'The sea! The ocean. This is going to the coast!' she exclaimed aloud. She hurried forward.

There was no mistaking it now: the air was cooler; there was a faint hint of salt water on the breeze, and a distant pounding. It wasn't her heart or the blood throbbing in her head. This was the thundering of waves on rocks.

The darkness was gradually lifting. The faster she moved forward the lighter it became, and the louder the pounding thud of waves against rocks. And then she saw a perfect craggy archway, opening to sea, sky and air. Almost crying with relief she stumbled forward, turning off the torch as she came into the daylight.

To Stella's surprise, the tunnel opened onto a ledge with stepping stones cut into the rocks leading to a small, sheltered spot where the water flowed in and bobbed calmly against a flat rock – a landing platform. It was a perfect place to retreat from the surging sea beyond. In the shelter of this cliff overhang one could stop and . . . what? Load? Unload? Was it for contraband? In or out?

A smugglers hideaway, Stella decided. But for what? And how to escape from here with no boat, and no return route except back through the cave to the locked door?

Standing on the exposed rocky platform, the wind whipping above her head but the water curiously calm around this secret inlet, she faced the wild sea, the dark tunnel behind her.

A voice hailed her. 'Madam, madam, are you coming ashore?'

Turning towards the source of the voice, Stella saw that a man in a squat little dinghy with a mast but no sail was rowing towards her, pulling at the oars, his muscular arms bulging beneath tightly rolled sleeves.

'Do ye want a ride to shore, lass?'

'Ashore? Thank you, yes! Anywhere!' Stella was almost weeping at the ludicrousness of it all.

'Stand by. I'll throw you a rope, you tie it on that bollard.'

She looked around, confused, as he lightly spun a lasso of coiled rope which landed at her feet, and she realised there was a loop, and there, in the rock, was a metal stake to tie it to, so as to moor the boat.

In minutes the little craft was snuggled beside the rocky landing and the short stocky man was helping her into the stern of his boat.

'Haven't had a collection here for a mighty long time,' he said, grinning, as Stella stared at the rocky coastline and the cliffs above, and sighed at the sight of the small inlet with calm water close to shore.

'I can't thank you enough, how did you know . . .?' she began.

'Me ship is out to sea; this is the quickest way in. I don't ask you how come you were where you were, and you don't ask me why I'm landing in here,' he said simply.

'How can I thank you . . .?' she said, but seeing his closed face as he concentrated on guiding them in, Stella realised with some primeval instinct that should they ever cross paths again, they would ignore each other.

When they arrived at a tiny stretch of beach, he held the little boat, reaching out his hairy arm to help her step ashore. If the tide were in, the sand would be covered. 'You follow the track up, lass. And never explain. You was lost and then you found your way.'

'Yes. I understand,' said Stella, who really didn't, but that instinct had kicked in and she trusted it. 'Thank you.'

'And we never see'd each other, lass.'

'No. Indeed we did not.' Stella almost smiled as the strange sailor pushed away and rowed out of sight, and she turned to face the path around the headland.

*

She was panting when she reached the top of the headland and saw Seawinds. Her husband and an older man were walking down the hill towards her.

'Stella! Stella, where have you been?' exclaimed Stephen.

'Exploring! Looking at the seabirds.'

'That's quite a trek,' said the unsmiling man beside her husband.

'Joseph, this is Mrs Stella Holland. My dear, Mr Broadbent owns Seawinds. He lives here with his sons.'

Stella started. Broadbent was the name of Stephen's first wife, Hilda. Stephen almost never spoke about her, and had certainly never mentioned that he was still in touch with her family.

Biting her tongue and avoiding frowning at her husband, Stella held out her hand. 'A charming and very interesting home, Mr Broadbent. Has it been in your family a long time?'

'Long enough. It's been here since settlement days when the island was known for its colourful history, which had a lot to do with its geography.'

'Its remoteness?' said Stella.

'It may be isolated, but over the years we've attracted archaeologists, inventors, snake oil salesmen, smugglers, thieves and lotharios to this area.' He gave a tight smile and glanced at Stephen. 'These are calmer times.'

'And your sons?' asked Stella, keeping her voice light.

'They keep themselves occupied since their mother died so tragically. My sister, your beloved wife, Hilda, was a great comfort to all of us,' he added to Stephen.

Stella blinked, even more surprised to discover that this man was Hilda's brother, not some more distant relation. Stephen had said nothing to her about it before they arrived. She kept her expression bland and said nothing.

'Yes. Well, we must be making our farewells, old chap.'

'A cup of tea, a sherry to see you on your way?'

'I would very much like tea,' said Stella quickly, as the men turned and strode back towards the house.

No one else appeared when Joseph Broadbent carried a small tray with tea for Stella into the library where they sat. Then he poured a small sherry for himself and Stephen.

'I appreciate your visiting me, Stephen.' He raised his glass.

'I'm pleased to find you in good health.'

'And do you and your sons plan to visit us?' asked Stella innocently.

'We don't travel far these days.'

'Oh, I see.' She glanced at her husband, who was sipping his sherry, eyes downcast.

'I'm sorry not to formally meet your sons. I thought I saw one of them in . . . the grounds,' said Stella.

'They're busy chaps. Working on a project, and running this place,' said Broadbent.

Stephen swallowed the last of his sherry.

'And what project might that –' began Stella, but her husband signalled her to rise.

'We must be leaving. Do say goodbye to your sons for me.' He followed the older man down the hall, and Stella had no choice but to follow.

*

As they drove into the nearby village, questions tumbled through Stella's head, but some instinct made her refrain from saying, *I am sure that the son, whatever his name is, has been to Arcadia. I'm sure I saw him in our woods. More than once. Nyx knocked him over one time. He sneaks around. And I did run into him today, though he didn't see me. And most of all, why didn't you tell me*

that we were visiting your first wife's brother and nephew?
She decided that talking about Stephen's first wife could be awkward in the confined space of the car, when neither of them could walk away. And she knew she couldn't admit that she had been poking around in the cellar. 'I saw a tunnel and a cave at the shore,' she said instead.

'You heard what Joseph said, there were smugglers around in the old days. A lot of ships were wrecked off the coast here.'

'And his sons, what do they do? What is this "project"?' asked Stella.

'I have no idea. I haven't seen either of them since they were schoolboys. They both went to university and I believe studied chemistry, science, some such thing. Before Hilda died I promised her that I would keep a friendly eye on her brother and nephews. Now, here is the guesthouse.'

Stella knew when a subject was closed. She drew a deep breath. Exhaustion now overcame her. She was physically tired from her ordeal, but her mind was spinning. She longed for sleep.

North-west Tasmania, 2018

'That woman was pretty strange. Didn't give us her name, and seemed to be a bit scared of her son,' said Jessica as she and Sally drove away from Shelter Bay.

'She didn't ask who Broadbent was, though,' said Sally. 'It seemed to me like she'd heard the name before. She knows more than she's letting on, I think.'

'Maybe she was afraid of us. Who do you think drove away from Seawinds while we were there, and who was upstairs? We need to go back there,' said Jessica.

'No way! I don't think we should delve into this family history any more. What my mother doesn't know won't hurt her. And when I think about it, I'd hate to disillusion her about her mother.'

'It's wickedly exciting, though. I can't imagine my grandmother ever having a secret lover,' said Jessica.

They drove through sleeting rain to the small harbour township where they were to catch the boat to Lone Island, and followed Carmen's directions to the little motel she'd recommended. Sally checked her phone.

'Carmen says the weather tomorrow should be fine. She's arranged for the boat to collect us,' she said, reading the text. 'Well, that's good, so we're off in the morning. Chrissie says we'll love it over there.' After thinking for a few moments, Sally added, 'Let's not mention the dreaded Shelter Bay or Seawinds to Carmen. I don't want to complicate things.'

Jessica glanced at her. 'Okay. You're right.' She paused then went on, 'We didn't get any answers, though. That woman back there knows who Broadbent is, I'm sure of it, and she knows we're asking questions. Maybe she or her son will come back to us if they get curious. You told her where you lived. Maybe they know your place.'

'Is that bad? Maybe she doesn't know anything about what went on in the cave.'

'Could be. But like you said before, I think there's more to this. A lot more.' Seeing Sally's worried face, Jess patted her arm. 'Hey, girl, lighten up. Who knows what we'll find on this remote island? Let's get back into adventure mode.'

'I've had enough adventures for today. I really hoped we'd find some answers to the things in the cave. The letter . . . Damn, we're out of range again. I want to Google Gordon Broadbent. The old lady said her son's name was Gordon but perhaps his surname isn't Broadbent.' Sally shrugged. 'But you're right, let's enjoy ourselves while we can. We'll be back in real life soon enough.'

'And another thing, I haven't thought about horrendous Hardy since we left,' said Jessica.

Sally managed a chuckle. 'Good. Let's go be girl explorers. Then we'll be able to say things like . . . *"When we were in Shelter Bay . . . and when we were on Lone Island . . . what, you've never heard of them? Fascinating . . . You must go!"'*

Grinning, Jessica reached over and hit play on Mollie's CD, and Aretha Franklin's throaty voice singing 'Natural Woman' filled the car.

South-east Tasmania, 1949

A thin trail of dust danced in the sunlight behind Dr Holland's car as he and Stella headed along River Road to Arcadia. Stella was happy to be back in their stretch of the river. The break at the coast on the dramatic Freycinet Peninsula at the holiday cabins by Rainbow Beach had been idyllic, but sometimes she found the great sweep of water and ocean overwhelming.

The windswept walks along the beach had been exhilarating, and the views from their small hotel spectacular, but she had preferred the picnics at Cooks Landing with the other couples they had met there. Some were holidaymakers like themselves and others lived in that picturesque setting. One was the owner of the cabins they'd stayed in, who talked about one day developing a larger hotel to attract visitors.

Stephen had revelled in what he called their second honeymoon, and he'd thanked Stella for suggesting the break away at the coast, as he generally preferred his trout-fishing expeditions in the mountains.

Stella gazed down at the shimmering stretch of river, the occasional small wooden jetty, the cluster of boats around the ferry and cargo wharf, the dots of boatsheds against the steep green hillsides as they drove home. Perhaps to some it looked a lonely and remote place, but to her, Arcadia and its setting had become utterly special. This was her home, her inspiration. She sat quietly, smiling slightly.

Stephen Holland reached over and patted her leg. 'Glad to be home?'

'Yes, very glad. I'm sure I'll have lots to do in the garden.'

Mrs James and Winsome were waiting for them at the front door as they pulled up in front of the house. Mr James, seeing them from the orchard, quickly headed towards the car to help with their bags.

*

At twilight, Stella walked down towards the forest, calling to Nyx.

She smiled as she heard his chiding screech. 'I know, I've been away. But here I am.' She walked into the emerald and gold light of the trees, stepping carefully over the fungi that clung to the lichen-covered roots and fallen branches. She inhaled the familiar dank earthen smell of the spores and decomposing wood. She saw new mushrooms, including odd-shaped gill-like specimens, which had erupted in soft explosions on the forest floor.

And there was Nyx, sitting on a branch, preening himself, grooming his feathers and studiously ignoring her.

184

She chuckled. 'Stop sulking, you silly old thing. I brought you something.' She flung him some food then reached for her camera to photograph the exotic-looking fungi.

She would ask Terry, the last of the James children living at home, if he would put her film in to have it developed next time he went to Burridge. Stella was pleased for Mrs James that her son was so well now and had grown into a strapping young man.

*

Life returned to its routine. Stella kept busy with her painting, toying with the idea of tackling a beach scene, but her heart wasn't in it, and the smell of her oil paints suddenly affected her. She packed her paints away and spent time in her rose garden instead, but directed Winsome on what jobs needed doing, avoiding digging, pruning or weeding as she really didn't feel up to doing those things which, until recently, she used to enjoy.

One morning she sat glumly at the table. 'I really couldn't face any breakfast, Winsome, thank you.'

As Winsome removed the eggs, Mrs James studied Stella. 'Not like you to refuse breakfast, Mrs Holland. Ever since you came back from your holiday you haven't seemed yourself. You look very peaky, if I'm honest. How do you feel?'

'A little wobbly. And you're right, I'm not myself.' Stella looked out the window and a tear suddenly ran down her cheek.

Mrs James sat beside her and reached for her hand, which was folded across her lap. 'I said to my husband this morning that maybe you're missing the relaxing time you had away with Dr Holland. You never get much chance

185

to really be by yourselves with all his patients taking up his thoughts and his days. Your little holiday was like a second honeymoon for you,' she said gently, 'but now, if I didn't know better, after all these years, I'd say you might be in the family way.'

Stella didn't react or answer. Then she slowly nodded. 'And you might be right.'

'Have you spoken to Dr Holland?'

'Not yet. I wanted to be sure. Not get his hopes up.'

'I see.' She studied Stella for a moment, still clasping her hand. 'It's nothing to be afraid of, you know.'

Stella nodded and looked down, tightening her hold on Mrs James's hand.

'Would you like to speak to my niece? She's a midwife. Very good lass. Just in case. Before you speak to Dr Holland. Husbands aren't always so observant,' Mrs James added with a small smile.

To Mrs James's obvious surprise, Stella nodded in agreement.

'I'll ask her over for tea at the cottage,' said Mrs James, getting up, sounding businesslike. 'Then you'll know how to handle it.'

*

Stella liked Sheilagh Pearson straight away. She was about her own age, with sunny features, a gentle voice and a soothing touch. As Mrs James made tea, Sheilagh examined Stella, asked a few questions and nodded, then smoothed Stella's hair back from her forehead.

'You are definitely in the family way, and you are certainly well enough along to break the news.' She gave a broad smile. 'Congratulations. These late miracles do happen. I suggest you tell Dr Holland straight away.'

'Thank you, I will. This evening. He will be rather surprised. Pleased, I hope,' Stella said, sounding a little apprehensive rather than overjoyed.

'Of course he will be. You're healthy, but you must take care. Forty is quite late for a woman to have her first baby, but there's no reason all won't be perfectly fine.'

Mrs James couldn't stop beaming when they told her. 'It was that holiday at Freycinet. No doubt about it. Well, this will put a spring in the old boy's step,' she said, making Sheilagh chuckle.

Stella joined in, giving a polite laugh in reply, and wrapped her hands protectively across her belly.

6

Lone Island, 2018

THE WATER WAS CHOPPY as they headed through the bar and out to sea. Angry currents crisscrossed the surface and surged against the boulders of the old breakwall. The headland offered little resistance to the crashing waves, or protection for the small but sturdy craft as it ploughed ahead. Relentless cascades of spray sloshed over its bow, rushing down the gunwale and obliterating the view. The horizon seemed to rise and fall, and seabirds hung motionless in the air, suspended by the force of the headwind, moving neither forward nor backward before dipping their wings to angle sideways and soaring higher, or skimming low above the troubled ocean.

Carmen stood at the wheel. Victor, her handyman-cum-caretaker who lived rent-free on the island in return for doing simple duties like wood chopping, was out in the open stern, an oilskin coat wrapped tightly around him while his sou'wester hat dripped rivulets of seawater. Suddenly he pointed. 'Look at those birds. Wonderful creatures. You know, most birds can't smell. But albatrosses can, that's how they search out food over such vast stretches of ocean. Same goes for vultures, and even kiwis have nostrils at the end of their beaks to help when they poke into the ground looking for worms. But look at those magnificent things.' He gestured at the shearwaters soaring beside them. 'They have great sight, and wings that keep them safe. That's why they never hide; their wings set them free.'

'Are there lots of birds on the island?' asked Sally.

'You bet. Heaps of rookeries. Be careful where you walk, the muttonbird holes can easily trip you up.'

'Thanks for the tip,' said Jessica.

'I suggest you go below, it's getting a bit wet up here,' Carmen called to them.

The two girls hunkered down in the compact cabin. Jessica tried to read a magazine while Sally scrolled through her phone.

'What are you doing? There's no reception out here,' Jessica said as she saw Sally frowning.

'Trying to figure out who's been calling me. Until the other day at Chrissie's I hadn't heard his voice.'

'Probably a crank. Or maybe you have a secret admirer?' said Jessica lightly, seeing the worry in Sally's eyes.

'Stalker, more like it.' Sally put her phone down. 'I'll try to ignore them. Phew, this is claustrophobic, I don't know how Bass and Flinders could bear being cooped up like this for months at sea.'

'Is the romance of the sea wearing thin already?' Jessica glanced at her watch. 'About an hour to go. No wonder Carmen and Victor don't leave the island too often. It's quite a commute. I can't imagine many tourists would come over.'

'Chrissie said the tourists usually go there by plane in good weather, as well as amateur naturalists, writers, those solitary kinds of people. Perhaps honeymooners. Definitely not the social hub kind of holiday spot.'

'Sounds like the perfect setting for a murder mystery.'

'Whose idea was this again?' Sally raised an eyebrow.

'Okay, okay. It seemed like a good idea at the time. Don't forget, you agreed. Carmen is kinda interesting, different. And we're going somewhere off the beaten track. I like that.'

Sally sighed. 'Well, there's no going back now. Jess, you can be impulsive. Hasn't that got you into trouble before?' she asked. 'I mean, it was harmless enough when we were kids, but I didn't think you'd still be, well, so rash.'

'Oh, I've been *very* rash,' said Jessica with a naughty smile.

Sally stared at her, then, sensing a story, settled herself more comfortably. 'Oh? Do tell! C'mon, Jess. We still have a lot of catching up to do.'

'I've had three lovers since I broke up with Hardy. Well, to be honest, I only slept with two of them.'

'Whaaat! I can't believe you never told me any of this, you minx!'

Jessica chuckled. 'That got you going, didn't it?'

'Oh. So you're joking . . . are you?' Sally paused. 'Did you ever cheat on Hardy? I mean, you don't have to tell me, of course.'

'No. No. I didn't. More fool me. When he moved out

and we had twelve months or more before the divorce came through, I did see some guys.'

'But the divorce was only final a couple of months ago, you said.'

'Yes. And then I got off the merry-go-round. But I was glad for the ride.' Jessica looked past Sally, obviously remembering.

'You didn't find anyone you liked? That's sad in a way,' said Sally.

'Actually, the three guys I found I absolutely *adored*!'

Sally looked stunned. 'Where did you meet them?'

'On a dating site, of course.'

'Oh, I couldn't do that. One of them could have turned out to be a serial killer!'

'Since when have you been so obsessed with killers? Online dating isn't stigmatised any more. Practically everyone is on there. It's the most normal way to meet people these days.'

'Not around my neck of the woods. You'd be spoiled for choice in Sydney, I suppose. I'd never go looking, of course.' Sally laughed. 'But I do sometimes pinch myself at how lucky I am that Toby and I found each other.'

'Living in a city can make it harder. And you do have to be careful. But maybe because I wasn't desperate, just lonely, I thought it'd be a bit of fun. I think I needed to prove to myself I could still attract someone. Hardy made me feel so . . . unwanted.'

Sally shook her head. 'That's dreadful. It was so mean and selfish of him. You are beautiful, Jess, and smart and funny, and generous, and . . . crazy.' Sally suddenly laughed, then leaned forward. 'So who'd you meet?'

'Oh, I chose someone totally out of left field the first time. American, bit of a hippy type – in a nice way – a geologist, but he was on a sabbatical, taking time out as he wasn't sure the path he'd chosen was the right one. He's a musician but was never brave enough to give it a go fulltime. We went to a few concerts, a few parties, but it turned out we had totally different tastes in music. We never slept together, but he was a great talker, articulate, not a bullshitter, you know how Americans can talk so persuasively. And he was quite poetic.'

'So nothing happened?'

'Something just didn't gel. After a couple of weeks we knew there was no point in wasting each other's time. So then I found Geoff.' Jessica rolled her eyes in a mock swoon.

'That good?' breathed Sally.

'Oh, yes. But it wasn't just the sex. We weren't lovers for ages, which was good. I didn't want to feel I was just hopping into bed with someone because I hadn't been truly loved and treated tenderly, or had great sex for, well, years. What I'd missed so much was – companionship. Someone to talk to, not in a deep and meaningful way necessarily, just to chat and laugh with. We went to the movies, had picnics and rode bikes around the park near where he lived. Nothing intense or committed. I really didn't know much about him and didn't want to; his family, his childhood, his future dreams. He'd been in a long-term relationship but on his own the last few years, and he liked it that way. So that suited me. No pressure.'

'That was nice for you. Did Hardy know about these guys? Or your mum?'

'Of course not. There was no way I'd bother telling Hardy. My mother did notice that I seemed calmer and happier, but I just told her I was glad Hardy was out of my life. Which was true. Then when Geoff and I realised we were looking for different things in life, I met Justin.'

Sally rolled her eyes. 'I hardly dare ask, but go on.' She leaned forward again.

'This time I fell for him with a crash. Very special person. An architect, he designs super-green environmental buildings in the city with gardens on the roof, hanging walls of living plants, quite amazing. He's in demand all over the world to reconstruct old towns and design new small cities and communities. Huge intellect, has read the philosophers, just looks at the world in a very different way. Visionary. Speaks several languages. He's a Buddhist. He could be intense, and then tell you a silly knock-knock joke. He married when he was in university but got divorced after his career took off as his wife didn't want to live overseas. We found each other then he landed a big project in Queensland, so I would fly up there, and sometimes he came down to Sydney. And then he asked me to move to China with him. Leave my job. Said he'd find me a research role or something. But I could tell it was all about him. And I get that; he's going to be super famous. It was an extraordinary time. It stretched me, romantically, intellectually, but I couldn't be an acolyte.'

'You must have been sad to break up,' said Sally.

'We didn't see it like that. It felt like we were planets orbiting each other briefly, then he sped off in a great whoosh towards the stars while I'm . . . just going round in circles.' Jessica said. 'However, I'm in no rush to "find" somebody. I just get annoyed, frustrated, when Hardy crosses my radar with some petty, arrogant demand. Though now the legalities are all done with, we hardly have much contact, which is a relief. The first months on my own I felt like a total tragic.'

'But still, you were married and had all that time together, don't you feel something?' wondered Sally.

'Not really. I'm sorry I wasted so much time with him. We don't have the tie of a child . . . I was just too young . . .'

'So was I!' said Sally, looking alarmed. 'But I can't imagine my life without Toby or Katie.'

'That's because you and Toby are so right for each other. You two hit the jackpot.' Jessica reached over and rested her hand on Sally's. 'You're the couple that proves the case. And gives the rest of us hope that we'll have what you have. One day.'

Victor stuck his head through the hatch. 'Approaching the island, come and see the cliffs. Bloody spectacular.'

Standing beside each other as the spray slicked over them, the two girls felt insignificant and the small boat fragile as it pitched in the swell rolling against the massive cliffs that towered above them.

'They look like giant sculptures,' Jessica shouted into the wind.

'The surfaces have been beaten by the weather and the sea for millennia, I guess,' said Sally. 'Do you suppose they were volcanic, exploding up from the bottom of the sea? And look at those crevices and caves. I wonder if anyone has ever set foot in there. Makes the hills near us look pretty tame.'

'Makes me wonder what the sea floor below must look like,' said Jessica. 'And see, up there, a plant is growing. How does it survive on that minuscule ledge?'

'There's a sea eagle's nest over there,' said Victor, who was standing next to them. 'See, where there's a tree hanging on, in the dip between the cliffs. And there are seals around here too. You see them over the other side, on the beach and rocks where it's more sheltered. The island is rugged but there are also some calmer spots. It's interesting to explore.'

'I don't think I want to climb to the top of that peak,' said Sally, clutching at the railing as the boat dipped to starboard. 'What made you move here, Victor? Hardly anyone seems to know about this island.'

He shrugged. 'There're no trendy bars, hotels or many people here. No entertainment, other than Mother Nature, or what you make yourself. Doesn't suit everyone, but I love it.'

Sally glanced at Jessica. 'I think even honeymooners might like some diversions.'

'Yep. No swim-up cocktail bars on this island, I'd say. But I'm keen to see what's here,' said Jessica.

'Another adventure you've got me into.' Sally smiled.

Victor nodded. 'I have one secret I'll share. There's a freak spot where you can get satellite reception. If by chance you need to make a phone call, let me know. And by the way, we have a couple of others visiting at the moment. Well, Dan isn't a tourist. He's a friend of Carmen's and often comes to do some fieldwork. There's another fellow here as well, and a fisherman comes in regularly.'

'Right. Thanks,' said Sally.

She looked at Jessica, who shrugged and whispered, 'I wonder what sort of people wash up on this rock?'

'Nice people, I hope,' said Sally, and they both knew she was thinking of the anonymous caller.

'Let me answer your phone if it rings,' suggested Jess. 'Well, it won't now; we're too far away from reception. So that's good. Forget about it.'

Carmen steered the small boat around the towering peak of the headland, and suddenly the wind died down.

It was more sheltered here, and the bay was dotted with pockets of pristine sand.

'Well, there won't be any queues for service at meal-times,' said Jessica. 'I can't see a single building.'

'That's the whole idea,' said Victor.

'There's a jetty,' said Sally. 'I can't believe how calm the bay is after those wild seas.'

'Yes, we're on the leeward side and the cape protects this bay. The airstrip is over here too.'

'Wow, look at all the birds,' said Sally.

'Bit of a circus when a plane comes in,' said Carmen. 'We all get out there with brooms to chase them off. Cape Barren geese, mostly. There's something of a zoo left here by the old-timers.'

'A family once lived here,' added Victor. 'They farmed cattle and sheep in the old days, and a few seafarers have washed up and left their mark.'

Carmen jumped down onto the jetty, helping Jessica and Sally with their backpacks as Victor started unloading supplies.

'Do people get together in the evenings?' asked Sally as they hefted their bags and followed Carmen along a sandy track towards a stand of trees.

'Sometimes, except for one odd bod who thinks he's pulling the wool over our eyes.'

'What do you mean?' asked Jessica.

'Says he's a geologist or some such. Brought some shiny new tools with him last time. But we know what he's after.' Carmen chuckled.

'What's that?' asked Jess.

Carmen turned around and winked at them. 'Buried treasure. Seriously. Back in the 1800s a ship was wrecked and as the story goes, the skipper sent a few men ashore with barrels to be buried, down by the Ti Tree lagoon, we believe. But then they were rescued and the captain never made it back to the island to retrieve his secret stash.'

'Was it rum?' asked Jessica.

'Nobody knew until the 1950s when an old beach-comber fellow came here, and then went back to the mainland and started paying for drinks with gold coins. After that he turned up here a few more times. Apparently there are rumours he left a map with a mate in Launceston. We still get the occasional hopeful treasure hunter, such as the man who is staying here now.'

'So there's no treasure here then?' said Jessica.

'Oh, there's treasures of all kinds here. Depends what you're looking for,' said Carmen quietly.

Jessica and Sally exchanged a glance.

'I'll show you to the guest cabin . . . and point out where my joint is. Victor will get you anything you need, including some provisions if you want to cook tonight. Otherwise, come over later for supper, if you feel like it,' she said. 'The geologist mostly keeps to himself, Dan is here again, Laurie, the cray fisherman, sometimes calls in, but please yourselves. Victor has maps of the walks and scenic spots on the island.'

The cottage Carmen showed them had been a family home back in the 1950s but was now updated in a simple rustic style, set among trees but within earshot of the sea.

'There're some basic groceries, clean towels, beach gear, fishing stuff, hiking gear. Plus water, soft drinks, milk and some wine and beer in the fridge. Also, there's wood for the pot-bellied stove if it turns cold, a few books and magazines, some games. Well, I'm sure I don't have to tell you how to entertain yourselves. Make the most of the island; you'll find there's a lot to see,' said Carmen.

'Thank you,' said Jessica. 'Where do we find Victor, if we need him?'

Carmen pointed to where the track divided. 'Left to the other guest quarters, right to my place. Victor is in Cabin 3, Dan next door to Laurie, and the geologist has his tent. There's the old barn and farmhouse in the middle of the island, but nobody is up there at the moment. Come over at around six if you want to meet the others.'

'Thank you, Carmen,' said Sally.

When they were on their own, Jessica said, 'Do you get the feeling we've dropped off the world map for a bit?'

'I do. This could be an adventure for Toby and Katie and me, when Katie's older,' said Sally.

'You mean when she's old enough to rough it, no screens, no internet?'

'Well, yes, but I think she'd love this. She's such an outdoorsy girl. Remember how we used to disappear for hours and hours when we were kids, exploring and playing in the woods and the creek?' said Sally.

'I loved those times. And there's no reason we can't do the same now. Let's take water, bread, cheese and some fruit and go exploring,' suggested Jessica. 'It's why we came, isn't it? It'll be fun. I'm going to pack my rain jacket. At this time of year it might turn cold or wet before we get back.'

They took the map of the island Victor had given them and decided to hike across the middle and up towards the headland. However, after three hours, they found they hadn't got very far as they were sidetracked by a beautiful golden lagoon surrounded by paperbark trees. The water, tinged brown by the button grass, was cool and fresh as they dangled their feet in the sandy shallows in the shade of the trees.

'People would pay a fortune for a treatment here,' said Jessica. 'Look at the colour of the water. It's like a mud bath.'

'So refreshing after that walk.' Sally sighed. 'I wish it was warm enough to go for a swim. Perhaps I'll come back in summer.'

'Right, which way next?' Jessica stood up and grabbed a towel to dry her feet, and then put her socks and runners back on.

The two girls were studying the map when there was a shout from the rise above them. 'Hi there!'

They glanced up in surprise to see a man giving them a wave. He looked to be a hiker, wearing sunglasses and a hat, with a canvas bag slung over one shoulder and carrying a bulky camera. He started to pick his way down the slope.

When he reached them he pulled off his hat, showing fair hair that flopped across his forehead, and gave a disarming smile. Jess recognised his friendly, handsome face immediately.

'You've found the best spot on the island. Hi, I'm Daniel Sullivan. Carmen mentioned she'd brought over a couple more guests.'

'Hi, actually we've met before,' Jess said with a smile. 'At the Botanical Gardens the other day. I'm Jessica and this is Sally.'

'Wow, of course. What a coincidence.' He reached out and shook their hands. 'You got shanghaied by Carmen to see this place, eh? It's pretty special.'

'Very unusual, such a mixture of landscapes,' said Sally. 'Before we came over, our friend Chrissie told us there's farmland, savannah, meadows, cattle grazing, this lagoon, massive peaks, and rocky overhangs. Is that where the caves are?' Sally pointed to the rocks behind him.

He nodded. 'I came down as the tide was going out. Have you walked around the rock shelf? It's stunning. There's a muttonbird rookery over this side. It's not muttonbird season, so there shouldn't be many snakes around. There's a lot of penguins, too. They breed around the island. Would you like me to show you?'

'Yes, sure,' agreed the girls.

'Better put your shoes on; the shells on the rocks are very sharp,' he said to Sally.

The three of them trailed slowly across the broad exposed rock shelf, marvelling that they were stepping over ancient natural sea art. The limpets were scattered like flowers, and the whorls and pools and holes carved by the ocean looked like abstract paintings. Each rock-pool was a small underwater theatre, a stage of swaying seaweed, shy creatures, sand and coloured shells. They lay on their stomachs, waiting for small crabs and trapped fish to dart onto centre stage.

'I think this one looks more like a ballet,' said Sally. 'We just need music!'

'Have you heard the ringing rock?' asked Dan. Seeing their incredulous faces, he explained, 'There are some special rocks at a couple of Aboriginal petroglyph sites on the island where, if you tap the large rock, which has carvings cut into it, with a smaller rock, it rings and sings.'

'How amazing,' said Sally.

Jessica glanced at him as Dan stood up. 'What else is around here?' she asked as she pushed herself up.

'Lots. I'm getting hungry. Should we have something to eat first?'

'Great idea,' said Sally, scrambling to her feet. 'We have some picnic things.'

'And I have this!' He suddenly brandished a knife from his canvas shoulder bag, and laughed as the girls recoiled.

He pointed at the rocks where the water was beginning to wash over the edge. 'Do you like oysters? Can't beat them shucked right off the rocks!'

'Oh yum, and we have bread. Perfect,' said Sally.

'Damn, no fresh lemon juice,' said Jessica.

'I can help with that. Let me show you.' Dan pointed into a rockpool where seaweed was growing in a cluster like a bunch of grapes. 'Pick a couple and squeeze. Tastes salty sweet, better than lemon.'

'I'll get the bread,' said Sally.

They sat at the edge of the wide rock ledge, their legs dangling in a pool, the bread and bottles of water spread on a jacket between them, as Dan shucked the oysters still attached to the rocks, handing the shells filled with succulent meat to each in turn.

Jessica sighed. 'These little beads of seaweed are amazing; so juicy.'

They talked easily because of their mutual connection with Chrissie and Paul, and now Carmen.

'So, do you know if there's any news about the plant samples we brought in?' asked Jessica.

Dan concentrated on lifting a fat oyster from its shell. 'Kind of. Firstly, I have to say I think the paintings are terrific. So they were done by your grandmother, Sally?'

Sally nodded. 'Yes, her name was Stella Holland. I want to do something with them, but I'm not sure what or how yet.'

'But you don't know where Stella painted them? I mean, where she sourced the subject matter?'

Sally looked at Jessica. 'Well, I assume it was at Arcadia, my family home. My husband and I, and my mother, now farm the land there; mostly saffron and truffles.'

Dan nodded. 'Makes sense. You have old trees?'

'We planted new trees.'

'The Far Forest is untouched,' Jessica reminded her.

'Yes, it's a mysterious place, and probably full of plants that've never been identified,' Sally said to Dan.

'It's an ancient stand of old-growth forest, covers quite a few acres, actually, on Sally's home down south,' Jess said. 'I grew up in that area too.'

Dan glanced at her. 'Ah, that makes sense. It's the fungi, the mushrooms in the photos of the painting your mother emailed me, Sally, that interest us. The little flower is uncommon, but I think it's a described species. Your grandmother has painted a ladybird known to eat fungus and a small cluster of the fungus itself.'

'Oh, how intricate! I've never noticed it, it must be very small on the painting,' said Sally.

'What's so interesting about it?' asked Jessica.

'Actually, it's quite involved. It's to do with the soil where these mushrooms grow. Do you know about the mycelium network?'

'Mycelium . . . that's the cobwebby stuff that spreads in the soil under mushrooms, isn't it? We noticed it around the truffles and fungi in the forest,' said Sally.

'Yes, that's right. For a while now I've been in contact with a mycologist guy from the States, Sean Hyland. We're still learning about the magic of mushrooms.' Dan smiled.

'You mean like fairy rings?' said Jessica.

'Ooh, Jess, remember our fairy ring? The one we found in our forest? A perfect circle of wild mushrooms.

Jessica wanted to pick them and take them home to cook and I thought it was bad luck,' Sally said to Dan.

'There's a lot of superstition about them. Some people think they're bad luck, others think they're lucky. They sprout from the network blanket of mycelium and the middle dies off, leaving the mushrooms around the edge in a circle. Those rings keep re-growing. There's a fairy circle in France that's believed to be hundreds of years old.'

'Is this what you're researching?' asked Jessica rather incredulously.

'Sort of, along with some other stuff. One of the mushrooms in Stella's painting is rare, so its spores would be valuable. Research about possible uses for mushrooms and mycelium has been going on for years, but it's becoming more important, so identifying where they can be sourced is of some interest.'

Jessica reached for another oyster. 'So are you attached to the Botanical Gardens, a museum, or a university?'

'At the moment I'm working for the Botanical Gardens in Hobart, but I also work for an international organisation, not quite not-for-profit but it gets some philanthropic funding to develop green farming practices on a large scale. Plus a few other projects that are a bit more my passion.'

'Like what?' asked Sally as Jessica studied Dan.

'There's a lot of people researching mycology, uses for fungi, mushrooms. The guy I mentioned, Sean Hyland, is an international expert. He's also Carmen's step-cousin. Lives in Canada, but he's working here for a month, in Hobart.'

'So what's the big interest in mushrooms?' asked Jessica.

'Ah, well, I know it sounds corny, but that's classified information.' He smiled. 'What I can say is that there's a bit of a race to get new products onto the market. Everything from products that enrich soil, enhance plant growth, clean up toxic waste, chemical spills, agricultural and industrial waste and radiation, to medicinal products for human health. And they're working on cures for diseases.'

'You're joking. All from mushrooms?' exclaimed Sally.

'Yes. Have you ever noticed how wood rots down in the forest due to the fungi? Fungi inhale oxygen and exhale carbon dioxide, as we do, and they are susceptible to many of the same germs. The mycelium network is like an underground computer system. Sean describes it as a neurological network of nature.'

'You mean the white mould under the mushrooms, like Sally said?' Jessica asked.

'Yes, it's actually thin, one-cell threads that interconnect and spread like a woven network of membranes, under the soil as well as on top. For every cubic metre of soil there's a kilometre of mycelium beneath.'

'So the trees and plants can talk to one another,' joked Jessica.

Dan smiled but nodded. 'Yep. It's a fascinating field to study. Mushrooms are the recyclers of the planet, essentially building healthy soils. They also filter water, help plants and trees to grow, and control insect pests. But fungi has also evolved natural chemical defences – antibiotics – against bacteria and viruses that cause diseases in humans. The study of mycology is huge and goes back to ancient times.'

'In what way?' asked Sally, fascinated.

'Well, you can make a fabric from mushrooms, and

there's a particular mushroom that the first peoples used to carry the embers of a fire in as they moved around. The firekeeper was an important guy. You can't do much if the fire goes out.'

'What can't you do with mushrooms?' asked Jessica.

'Not much, it seems,' said Dan. 'I know one researcher who's experimenting with making flameproof clothing from mushrooms.'

'Someone's going to make a fortune,' Sally said.

'Hence the race?' said Jessica.

'Yep, patents have been taken out by people all over the place for specific products. But Sean, the guy I'm working with, decided the best and fairest thing to do was to release the details into the market as free commons, so they can be used by the poorest nations, and whoever wants to can develop, produce and sell them.'

'It all sounds so . . . unreal,' said Sally. 'Have you seen these ideas actually working?'

Dan nodded. 'Sean puts them out on the internet and there've been all kinds of formal tests and trials by reputable outfits. I went up to observe some experiments in outback Queensland where contaminated from soil oil and gas fracking was putrid, salty, killing everything around where it leached out of the ground. Not only was it cleaned up by the mushroom "compost", but the people there grew a whole crop of nutritious food on it after the first crop of mushrooms had sprouted.'

'Sounds like trailblazing work,' agreed Jessica.

'Do you think my grandmother had any idea about this?' wondered Sally.

'If she did, she wasn't much of an entrepreneur,' said Jessica, laughing.

'Who knows?' said Dan. 'But she certainly had an eye

for nature. And it seems that some rare species could be living in the forest on your place. I'd like to investigate what's still growing there, if that's all right?'

'Of course. Toby, my husband, will be very interested in all of this.'

'What about you, Jessica? What do you do?' asked Dan.

'I used to work in a pharmacology laboratory in Sydney, so I never went outdoors. It got me down,' confessed Jessica. She paused, bowing her head, and didn't seem to want to say anything more.

'Where are you based, Dan? Are you a Tassie guy?' said Sally, sensing her friend's shift in mood and wanting to move the conversation away from her.

'I'm originally from regional New South Wales but home now is a small flat in Sydney. I travel a lot – you could say I have a portable profession.'

'So why are you here on the island?' asked Jessica.

'Well, I always enjoy catching up with Carmen, and this time I've come over to follow up investigations into the degradation of the ancient rock carvings, and examine the soil and plants around them. The debate over whether they were done by first inhabitants or are a result of weathering and age is still a hot potato in some circles. They're fascinating; some scientists say they go back to when Lone Island first broke away from the main island. Not much Aboriginal history has been documented in Tasmania as the colonists tried to wipe out the local people. Introduced diseases were killing whole tribes, and the Black War decimated them, of course.'

'But not quite,' said Sally. 'The Black War . . . how come we never learned about it at school?'

'It was a war for country and the survival of a race, which was almost erased here in every way. We all know when the so-called "last Tasmanian", Truganini, died, but there is so much history we don't know,' said Dan, frowning. 'Tragically, the Indigenous people were seen as a disposable species by the colonisers.'

'Yes, it was shocking and terrible,' said Jessica.

'The colonisers had no respect for people, animals or nature. Think of the thylacine, the Tassie Tiger,' said Sally. 'Poor thing, the last of the species died in Hobart Zoo in the 1930s. It makes me so sad to think about it.'

'Yes, me too. And they saw it coming. Well, John Gould, the naturalist, did. I've got a reproduction of his thylacine painting on my office wall. I memorised the caption . . .' said Dan.

'Go on then,' Jessica prompted.

'Okay . . . "*Numbers of this singular animal will speedily diminish, extermination will have its full sway, and it will then, like the wolf in England and Scotland, be recorded as an animal of the past . . . John Gould, 1851.*"'

Jessica smiled sadly. 'I'd love them to come back. They're sort of like dingoes on the mainland . . . a wolf dog.'

'Scientists are trying to clone one,' said Dan. 'They've found fully formed foetuses of the thylacine preserved and sent abroad to collectors a century ago. Who knows . . .'

'Are there records from old Aboriginal cave paintings?' asked Sally. 'Paintings of the Tassie Tiger?'

'The early French and Dutch explorers did drawings and made observations, and some of the early settler artists recorded colonial life in their work. But it's only been in relatively recent times that we've become aware of what was here first and what's been lost,' said Dan with a sigh. 'The rock art in the Tasmanian Wilderness

World Heritage Area is up there with the rock art on the mainland in terms of antiquity and cultural significance.'

'Is the rock art protected?' asked Jessica as they started to pack away their lunch things.

'Not well enough,' said Dan. 'Despite national heritage protection, the place is threatened by unauthorised off-road recreation vehicles and bikes driving along the beaches and sand dunes, and the bush, and running over the middens and petroglyphs, sacred places. Often people destroy them without even knowing they're there.'

'Or, if they do, they don't care,' said Jessica.

'So are the mushrooms or this sort of thing with the plants around Indigenous artefacts your main field of study?' asked Sally.

'Both, in a way, as it's all tied up with nature conservation. Looking at how we can save our planet.' He smiled.

'Oh, just the regular stuff,' added Jessica, chuckling. 'Nothing too challenging.'

They laughed and Dan stood up. 'Shall we get going?'

'Thanks for the oysters, by the way,' said Sally.

Dan reached out his hand and helped pull Jessica to her feet, then turned to Sally.

'I'm fine, thanks.' She smiled and picked up her small backpack.

They made slow progress, stopping regularly as Dan showed them bird rookeries, small nests and animal habitats, unusual plants, strange rock formations, and a spectacular outlook where, on the windswept crest of a craggy hillside, he parted the button grass to reveal intricately carved ancient rocks.

They all fell silent, staring at the dramatic expanse of sky and sea.

'It's like a great art gallery,' said Jessica finally.

'Or a church,' murmured Sally.

'Definitely a hand-picked site, not a random scattering. I always feel this,' agreed Dan. 'The art and landscape are as one, in a way.'

It didn't strike Jessica, or Sally, until much later, that they hadn't felt the need to document such a special place by taking photographs, selfies, or sharing it on social media. 'Being there was enough,' Sally concluded when they talked about it.

Dan took them cross country past windswept trees standing like sculptures, down to the old forest and sheltered cove where Carmen's farm was nestled.

'This is my sort of territory,' he said as they walked single file through the weathered ancient trees, treading gently on the spongy moss underfoot. 'It's like something out of *Lord of the Rings*,' he said, laughing.

'It's like the Far Forest,' said Sally quietly.

Jessica paused. 'So it is.'

Dan, in the lead, turned around and stared at them. 'Your home, Sally? It's like this? Then I'd really like to visit it sometime.'

'Sure,' said Sally simply.

Jessica was staring at the good-looking, easygoing man in front of them. Then she turned and strode ahead.

They reached their cabin and said goodbye to Dan.

'See you up at Carmen's place,' he said cheerfully.

'Yes, see you there,' said Sally.

Inside, she pulled off her shoes and flopped in a chair. 'Wow, what a day, I'm whacked. Are you okay?' She noticed that Jessica was looking pale.

'Bit tired.' Jessica sighed.

'Me too. I'm not sure I want to go to Carmen's place. She can be hard work, bit of a rough diamond.' She yawned and went on, 'Dan sure knows a lot. But, I mean, what he was saying about mushrooms sounds a bit out there. Do you think it's feasible?' she asked.

'Who really knows? The studies and tests must be legit if they've been peer reviewed, I s'pose. And if people are taking out patents that means they smell big bucks.'

'The mushroom man from Canada sounds really interesting. And the fact they want to make this all available to the world is good news,' said Sally.

'Yes, very altruistic. But I bet big corporations will try to muscle in,' said Jessica.

'Or stop them,' added Sally.

Jessica looked thoughtful. 'Greed. Secret money, secret deals. Sign of the times. Everyone is selling something; pitching something for money.' She bent down and took off her shoes too.

'So, what's rattled you?' asked Sally, watching her friend.

'What do you mean?'

'Just now. Come on, I *know* you, Jess. I saw you go white as a ghost when we were saying goodbye to Dan earlier, and then you rushed off.'

'It's nothing. Well, you know me, I just get these flashes, these strong feelings. Something about Dan intrigued me.'

'Really?' Sally left the question hanging, waiting for more.

'I was just surprised to feel like that, I guess. After all, I don't even know the guy apart from the walk today.' Jessica shrugged.

'His job sounds pretty interesting,' said Sally. 'C'mon, let's bite the bullet and go and have one drink at Carmen's place. We don't have to stay, there's some food here and we can ask Victor for more.'

'Well, we don't have to dress up for dinner, that's for sure!' said Jessica. 'I'll just have a shower.'

*

They walked through the trees in the dusk, smelling woodsmoke before they saw the glow of lights from Carmen's cottage. As they drew closer they both stopped. The sound of music drifted towards them. 'Chopin?' Jessica tilted her head.

'I don't know. Surely it's not Carmen playing? Must be a CD.' Sally hurried forward. The door was ajar, and they knocked and waited.

The playing ceased as Carmen called out, 'Yo, come on in.'

Sally looked at Jessica and raised an eyebrow.

'Hey, how was your day? Come on in to the fire.' Carmen met them with a smile and ushered them inside.

'You play the piano?' said Jessica. 'It was lovely.'

'Piano needs a tune, don't think it likes the sea breeze.'

'How did you get it over here?' asked Sally as Carmen led them into the main room.

'Well, that was an exercise and a half. Wish I had a video of that day. Here we are. Now, what can I get you? I have very nice wine from a friend's vineyard on the east coast.'

'Thank you, that would be perfect,' said Sally.

'I love this room,' said Jessica, looking around. 'Indeed your cottage is . . . well, wonderful. You have eclectic taste.' She glanced at Sally, who gave her a wide-eyed look behind Carmen's back as she poured their wine. Jessica knew they were both thinking the same thing, *How did we misjudge Carmen so badly?*

The small house was filled with Carmen's life and

·211·

interests – music, books, a spinning wheel, a painting easel, a kitchen crammed with copper saucepans hanging on a rack, bunches of herbs, baskets of fruit and vegetables, and a delicious smell of something cooking. In the living room, the piano was in a corner by the windows that faced the sea. A violin case rested on sheets of music on top of it.

'How on earth do you find time for all . . . this?' exclaimed Jessica, waving an arm at the spinning wheel, where a basket of fleece was half spun.

'I'm thinking of getting some alpacas. As well as the goats, there're some old sheep here – the original farmers had dear old Romney ewes they crossed with Polwarth rams and they did well with them. I like keeping a few sheep about the place. Spinning wool is very calming.'

Sally picked up a soft creamy throw rug from the edge of the sofa. 'Did you make this from your wool?'

Carmen handed her a glass of wine. 'I did. Amazing what you can get through with no TV!'

Jessica sipped the crisp sauvignon blanc, putting it down to carefully lift a book from the top of a stack on a small table. 'These books are very impressive, and this is a first edition, too,' she said as she gently turned the pages.

'I come from a family of readers and musicians. Lucky I like my own company, eh? Ah, I hear another arrival.'

As Carmen left the room, Jessica opened her mouth in mock surprise and Sally shook her head in wonder at how they had underestimated the talented intellectual within the down-to-earth Carmen.

'G'day, Vic. Come on in and warm up. How're things out there?' said Carmen as Victor appeared in a clean faded shirt, shrugging out of his jacket.

'All checked and animals done. Say, how'd your day go, eh, girls?'

'Amazing. We ran into Dan, so he showed us around,' said Sally.

'Bright fella, that one. Did ya hear how the treasure hunter went?'

'He's still being cagey about what he's really looking for. Asked for a decent spade, said he was digging up mussels,' Carmen said, and rolled her eyes.

Dan tapped at the door and came inside. 'Hi, sorry, am I holding up the party?'

'Not a party. Just a quiet get-together, to appreciate the day,' said Carmen, handing him a glass of wine.

'Thanks for showing us around today,' said Sally.

'Glad you enjoyed it. It's a special place.' He glanced at Jessica. 'What did you enjoy most?'

'Many things. I couldn't live here, though.'

'Too quiet?'

'No. It's peaceful and beautiful.'

'Too wild?'

'Not at all. I grew up in the south-east, so I'm used to wild.'

'Because it's an island?' Dan stared at her.

'Exactly.' She gave him a brief smile. 'You get that?'

'That's the very reason I like living here,' said Carmen. 'Breathing space. No one unexpected is going to knock at your door.'

'Unless they're shipwrecked,' said Victor.

'True. But islands can be little time capsules, hopefully delaying the onslaught of being loved to ruin,' Carmen said, and sighed.

'Tourism, you mean?' said Sally.

'And development and greed, and ignorance,' said Dan. 'Sorry to be a party pooper.'

'It's your job,' said Carmen.

There was a bang at the door and the girls jumped.

'Ship ahoy,' said Victor. 'I'll go.'

They heard Victor talking and Carmen, who'd turned on music that played discreetly in the background, joined him. Victor returned and told them, 'It's Laurie, the cray fisherman I told you about. He's found an injured penguin.'

'Oh really, is it badly hurt?' asked Jessica.

'Not serious. Carmen knows what to do.'

Jessica and Sally jumped up and hurried after Carmen.

In the glow of a dim light bulb on a table on her side verandah, Carmen expertly examined the penguin's foot, murmuring quietly to it as Jessica held its wings still, and Sally helped Carmen with tweezers, disinfectant and a small bandage.

'Cut himself on something sharp. There wasn't broken glass, or a tin can or something anywhere, was there?' she asked Laurie, who told them he'd been fishing down on the shore in the shelter of the boulders. 'Sometimes inconsiderate visitors dump stuff.'

Sally thought Laurie looked the perfect image of an old salt – weather-tanned, stubble covering his chin, seafarer's knit jersey, untamed salt-and-pepper hair under a mashed sea captain's cap.

He gave a shy smile. 'No, not that I noticed. I saw he was limping and I just scooped him up. Didn't know what else to do.'

'Well, you did the right thing. I'll put him in a cage I have for wounded wildlife. Vic, could you please take Laurie inside and give him a drink?'

They went into the living room and the girls sat down on a small settee as Victor handed Laurie a beer. Dan smiled at Sally and Jessica. 'Carmen is a surprise, isn't she? Multi-talented, you could say.'

'Yes, she certainly is. You seem to wear several hats, too,' said Jessica.

'Not really. As I said earlier, everything comes from, and goes back to nature.' He paused. 'Are you living in Tassie, Jessica?'

'I'm kind of between lives. I'm not sure where I want to be at the moment. I grew up here. Sally is my oldest friend.'

'Ah. I understand. This is a good place to be then.' He paused, glancing at Jessica. 'I'm going to help Carmen with the food, want to join me?' he asked them both.

Carmen served a hearty moussaka, a green salad, home-grown tomatoes and basil, and fresh-baked bread. They all helped themselves, then gathered informally around the table.

Victor and Laurie were deep in conversation, Sally was talking to Dan about truffles, so Carmen turned to Jessica. 'Did you enjoy today?'

'I did. So much to explore. History seems embedded here. There are so many things I know only vaguely or simply have no knowledge about. Talking with Dan and Sally today made me realise I hardly know anything about the lives of the Indigenous people here in Tassie, before the English came,' she said.

'The colonists did a pretty thorough job of eradicating the first Tasmanians,' Carmen said. 'Well, they thought they did.'

Jessica shook her head. 'How do the local Indigenous people feel about their story, I wonder? We never hear their side.'

Carmen sipped her wine. 'You will, but it could still take a while,' she said softly. 'It's taken a long time already for non-Indigenous people to acknowledge that Aboriginal people control their own history and stories.'

'Aboriginal history is part of World Heritage history and it can contribute to cultural pride, information and understanding, yet so many politicians still ignore this fact,' Dan said, joining their conversation.

'Do you think people find it easier to believe one version of the past rather than recognise what really happened?' Jessica asked.

'Maybe,' Dan said. 'In some places around Tassie now the local Indigenous people are working with the academic and scientific community, directing the research to record their history.'

'That's so great. I've realised I miss that challenge, being collaborative, unravelling puzzles, even if it's just peering down a microscope or collating computer print-outs. I worked in a pharmacology lab,' added Jessica, turning to Carmen.

'And now?' Carmen asked.

'Taking time out. Reassessing, I guess,' she said.

Carmen touched her hand. 'This is a good place to do just that. Right, dessert.' She rose, and Sally and Victor started to clear the plates.

Dan leaned towards Jessica. 'Does that mean you might be available for some fieldwork tomorrow morning? I'd love a hand if you have nothing else to do.'

'Me? I'm on a holiday! Just joking. Really, I'm not sure how I can help you, though I'm happy to tag along if you like.' She studied Dan. 'Why do you ask?'

He gave a slight shrug. 'I just thought you seemed interested in our work. Sally is welcome too, of course.'

'I'll talk to her. We'll probably head back when the boat comes in the day after tomorrow.'

'It's up to you. There's a cave complex where I have permission to study the plants. It's where some of the earliest human occupation of this state was found. I was first taken there with one of the local custodians. We had a young Aboriginal graduate student with us and he got so spooked.'

'Scared, you mean?'

'Yes, he suddenly felt, heard, could see, his ancestors in there, sitting around a fire, wrapped in possum-skin cloaks. He swears he heard singing and clapsticks. It was thought that perhaps a few Indigenous people survived on the fringes of the rainforest, but the true wilderness was uninhabitable. Yet people co-existed with the wilderness, which survives today thanks to the world's first green movement to save the rivers and the forests here.'

'We lost Lake Pedder,' Jessica reminded him. 'A pristine glacier lake flooded for hydro-electricity. My parents still talk about it; they wish they'd seen it. Now tourists want to come to Tasmania for the wilderness experience.'

'That's becoming a worry. The experience part . . . we need to quietly observe the wilderness. Untouched. Like this cave, forgotten, for thousands of years.'

'Caves hold secrets,' said Jessica slowly. 'So what did the young guy do?'

Dan smiled. 'He became an archaeologist. We work together now and then. He wants some samples of plants from here. There're some buried in clay in the old strata. The local custodians now work with scientists and other academics who are trying to piece together the very big pre-history picture. I help out every so often.'

Sally came over and put a cheese platter on the table. 'What are you two plotting?'

'Dan's asked if we want to go out tomorrow as field assistants.'

'Only if you want to, but it's a pretty interesting area. I have permission,' he added.

'It's a cave shelter,' added Jessica. 'Do you want to come along?'

'I thought we were over caves?' Sally raised an eyebrow, but she was smiling. 'Sure,' she said. 'I'm going to call Toby first thing, though. Victor has explained where the spot is where we can get phone reception.'

'I know it. It's on the way, I can take you there. We'll head out after breakfast then,' said Dan. 'Is eight too early?'

'We weren't planning on going clubbing tonight, were we?' Jessica said to Sally.

Sally chuckled. 'I'm helping Victor with the drying up. Give me ten minutes, then we'll hit the sack. I'm too tired to even read.'

The girls hugged Carmen goodnight, thanking her for a wonderful evening.

'It's not even ten o'clock,' she said with a laugh. 'Some nights the talk goes on for hours, or we listen to music. I'm glad you've enjoyed the day. You'll have an interesting morning with Dan. He's a wise little owl, that one. Laurie might head back to port late-ish tomorrow, can't promise, depends on his catch but mainly on the weather, if you want to go with him. Victor will be heading out at first light the following day, again weather permitting.'

*

Dan walked with them back to their cabin. 'I have everything we need for tomorrow. Just bring a hat, water, and a jacket in case the weather turns. As well as any snacks you want.'

'You sure you don't mind if we stop to make a phone call?'

'Not at all. Sometimes the reception can be dodgy, but it's worth a shot.' He paused. 'Sally, what did you mean about you being over caves? If you're claustrophobic, don't worry. This cave complex is really big, you won't feel it in there.'

'No. No, it's all right. Jess and I had a secret cave hideout at Arcadia when we were kids,' Sally said.

'Yeah, we made a pilgrimage back there not long ago, which kinda prompted this little jaunt,' added Jessica.

'What happened?'

Jessica nudged Sally, who shrugged. 'We found some old stuff in there, connected to my family, going back to my grandmother's time. There was a letter . . . with the name of a house in Shelter Bay.'

'So we thought we'd check it out,' added Jessica.

'The grandmother who did the paintings – Stella?' asked Dan. When they nodded, he asked, 'Well, what did you find out?'

'Not much. It was all a bit weird. And Sal is being stalked.'

'Not really! Well, I hope not,' exclaimed Sally.

'Someone is following us. Phone calls and heavy breathing. He did speak once . . .'

'Bloody hell . . . what did he say?' asked Dan.

'"*I know where you are . . .*"' muttered Sally, now looking upset.

'Whoa, that's full-on.' Dan shook his head. 'But you went to the house in Shelter Bay? What did you find?'

'Nothing. Just this big house and a nervous old lady who told us to go away, but I'm sure she recognised the name of the man we asked about,' said Sally.

'There was someone else there too,' added Jessica. 'And a big shed . . . I mean, like a huge greenhouse with lots of security . . . it was weird. And there was some sort of a tunnel with a massive old lock on its door that just about fell open when I touched it. Actually, Dan, you would have been interested. They were growing mushrooms in there.'

Dan raised his eyebrows but was silent for a moment. 'Was this your grandmother's house, like where she grew up or something?' he finally asked, looking at Sally.

'No, she came from the mainland. She was my grandfather's second wife, and much younger than him,' said Sally, as they reached their cabin. 'We're not sure who or what is the connection between her and Shelter Bay.'

'Look, I wouldn't worry about it, but if you like I can look into it. I have a feeling I know who they might be. It sounds like a place I've heard of through someone who works at the Gardens.'

'Really?' chorused both girls.

'Listen, I'll be heading out your way to meet Sean Hyland. I'll call in and see you at your farm, Sally, if that's okay, and I'd really like to meet Toby too. We can talk more about it then.'

Sally nodded.

'Get a good night's sleep, and I'll see you in the morning.' He smiled at them. 'Have breakfast before you leave!'

*

The girls were snuggled in their beds in the small bedroom.

'What an amazing evening,' sighed Sally. 'I'll be asleep in a flash. Did you set your phone to wake us up? We can make tea and toast, that'll do us.'

'Yep. Listen to the wind, it's nice, not too strong, and I'm so comfortable and warm. No distractions.'

'You don't think Dan is a distraction?' Sally's voice was muffled as she curled into her pillow.

'What's that mean?'

'Nothing . . . It's just, he's such a nice guy. Sounds

like he's well known in his field. Carmen filled me in,' said Sally. 'But I keep wondering, do you think all that stuff he told us about the mycology, the mushrooms and stuff . . . all those experiments, is for real? How come nobody seems to know about it?' she added.

'My guess is, they soon will,' said Jess.

'Maybe. Mum is always saying that she pooh-poohed the internet when it first launched. And there are so many other examples like that. Who knows what's in the rainforest and old-growth forests right here in Tassie?' said Sally.

'Yeah, but it's much more complicated than that. You might find something quite extraordinary, but if someone else beats you to it, they might lock it up with a patent, and use it to benefit and profit just a few. Look at the pesticide moguls.'

'That's why I'd love to meet Dan's mycologist guy,' Sally said. 'He sounds amazing.'

Jessica smiled to herself. Sally sounded like her old self. Daniel Sullivan had settled her fears, and Jessica knew that Sally was quite looking forward to seeing the cave tomorrow.

For the first night in a long time, Jessica was sure she would sleep soundly, like the inevitable tide rolling in and submerging the anxieties of past days. She looked out the window where a pale moon rose, a glimmer through clouds. She heard the wet wind wrapping around the trees, and imagined it sweeping through the grasslands, across the rocks and high headland, crossing the sandy cove, ruffling the surface of the lagoon before bravely dancing off the coast to be pushed away by the great seas and winds of the Roaring Forties.

She closed her eyes and let sleep overcome her.

Stella's footsteps were muffled as she walked slowly down the hall and tapped on the door to Stephen's study, which served as office and library.

'Yes, Mrs James, come in.'

'It's me, dear. I let Mrs James go home, she's had a big day. Here's your brandy nightcap.'

'This is a nice surprise, thank you, dear.'

Stella hovered as he placed the small glass on the table beside his wingback chair. He glanced up and gave her a querying look. 'It's late, you're not dabbling with your drawings, I hope. Tomorrow will be busy and I have an early start. I thought I'd take the *Charlotte-Ann* out tomorrow afternoon. Would you care to come along?'

They hadn't been sailing together for quite some time, so he seemed put out when Stella shook her head. 'I don't think so. Thank you.'

'Oh. Do you have an appointment?' His tone was faintly facetious. Stella knew that he expected her to accompany him whenever he extended an invitation. He reached for his brandy, taking a small sip through pursed lips.

'Yes. Actually I do. May I take the car into Burridge?'

Stephen looked surprised. 'To the village? What are you going there for?'

'I'm seeing Mrs Pearson. The midwife.'

'Ah, what are they roping you into now, my dear? Do they want you to be involved in some fundraiser or other?'

Stella sat on the footstool near his chair. Frowning, Stephen put a bookmark in his book and closed it.

'The appointment is professional. For me. I believe I am expecting a child.'

Stephen blinked, a swift expression of hope then solicitous concern flashing over his face. Then gently, faintly condescendingly, but nonetheless in a rather fatherly tone, he said, 'My dear girl. Much as we might welcome such an event, I'm afraid you're misreading matters. Sometimes symptoms begin to appear at this stage of your life and your functions change –'

'Stephen! I'm still quite young. I am not forty yet!'

He leaned forward and took her hand. 'Although we have wished for a child, sometimes these matters are not to be . . .'

Stella's face was flushed and she struggled to remain composed. He reached for her other hand, making a soothing noise.

Stella couldn't help it; she pulled her hand away. 'Stephen! I wanted this to be a surprise. I have already visited Mrs Pearson, and she confirms that I am having a baby.' Seeing the shocked expression on her husband's face, she quickly added, 'She says it's not totally unexpected. It happens. When husband and wife are relaxed and . . . loving . . .'

'*She is not a doctor!*' he exploded.

Stella straightened. 'Aren't you pleased, Stephen?'

Flummoxed, he grabbed his brandy and took a large mouthful. 'Stella, dear girl, I don't want you to be disappointed. Of course, I'd like nothing better . . . but this woman, she's not trained, she's not a doctor, I don't want you to get your hopes up . . .'

Stella stared at him and almost burst out laughing, but bit her tongue and lowered her eyes. She knew the dynamics in the room had swung to her side.

'She says it's confirmed. But I am happy to see one of your colleagues as well, anyone you may suggest. However, even Mrs James, who's quite experienced in these matters after so many babies, believes I am at last . . .' she tried out the word, 'pregnant. I hoped you would be pleased.' She lowered her head again, and Stephen clutched for her in a convulsive movement.

'My dear . . . I am at a loss. Of course, professionally, I know these things sometimes occur, but . . .'

Stella looked at him with brimming eyes as she held his hand. 'Stephen, dear, I . . . we are so blessed.'

He patted her hand. 'Of course, dear, of course. It's just . . . well, a surprise.' He gave a small smile and placed his book beside the brandy and rose, drawing Stella to her feet. 'Now, indeed, you must rest.' He kissed her cheek. 'You must look after yourself.' And as Stella turned, he added, 'Best we keep this our little secret, just for now.'

'Of course, Stephen.' Stella walked carefully from the room, conscious that every step was important, that she was, indeed, carrying a precious gift.

*

Stella retreated into herself during the next months, though she painted and worked in her studio with some fervour. Stephen told her to stop her garden work altogether, forbade long walks and asked Mr and Mrs James to monitor her during the days when he was away seeing patients or at his surgery.

Nonetheless, Stella continued to visit the woods, calling to Nyx, sketching and photographing the trees, plants and fungi. She also found it relaxing to walk along the edge of the river and sit near the boatshed, watching the occasional boat pass by.

Stephen insisted they move into Hobart prior to the birth, and Stella arranged for Sheilagh Pearson to be with her when her time came.

After a long labour, she gave birth to a healthy baby girl.

'I'd like to name the child after my mother – Cecilia,' Stephen said. But Stella was firm.

'Mollie. Mollie Cecilia Holland. My dearest friend was Mollie. She died when she was sixteen.'

'Very well,' he said with an indulgent sigh.

Mollie's christening was a modest gathering in the church at Burridge. Mrs James was a grandmother to many these days, but said she was deeply touched when Stella asked her and Mr James to be Mollie's godparents.

At the baptismal font, Stella noticed Mrs James discreetly wiping a tear from her eye, then Stella's gaze returned to the infant in her arms, the baby's blue eyes trustingly searching her mother's face.

Baby Mollie was wrapped in the shawl Mrs James had sewn from fine woollen cloth. She had crocheted around the edges and, along its border, had painstakingly embroidered flowers, ferns and birds, including the unmistakable guardian of an owl.

7

Lone Island, 2018

THEY WERE BOTH CROUCHING down on a patch of stubby dry grass, wrapped in jackets as the sun had yet to take the night-time crispness from the earth. It was a morning where in the sharp, fresh air a deep breath would catch in the lungs. Dan had described it as 'one of those cut-glass clear mornings', adding, 'But it won't last. The weather is unpredictable here.'

Jessica, wearing cotton gloves, was gently cutting samples of a grey–green grass that was growing in a small crevice beside the petroglyph, as Dan had directed. Sally was perched on a nearby rock, peering at her phone. 'Dan, there's only half a bar, does the reception get any better? The phone won't work here,' she called.

'You'll have to walk up the hill a bit more, Sally,'

he said. 'See the two big rocks that look like an arch? There's a spot beside them; face the north.'

'Okay, I'll give it a go. Thanks.'

When Sally was out of earshot, Jessica said, 'Sal misses her family. She has a darling little girl, only four years old.'

'That's understandable. Did you both just set off on a road trip for fun, or are you serious about tracking down this family connection?'

'We're not sure if it's actually a family connection . . .' Jessica said, and hesitated.

'Oh, I don't want to pry, but I get the feeling there could be more to this. If Sally doesn't mind, I'd like to pay a visit to the farm you mentioned at Shelter Bay. Seawinds, was it? From what you've described, they could be manufacturing or growing something of real interest. We heard a rumour about someone in that area doing interesting soil and plant experiments, which crosses into my field of plant physiology. But they haven't been very forthcoming with their results, if they have any.'

'I keep wondering why they are being so secretive,' said Jessica. 'The security for the shed seemed really tight.'

'They might be protecting a possible money earner. Trying to register a patent and be the first to get it out on the market. Not everyone is as altruistic as my friend Sean.'

'Well, the old lady who answered the door there didn't seem to recognise Sally's family name or Arcadia. On the other hand, although she ignored us when we mentioned the name Broadbent, her reaction made us think she seemed to know it. But she was pretty anxious to see us leave.'

'You'd think a couple of women making inquiries about a family in the area wouldn't be a threat,' mused Dan.

'Ooh, what's this!' Jessica's attention was drawn to something in the crack in the old rock where she'd been carefully scraping away the soil around the wild grass's roots.

'Wait. Don't pull it. Just gently brush around it. Hang on, let me photograph it. We need to record things in stages . . .' Dan reached for his camera.

Jessica wriggled to one side as Dan leaned in, focusing the lens on the small protrusion, which was no larger than the top of a pencil.

'It doesn't look like part of a plant,' said Jessica.

'Okay, brush around it carefully. It could be fragile, maybe an old bone or something, you never know,' said Dan as he lay flat down beside her to get a closer look.

'Really?' Jessica swept the soil away with the soft brush Dan had given her, then paused. 'I don't want to do anything more in case I damage it.'

'Can I have a go?' Dan took a small trowel out of his backpack and carefully shifted more soil away. 'It's not botanical . . . it looks hard . . .' He carefully dug at the earth and then handed Jessica the trowel. 'Here, keep doing this very gently while I take another photo.'

'It's metal! Or stone,' Jessica said.

'See if you can lift it out . . . gently.'

'What is it?' breathed Jessica as she extracted a flat stone and held it in her gloved hand.

Dan bent close to look. 'Flint of some description . . . perhaps it's a tool for cutting or chipping.'

'You mean it could be ancient? An artefact?'

Dan chuckled as he took her hand and posed the piece of flint on her palm in front of the camera. 'Maybe. Hold it for a photo.'

'It's heavy, and look, it's been shaped to a point,' said Jessica.

'It could have been used to carve the markings on the rock face here,' said Dan. 'If we could match the cuts and gouges to the cupules and find it's the actual tool, that'd be quite a coup. Can you put it in here?' he asked, handing Jessica a small, secure box. 'I'll take it to the museum guys.'

'Jess!' There was a scream from Sally.

Jessica and Dan scrambled to their feet as Sally came stumbling towards them.

'What's up?' called Jessica.

'Was it a snake?' shouted Dan.

'Snakes?' Jessica said in alarm.

'There're copperheads and tigers,' said Dan grimly. 'Docile unless provoked.'

Sally was waving her phone wildly as she ran, and Jessica hurried towards her. 'What's happened? Is Katie okay? Toby?'

Panting, Sally reached them and grabbed Jessica's hand. 'The farm has been raided. The truffles, Jasper is injured . . .' she gasped.

'What!'

'Sally, here, sit down. Take a few deep breaths for a moment,' said Dan as he took her arm and guided her to a small boulder.

Jessica sat beside her friend and held her hand.

'It's the farm . . .' Sally said, close to tears.

'Katie, Mollie and Toby, are they okay?'

Sally nodded, and Jessica drew a breath of relief.

'Someone got in and raided the truffles. Jasper was hurt, but he's okay. Why would someone do that?' Sally let out a sob.

'Did they actually dig up the truffles?' asked Dan as he squatted down beside her.

'Some. Jasper must have heard them because he went after them. They threw something at him, a spade, I think. Toby says he'll be okay. But they got some truffles . . .'

'Anything else taken?' asked Jessica.

'Toby doesn't think so. Luckily he'd already collected the first batch of ripe ones and packed them ready to send to Sydney.'

'It's okay, Sally, probably just some random grab; someone trying to make some money thanks to your hard work. You might have to increase your security, though,' said Jessica.

'I want to go home now.' Sally looked at Jessica. 'Is there any way we can get over to the car today?'

Dan glanced at the sky. 'There's a storm brewing, so the seas might be too rough. And I doubt the pilot would want to chance it in bad weather in a small plane. But let's check with Carmen.' He gave Sally a smile. 'Tomorrow morning is meant to be fine.'

'I just feel sick I'm not there.'

'C'mon, Sal, let's head back,' said Jessica, helping Sally to her feet.

'Let me quickly finish up here and I'll walk back with you,' offered Dan.

'No, we're fine, Dan. You keep going here. I know it's important,' said Jessica.

'Oh, sorry, Dan. I'll be okay.' Sally drew a breath.

'Why don't you call your husband back again now, or your mother, and just reassure them that you'll be home by tomorrow night. Also, maybe ask if there's been any other . . . interference at your property.'

'Yes, talk to your mum, that's a good idea. While you've got phone reception,' agreed Jessica.

Sally walked back up the hill to the pocket of reception.

'That's all a bit of a worry,' said Jessica. 'Arcadia is such a sheltered, out-of-the-way place.'

'Yeah, but lots of people would know about it, and good truffles can fetch two grand a kilo,' he added.

As Jess carefully packed up the tools she'd been using, Sally walked back towards them, looking a little less anxious.

'I spoke to Mum. She's upset, of course. Feels violated that someone got in and stole from us. She's worried about Jasper too, and about insurance. She thinks Toby is downplaying it a bit so she doesn't get anxious. She knows he's nice like that.'

'Well, at least there's no immediate emergency or danger,' said Dan. 'Thanks for your help, Jessica,' he added as he noticed the neatly packed toolbox.

'Oh, don't stop on my account, Jess. We haven't even gone to the cave yet. I'll head back to the cottage if you want to stay awhile and work. It's too early for lunch,' said Sally. 'I'll see if I can find Carmen and double-check that Victor is heading over to the mainland tomorrow morning. She might even have time for a coffee.'

'I don't want you to go on your own, Sally. You've had a horrible shock,' said Jessica.

'It's fine,' Sally said. 'I feel like a quiet walk to put my head back in order.'

*

While her contribution was straightforward – taking measurements, marking plant and soil samples in little plastic bags, taking photos and listening to Dan's explanations and theories, Jessica found it all absorbing. It was just nice being involved in something again, outside of her own personal issues.

After a while, Dan sat back. 'Let's take a breather.' He passed her a flask from his knapsack. 'Some fresh orange juice. I have another one here.'

'Great. Thanks.' Jessica took a sip. 'Poor Sally. It's scary to think strangers can get in and rip up your crop.'

'It's an interesting crop to grow. Do you know what got them started?'

'I think they got the idea when they found a wild truffle down in their old-growth forest.'

'That forest is obviously something to treasure. Has it ever been logged or damaged?'

'Never been touched, as far as I know. Amazing trees hundreds of years old. You'd love it – they also find wild mushrooms growing there,' said Jessica.

'Mmm, yes, sounds like it would be the perfect breeding ground for fungi,' said Dan.

'Could those wild mushrooms be valuable? Like the ones you mentioned being used in those experiments?'

'Possibly. When you have the wild spore you can start breeding, cultivating them. They only have a short life span but they multiply quickly. Some fungi are quite rare. Do you know if there are more paintings in Sally's grand-mother's collection with fungi in them?'

'Gosh, we didn't look that closely and didn't pay much attention to the mushrooms,' said Jessica. 'All the plants and flowers she painted were stunning . . . we'll have to look as soon as we get back to Arcadia,' she added.

'The forest at Arcadia sounds right up my alley,' Dan said.

'It was one of our favourite playgrounds when Sally and I were growing up. The whole area – the forest, the creek and the cave.'

'The cave that somehow sent you on this hunt to Shelter Bay?'

'Oh, yes.' She'd forgotten she'd told Dan about it. 'Well, you don't know the whole story. Nor do we, actually,' said Jessica. 'Sally and I used the cave as a hideout when we were kids. Then one time Sally tripped off the ledge when we were climbing back down and she fell down into the creek . . . could have been terrible, but she was okay.'

'You rescued her?'

'Well, yes. But she'd have jumped in to help me if I'd fallen. We've never told anyone . . . now you know our big secret.' Jessica smiled, surprised at herself for mentioning it. 'Anyway, we never went back there again. Until a couple of weeks ago.'

Dan nodded, listening quietly.

In a rush Jessica told him, 'And we found this old tin hidden behind a bed in the cave. I don't think anyone had been in there since us, and who knows how long before that. But we think we know who was there . . .'

'The Shelter Bay people? Whoever they might be?'

'Partly. There was a map that had the address "Seawinds, Shelter Bay" on it. Also, we found a note on pretty writing paper. A love note, as it turned out. A farewell message . . .'

'A "Dear John" letter, isn't that what they're called? These days you get a text message. Sorry, go on,' said Dan.

'Yes, she said she couldn't see him again, she'd always love him . . . that sort of thing. No signature. But we found some photos so we think we know who wrote the note.'

'Really? So, who was it?'

'Sally's grandmother, Stella, the artist.'

'Wow. Was she married at the time?'

'She was, to Stephen Holland, who owned Arcadia.'

Dan gave a low whistle. 'Oops. So where does Shelter Bay come in?'

'Well, if the items in the cave, including the map, belonged to the Adonis we saw in one of the photos, then maybe that's where he was from. We think the cave was their trysting place.'

'How come the map was in the cave?'

'We don't know. We haven't delved into it too much. I mean, Sally hadn't expected to discover that her grand-mother had a secret lover. It was a real shock. From the photo of him and the shots of Stella in the family album we know they were both very good-looking. Her husband, the doctor, was much older, so . . . I guess it's understand-able, but at the time it would have been a pretty daring thing to do.'

'You're right,' said Dan. 'Do you think she was seeing him before she was married?'

'I doubt it. Stella was from the mainland. She met Dr Holland in Hobart when she was studying art.'

'Maybe she broke it off, and he came back, watched her from afar, that sort of thing. Which might explain the letter in the cave.'

'Well, if she broke it off, I doubt he'd risk hanging around. There's a sinister side to it, too.' Now Jessica had revealed this much to Dan she kept going, keen to hear his thoughts.

'How sinister?'

Jessica told him about the sketchbook and the sadistic drawing of Stella and the dead owl.

'That's pretty threatening. Was the lover angry at being dumped?'

'Who knows? All I know is that Sally's grandparents definitely stayed together and I think they both lived to a decent age.'

Dan shrugged. 'Every family has its secrets, I guess.'

'I suppose so. I can't imagine we all have such dark and troubling ones, though.' Jessica handed the flask back to Dan. 'Thanks for that.' She gave a small smile. 'Please don't mention to Sally that I've told you.'

'Of course. So tell me again, what did you think you'd achieve by just rocking up at this place, Seawinds?'

'Well, we had a name, we were going to pretend we were doing family ancestry research or something.'

Dan frowned. 'Seems a long shot. Like I said, I know a bit about Seawinds – it's something of an historic house because of its connection to smugglers in the old days, and whalers and seafarers. The house has a tunnel that runs from the coast into the basement. It's old, so I guess it's too dangerous to use now.'

'How do you know that?' asked Jessica.

'The fellow at the Botanical Gardens knows about the house. There was talk of opening it up as a tourist attraction, some tourism group's idea, but it never happened. The family who live there put the kibosh on it. The smugglers' tunnel is known in the boating fraternity. It took a skilled sailor to get in there.'

'It sounds fascinating.' Jessica sighed. 'I wonder if that has anything to do with Sally's grandmother's secret? At first it was a surprise, a bit of a shock for Sally to find out her grandmother had been having an affair. But now I think it really bothers her as there's something not quite right about it all . . . especially with the anonymous phone calls and now the terrible news this morning.' Jessica stopped.

'Yeah. I agree,' Dan said. 'Let me help. As I say, I'll try to go to Seawinds and then call you if I find out anything. Perhaps I can call in at Sally's place soon too. Are you going to see Chrissie and Paul on your way back?'

'No, I think Sally will just want to get home.'

Dan began packing up his tools and samples. 'So where's your home these days?'

'Good question. I've yet to make that decision. I walked out of a marriage and a good job. I know I can do better. So I'm just taking time out.'

'That's a gutsy move. But you sometimes have to do that. Take life like the proverbial bull by the horns.'

'I'm tending more to tiptoeing through the tulips,' said Jessica wryly.

'And man, aren't those tulips beautiful. Tassie can almost rival the Netherlands for them.' Dan laughed.

'Ha! Yes, you're right.' She smiled and handed Dan the notes she'd taken. 'But being here has made me appreciate trees again. I took them for granted growing up in Tasmania. But living in Sydney . . .' She shuddered. 'Cement canyons, high-rises, traffic jams. I cringe when I see photos of crammed housing estates covering land that used to be old market gardens. Heritage homes and buildings knocked down. It's shameful how they're destroying a beautiful city.'

Dan held out a hand and helped her to her feet. His hand was warm, firm.

Jessica shivered, then busied herself slinging her bag on her shoulder. 'Have we got everything?'

'Yep. Thanks for your help.'

'It was interesting. Your job is certainly varied.'

'Plant physiology and plant biochemistry covers a lot of fields. Nature is an amazing canvas,' he said. 'My passion is the old-growth forests. Sean considers the old trees a resource of incalculable value. Those habitats have immune systems, just like people, and mushrooms are the cellular bridges between the two. His research is coming up with medicinal immune enhancements for humans, bees and animals.'

'Wow. Your mushroom guy sounds like a fount of knowledge. When are you seeing him?'

'He's giving a public lecture in Hobart soon. After that he's heading to Europe. More and more he's being contacted by government agencies and organisations around the world that see the need to take drastic action to protect the environment. Trouble is, big money gets in the way of good government. Don't get me started.' He looked at Jessica. 'Would you and Sally like to come to his talk? I can arrange tickets.'

'Absolutely. Thank you. Let us know when it's on.'

They walked together quietly for a while until Dan said, 'I might just head over by the airstrip, is that okay? There's a little flower that grows there, rather inconveniently, but we like to keep an eye on it. It's endemic to this island and nowhere else that we know about.'

'Of all the places to choose to grow.' Jessica laughed.

He stopped and pointed. 'Look . . . here's one.'

'It's a spiky little thing, but sweet,' said Jessica as they crouched down and Dan snapped a photo on his phone.

'I'll forward you the photo. Seeing as I'd better not pick the actual flower for you.' He smiled.

'I suppose plants and animals are safe here on the island. Carmen wouldn't let anyone touch them.'

'You're right in one way, but this little flower has to tackle the same problem that the big trees around the world are facing,' Dan said.

'What's that? Climate change?'

'Yes, sadly. And it'll only get worse, even if we act as fast as we can now.'

'You just have to look around,' agreed Jessica. 'From

melting arctic ice and glaciers to warming oceans. Scary.'

They stood up and Dan went over to the airstrip while Jessica headed back to the cottage for lunch with Sally, deep in thought.

*

At the jetty the next morning, Victor slung their backpacks onto the boat as Sally then Jessica hugged Carmen.

'It's been really special,' Jessica said.

'Come back anytime.' Carmen smiled. 'Whenever you want a little escape.'

'It's the perfect hideaway, that's for sure,' said Jess.

Dan untied the rope from the bollard and jumped on board. Then Victor reversed and turned the bow towards the open sea.

Sally went below, but Jessica stayed on deck, waving to Carmen then watching the cliffs of the headland recede.

'Is Sally okay?'

She turned to Dan. 'Just anxious to get home. As soon as she can call Toby, she'll feel better.'

'Too bad you couldn't stay longer on the island, there's still a lot to explore.'

'Well, thanks to you, we've seen heaps. I had a really wonderful time.'

They were quiet for a moment, then Dan said, 'You have a science degree and lab experience, Jessica, maybe you should think about investigating new fields to work in. I'd be happy to make any introductions. You could spend a couple of days at the museum and the Botanical Gardens to see what projects they have on there.'

'Perhaps. But I don't want to hurry into anything. I'll just hang with Sally and Mollie for a bit. I'm getting used to the freedom of being unemployed, although I'll have to face up to the reality of earning a living soon; my savings won't last forever.'

She went below deck and found Sally hunched over her phone.

'No reception yet,' Sally said when she looked up. 'It's awful being away from Toby and Katie when something horrible happens. It's rattled me. I feel like I'm unravelling or something.' She looked stricken.

Jessica was about to say 'rubbish', but she hesitated then said gently, 'It is a bit unnerving, Sal, but I'm sure everything will be okay. Dan is going to check out the people at Seawinds, and come see you and Toby at Arcadia, which is good of him.' She paused. 'I suppose it's just those odd things that have shaken us . . .'

'So you feel it too?'

'Well, sort of. Now don't you go spooking us!'

'Who, me?' Dan stuck his head through the hatch. 'When we get there, would you like to have a late lunch with Victor and me before you head off?'

'We should get going . . .' began Sally uncertainly.

'Talk to Toby as soon as you get phone reception,' suggested Jessica. 'I'm sure you'll feel better after that. If we have lunch then we won't have to stop later.'

'Good idea,' said Dan, and Sally nodded, glancing at her phone.

*

Once ashore Sally was her cheerful self again. 'Toby and Mum are fine, Katie has a friend over to play, and they're looking forward to meeting Dan.'

Jessica sighed. 'Phew. Well, that's good. Let's go eat.' The four of them walked along the waterfront to the seafood café Victor had suggested.

'You know, this seemed like the end of the world a few days ago,' said Jessica as they arrived at the simple eatery that had once been a general store. 'Now it feels like a teeming civilisation!'

'This is the best place for battered flathead fillets and potato wedges,' Victor told them.

He turned out to be amusing company, and Dan and the girls kept exchanging glances as Victor regaled them with funny stories of his time as a landlubber on an outback sheep station.

'That fish was delicious, light and flaky, freshly caught, I s'pose?' said Jessica.

'Yep, old Angelo, one of the local fishermen, knows all the spots if you want to have a fish any time,' said Victor. 'I swap him oysters and crays.'

'Well, we'd better make a move,' said Sally.

They split the bill between them and Dan walked Sally and Jessica to their car after they'd farewelled Victor.

'You've got a full tank? Don't forget, there's not a lot of places to get fuel if you take that back road I told you about.'

'Yes, we'll be fine. So we'll see you at Arcadia in a day or so?' said Jessica.

'Sounds good. Safe trip, and I'll let you know what I find out if it's anything exciting. Otherwise, see you at your place, Sally.' He opened the driver's door for Jessica and gave Sally a wave. 'Don't miss the turn at River Bend, it's a bit rugged but saves you time.'

'See you, Dan,' said Jess.

They lapsed into silence as Jessica drove through the quiet countryside, the lingering afternoon light mellowing the fields, paddocks and meandering rivers.

'Did you want music?' asked Sally.

'Not really.'

As they drove higher into the hills, turning around the curves of the incline, stately trees, their upper branches and canopy too high to see, leaned benevolently over the road. They seemed to watch and guard the small red dot of the car as it slid steadily through the golden shadows.

'Stunning scenery. How old must these trees be?' Jess said.

'You wouldn't want to have an accident and go down there, they wouldn't find you for yonks,' muttered Sally, staring at the steep drop beside the road.

'Don't look. Anyway, we haven't seen another car.'

'Just as well, there's nowhere to overtake.'

'I wonder what's the longest stretch of straight flat road they have in this state,' said Jessica. She flipped the sun visor down as the setting sun began to angle into her eyes. Then she glanced in the rear-vision mirror. 'Oh, rats. Someone is behind us.'

'Well, they'll have to be patient, there's nowhere to pull over and let them pass.' Sally shuddered, looking down again at the mountainside disappearing in layers of forest.

Jessica tapped her brakes, flicking a 'slow down, back off' message to the driver behind. And the four-wheel drive dropped back.

'Good. They got the message. How many mountains have we driven over on this jaunt?'

Sally shrugged. 'I didn't sleep well last night. I might close my eyes for a bit, okay? Let me know when you're ready to trade places.'

'Okay. I'm good for now.'

Jessica silently reflected on her conversations with Dan and what he'd said about the environment, and about Sean's work. From there her mind tumbled into thinking about how she lived day to day, week to week, month to month. The years had begun to blur, one into the next, and yet, how often did she ever take a step back and consider the big picture for the future? Really think about what sort of world children like Katie would inherit?

The light was fading, and as she reached a short straight section of road she glanced in the mirror to see that the four-wheel drive was back behind her again. And it was annoyingly, dangerously, close. Its lights were on high beam, obscuring her view of the driver behind the tinted windscreen.

As she rounded a bend there was a wider section of the shoulder, so she quickly pulled over and the car sped past her.

'What's going on?' Sally sat up, woken by the sudden jolt of the car braking.

'Just letting that car past. They must have known the passing shoulder was here; they came up right behind me.' Jessica pulled back onto the road.

'It's getting dark early.'

'All the trees, I guess. We're almost down. Oops, what the –'

The black four-wheel drive with the tinted windows had pulled over ahead of them, and as Jessica swerved past it, a bright light flashed.

'Did they just take a photo of us?' exclaimed Sally.

'I don't know what's going on.' Jessica put her foot down.

'Hey, Jess, ease up. You're over the speed limit.'

'At the moment I wouldn't mind being pulled over by a traffic cop. That car is giving me the creeps.'

'There's no police on this road,' said Sally. 'There's no one on the road. Full stop.'

A few minutes later Jessica said quietly, 'They're back.'

Sally turned and looked behind at the headlights. 'Probably some yobbo trying to frighten us. Saw two women in a car.'

'It's ages till we get to a town and there's nowhere to pull over.' Jessica gently increased her speed again, but the gap quickly closed as the black car kept pace on their tail.

'I know you're a good driver, Jess, but this is scary!' Sally sat rigid in her seat, her foot pressing on an imaginary brake, her eyes glued to the darkening road as they twisted downwards.

'We're levelling out,' said Jessica grimly as they hit the lower section of the mountain road, passing paddocks and old wooden fences.

'Jess! There's a light over there.' Sally pointed. 'A farm.'

Without hesitating Jessica turned onto the stretch of dirt road at the milk-can letterbox on a post, rattling over the metal bars of the cattle grid and raising a dirt cloud behind them, and then sped up the driveway.

'Are they following?' Jessica's voice was high and strained.

'I can't tell, there's so much dust. Slow down! I can't see any lights . . . I don't know. Ooh, look out! Cows . . .!' screeched Sally, as two cows were suddenly lit up in the headlights.

Jessica swerved as the startled cows loped to one side.

'Oh, no, they've turned in the driveway! Watch out!' said Sally, her voice shaking. 'Get to the house, quick. There's a light on at the door.'

'But there're no lights on inside, they might be out. Damn.'

Sally looked back over her shoulder. 'That car's slowed; they're waiting. Do you think the house is locked?

We could get in, lock ourselves inside and call for help . . . What're you doing?' she yelled as Jessica drove across the grass in front of the house and bumped around the back where bushes screened them. Their headlights swung across a barn, sheds and a vegetable garden.

'Oh, shit,' said Jessica. 'Get your phone. You go to the barn, I'll try the back door.'

'Are you nuts?'

'Just run, Sal! Hide. Then text me if I don't come straight away.'

They stumbled from the car, running in opposite directions as they heard the four-wheel drive clatter over the cattle grid at the bottom of the drive.

Jessica stumbled up the steps to the back door and yanked at the doorknob, but it was locked. Then, seeing a light switch, she stabbed at it and the back verandah and yard were illuminated by two spotlights. She bolted across the yard into the barn. 'Sal?'

'In here . . . the second pen,' came a muffled reply.

Jessica slammed the heavy barn door shut. 'Is there a back door?' She paused, hearing a car door close. 'Shit, they've driven up here. Sal . . .?'

'Over here, careful.' The barn was dimly lit, and when Jessica reached the stall she gasped.

Sally was squatting beside an enormous sow, which was lying on her side on thick straw as a dozen fat piglets suckled the teats along her large belly.

'What the . . . Holy cow, Sal . . .'

'No, holy sow,' hissed Sally. She giggled, but looked terrified.

Jessica clambered into the stall as the sow gave them a beady-eyed glare.

'Should we call the cops?' whispered Sally.

244

'I don't know. I've no idea where we are, and it'd take them ages to get here.'

'Why is that person following us?' asked Sally nervously. 'Is it the man from the phone call? He said he knew where we were . . .'

'I don't know. Let's think . . .'

'We can't stay here, he'll come looking for us,' Sally said. 'It pongs in here. Back there is awful, where she pees . . .'

'That's good . . . go and hide there. Whoever it is won't look back there, and it's dark.'

'Is there more than one of them, do you think? Where're you going, Jess?'

'I don't know, the windows are tinted. We need a photo of the number plate. I'm going out the back door. Hand me a couple of the piglets – ones that're sleeping, not eating,' Jessica said. 'Leave this door to the pen open so the mum can get out . . .'

'Jess, what the hell are you doing?'

'Not sure. Need a distraction. He'll probably look in here, so just keep out of sight. Give me those piglets. Quick. How can I keep them quiet?'

'I don't know. Hold their mouths shut, stuff them up your jumper, they're asleep.' Sally shoved two piglets at Jessica as the sow lifted her head.

Her heart beating wildly, Jessica pushed the piglets under her jacket and moved quietly to the back door of the barn, which led into a small fenced pen. Clutching the piglets to her chest, she clambered over the rails and crept around the side of the barn in the shadows.

Straight away she saw a man in a pool of light near the house. He had his back to her and was looking at the door, possibly wondering, as she had, whether he could open it.

Jessica walked slowly around the far side of the house in the darkness, hugging the baby pigs close and pulling her phone from her pocket with her free hand. As she tiptoed around to the front, she prayed there wouldn't be another man standing by the car.

The top-of-the-range vehicle was parked in the driveway, the driver's door open. There was no sign of anyone else.

Edging closer, Jessica snapped a photo of the car and its number plate, then hurried quietly back around to the barn. The driver had checked the back door, and must have seen the light switch and turned it off. The yard was in darkness. But Jessica could make out his silhouette trying the door handle of a shed before heading towards the open back door of the barn.

She froze in the shadows as he hesitated at the barn entrance, then turned on the torchlight in his phone and stepped inside.

'Sorry, kids.' She wrenched the dozy piglets from her jacket, put them on the ground and gave their curly tails a sharp tug before sprinting for the front door of the barn in the darkness. To her relief, the piglets squealed loudly behind her.

For all her gross bulk, the enormous sow must have been on her feet the second she heard her babies' cries, because from her position in the doorway, Jessica, now saw the animal sprint at full charge to the back door on her tiny, dainty feet, bowling over the figure as she rushed to rescue the enraged little piglets dropped so unceremoniously onto the cold ground.

While the man was picking himself up, Jessica dashed to the sow's stall and pushed her way to the back, near a feed trough. 'Sal, you here?' she whispered.

'What's happened?' hissed Sal. 'You didn't hurt those piglets?'

'Only their pride . . .' She shushed Sally as they heard curses and, peering through the pen, they saw the figure of a man limping outside as the angry screeches from the sow and irate squeals from her piglets ricocheted around the yard.

'Urgh, it stinks in here. Let's move.'

'Where is he?'

'Heading back to his car, I'd say.'

'Shh, is that an engine? Is he driving away already?' whispered Sally.

'No, that's a car driving *in* . . .' said Jessica.

There was a screech of brakes and some shouts, and then the girls heard the four-wheel drive rocketing away. Voices continued to yell and the sow started honking as her piglets screamed in fury. As the two women moved towards the barn door, they saw light flood the backyard, then someone picked up the piglets and came into the barn. The person turned on the main light as the sow trotted worriedly behind them.

They were middle-aged couple, and they were fussing over the piglets. 'The rest are here. Now how the hell did Sheila get out . . .?' the woman said.

Sally and Jessica emerged from the shadows. 'Sorry, we did that . . . are the babies okay?' said Jessica softly.

The woman screamed and the man started in astonishment.

'Who the hell are you? What're you up to? What's going on?' he stuttered.

Sally put her hands up. 'It's all right, we can explain. Some of it, anyway . . . Do you mind if we go outside? The smell is getting to me.' Sally hurried from the barn.

'We're so sorry to alarm you. I'm Jessica Foster and this is Sally Sandford . . . That man in the four-wheel drive was following us, I mean seriously shadowing us down the mountain. We came in here to get help, but when no one was home we looked for somewhere to hide. It's a bit of a story, would you mind if we washed up first and then told you?'

The woman had regained her composure and her frightened expression had turned to one of concern. 'Oh, you poor dears, that's terrible. Yes, yes, come in, have a shower if you want. Roger, can you please settle Sheila and the babies and lock up? I'm Barb. Barbara Brown.'

'We're so lucky you came home when you did,' said Sally as they walked towards the house.

'We were only over at the neighbours' place. We have an alarm security system that alerts us if anyone comes near the house. It went off, so we came back. Why were you being followed?' Barbara asked.

'We wish we knew,' Sally sighed.

Over coffee, after a thorough scrub of their faces and hands, they gave an edited version of the events of the afternoon, as well as the mysterious phone calls and the fact that Sally's farm had been raided. The Browns were very sympathetic.

'Would you like to stay for dinner, stay the night?' Barbara offered.

'Thank you, but no. I'm anxious to get home,' said Sally quickly. 'I've already called my husband to say we're just having a coffee break and will be back on the road soon.'

'What did you tell him?' asked Jessica.

'Oh, nothing, I didn't want to worry him. He just assumed we were tired and stopped to take a break.'

'Do you want to call the police?' asked Roger.

'No. Not yet, anyway,' said Sally. 'I'm so sorry we've caused such a disruption.'

'It's up to you,' Jessica said to the Browns. 'I don't want you guys to feel threatened, but frankly, I think that man was following us. I doubt he'll bother you again.'

'Well, okay. Here's our number. Call us when you arrive so we know you got home safely,' Roger said, then shook hands with both girls and walked them out to their car.

'Please apologise to Sheila for borrowing her babies,' said Jessica.

Sally drove and Jessica called Dan and told him what had happened.

'I can't believe it,' said Dan, aghast. 'Send me the photo of the number plate and I'll be right on it. I have a friend who can trace it for us. Would you feel better if we called the police? Trouble is, this guy probably knows you got his number plate, so he won't be on the road now.' Dan paused. 'Look, I plan to go to Seawinds in the next day or so, and I'll call as soon as I hear anything.'

'Thanks, Dan. Sally and I just want to get home now. We'll think about calling the police later,' said Jessica. 'See you soon.'

*

Katie was in bed when they got home, but as Sally crept in she stirred and smiled, holding out her arms to her mother. Sally kissed her and tucked her in, adjusting Mr K, her favourite koala, beside her. 'See you in the morning, darling girl,' she whispered.

Mollie had fallen asleep, but she hurried over from her cottage, saying that she'd woken up when she heard their car pull in. Jessica had showered and was wrapped in a bathrobe, drink in hand, talking to Mollie and Toby about the island when Sally joined them in the sitting room. A small fire glowing in the grate below the mantelpiece made the room feel snug and safe.

Toby and Sally sat close, holding hands. The girls were still rattled but had decided to try to downplay what had happened. After retelling the bald facts, however, Mollie and Toby were both alarmed.

'We need to call the police,' exclaimed Mollie.

'We don't have much to go on,' said Toby. 'We could get them to check out that number plate. But it might be hard to prove what that man was up to.'

'I'm sure the Browns would back up our story,' said Sally.

'Let's wait and see what Dan's friend finds out,' said Jessica.

She and Sally were worn out, and by unspoken agreement neither mentioned the phone calls or their visit to Seawinds. Instead, they talked about meeting Carmen and Dan. 'Carmen's a very no-nonsense woman,' Jess told them. 'Down-to-earth, and we discovered she has a very artistic side. Interesting. I liked her. Don't think she's one to suffer fools gladly, though,' she added, making Sally smile.

'How are you going?' Sally said, turning to look at Toby. 'It's upsetting enough to lose a valuable crop, but the fact that someone came onto our land and went digging for it is even scarier. Gives me a creepy feeling.'

Toby drew her into a hug. 'Let's talk about it tomorrow. It's late and you must be exhausted.'

*

The following morning Toby walked with Sally and Jessica along the rows of trees that had been inoculated with the truffle spores. 'See, they missed some. Without a good nose, they're difficult to find.'

'How is poor Jasper?' asked Jessica.

'He's okay. I think he's more upset that he let us down,' said Toby. 'He's such a loyal dog and takes his job very seriously. We heard him barking, which isn't too unusual. But it went on for so long, I finally got up and let him out, and that's when we heard him yelping and a car drive off. He limped back to me. He'd had a bit of a whack, hit with their spade, I think. Fortunately his leg is healing. Could have been much worse.'

Sally shuddered. 'Let's not go there. How is the saffron doing?'

As Toby and Sally talked, Jessica stared at the tall trees. 'I'm going to head down to the Far Forest and look around,' she said. Sally nodded as she and Toby turned towards the saffron field, arms around each other.

Jessica strode down the hill, walking from the bright sunlight into the mellow shade of the cool, damp forest. She took a deep breath, inhaling the sweet earthy smell, enjoying the moist softness around her. It was as if a million leaves or more breathed with her. In and out, the dampness from dripping leaves and spongy moss was cleansing and refreshing, and strangely calming. Apart from the faint gurgle of the creek, all was quiet. The eeriness, the other-worldliness she'd sometimes felt in the great old forests in the national parks around the state wasn't present here, but the stillness created its own atmosphere. Her footfalls on the lichen and the rotting wood and leaves were muffled. She imagined that if she stood still and quiet, she might hear the busyness of insects and small creatures, the trees taking in carbon dioxide and faintly dispersing oxygen. It occurred to her that she *knew* these giant trees. She would never get lost in here; she recognised each and every tree from years spent wandering and playing in here with Sally. They were familiar, like old friends.

Jessica took a long, deep breath and suddenly felt she had X-ray vision. That beneath her feet she could see the flickering membranes of mycelium, which Dan had described; they were alive, like miniature underground powerlines, zinging messages from roots and fermenting earth, from tree to tree, plant to plant, hill to hill.

She looked for the familiar fungi that always grew here and realised with a jolt that there were none. Very unusual. Bending down, she saw the disturbed soil among the massive roots, and as she wound her way deeper into the thicket of trees leading from the creek, she saw that the mushrooms had all been picked.

They had always been here but were such an integral part of the forest floor that she'd taken little notice of them before. Stella's painting had awakened her to their unique beauty, and now Dan had sparked her interest in them and she was keen to know more. A worrying thought struck her and she quickly headed to the clearing.

Jessica let out her breath with relief. It was still there – the fairy ring. It was a large circle of broad mushrooms, and, after talking to Dan, Jessica now realised she was looking at the outer edge of the mycelium mat of fungi filaments. Like lace at the hem of a skirt. She knelt down and poked her finger into the earth. It was damp and crumbly, rich smelling. Did the intruder who'd taken the mushrooms from around the trees not know these were here? Or did he go along with the belief that to break the fairy ring would bring bad luck?

Jessica glanced across the clearing, sensing she was being watched. She strained to see into the trees on the far side. Was she imagining it, or was that the hunched bulk of a bird? She looked across at the creek, calm before the seasonal rains, and up at the trees and plants that hid the path to the cave. What had happened here? It seemed very likely that the same people who stole the truffles had taken the mushrooms too.

Deep in thought, Jessica retraced her steps. For the first time in a long time she felt the bite of scientific curiosity, the desire to find out more, to untangle the strands of questions, to see where they led her. She walked swiftly, her senses sharpened, her observational skills switched on, as if a great thirst had been quenched.

She'd always been drawn to this quiet green world of ancient giants. This was more than schoolroom rhetoric of the great rainforests being the 'lungs of the planet'; there was a reason these trees had stood as sentries for centuries. And yet how many millions of them had died in such a short amount of time, due to the actions of humans and climate? We've learned so little, she thought.

*

Sally and Toby were out in the fields, and Mollie and Katie were looking after Jasper, so Jessica made herself a coffee and brought it into the sitting room. Seeing the folder of Stella's unframed paintings, she put her cup to one side and slowly looked again at the beautiful images, which were filled with life and atmosphere, capturing the forest where she'd just been. And it came to Jessica that Stella had intuitively understood its value, the magical importance of this place, her Arcadia, even if she possibly hadn't known why. As she sat there thinking, her phone rang and she pulled it from her pocket.

'You got home okay?' said Dan. 'How do you feel this morning?'

'We were a bit wobbly last night. We made light of things because we didn't want to upset Mollie and Toby. Though maybe Sal has told Toby more this morning.'

'Are you okay?'

'Yes. You bet. I've had a bit of an epiphany.'

'Really? Good or bad?'

'I don't know.' She laughed. 'I'll tell you more when you get here. Any news?'

'Yes. That's why I'm calling you first. We got a lead from my mate in the police department on the number plate you sent.'

'And?'

'It's registered to a Gordon Broadbent, Seawinds, Shelter Bay.'

Jessica gasped. 'What? Holy moly . . . That has to be the Gordon the old lady at Seawinds was talking about. And almost certainly related to the guy in the cave. Ooh, I have goosebumps. What else?'

'Not much; he has no criminal record. I Googled the name but nothing came up, which is interesting: you have to be really private these days to have no internet foot-print at all! Tell me, any leads on the truffle mugger?'

'No. Well, I haven't quizzed Toby too much. But . . . I've just been down in the forest. I'm deeply intrigued by your mycology man and what you told us, so I went for a closer look. But all the fungi that were around the old-growth trees have been yanked up. Gone.'

There was an intake of breath at the other end of the line.

'So. Curiouser and curiouser, eh?' said Jessica.

'Actually it makes sense. I'll be there sometime tomorrow or the next day. Can you check with Sally and Toby if that will be all right?'

'Oh, they're all expecting you,' said Jessica. 'And Dan, tell Sally about the Broadbent connection, but it might be best to let her decide how much to tell her mother,' she added. 'We don't know what she knows. We're still fumbling around the fringes of the story.'

Arcadia, 1951

On a golden, sunny morning, Stella sat on a picnic blanket in the rose garden, watching Mollie playing peekaboo with Mrs James. It was cool in the shade, and reminded Stella of the blissful days she used to spend in the Far Forest.

Before Mollie was born, Stella regarded her regular visits to the forest as the most important part of her life; the trees inspired her art, and she always admired their size, strength and power. These days, however, her darling Mollie kept her so busy, she could rarely make it down to the forest. Sometimes she allowed her mind to drift and imagined herself back there. And if ever there was a memory she clung to over the years it was one particular day, not too long ago, etched forever in her mind and heart like a fleck in amber.

Two years earlier . . .

Stella noticed that Mrs James was watching her as she walked towards the woods, so she stopped swinging her small picnic basket and strode on. Glancing back a few minutes later she saw Mrs James pulling the door of the main house closed and heading towards her cottage.

She wore a cardigan across her shoulders. Her field glasses hung around her neck and her leather bag was slung across her body, packed as always with her notebook, pencils, pen and camera. Checking her reflection in the mirror before she'd left the house, she'd smiled at her herself and dabbed some perfume onto her wrists and collarbone.

The woods were motionless; no breeze ruffled the early summer stillness. And while it was tranquil, Stella felt the life and energy in here.

She reached the clearing, put down the basket, gave a short whistle and waited.

There was movement by the pine tree and as Stella smiled, a figure stepped from the shadows. He strode across the clearing and when he reached Stella, her outstretched arms clasped him to her heart.

'How I've missed you,' he murmured. He kissed her deeply and then lifted his head, putting a finger beneath her chin to study her dancing eyes and smiling mouth.

'Now, Tommy, first things first,' said Stella, 'or we'll have no peace.'

He chuckled and took a step behind her, watching as Stella whistled again, holding a wriggling mouse in cupped hands.

There was movement but no sound as the owl flew to the tree closest to her.

'He's watching you,' she said.

'I think he's getting used to me. That's good.' Tommy smiled.

Stella cajoled and spoke softly, tilting her head as the owl mimicked her, tilting his own head, his steady eyes never leaving her face. But as she leaned down, the bird was poised, his eyes on her curled hand, and when the mouse tried to make its dash for freedom, the owl swooped, scooping it up and flying to a further tree.

'So fast, so quiet. So deadly,' said Tommy.

'He expects it,' sighed Stella. 'At least one more little marsupial from here in the forest has escaped Nyx's talons. I'll have to get some more mice from my farmer friend. I'm pleased Nyx is finally accepting you. I doubt that his father would have been so kind.'

He laughed. 'Me too! I thought I was going to lose my head the first time I met you here!'

'Nyx Senior was my protector and now Nyx Junior is too. I think he gets jealous of you.' Stella smiled, and together they spread the blanket and settled themselves, Stella lying with her head in Tommy's lap.

'I've missed you, my darling. How long do we have?' He traced the edge of her face, winding a tendril of her hair around his finger.

'Stephen is away until tomorrow evening.'

'I hate it when we are apart. I wish I could take you to the coast with me. I wish I could sail away with you so we could be together,' he whispered hoarsely, and lowered his face to hers as she touched a finger to his lips, stilling his words.

She wished it too, sometimes. Here, in these woods, and in the cave Thomas had found, they had their own world, if only for brief stolen sojourns.

It had been almost two years now since she had set up her sketching easel to paint her favourite tree early one morning before the sun had penetrated the deep forest and dried the dew on the lichen and fungi. She'd thought she heard noises coming from the creek, but who would venture here so early? she'd wondered.

Nyx was grooming himself, preparing to settle down

to sleep after a night hunting and guarding his territory. He'd made a nest in the deep hollow of an ancient tree, once seared and split by lightning. But his attention must also have been caught by the sound of breaking twigs and movement, as he gave a piercing warning screech.

Stella had paused and looked around, suddenly fearful, then dropped her brush as she saw a figure through the trees.

'Who's there?' she'd called, memories of the man in the deerstalker hat flooding back, the fear just as sharp as it had been all those years before. She had last seen the man at the house with the tunnel to the sea, when she'd visited the place with Stephen. Had he dared to return here? But the man who suddenly appeared seemed taken aback to see her and raised his hand.

'Ahoy, don't be afraid. Sorry, I had no idea there'd be anyone here. I didn't mean to startle you . . . Oy!' He ducked and yelped as Nyx flew low over his head.

'Sorry! Nyx! Come back,' called Stella, lifting her arm to calm the large owl, who silently swept between them and sat low on a branch, alert, studying the tall blond man.

'What a magnificent owl.'

'Stay still, if you don't mind,' she warned the man. 'May I ask who you are, why you're here?' Stella drew herself up and tried to sound more authoritative than she felt. Then, looking closely at his face, she realised she'd met the man once before, years ago, down at the river. He hadn't introduced himself but she recalled that he had somehow known who she was.

'Sorry, I'm Tommy, I came down the creek in my canoe. The water is low. I was keen to inspect the fungi in here.' He peered at her easel. 'Is that what you're painting?'

'It is. Why did you come to see the mushrooms?'

'I study them. My brother has a farm and we cultivate mushrooms. The rarer varieties like these wild ones.'

'This is private property, sir.'

The man looked genuinely shocked. 'Are you sure? My brother told me otherwise. I know these woods back onto a large property . . .'

'Yes. Arcadia, which belongs to my husband.'

'Is that so . . .?' He frowned. 'My older brother is a bit of a . . . scallywag,' he said finally.

'I'm sorry, you cannot disturb these plants,' Stella said firmly.

He gave a slight grin, and Stella couldn't help but notice how very handsome he was. He moved closer, glancing at her easel, and was quiet a moment. 'You are a very fine artist, madam.'

'Thank you. What is your interest in mushrooms, anyway?' she asked.

'We believe they have important properties, medicinal and otherwise.'

'Really? I see . . .' She frowned. 'I will ask my husband, Dr Holland. I'm Stella Holland, but of course, you know that already.' She gave a brief smile and glanced up at Nyx, who had been glaring at the intruder. She gently clapped her hands. 'Goodbye, Nyx.'

The man, Tommy, looked up at the owl. 'Beautiful creature. My brother told me he was once attacked by one here. Take care.'

'Oh, Nyx and I are old friends,' said Stella. 'Tell me, have you and your brother come here before . . . collecting?'

'I was only here once. My brother, John, has been here more often. He showed me how to get here. I apologise, I thought these were, ah, wild woods. Not your property.'

'They are wild in one respect. These acres are on our land but have never been touched. My husband's family has always protected them. Some trees are many hundreds of years old.'

'Your husband's family?' He raised an eyebrow.

'I believe so,' said Stella, feeling uncomfortable at his question. 'He was widowed before I met him,' she added.

'He's a physician, isn't he?' said the man, who Stella now guessed was only a little older than herself.

'Do you know him?'

'No, but my brother does.'

Stella paused, then asked, 'Does your brother by chance favour wearing a deerstalker hat?'

'Yes. He does. And he has a messy moustache.' He smiled. Then, seeing Stella's expression, he added, 'I'm sorry, Mrs Holland, is there a problem?'

At that moment Nyx swooped above them once again and landed in his tree. Turning his head almost full circle he glanced over his back at Stella and then hopped into the tree trunk hollow.

*

'Stella . . . Darling, where have you gone?' Tommy touched her cheek. 'What are you thinking?'

'I was remembering when we first met . . . here in the forest. How shocked I was when I realised who your brother was.'

'Please, forget about John.' Tommy had told her he'd had a falling out with his older brother a few months ago. John was angry and bitter over something to do with their aunt, and held a grudge against Stephen Holland. Tommy didn't want John to confront Stephen, knowing it would only cause trouble for Stella, and so John had cut him out of the family. Stella couldn't stop thinking about it.

Tommy tightened his hand on hers. 'Please, darling, let's not spoil our time together.'

Stella shook her head. 'I can't believe that he's cut you off from the family. Perhaps I can help you. Maybe I can sell my paintings . . . something.'

'You have a great talent, but I'll be alright. Give me time, Stella, I really believe I can be somebody.'

'You believe so strongly in what you're doing. But you said John has taken over your experiments.'

'I didn't tell him everything.' He jumped to his feet. 'Enough of that. The sun is out, let's go for a swim, and then have a picnic in our cave.'

Stella laughed at his enthusiasm. Such a beautiful man, who behaved like a mischievous boy at times. He made her feel a different person. Carefree, happy, loved and adored. Apart from that day at the river, she had never seen Tommy outside the forest; this was their magical world. Sometimes she wondered if it was all a dream or that she'd imagined, like Alice in Wonderland, that she had fallen down the rabbit hole. What they were doing was wrong, she knew, but she couldn't give him up. Where he went and what he did between their trysts, she didn't ask.

How free she felt, pulling off her clothes to slip into the clear, cold water, shivering into his arms, where their bodies came together as they kissed and clung to each other tightly.

Laughing, Tommy stepped from the water and clambered up the bank, looking back at Stella's slim, milky body as she smiled up at him.

'Stay there.' He pulled her camera from her bag and

snapped a photograph of her as she floated just beneath the surface of the water.

*

Tommy tramped ahead, carrying the picnic basket and holding her hand, helping her as they hiked up to the cave he'd found and made their special place.

She'd never asked when or how he'd brought the few small comforts here, or indeed, when he came here on his own. She suspected he sometimes visited when she was trapped in the routine of her life at Arcadia. But, at times like these, when she knew Stephen would be away, she left a note in the small hollow of a tree close to the creek.

They shared her picnic, then, naked once more, they fell upon each other on the improvised bed, and languidly, lustfully, explored their bodies until, passion spent, they held each other close and slept awhile.

*

Stella woke, feeling chilled, knowing the sun must be going down. She stood up and for a moment looked at the sleeping man, one leg flung out from under the coverlet, a hank of blond hair across his forehead. Quietly she in turn snapped his photo. And quickly dressed, smoothing her hair.

She knelt beside him as, smiling, he dozily reached for her.

'Tommy, I have to go,' she whispered.

'Wait, I'll come with you.'

'No. It's better if you stay. I'll be all right.' She kissed him quickly and picked up the basket.

As she slid through the cave entrance to the bush track he called out, 'I love you, Stella . . .'

Smiling to herself, she crossed the creek where there were large flat stones and headed along the bank. Then she heard, 'Mrs Holland, where are you?'

'Here, Mr James. Just coming . . .'

Blackie James came towards her through the trees, his forehead creased, and took the basket from her. 'It's getting dark, we were a bit worried. You've been gone all day, apparently . . .'

Stella settled a neutral expression on her face. 'I'm sorry to worry you. I was in the forest. You know how I love it there . . .'

Mr James didn't answer but turned and plodded ahead up the hill, where the last of the sun's rays, reflected in the windows of Arcadia House, flashed like a beacon.

For Stella that day was a memory of many, which never faded, all her days.

8

Arcadia, 2018

'Four women and a forest,' whispered Jessica. 'Sounds like a movie, doesn't it?'

'It looks like one too,' agreed Mollie softly. 'It's been a long time since I came in this far. Into its heart.'

'I always feel so safe in here,' said Sally. It feels protective, embracing. No wonder Stella loved it.'

'Who's Stella?' asked Katie, holding her mother's hand tightly.

'Your great-grandmother, sweetie. Granny's mummy.'

'With the birdie?'

'Boy, she doesn't forget anything.' Mollie chuckled. 'I told her once about Nyx and showed her the painting.'

'Are you getting tired, honey?' asked Jessica. 'I can piggyback you.'

'I'm okay, but where are the fairies?' Katie said.

'They're sleeping. But we can show you where they play,' replied Jessica.

'And dance,' added Katie.

'Sure. But they only come out in the moonlight to do their dances. When you're in bed,' said Sally.

They crossed the clearing, which was bathed in shafts of sunlight, and stopped by an ancient eucalypt.

'My mummy brought me here when I was the same age as you, Katie,' said Mollie. 'It's a special place.'

'Look! I can see the fairy seats you told me about, Mummy!' cried Katie, pointing to the spreading circle of mushrooms a little way ahead. She dropped Sally's hand and hurried to the base of a tall tree, staring up into its branches. 'Are the fairies up there?'

'Could be. Maybe they sit under the leaves and in the hollows and behind the walls of the big roots,' said Sally. 'But you know you can never see them.'

'They come out and dance at night for all the creatures and the night birds,' said Jess.

'Like Nyx, the owl?' asked Katie.

'Maybe Nyx has grandchildren too,' said Mollie. 'Owls live a long time. I always felt safe here because of him. Looking back now, there was an extraordinary bond between my mother and that owl, and its offspring.'

'This whole place is special,' said Jessica. 'I hope it always stays just like this.'

'That's what my grandfather wanted, wasn't it, Mum?' said Sally.

Mollie nodded. 'There's some history here, though I never knew what, exactly. Dad never talked much about it. I guess he might not have known the whole story.'

'Oh, really?' Sally looked up with interest.

'Dad always told me Arcadia would be mine and I was never to sell it, nor touch the forest,' Mollie said. 'When Graham and I got married I moved away, but Mother was alone for so long after my father died, even though Mrs James stayed on till she died. When Mum's health was failing, we decided we should move back here.'

'Was that okay with Graham, Mollie? He had a farm too, didn't he?' asked Jessica.

'Graham was happy to move here and his brother took over their family farm. He was very easy-going. Such a lovely, gentle man. I still miss him terribly,' sighed Mollie.

'Me too,' said Sally softly.

Katie was restless and called out, 'Let's go to the fairy seats.'

'That sounds like a good idea,' said Jessica, holding out her hand. 'C'mon, Katie.' Katie skipped over to Jessica and they took the lead.

Sally slipped her arm through her mother's. 'You must have been lonely all these years without Dad.'

'Yes, I miss him. But having you and Toby and Katie makes up for a lot. I don't think I would have managed on my own.'

'You never wanted to find someone else, a companion?' asked Sally, something she'd often wondered about.

'No. With you guys and the farm I have plenty to keep me occupied. I'm lucky compared to some of my friends, who I know are very lonely. I can have meals with you and Toby and Katie when I want to, and watch telly together with you some nights. I can read my grand-daughter a story, or sit and chat to you and Toby over a glass of port . . . and of course we entertain a lot, don't we? Life is good. I contribute to the business, my brain still works, I'm fit . . . what more could I want?' Mollie laughed. 'Sal, I'm in my seventies but in my head I feel thirty-something. I have wonderful memories, including some that you'll never know about!' she teased. 'You have to accept life as it comes along and make the most of it while you can.'

'Come on, Granny!' squealed Katie, and the women laughed as Katie danced in and around the fairy ring.

'You know the man I told you about, Sean Hyland, the mushroom expert?' said Sally. 'We're going to his talk in Hobart. He sounds so interesting.'

Mollie nodded. 'Very. I've been researching his work on the internet since you mentioned him. He's not alone, you know. It's like the minute one person puts something out there in the ether, ten other people independently come to the same conclusion. It does seem that those mushrooms, and that network beneath the ground, hold a whole lot of answers we're yet to explore properly. Your father always said the soil was the most important ingredient on this farm. And the trees, too, of course. It breaks my heart how so many ancient trees are dying here and all over the world. Millions of them. Something's not right. It has to be the changing climate, as well as logging and development, of course.'

'So tragic, when we can do something about it,' said Sally, watching Katie twirl around the mushrooms.

'Shall we have our morning tea picnic down by the creek?' said Mollie.

Settled on the grass with a thermos of coffee, fruit juice for Katie and fresh buttered scones and honey wrapped in a tea towel, Mollie lifted her face to the sun. 'I see why you girls always loved to come down here when you were young,' she said.

'Didn't you do the same when you were growing up?' asked Jessica.

Mollie sipped her coffee. 'Hmmm, not really. My mother loved coming here, but it was something of a sacred pilgrimage to her. And of course she'd spend hours sketching and painting, which was a bit dull for me when I was little, so I didn't join her.'

Sally and Jessica exchanged a glance. 'Did she ever mention a cave?' said Sally.

'A cave? Here? No, I don't think so. She wasn't the athletic sort.' Mollie laughed. 'We never went hiking, though Dad was big on brisk walks. So I can't imagine her doing that sort of exploring.'

Jessica gave a faint frown and Sally changed the subject.

They shared the scones, then Katie threw some crumbs around a tree for the birds as the women talked. Sally and Jessica decided they would stay in Hobart overnight after Dr Hyland's lecture, and maybe check in with the Botanical Gardens people while they were there.

'Though Dan might have some news before then. I wonder how he got on up the coast? Have you heard from him?' asked Sally.

'Yes, he rang and said he'd be back in the next day or so. He seems to be involved in so many different things,' Jess said. 'It's certainly not a mundane job.'

'Speaking of mundane jobs, we'd better start heading back. I need to clean out the chook pen this afternoon,' said Mollie.

'Katie can help, she loves those chickens,' Sally said, and turned around. 'Katie, darling, do you want to help . . . Katie?'

'Katie?' echoed Mollie.

'Now where has she gone? Is she feeding the birds?' muttered Sally, jumping to her feet. 'C'mon, Katie, we're going home . . . Katie?'

Jessica shoved her fingers in her mouth, letting out a loud shrill whistle, then called, 'KATIE . . .'

'She can't have gone too far. Oh my God, the creek!' Sally ran towards the water. Mollie and Jessica both headed into the forest, both shouting the little girl's name.

After a few minutes they saw her. She was running and stumbling towards Sally, arms outstretched, crying hard.

Sally scooped her up, hugging and kissing Katie's white, tear-streaked face.

Jessica called out to Mollie, 'She's here. Sally's got her. She's okay!'

Mollie and Jessica hurried over to where Sally was sitting on a log, cradling Katie, murmuring softly. 'You're safe, darling girl . . .'

Jessica spread her arms and raised her eyebrows, signalling, *What happened?* But Sally shook her head. *Not now.*

'Well, that was a bit of excitement,' Sally said. 'She's fine. Just wandered off.'

'I've never seen her this upset,' whispered Mollie.

Sally continued cuddling a whimpering Katie as Jessica and Mollie packed up their little picnic.

'Go and ask Granny for the last scone, I'm sure there's one left,' said Sally.

As Mollie quickly pulled out a scone for Katie, Sally took Jessica aside. 'She says she saw a scary man.'

'What!'

'When we all shouted, she says he ran away.'

'Do you really think she saw someone? She didn't just imagine it? Would she make something like that up?'

'She wouldn't be this upset unless it actually happened,' said Sally. 'It's just not like her. But I don't want to push her. Let's go home and I might be able to ask her more later. Do you think that man with the four-wheel drive is stalking us? Maybe he had something to do with the truffle raid, too?'

'I'm going to have a look,' said Jessica, but Sally put a restraining hand on her arm. 'No, don't. I don't want to worry Mum and Katie. Let's just not mention it for now. We can talk about it later.'

Mollie was holding Katie's hand as they walked home. Sally hurried ahead and caught up to them, taking Katie's other hand while Jessica held back and pulled her mobile out of her jeans pocket. She sent a quick message to Dan.

He replied to her text message before they reached the house.

Sorry to hear the little one got a scare. Seems there's a lot going on for Sally and her family at the moment. Am heading to Arcadia tomorrow morning. See you soon.

Back at the house, Jessica told Sally about Dan's text then smiled when she saw that Katie had settled down and was playing with some toys. 'She seems fine now,' she said.

'Yes, but I wonder if we should go to the police?' said Mollie. 'After the truffle theft they said to let them know if we noticed anything untoward.'

'Actually, I did ring the local station just after we came back, when you were looking after Katie,' said Sally. 'The officer I spoke to was pleasant and concerned but explained that she couldn't act on the word of a four-year-old, especially without any further evidence, even though we know Katie probably did see someone. She made a note of the incident, though, and said that if we see the man ourselves it would be another matter and we should report it immediately.'

*

The following morning, as they were sitting in the conservatory, reading and working, Toby walked in with a smiling Dan. 'Look who I found at the front gate,' he said.

Dan greeted Sally and Jessica and gave Mollie a hearty handshake.

'I feel I know you already. Sally and Jessica have told me so much about you,' Mollie said.

After making a fuss over Katie, Dan accepted Toby's invitation to look around the farm.

'It's an impressive place you have here,' he said to Sally and Toby after lunch. Mollie had gone back to her cottage and taken Katie with her, leaving the others to linger around the dining table.

'Yes, it's a great property. Apart from the incident with the truffles, the farm is going great guns,' said Toby. 'And of course there's a big sentimental attachment with Sally's family being here so long.'

'So, Dan, what did you find out at Shelter Bay?' Sally asked.

'Not a lot, but they're definitely manufacturing something there. I snitched a sample from the laboratory set-up in that tunnel you found. When I'm in Hobart I'll try to get some info from the Botanical Gardens. I spoke to the old lady, who must be Mrs Broadbent, but as you said, she wasn't friendly. She did say her son was "away", but that could be anywhere.'

'Like here?' Jessica asked.

'Tell me, how is Katie after her scare?' Dan said. 'I didn't want to ask while she was here.'

'Well, we rather downplayed it,' said Sally, and she explained that while they were taking it seriously, she wasn't sure the police would be able to act on it.

Toby rubbed his eyes. 'I'm losing sleep over this! If he was the man who was following you, he could have come here and still be hanging around. I don't want to rattle you, but it's really worrying me.'

'It's scary. Just what is he after?' asked Sally, then paused for a moment in thought. 'Maybe he was responsible for the truffle raid, as a diversionary tactic, and the mushrooms in the Far Forest were his real target? The farm at Shelter Bay is clearly doing something with mushrooms. I can see why he might want our wild fungi,' she added slowly.

'Speaking of which, I can take you to the Far Forest – the old-growth forest – this afternoon, if you like, Dan,' put in Jessica. 'Is that okay, Sally?'

'Sure. I have a few things to do so I won't join you. We've asked some friends over for dinner, so come back any time before six,' said Sally.

*

As they headed into the green-lit cavern of the old forest, Jessica gave Dan a sidelong glance as he gazed around. Then he reached out to touch the trunk of a massive ribbon gum.

'This is a grand sight. These *viminalis* are dying out by their thousands, all over the country. But this one looks really healthy. This is such a special place . . .'

When they came to the trees whose roots and some parts of their trunks were normally studded with fungi, Jessica pointed out where the ground had been disturbed.

Dan crouched down and crumbled the soil, sniffing it.

'Still some mycelium in here. These trees are so old, they're probably harbouring some rare mushroom species. You need the original spores to start a breeding program, so these would be very useful to someone who knows what they're doing. Look, there's a piece of mushroom; must have broken off when it was picked. I'll take it in case we need to have it tested,' he said, carefully wrapping it in a tissue.

'Whoever took the mushrooms didn't touch the fairy ring . . . superstitious, I suppose.'

They walked to the creek and stood looking at the peaceful setting.

'This is beautiful. What an amazing backyard Sally and Toby have,' Dan said.

'Yes, it's only really in retrospect that you realise it, but this was an amazing place to grow up in.'

Dan studied her. 'Would you settle back here again?'

'I'm not sure. It'd be hard to find a place like this these days. I see why Dr Holland never wanted it touched. But Sally and Mollie have always been generous and let me feel as if it's my magic place to come to when I need to . . . like now.'

'Are you okay now?' He raised an eyebrow. 'You seem pretty strong to me. I wouldn't steal piglets from a cranky sow. I thought that was an inspired move, by the way.'

Jessica laughed. 'Needs must. Anyway, it was Sally who grabbed them. I'm all right but I suppose I feel my life is on hold.'

'That's hard, but I'm sure something will turn up.' He gazed across the creek. 'Is that still Arcadia's land?'

'Yes. You can cross over the creek down there. Unless it's raging,' she added. 'That's where the cave is.'

'Where you found the incriminating evidence? Can we go up there now?'

'We took everything of interest, which was just a tin box.'

'Oh, come on, it'll be an adventure,' cajoled Dan.

'Okay. I guess so.'

'I'd like to see it – sounds fascinating. Though a pretty uncomfortable love nest.'

They followed the barely discernible track but found it easy going. Jessica thought about how rattled she and Sally had been when they last left the cave.

When they neared the top of the cliff overhang, Jessica pointed to the narrow passageway. 'You have to squeeze behind here.' They went through and Dan followed her into the cave.

'There's a fantastic view to the left at the back,' Jessica said as she straightened up.

'This is amazing.' Dan was staring around. 'What's up?' he asked, seeing Jessica's shocked face.

'Someone's been here. We didn't leave it like this . . . it was a mess before. Oh no . . . the guy Katie saw . . . what if it's *him*?'

'What do you mean?'

'This has been tidied up. Someone has *slept* here . . . and . . .' She sniffed again, then pointed at the floor.

'Oops.' Dan leaned down and looked at the fresh cigarette butt stamped into the dirt floor. He pulled out a tissue and carefully scooped the butt into it.

'This is creepy,' she said. 'Why would someone come here? How would they even know about this place? When Sally and I were here a few weeks back, it looked like no one had been here since we were last here, about twenty years ago. Now . . .' She shuddered.

'Do you think there's some connection to Shelter Bay? It's the only link,' said Dan.

'Yes, it's the only thing that makes sense,' said Jessica slowly. 'And the woman at Seawinds said her son, Gordon, was away, didn't she? That's the Gordon Broadbent who owns the four-wheel drive that followed Sal and me.'

'Yeah. That's right.' Dan frowned. 'Let's look around.' He checked out the cave, then took in the breathtaking panorama of the trees and creek, and the distant hills.

'What's up there?' He turned away from the view, pointing to the back of the cave, where a small opening led into darkness.

'More caves, we think. It gets too small to explore, and it's wet. We tried once but never bothered going back there.'

'Might be worth going in a bit to see,' he said, hunching over as he moved forward.

'Here, use my phone light.'

Jessica crept behind Dan as he stepped into the cramped, dank side tunnel, shining the beam from Jessica's phone from side to side. It smelled earthy, and a rivulet of water dribbled between their feet.

Dan moved the light from side to side. 'It's getting narrower; I guess it just goes further back into the hillside.'

'I feel like a water rat or something,' said Jessica. 'We won't be able to turn around if it gets smaller, we'll have to back out. No one would come in here.'

'Yeah, okay, let's head back.'

'Can I have the phone . . .?' Jessica turned until she was again facing the chink of daylight. She reached behind her as Dan rose to hand her the phone, almost bumping his head on the roof of the tunnel.

'Oops . . . hell . . . what's that?' He flailed his hands, and Jessica grabbed the phone, just as she felt something drop into her hair.

'Yikes, don't tell me there're bats in here.' She flapped her arms, the beam of light swinging wildly around them.

'Hey! What the . . . Hold the light, Jess, over here,' yelled Dan.

'There's something on me . . .' Jessica was brushing at her hair. 'Here, take the phone.'

Dan grabbed it back and trained the narrow beam of light on her. 'Oh, shit, Jessica, stay still . . .'

Jessica froze. 'What, what is it?'

'Just a minute, I'll get it off you.' Dan leaned over, shining the phone above her. Then Jessica felt something moving in her hair and she screamed, fighting the urge to beat at her head. Dan flicked his hand, and Jessica felt her hair pulled lightly. She grabbed at it.

'Jess, it's gone! Stay still!'

She froze again, gingerly touching her hair and, feeling nothing, smoothed her hands over her head as Dan shone the light above them.

Jessica followed the beam and screamed again. 'Holy shit!'

'Stay still . . . they're more afraid of us . . .' The torch-light illuminated a dozen or more giant spiders, the size of dinner plates, hanging from the cave roof. 'Tassie Cave Spiders . . . a local specialty.'

'I've never seen them before.' Jessica shuddered. 'They're awful.'

'Yes, they are. The females eat the males while mating, if the males are not careful. Something like that.'

'Come on, Dan, let's get out of here.'

At the cave opening, she glanced back. 'I feel like leaving a note for whoever is staying in here . . . although maybe seeing a cave spider might scare them off.'

'Yes, let's hope so. Whoever came here was trespassing.'

'This place has been forgotten for years. It was aban-doned when Sal and I first came across it as kids . . . but now it seems someone else knows about it. Might have always known about it,' mused Jessica.

'Should we tell Sal about this?' Dan asked.

Jessica thought hard about it. 'I think we shouldn't, not for now, at least. She was really rattled by the whole truffle affair. Until we know for sure whether it's related, best not to worry her with it.' She sighed. 'Come on. I've had enough surprises for now. Let's head back.'

Arcadia, 1968

Mrs James paused while sweeping the front steps and watched Stella walk slowly down the hill to the forest. It was a familiar path for her, but she walked more slowly and carefully these days and carried a strong stick. Mrs James gave a heartfelt sigh.

'Mum, I'll finish that for you. Take a breather.' Her youngest son reached for the broom.

'It's all right, Terry. Does me good to do something. Can't sit around in the sun all day.' She smiled as he took the broom anyway, and noticed that he followed her gaze.

'I think Mrs H is lonely, ever since Dr H died and Mollie left to go travelling,' he said. 'Good thing she's got you, Mum.'

'And I'm very lucky to have you, my dear boy. But you should travel, too, like you've talked about. Don't stay here just 'cause of me. Your brothers and sisters shouldn't leave everything up to you.'

'They've all got families, Mum. Anyway, managing Arcadia for Mrs H is a good job. I enjoy it.' He smiled and began sweeping energetically, moving carefully on his awkward bent feet.

'I don't know how I'd cope without you now that your dad's gone.' She sighed. 'You're doing a grand job with the farm. Your father taught you well.' She smiled at her grown son, feeling a tug at her heart. She was glad he was here to help and watch out for her and Stella and Arcadia. But it didn't seem fair for him to sacrifice his own life and adventures. He'd taken a few holidays, but she knew he felt responsible for her, and for Arcadia.

'When Mollie comes home here to live, you can travel and do what you want, son.' She knew that Mollie had been raised to understand that Arcadia was special, and would be her forever home and, one day, her children's home.

'That's a long way off. I'm happy being here with you.' He went to put the broom away. 'Right, I'm going to check on the animals before the sun sets.'

Mrs James sighed as she walked inside her cottage, which Stella had let her live in rent-free after Mr James had died, not so long after Dr Holland had passed away.

In her view, Stella was too young to be a widow, even though she kept herself occupied with her art classes and her own artwork. Still, she hoped Mollie would come back soon, at least for a visit. She knew Stella missed her daughter now that she was on her own.

*

Stella walked slowly but sure-footedly, her back straight, into the old forest, inhaling its familiar earthy smell of fungi and damp moss. She chose a place to sit, not because she was tired but sitting surrounded by the soft busy sounds of the forest always soothed her. It was her healing place, a calm place, where memories returned to her.

Once more in her mind she was at the bedside of her failing husband, smoothing his hand, his grim jaw the only clue to his battle as he clung to life, refusing to succumb. Silently Mrs James came and stood behind Stella, her hands folded. And then in a gasping breath, Stephen managed to speak. '*Hilda . . .*'

Mrs James rested her hand lightly on Stella's shoulder as Stephen's eyes flew open, staring ahead, and then he turned his head towards Stella, taking in a breath, his face calm. And did not breathe out.

After a few quiet minutes Mrs James began to bustle about, knowing what to do.

It wasn't till weeks later that Mrs James and her son, Terry, sat down with Stella, and Mrs James told them of the lingering death of Hilda, Stephen's first wife.

Stella didn't know why this memory had floated through her consciousness now, but she didn't question it, instead letting it slide away. Then she rose and headed to the creek, crossing carefully, using her stick for balance, before moving steadily along the overgrown track.

She slowly climbed up to the cave and drew a deep breath. Everything was as she'd left it, so long ago. She wasn't sure what she might find, and the tiny glimmer of hope in her heart quickly faded. All was as it had been the last time she was there. Or so she thought. Looking more closely, opening the tin box, feeling along the shelf, she saw that nothing had been touched – the tiny silver eggcup with the Arcadia crest, the pretty pebble from the creek, a dried flower plucked from the forest, all still there. She closed her eyes, hearing, remembering their laughter, the tender touch of a hand on her cheek, the pained blue eyes she'd never be able to forget.

She was about to leave things as they were, as he had

left them, then changed her mind. With every ounce of her strength, she pushed the tin box as far as she could into a hollow in the rock wall and covered the opening with some hessian bags that had been on the bed. Finally, she dragged the bed over and jammed it up against the bags, satisfied that the box was safely hidden.

With shoulders stooped with sadness, Stella made her way back down the track, crossed the creek, and walked into the heart of the forest.

She sat and rested on her favourite log, deep in thought. Then felt the movement of air and her heart lifted. She turned her head to one side.

Nyx the Third was sitting on a stump beside her, pretending not to notice her.

'Hello, old fellow,' she said softly. 'Haven't got anything for you, I'm afraid.'

Slowly, methodically, the old owl shifted and began preening his feathers, which were sparser now, though still glossy.

'I miss them, Nyx,' she sighed. 'All of them.' A tear dropped onto her cheek. 'Did I do the right thing? Tell me, wise old bird.' She paused, letting the tears continue. 'If only I could go back . . . would I? Would I? How do you know, Nyx, how do you know that you made the right decision?' She bit her lip. 'But I can't help thinking about what might have been . . .' She caught her breath, swallowing hard. 'And now it is too late, there is no going back, no changing anything. No knowing . . .' She turned to look at the dear heart-framed face, the dark, intelligent and soulful eyes, the startling dramatic white mask, this expressive knowing creature, son of sons she loved and knew so well through three generations. And who knew her, and her secrets. Each had shared so much . . .

The bird blinked. 'No, no, don't you cry, Nyx,' she tried to joke. And, as she knew he would, he leaned, lifting a wing, so she could gently scratch his favourite spot.

'Do we get to meet again, Nyx, start over, do things differently?'

Stella sighed and straightened up. The owl, shaking his feathers back into place, settled his wings, giving her an implacable stare.

'All right, Nyx, my dear friend.' She drew a breath and stood, picking up her stick. 'Thank you. Thank you for looking out for me all these years. You and your dad and your grandpa.'

Stella turned her back and walked slowly towards the clearing. Before she left the canopy of the old trees, she felt the movement in the air as Nyx swooped above her, the gentle touch of a wingtip on her cheek. She did not look back. She had a feeling she would never see her protector again.

*

'It's like she's given up, she's in another world,' Mrs James whispered to her son. 'I worry about her. She practically lives in her studio, with Mollie's shawl over her shoulders.'

'The one you made?'

Mrs James nodded. 'How I managed to embroider those tiny flowers, and the little owl she wanted, I'll never know. My fingers couldn't do that intricate work now. I made it for Mollie's christening, you know, and I hope she can use it for her babies one day.'

'Well, she's only eighteen, plenty of time for all of that,' Terry said.

Mrs James sipped her tea. 'Son, you're a sensible boy. You keep an eye on Mollie, promise me that, all right?'

'Of course, Mum.' He leaned over and squeezed her frail, work-worn hand.

Arcadia, 2018

Jessica looked around what Sally called 'the long table', where she and Toby entertained when they had lots of guests. It was an interesting group and everyone seemed relaxed. She could see that Dan was enjoying himself, talking to two couples who were Sally and Toby's neighbours. Mollie had invited a friend from her book club, a retired solicitor, who she said didn't get to enjoy home cooking too often. Katie's babysitter, a teenage girl from a farm nearby, was helping to serve the food and clean up the kitchen, having put Katie to bed earlier.

'So when are you going to hear this professor guy speak at the uni?' asked Juliet, their neighbour on the western side. 'He sounds pretty out there.'

'I've heard of him,' said her husband. 'Saw a clip of him on the internet. All that mushroom stuff is so interesting, worrying, and fascinating.'

'Day after tomorrow. I'm looking forward to it,' said Jessica.

The conversation ranged across Dr Hyland's work, the environment and what they were all doing on their own farms until Sally and Toby came out with dessert. Plates were passed around and wineglasses refilled.

Later, when the guests had gone and Mollie had retired to her cottage, the four of them gathered around the fire for a nightcap. Sally asked, 'So, you're heading to Hobart tomorrow, Dan?'

'Well, I had a call from a mate,' said Dan, sipping his drink. 'He's going to do some filming at a fairly isolated spot tomorrow – I've always been keen to go there, and so he's arranged for me to tag along. There's room for one more, though – would you like to come, Jess? Five in the big chopper will make it a full house.'

'Where're you going?' asked Jessica.

'It's kind of a secret.' He grinned. 'But come along, I think you'll find it pretty eye-opening. We could have dinner back in Hobart tomorrow night and then you'll be there to meet Sally and Toby the following day. I spoke to Carmen yesterday and she said you could stay at her city place; she's coming over to hear Sean, too.'

'Now that sounds very mysterious!' said Sally.

'I can tell you this much – it's to do with my work, and it's a chance to see something really rare,' said Dan.

'Okay, I'm hooked,' said Jessica with a smile.

'Pack a jacket, might be cold up there. Misty. It's up a mountain, hence the chopper,' were all the clues he'd give her.

'So where do we rendezvous?'

'We'll need to leave here early in the morning. Then afterwards, late afternoon-ish, we'll drive to the city.'

'Right, so I'd better go and pack,' said Jessica. 'It's been a great evening, Sal. G'night, all. See you for an early breakfast, Dan.'

Sally followed Jessica as Dan and Toby finished their drinks. 'Well, sounds like you're in for a treat,' she said to Jessica. 'You okay about zooming off to the wilds in a chopper?'

'I think so. I'll see you at the talk, and text you before then.' Jessica hugged Sally. 'Sleep in, Dan and I can get ourselves off in the morning.'

*

The sun was up and the early morning mist had cleared by the time Dan parked the car beside an isolated airstrip. The only buildings in sight were a tin shed and a hangar.

'Who owns this place?' asked Jessica.

'Government environment agency. An official from the agency is coming with us. There's my mate Leo, the cameraman.' Dan waved at a man standing outside the hangar, who began to head towards them. 'We've worked together a few times before. I've even acted as his sound man.'

'Why is the official guy coming?' asked Jessica.

'Ah, top secret!' he joked. 'Seriously, though, you'll find out soon. By the way, you're my associate for today.'

'I'm not carrying anything,' retorted Jessica.

Leo arrived and slapped Dan on the back. 'Long time since I've seen you, buddy.' The older man smiled at Jessica and held out his hand. 'Leo Andrews.'

'Jessica Foster,' she replied.

'Dr Foster is helping me out,' said Dan.

'Good to meet you, Dr Foster,' said Leo.

'Just call me Jessica,' Jess laughed. 'No one at home here in Tassie ever uses the "doctor" part.'

'How're things with you, Leo?' Dan asked.

'Up and down. Been doing some interesting stuff for *National Geographic* and one of the streaming channels. They'd love this.'

'Today's just a check-up. Don't think we'll see anything too dramatic. I'm looking forward to it, though.'

'I prefer run-of-the-mill over dramatic when it comes to helicopters,' said Jessica firmly. 'I'll just enjoy the view.'

Leo raised an eyebrow and chuckled. 'I don't think so.'

The pilot, recognisable by his khaki shirt with an insignia on the pocket, came out of the hangar and walked towards them. 'G'day. Let's get ready, we're cleared weatherwise.' He shook their hands as they introduced themselves. 'Tony Lord.'

'Known as his lordship,' Leo said, and smiled.

The pilot gave a brief smile. 'The government guy can't come, so it's just the four of us today. Okay, let me stow the gear. Leo, you better nurse that machine of yours. Here you go. Shoes off, easier here than at the other end.'

'Bare feet?' said Jessica.

'Nah, socks with special rubber soles.' He handed them each a pair of soft booties. 'And the blindfolds. Sorry, but regulations. I'll let you know after take-off when to put them on.'

'Blindfolds?' Jessica looked at Dan, who shrugged.

'Sorry. Can't afford just anyone going in there and contaminating the area, or finding out where it is. Too rare and precious. Right, hop on board.'

Tony showed them where to sit; Leo beside him, and Dan and Jessica in the back. Then he ran through the safety drill, adding, 'After take-off I'll instruct you to put the blindfolds on. It's not for too long.'

Seatbelts clicked on, then the helicopter lifted off the strip, circled and rose into the blueness towards the mountain ranges.

'It's rugged country down here in the south-west,' Leo said, his voice crackling through their headsets.

'Where on earth are we going to land?' wondered Jessica, looking at the blanket of green below.

'There's a handkerchief strip cleared for us in the scrub,' said Leo. Turning to Tony, he asked, 'Can I take a couple of quick shots from here?'

'Yep, but make it quick and no landmarks.'

After what seemed to Jessica just a few minutes' time, Tony instructed them, 'Put the blindfolds on, please.'

It felt weird sitting in the vibrating helicopter, sensing its change of direction but unable to get her bearings. She clutched her seat as she felt them tilt.

'Okay back there, folks?' Tony's voice crackled. 'We're starting to descend.'

Suddenly there was a scraping noise and a bump as the skids hit the ground. 'Stay seated. Right, you can take off the blindfolds.'

'You okay?' asked Dan as Jessica drew a deep breath.

'Was that absolutely necessary? The blindfolds?'

He gestured around. 'Any idea where we are?'

'Nope. I can only see scrub and a distant peak.'

'That's the idea. I suppose we could be almost anywhere in Tassie.'

As the rotors stopped, Tony and Leo jumped out. Cradling his camera, Leo ran from the chopper and, turning, quickly began filming Jessica and Dan getting out and staring around.

'What's Leo doing?'

'Ah, bit of human interest, I guess. Is that okay?'

Jessica shrugged. 'What's it all for?'

'The university or Botanical Gardens, I s'pose. He does a lot of stuff for them.'

'Ready?' Tony called across. 'Follow me. You've been here before, Dan?'

'No. I've seen a sample in the Seed Conservation Centre. I know what to check for.'

'We're looking at seeds, a plant? Why the secrecy?' said Jessica.

'It's rare.'

'Must be,' she muttered as she stumbled slightly on the rough track in the thin booties they had to wear. Then she paused, looking at the rainforest peaks above them and the thick understorey. 'We're not so high up, are we?'

'No, there's a river below us. Do you hike?' Dan said.

'Not really. I prefer the water or the forest on flat land. Hate this wind.'

'I'm a water man. Used to have a boat in Sydney. Had a dream once to sail around the world. I've put that on hold.'

'Yes. We like sailing too.'

'We?'

'Sal and me. We used to take her grandfather's boat out. Classic Huon pine. The *Charlotte-Ann*.'

'Nice.'

Tony paused in front of them. 'Leo has gone ahead to get into position. He wants you to say a few words, bit of a description.'

'Now he tells me.' Dan laughed. 'I'll talk to you about what we're seeing, if that's okay, Jess?'

'I have no idea about anything, so sure.'

'It's closed in a lot, and it's much wetter than it was when I was here last, a couple of years ago,' Tony said.

They slowed as they came to a tangle of bushes and trees where Leo was busily filming.

'All right, let's just wing it,' he called, signalling to Dan.

Dan led Jessica towards the closest bush and pointed to the spiky shiny green leaves. '*Lomatia tasmanica*,' he said to her, and Jess stepped closer and stood beside him. Dan spoke quietly, reverentially. 'This plant and its clones – they're all connected as one – has been growing here for at least forty-three thousand years.'

Jessica gasped. 'This plant? All that time? Here?'

Dan nodded with a slight smile. 'It's the world's oldest living plant. It's also known as King's Holly.'

'It does look like holly, does it have red berries?' asked Jessica, awestruck.

'We've never seen seeds and only once a flower sample. It was discovered by a wonderful local man, Deny King, in 1937. He was mining for tin around here and was something of an amateur naturalist. It wasn't formally identified till 1967.'

'It's so hard to believe!'

'We're here to check on it, as the plant has been suffering root rot. Maybe the overstorey has shaded it too much, and climate change is affecting it.'

'May I touch it?' When Dan nodded, she reached out and lightly stroked a leaf with the tip of her finger.

'What was the world like when this plant was young, I wonder?' Dan said softly.

Jessica couldn't speak, and felt tears spring to her eyes. 'This is so . . . special,' she managed.

'I'm taking samples for the Botanical Gardens in Hobart. Scientists there have been slowly propagating it from tissue samples, which is unusual. It's been a very difficult process, but they have maybe fifty plants in the nursery now.'

Leo moved in with the camera as Dan looked in his shoulder bag for his sample materials.

'Thank you, Dan,' said Jessica quietly.

He glanced at her. 'I thought you'd appreciate seeing this.'

By the time the helicopter had taken off and they'd removed their blindfolds, Jessica realised it was well into the afternoon. Time had seemed to stand still when they were doing the filming.

'Sorry we've missed lunch. What do you fancy for dinner?' asked Dan.

'I'm easy. But I'll buy you a glass of champagne first up to thank you for today. It was just incredible.'

*

Dan and Jessica drove to Carmen's house after dinner, and she had just come in from Lone Island when they arrived. Her city house was as eclectic as her island cottage, but far more upmarket. 'Parents' and grandparents' furniture,' she explained, waving an arm at the beautiful antiques and baby grand piano Jessica admired.

Over coffee and cake Carmen said, 'Dan, don't forget that Sean has made arrangements to go up to Mt Field tomorrow. He's meeting one of the science guys up there. Would you like to go too, Jessica?'

'Absolutely, I'll put my hand up!' said Jessica. 'There're those glacier lakes up there, right?'

'Yes, the Tarns, and beautiful waterfalls as well as hikes through the rainforest,' added Carmen. 'It was the first nature reserve in the state.'

'Isn't it where they caught the last thylacine?' Jessica said.

Dan nodded. 'Yes. Though Sean reckons he knows people who say they saw a thylacine up there a few years back. But there was a baiting scheme with 1080 poison some years ago that would have wiped them out, as well as wallabies and whatever else,' he said with a grimace.

'Why is Sean going there?'

'Fungi,' said Carmen and Dan together.

'There's a great variety up there. We'll be back in time for you to relax a bit before his lecture,' added Dan.

'Count me in,' said Jessica.

'See you around eight in the morning, then. I'll bring Sean with me,' said Dan.

'Wonderful, I'm looking forward to meeting him. Thanks for today, Dan.'

After Dan had left, Carmen led Jessica upstairs. 'Come and I'll show you your room, you must be pooped,' she said. 'Victor sends his best, by the way.'

'Thank you.' Jessica yawned.

'How was dinner with Dan?'

'Lovely. I couldn't get over where we went today . . . that plant . . . it was so sweet of him to think of inviting me.'

'He likes you. Thinks you should be working in the field. Move out of a lab and in with the plants.' Carmen smiled as she handed Jessica a fresh towel.

'Botany? I'm not sure where my experience would fit in. But I will have to start thinking about picking up my life again.' She sighed. 'Getting a job.'

'Hang out with Dan a bit,' suggested Carmen. 'He seems to know people in a lot of different fields. And he is good company.'

'Yes, he is,' said Jessica.

'Here's your room. See you in the morning. *Bonne nuit*. Sweet dreams, Jessica.'

*

'Dan's just arrived,' called Carmen.

Jessica grabbed her jacket and bag and gave Carmen a quick hug at the door. 'Thanks for everything, Carmen. See you later.'

'Enjoy the mountain.'

Dan opened the garden gate for her as Sean Hyland seemed to explode from the front seat of Dan's car. He was tall and solid, with a ruddy complexion and hair that struck Jessica as 'electrocuted' – frizzed and standing on end in a bushy red-grey halo. He was beaming and chuckling as he talked. 'Splendid, wonderful. You're Jessica. Lovely to meet you.' He grabbed her hand and pumped it.

'This is Distinguished Professor Dr Sean Hyland,' said Dan.

'Call me Sean, call me Sean, now that you know I am "distinguished".' He laughed. 'Here, you take the front.'

Dan winked at Jessica as he got behind the wheel and Sean settled himself in the back seat.

The hour's drive to Mt Field melted away as Sean talked and laughed. Occasionally he railed in mock horror and despair, but almost every sentence was punctuated with a peal of laughter, even as he described his frustration with the tourism industry's tactics in wilderness areas.

'The great shadow of ecotourism, garnished with gourmet food and vintage wines, is served up to lure people to pay exorbitant rates for experiences they could have – and have better – for free!' On a roll, he continued, 'It's development at all costs from government and business, no matter how tacky or tawdry, or even tasteful, so long as it caters to tourism. It will ruin more than we realise.'

'And you'll hear more about that tonight!' said Dan as he parked and they all got out.

They were walking through the great forest of tall swamp gums on the mountain when Sean sprang into a pose like a Samurai warrior.

'Aha! Here, behold, the beauties!' He pointed to a cluster of bright yellow mushrooms. '*Cortinarius sinapicolor*. Also called Slimy Yellow Cortina,' he said to Jessica with a chuckle.

'I can see why,' she said. 'And we're standing on kilometres of mycelium filaments under there, right?' She pointed to the roots of the trees.

'*Brava*!' He laughed. 'Yes, the superb interconnectivity of fungi, they're unique in fulfilling ecological roles not provided by other organisms. Mycelium is a framework, literally and metaphorically, for nature and society, from making soil to providing food and medicine. It's an example of interconnectedness in all conceivable ways. Miraculous, magic and mysterious, eh?' He chortled.

Two hikers standing close by came over to see what they were looking at and one said, 'They don't look edible!'

'Too pretty to pick,' added the woman.

'Definitely. Don't eat these guys,' said Dan.

'They're too important working just where they are,' said Sean cheerfully. 'You know how to tell if a mushroom is edible?'

When they shook their heads, he laughed. 'Don't risk it! Go and look up Fungimap. Tells you everything you want to know about fungi. Join them, it's a great organisation! You'll be amazed. There're about three hundred species of fungi in this national park alone. See if you can find some more. Become a citizen scientist!'

His enthusiasm was infectious, and the hikers were grinning. 'Really? Terrific. Okay, we'll check it out.' The couple wished them a good day and walked on.

Sean clapped his hands. 'How's that then? C'mon, there's more to look for. We have to get the park's management to promote the fungi up here, make it an attraction. People need to know that fungi rules!'

'Do we have time to go to the waterfalls?' Jessica asked. 'I remember that Horseshoe Falls are spectacular.'

'Yes, we can head that way now,' said Sean. 'Let's go.'

*

On the drive back to Carmen's, Jessica was feeling overloaded with the endless stream of information and laughter from Dr Sean Hyland. She could imagine his talk that night would be just as insightful and entertaining.

'I hope Sean didn't overwhelm you,' said Carmen, almost reading her thoughts when she arrived back. 'Would you like a coffee or something stronger?'

'Thanks, Carmen, a coffee would be great. Well, I am just amazed at what a broad subject mycology is, how it covers so many disciplines, and how little awareness there is about fungi.'

'Its time is coming. You know how it is when you put something out there into the universe and it just starts to build its own momentum. Suddenly something you think only you know about is being talked about and written about, and so on. Sean isn't alone; many other people have been following their own path to this for decades, and there's a young Canadian guy in his thirties who's working with Sean, who is writing books about fungi and doing wonderful things.'

'Sean said that some important mushroom products are starting to be manufactured,' said Jessica.

'That's right. Products that can help clean up toxins, save our soil and trees and water. Sean's been working on some, and he's the kind of person who shares his research, motivates others, and tries to have altruistic bodies market it freely.'

'But the cost of researching, experimenting and producing these products has to be paid by somebody,' said Jessica.

'Sean took out some patents, then found there was such a dark underbelly of individuals, big pharmaceutical companies, all kinds of businesses that could see a way to make a buck rather than trying to save the planet . . . Well, he threw the proverbial spanner in the works by telling everyone he could about his research.'

'Yes, Dan mentioned that. Good for him!'

'It's earned him the label of being a bit of a nutty professor. But the fact that massive chemical companies, mining people, drug companies, agriculture, food people, you name it, spy on him, hack him, break into his lab, nobble his students . . .' Carmen sighed and leaned back. 'Well, he must be on the right track, eh?'

'Really? Yet he seems so happy,' said Jessica.

'That's his way of dealing with things, I suppose. He's strong in himself. But I don't really know; he's my step-cousin and I don't know his side of the family in Canada that well. I tend to deal with things in my life, though of far less import, in a different manner. Sean sails into the gale full of optimism and confidence. I retreat to the island.'

'He must like staying over there with you,' said Jessica.

'He does. While I've never seen him down or dispirited, he comes when he says his batteries need a bit of a recharge. I guess we all need that special place, don't we?'

'Yes. I'm so grateful to Sally and her family. I find that at Arcadia. As they do. Though we have our own sacred spots. Toby likes the top of the hill where he's planted his trees for the truffles. He likes that open view. Sally and I had our own secret spot in their forest when we were kids. Her grandmother had her special place . . . and this trip, I've found sitting by the creek and in the forest, well . . . healing.'

'Wounds do heal. Music does it for me,' said Carmen quietly.

They both sat in contemplative silence for a while. Jessica didn't pry but wondered what had happened in

Carmen's life. She knew well that sometimes you had someone in your life, be it friend, family member, colleague or acquaintance, and thought you knew them well, and then one day you found out you never knew anything about them at all.

*

Jessica was getting dressed for the talk when her phone rang. It was Dan.

'Hi. Hope you've recovered from the day! The Distinguished One can be a bit overwhelming.'

'Ha! Carmen said the same thing,' Jessica replied with a chuckle. 'I'm fine. I have my second wind, thanks to a strong coffee.'

'Would you like me to pick you and Carmen up? The talk's on at the Sandy Bay campus of the uni. And there are drinks afterwards. Sorry, I should have mentioned that earlier. Sean had some media to do this afternoon, so I've been driving him around.'

'Thank you. Boy, you must have had a big day. Are you his minder as well?'

'No, no. We overlap in some areas, and besides, Sean is amazing company. That mind and mouth never stop!'

'Nice of you to think of us, Dan. Let me just go and check with Carmen.'

Carmen was dressed in a floor-length embroidered coat over black leggings and a long top with a dramatic necklace. She was tying a silk scarf turban-style around her head when Jessica walked into the kitchen.

'Wow, how great do you look! Dan is on the phone – he's offered to drive us there.'

'Sweet of him. Yes, please, a lift would be good. I'll be fine getting home as I'm meeting someone afterwards . . .'

she said with a smile. 'Tell Dan we'll see him in, say, forty-five minutes?'

*

There was quite a crowd milling at the entrance to the Stanley Burbury Theatre.

'We'll find you inside, thanks, Dan,' said Carmen as she and Jessica got out and Dan drove off to park the car.

'There's Sally and Toby,' said Jessica, waving.

'I'll see you inside, Jessica. I can see a few friends I want to catch up with. You have the spare key? Our paths might diverge this evening.'

'I do. Thanks, Carmen.'

'See you anon. Enjoy!'

Jessica grinned. 'Yes, see you in the morning.' She caught up with Sally and Toby and they walked over to the theatre.

Jessica spotted Sean immediately, hearing his booming laughter as he talked to a group in the foyer. In contrast to his sweater and jeans of the morning, he was dressed in a midnight-blue velvet jacket, a loosely knotted red silk tie and a brocade waistcoat teamed with dark pants and polished boots. His wild hair had been somewhat slicked back but not entirely tamed. He waved to Jessica but continued talking.

'We'll catch him later,' she said to Sally.

'Good roll-up,' commented Toby, looking around at the crowd.

As they settled in their seats, Sally nudged Jessica and pointed to Carmen a few rows in front, talking to a tall man with salt-and-pepper hair and a neat beard.

'He looks rather professorial,' she whispered.

'So handsome! Good for Carmen.'

The lights dimmed and a young woman placed a small carafe of water on the lectern as a stately, white-haired lady walked onto the stage.

Just then someone sat in the empty seat beside Jessica. It was Dan.

'Hi,' he whispered.

'Hi. Who's that doing the introduction?'

'Director of the School of Environmental Science. Very impressive lady, Doris Pyke. Big philanthropist,' he whispered back.

For the next fifty-five minutes, the audience sat mesmerised while Sean Hyland spoke. He projected a few PowerPoint slides onto the screen behind him, but the audience hung on his words, which were punctuated by Sean's now familiar laughs, gesticulations and some-times dramatic sighs, as he talked of many things without glancing at a single note.

Like a brilliant, cheerful spider at the centre of every-one's attention, Sean spun a silken word thread of ideas, of observations, of history, of science, of nightmares and dreams and of facts; a web that linked together what has been, what is occurring, and what might be and what will be, in a frightening and believable scenario.

'Everything on this planet is interconnected. And we are the masters of our own extinction,' he said.

Sean reminded them that Aboriginal occupation of more than sixty thousand years had kept the conti-nent intact, but it had taken barely a generation for white settlers to begin the extinguishment of Aboriginal people, wildlife and flora, environmental destruction that continues today, faster than in any other country in the world.

'Trees . . . now the old-growth forests that remain are

the saviours for us all. Nothing can replace an ancient tree. These forests, and our mangrove forests on the coast, are Australia's lifeblood for air and water. Cut down the forests and we will be left with rising temperatures, drought, fires, insect epidemics, more carbon dioxide in the overheated atmosphere, and clouds will lose their ability to make rain. Lose the rainforests, and we lose life. Trees are climate stabilisers, but worldwide they are dying at unprecedented rates.' He paused in the shocked silence. And then lifted a finger . . . 'But if we keep the forests alive, we preserve another saviour, and that is . . . the forest fungi! New soil, new life!'

Sean swept into an overview of the mycelium network, and details of the various mushrooms with their powerful properties for the enrichment of soil, plants and humans. He ended on a philosophical and heartfelt note that touched the audience, who gave him a rousing cheer and a standing ovation.

'Makes you want to go out and march in the streets, doesn't it?' Dan said in Jessica's ear.

She nodded. 'Certainly does. It all seems so bleeding obvious. For over thirty years, he said, we've known about global warming . . . and so little has been done!'

'Politicians have their priorities all wrong,' said Dan.

Toby leaned over. 'Wow, that was fantastic. And we've got mushrooms and old-growth forest all over Arcadia!'

'Let's head for the reception.' Sally linked her arm in Toby's. 'It's been ages since we didn't have to rush home to the babysitter.'

'We can all go in my car,' Dan suggested.

'Where exactly are we going?' said Jessica.

'Professor Pyke's house; it's a lovely old place in Battery Point which overlooks the waterfront.'

'Ooh, I can't wait to see it,' said Sally.

Dan drove up the circular driveway to the Pyke residence, where two young uni students were working as valets, parking the cars. On the floodlit portico, two more students were ticking off names on the guest list, and directing guests to the cloakroom. From there guests were ushered down the hallway to the reception room.

'How many people are here?' wondered Sally.

'About sixty, I think,' said Dan.

'More speeches?' asked Toby.

'Maybe just one. Professor Pyke will want to thank Sean and I think she's giving him some award. There's food coming round.' Dan pointed to wait staff carrying trays.

'Seems like a few uni students are making some pocket money tonight,' said Jessica.

'Come out onto the terrace. The view's worth seeing,' said Dan.

'How beautiful,' said Sally as they stepped through the open doors.

'You come here often?' Toby said to him.

'Yes, I'm involved in the Bookend Trust, which Professor Pyke supports.'

'What's that?' asked Jessica as they moved along the stone terrace dotted with comfortable settees and chairs and tables; standing gas heaters were set up along the walls. Candles in tall glass holders and low lamps gave a soft glow to the setting.

'I'll tell you all about it later. I think the Bookend Trust is something you might be interested in,' said Dan.

'I see a bar, what can I get you all?' asked Toby, spotting a long table covered with a white cloth, an ice bucket, glasses and bottles of water and wine.

'Just water for me. I'll help you. Jess?' said Dan.

'A white wine, please.'

'Toby, if there's something exotic, surprise me.' Sally smiled. 'I wonder if a photo would come out. I love the lights from the boats.' She got out her phone and moved to the edge of the terrace.

Settled with their drinks, Dan leaned towards Sally and Toby. 'Okay, guys, I have some news from my friend at the Botanical Gardens; I saw him when he was waiting to go into Sean's talk and he told me the main details. I'll need to catch up with him during the week to find out more, but I think it could tie in with a few things.'

'About the truffles?' said Toby.

'Possibly. I'm wondering now if the truffle theft was opportunistic. Not what they went for in the first place, as you suggested the other day, Sally. I was actually talking to my friend about Shelter Bay, as he knew the place, and when I mentioned Seawinds, he said he knew the family. Well, not personally, but he knows of the family.'

'The Broadbents?' said Sally.

'Yes. My friend told me the woman we met is the mother of Gordon Broadbent. She was married to a John Broadbent, who had a brother called Thomas, or Tommy.'

Sally and Jessica exchanged startled glances.

'Sally, Thomas Broadbent! The man from the cave!' Jessica exclaimed.

'You're right!' said Sally. 'What else can you tell us about the Broadbents, Dan?'

'Gordon is now running Seawinds, which is quietly producing some sort of substance from unusual fungi. It's all a bit secret.'

'Intriguing,' said Sally.

'Yes, but keep going . . . I want to know how all these pieces fit together,' Toby said.

'Well, John and Tommy's aunt was called Hilda. Hilda Broadbent.' He paused. 'Recognise that name?'

'Mmm, the name's familiar but I can't remember why. Who was she?' Sally said.

'Hilda Broadbent married Stephen Holland – your grandfather, Sally. The Broadbent family had owned Arcadia as well as Seawinds. Apparently there was some argy-bargy with the family over Hilda leaving Arcadia in its entirety to Holland in her will.'

Sally was staring at Dan, wide-eyed. 'That's incredible,' she said. 'I didn't know any of that. I've only heard the name of my grandfather's first wife once or twice, and only her first name. That's not surprising, I guess, when you consider that he died so long before I was born and Mum doesn't speak about him much; she mainly talks about her mother.'

'I'm sure your mum will know more,' said Toby.

'Yes, I'll ask her,' said Sally. 'It's strange that I never wondered about who my grandfather was married to before my grandmother. Of course, he didn't have any children with his first wife.'

'What else do we know about the son, Gordon? How old would he be now?' asked Toby.

'Not sure, but probably in his sixties. Sally, could you check with your mother, see if she knows anything about him?' said Dan.

'I will, but I don't think she would. She's never mentioned any family connection up north. And Stella's family came from Victoria,' said Sally.

'But the Broadbent family are, or were, obviously closely connected to Arcadia,' said Jessica. 'This is starting to answer a lot of questions,' she added.

'Do you think that because the property was once in

their family they might believe they still have the right to sneak around and steal from us?' exclaimed Sally.

'It's okay, Sal,' said Toby gently. 'We don't know it was them at all.'

'Listen, we should go in soon, Professor Pyke will be saying a few words,' said Dan. 'But just quickly, there's more to tell you.'

'Like what?' said Sally as they finished their drinks.

'I spoke to Denyse at the Seed Centre. She got a lead on your grandmother's painting. She's quite excited.'

'Why is that?' asked Jessica.

'The fungi in the picture were easier to identify. But the little flower is rare, a previously unknown mycotrophic which means it derives its nutrients from a fungus. When I saw it I didn't realise it was that plant; the photos Mollie sent of the painting were a little out of focus. But Denyse was able to blow the images up and work out what it was. It's a *Thismia*, commonly known as a Fairy Lantern because they grow underground and only pop up when in flower. And this one, presumably growing at Arcadia, has a never-before-seen colour. Unless your grandmother took some artistic licence, this is a realistic reference for us that we haven't had before.' Dan stood up.

'Were the dried flowers we found useful in identifying it?' Sally asked.

'The colour has gone from them, but they could be useful in other ways. Denyse said she's still working on them.'

'Is it still growing there?' Jessica asked Sally. She couldn't remember seeing any when they were last there.

'I don't know,' said Sally. 'To be honest, I'm more concerned about looking into the connection between the Broadbents and our family, and Arcadia.'

Toby put his arm around Sally. 'Cuppa tea and a good chat with your mum might get a few more answers.'

As they moved towards the doors, Sally turned to Jessica and lowered her voice. 'I keep thinking about Stella's notebook, that horrible drawing . . . What if the Broadbents had something to do with that?'

*

It seemed perfectly natural at the end of the evening that Sally and Toby grab a waiting taxi, while Dan drove Jessica back to Carmen's, as it was on his way.

'Sally seemed a bit perturbed at the news about the Broadbents. Strange that she didn't know more about them,' said Dan as they drove.

'Not really. Mollie's mother married a lonely widower who didn't talk much about his younger years, from what I can gather,' Jess said.

'I've discovered that in-laws and relatives often have a habit of sticking their nose into things, especially if they smell money,' said Dan grimly. 'My sister's husband had a loose cannon of a relative turn up and cause trouble for a bit.'

'Ooh, that sounds nasty. Do you have many sisters and brothers?'

'An older brother and a younger sister. I'm the middle one. I'm lucky as I get to roam, particularly in my work, while the others keep an eye on the folks. Not that they need it. My parents are addicted to cruises.'

Jessica laughed. 'Lucky them. My parents are happy, healthy . . . Touch wood they stay like that. I often think Mollie must be lonely. She rarely leaves Arcadia, Sally says.' She yawned. 'It was an amazing evening. Dan, thank you for taking me up to see King's Holly, introducing me to Sean, and the hike today and everything tonight . . . it's all taken me completely by surprise. In fact, my whole time back here in Tassie has been incredible. I ran away feeling shattered, but coming to my best friend, and to the place I've always known as a second home, was the best thing I could have done. And now all of that stuff, that baggage I ran from, doesn't mean a thing.'

Dan nodded, smiling. 'Sitting in a forest will do that. Having good friends around helps too.' He pulled up outside Carmen's place. 'All looks dark; Carmen must be in bed already, or still out and about. I didn't see her at the Pykes' place.'

'No, I think she has a date.'

'Go, Carmen!'

For a split second Jessica thought about inviting him in, but it wasn't her home. 'Thanks again, Dan.'

'Let me get the door.' He walked around and opened Jessica's car door.

'Thanks for all you're doing for Sally, too,' said Jessica. 'I'll call you tomorrow.'

'I'll look forward to it.' He leaned over and kissed her lightly. 'Sleep well.'

Jessica found the key in her bag and opened the front door, then turned and saw Dan standing by his car, arms folded, waiting till she was safely inside.

It was a nice feeling. She latched the door behind her with a smile.

9

Arcadia, 1976

STELLA SAT IN THE chair in her rose garden, which overlooked the untouched forest and the distant mountains. These days more cars travelled their road than had when she'd come here as a young bride, and there were new shops in their growing but still isolated township. The river traffic had increased too, with more leisure boats, yachts from the sailing club, fishing craft, and occasional scenic cruises. The farms in the area were expanding, with apple orchards being replaced by different crops, as well as some sheep and cattle.

Arcadia hadn't changed. But it wasn't the same without Mrs James. She'd died as she'd lived – peacefully, not wanting to be a bother to others. She'd fretted about Stella being on her own as Mollie had moved north with Graham after their wedding. 'Nonsense. I have your Terry, who is wonderful. I am doing perfectly well here, and I can get any help I want. And one day soon, Mollie and her family will come home here, to Arcadia.'

Mrs James had smiled. 'Yes. That's a fine plan. I hope she doesn't leave it too long.' They'd reached out to each other, Stella's long fingers stroking the older woman's careworn hands.

Within two months, Mollie and Graham had moved to Arcadia, leaving Graham's family farm in the care of his father and brother.

Stella remained in her old bedroom, and kept her studio unchanged. Mollie freshened up the master bedroom with new curtains and paint, but she focused mainly on tidying up the garden and running a few cows. Most of Graham's time was taken up with his job as principal of the small primary school in Burridge.

The Jameses' cottage became guest quarters, though Stella contacted all the James children to tell them that the cottage would always be available any time they and their own families might wish to visit.

Ever since her husband's death, Stella had become more and more involved with the Art Society, which she enjoyed for the social contact as much as the exhibitions, the lectures, the painting trips and occasional master classes conducted by renowned visiting artists.

Mollie found her mother clattering away in her studio one evening as she sorted through stacks of canvases and unframed pictures in the set of drawers wide enough to hold her artworks. 'Mother, dinner is ready. What are you looking for?'

'I've been asked to enter a piece in a rather special art show, an invitation-only event.'

'Well, that sounds prestigious. What are you going to paint?'

'Mollie, dear, my eyes aren't up to scratch these days. In her letter, the director asked for a botanical work, and that requires a steady hand and good eyes. So I was thinking I might enter something I did some time ago. The one with Nyx or that purple–blue plant with the fungi.'

'Okay, good idea,' said Mollie. 'Come and have dinner and I'll help you later.'

So after dinner Mollie and her mother rifled through the stacks of pictures. 'Mother, you should do something with these. Sell them or give them away, or store them somewhere temperature controlled so they won't get damaged by the weather.'

'Perhaps, but I rather like having them around. They are dear old friends.'

'Is this it?' asked Mollie, pulling out a large painting of delicate fronds with mushrooms and the odd little purple flower in the corner. 'It's very good. So is the owl, of course.'

'That's the one! Thank you, dear. I remember the day I did the sketches for the Nyx painting very well.' She smiled. 'It was in 1935. Then I exhibited it in 1939, and it won a prize, which was a great surprise. But for some reason, I've never shown this one of the fronds before.'

'It's the perfect choice for the exhibition. Is there a prize this time?'

'I don't believe so. A piece of paper, perhaps. And the honour of meeting the curator, who's an artist from America, I gather.'

'What's that little flower?' Mollie peered at the picture.

'I haven't been able to find out. It pops up every year or so down under one of the big old trees. It seems to sprout from the fungus. I haven't been there for a while, I must take a look again,' said Stella wistfully.

'Mother, do you think so? Please don't go alone, you could trip and fall. Wait till Graham or I can go with you. It's funny, I've never found that forest as romantic and fascinating as you seem to.'

'I feel I know every inch of it. I'll take my stick if I go, and let you know,' she added.

Mollie and Graham didn't like Stella spending hours alone in the forest with no means of communicating with them if anything went wrong. When she went off to paint or draw or simply to birdwatch, one of them would go down with morning or afternoon tea to check on her. 'I don't know how she can just sit there for hours on end, with only her sketchbook and binoculars,' Mollie had once said to her husband.

The next day, Stella took a walk to the woods with her camera and notebook, treading carefully along the track that was imprinted on her heart. As she always did, she paused at one particular old tree and rested her hand in the shallow hollow in its trunk. She knew it would be empty, but the gesture brought back memories of the small notes that had been hidden there, which still made her heart leap.

*

The night of the Art Society reception to open the exhibition and announce its plans for the coming year, Mollie drove her mother to the gracious sandstone building, fashioned after a Greek revivalist–style temple, in a little park at the foothills of Hobart's Wellington Park. Ancanthe, as it was first named, had been built by convicts in the 1880s and was now known as the Lady Franklin Gallery, after its creator, the wife of the then governor.

'The Art Society is so lucky to be housed in this lovely building,' said Stella as they drove up and parked the car. 'After the Franklins left, the place became so neglected. Did you know they used to store apples and cattle fodder in here? Thankfully it was restored. Your father and I came to the opening, in 1948 I believe it was.'

'That Lady Jane was quite a woman. We're only just finding out about her,' said Mollie. 'Typical, isn't it? The wives were never written into history. Like Elizabeth Macarthur in Sydney.'

'I'm thrilled to be exhibited tonight,' said Stella, linking her arm through Mollie's.

'I hope there'll be photographers here and you get your photo in the paper. You look just beautiful.' Mollie squeezed her mother's arm, glancing at her elegant silk trouser suit and lace shirt, her hair coiled on top of her head, tendrils threaded with silver falling around her face, soft make-up and sparkling earrings.

And Stella *was* photographed, standing next to her painting. When the director of the Society asked her to say a few words, Stella smiled shyly and, speaking quietly and graciously, she thanked the Art Society for its loyal support for the advancement of art in the community.

'I believe artists can see in their mind's eye the masterpiece that consumes their heart and soul, and the translation from mind to canvas can be a mysterious, unfathomable, uncontrollable journey to convey the same vision to the outside world. It can be frustrating, certainly, but it's an unquestionable and unquenchable desire only a fellow artist, in whatever medium, can appreciate,' said Stella with a small smile. 'We tend to be a solitary breed, so on occasions such as this, we are grateful for the appreciation and also for the opportunity to share our passion. So thank you.'

The director smiled broadly and led the applause as she shook Stella's hand warmly.

*

Mollie stood back, watching her mother being feted and feeling proud as the director escorted Stella around the room. She was sipping a glass of sherry when a man she didn't know approached her.

'You're Mrs Holland's daughter?' When she nodded, he added, 'Do you still live at Arcadia? I am intrigued by your mother's painting. I wonder if it is a composite, a fantasy, or botanically accurate?'

Mollie felt a bit taken aback. 'I really couldn't say for sure, Mr . . .?' She gave him a questioning look. When he made no move to reply, she continued, 'I believe she paints what she sees around her.'

'A very interesting composition. Especially the fungus,' he said with a twisted half-smile.

'Are you an artist?' asked Mollie.

'Not at all. More a collector.' He gave a nod. 'Nice to meet you.' He slid away, leaving Mollie feeling uncomfortable. She glanced across the room and saw him approach her mother.

Stella smiled as he walked over to her, but then her smile faded, replaced by a puzzled look, and finally her face closed and she turned away abruptly. As Mollie hurried across the room towards her mother, she saw a photographer get there first and start talking to Stella, who now looked rattled.

'Oh, Mollie, dear, ah . . .'

'Are you all right?' Mollie linked arms with her mother.

'Hey, that looks great, can I take a photo of you both for *The Mercury*, please?' said the photographer. 'Thanks. Great painting, Mrs Holland.'

'Thank you,' managed Stella.

'Okay, smile, this way. And one more.'

As he wound the film on, Stella squeezed Mollie's arm. 'I think I want to leave now. I'm not the social butterfly type.'

They thanked the director and headed for the door.

'Who was that man?' asked Mollie.

'I'm not sure. He made me feel uncomfortable. Brought back a memory, things I haven't thought about in years,' said Stella. 'Silly of me. I suppose I need to get out more and mingle.'

'No. He was creepy,' said Mollie. 'Still, it was a wonderful event. Are you inspired to do more paintings? Just before the speeches started, I was talking to a woman who owns a gallery outside of Hobart. She said she'd love to sell your work.'

'Oh, I don't know about that. It's not only eyesight that would hold me back – I do them for my own pleasure. I'd feel too constricted if I knew I was painting something to please someone else who had to pay for it.'

'Well, it's nice to be recognised for what you do,' said Mollie.

*

A few days after the exhibition opening, Stella left Mollie a note on the kitchen table to say where she was going, and set out to walk to the forest, carrying her trusty bag slung across her chest packed with camera and notebook. Using the solid walking stick that Mr James had cut for her long ago, she walked at a careful but determined pace, knowing exactly where she was going.

In the misty air of a crisp morning she smiled at the dew lingering in patches the sun had yet to find. She saw her tree and crossed the clearing, heading towards it, and then stopped to look at its protruding roots. Some fungi, moss and ferns were growing around it, as she remembered. But the particular mushrooms she knew should be there were missing, as was her little lantern flower, which she'd seen pop up to bloom briefly before returning to its life beneath the soil – the same kind young Flora had first showed her all those years ago. She'd seen orange ones flower as well, but this purple one had only occasionally appeared, which is why she'd chosen to paint it all that time ago. From her last visit before the event at the Art Society, she had spotted the pale purple–blue tip bulging through the surface of the soil, and by now it should have been at full flower in its brief appearance above the ground.

She knew it must be rare, or an anomaly she'd witnessed every few years. She wanted to photograph it for a botanist at the Botanical Gardens who'd asked for a picture after seeing her painting at the Art Society. And now, after all these years, she was keen to put a name to the little lantern-like bell that appeared among the fungi.

How disappointing; it had not bloomed. She had never seen another growing anywhere else in all her years here, just the one at the base of this tree. She didn't like to disturb anything in the forest so she had only ever once picked the little flower, and that was years before when she'd done the painting and had plucked the rare bloom to take to her studio so she could paint it in a better light. Once she'd painted it, she'd tucked the flower into her sketchbook, a special reminder, and later she would give it to a friend.

She sighed, and was about to turn away when something caught her eye. She stood still, gazing at the ground. Something didn't look right. The lichen, a twig atop the rotting leaf matter looked . . . with her artist's eye . . . composed. Arranged, almost. She stooped and gently brushed away some leaves. The topsoil was pressed down and smooth, not moist and crumbly as it usually was. She knew the bulbs and roots of the flower were spread beneath, and she gently scraped the surface. Then she crouched down and, with the top of a twig, began scooping away the soil. It quickly became apparent that the network of rhizomes and filaments that fed the underground plants and bulbs had been severed. The plant that bloomed so briefly and rarely was gone. Entirely separated from its host. This had not been an accident; the careful replacement of the soil attested to that. She knew there were no more. And now it was gone. It would have been easy to spot, the small dash of purple against the emerald dampness, if you were here at the right time. It had disappeared in the last two or three days.

A face, a figure, a familiar voice, flashed through her mind. Shakily she got to her feet. She turned her back and walked away, as quickly as she could, her knees trembling, her mind racing, her usually gentle face set in an expression of fury and sadness.

Hobart, 2018

Jessica leaned back, closing her eyes, tilting her face to the sun. 'You can't beat the smell of good coffee, croissants and car fumes,' she said.

Sally and Toby laughed. They were sitting at a table outside a trendy local café close by Carmen's house.

'So what do you two want to do this morning? I have to go pick up some things from a produce supplier,' said Toby.

'I'm easy,' said Sally. 'I might look for something to take back to Katie. There're some cute boutiques around here.'

'My niece has a birthday coming up and I should buy her a present, so I'll come with you,' said Jessica. 'She's three. Mum keeps saying we should get her and Katie together one day when they're both in Sydney. Speaking of which, do you two have any plans to head over to Melbourne or Sydney soon?' she asked.

Toby shrugged. 'Gosh, that's up to you, Sal. We have to fit in my dad's birthday. His sixtieth is coming up, and that might take up any spare time I have for a while.'

Sally sipped her coffee. 'I'll see what Mum wants to do. She hasn't been over to the mainland for a bit. She has friends in Melbourne she wants to catch up with.' She paused. 'No pressure or anything, but what about you, Jess? Any plans?'

Jessica put her cup down. 'No plans. But a few ideas starting to bubble away.'

'You can stay with us as long as you want, you know,' said Toby.

'Thanks, Toby. You guys are so kind to me. This has been such a break. I kinda put my life on hold and that's been good. I can't thank you enough.'

'Jess, we're not pushing you out,' said Sally quickly.

'I know. I realise that I just needed breathing space, a little healing time. A chance to find a new direction. The thought of going back to live in Sydney with all the over-building, traffic and the exploitation of everything, is . . .' She shuddered. 'I see it all more clearly from this distance.

314

The greed is depressing. After meeting and hearing Sean Hyland I feel, well, that I want to do something that means something . . .'

Toby nodded. 'We felt like that when we moved to Arcadia, didn't we, Sal? We took a sideways step and gambled on something different. Sometimes I worry about it in the middle of the night, but I wouldn't change anything.' He smiled at Sally and she grinned back.

'So many people feel the same way, it's kind of catching. Perhaps it's the surroundings – this is a special place, this whole state. People come here to get out of the rat race, follow a dream, prioritise family and health and lifestyle. We just have to be careful that we don't get loved to death, overrun or sold out,' said Sally.

'Careful, Sal, you don't want to sound like a NIMBY,' said Toby, chuckling.

'You don't read the independent papers and listen to ABC radio, and follow what's happening in Canberra, like I do,' said Sally.

Jessica laughed. 'You should get involved in local politics, Sally.'

'She's already stirred up the P&C group at the local school,' said Toby, 'and Katie's only been going to preschool for a few months.'

'Good for you, Sal,' Jessica said. 'By the way, what about your mum?' she added. 'When are you going to sit down and ask her about her mother, Shelter Bay, the Broadbents? Surely she must remember something?'

Sally drained her coffee and put down her cup. 'It's tricky. I really don't think she knows much or she would have said something over the years. She's not the type to keep anything from me.'

'Maybe see what Dan has to say first,' said Toby.

'I'm meeting him for lunch at the Botanical Gardens,' said Jessica. 'He wants to introduce me to a few people who work there, although I guess they might not be there on a Saturday. Had you heard about the Bookend Trust before he mentioned it last night?' she added. When Sally and Toby shook their heads, she continued, 'Me either. Dan said it's a not-for-profit group of educators, academics and scientists who want to inspire students to choose environmental careers. Founded here in Tassie, but it's Australia-wide and starting to spread overseas too. Great idea. Dan thought I might like to get involved.'

'It does sound like a good idea, but surely you need a paying job?' said Sally.

'I know. Anyway, they'll be interesting people to meet.'

'Well, I better get going,' said Toby.

'Want to meet for lunch, darling?' Sally asked him. 'Take advantage of having a day in town?'

'It's a date. I'll get this.' He reached for his wallet. 'See you later, Jess.'

*

Sally and Jessica plunged into their shopping, hitting the many boutiques that lined the main street. Having bought gifts for the young girls, they headed to a small fashion shop to browse.

'Oh, I love this top.' Jessica sighed as she held up a silk blouse with a long lace cuff, full gathered sleeves, and a lace inset at the throat and around the neckline.

'Try it on, it's so soft and feminine,' said Sally. And when Jessica poked her head out of the change cubicle, Sally clapped her hands. 'Oh, that's stunning! Pull your hair up, you look like a Brontë heroine! You have to buy it!'

'I'm unemployed and poor,' said Jessica.

'Maybe, but you look fabulous. Get it, Jess! How long since you bought yourself something so gorgeous?'

'I feel gorgeous. What the heck. I'll take it. You're a bad influence, Sal.' She laughed.

'Leave it on and wear it to lunch. And keep your hair up.' Sally stepped forward and fiddled with Jessica's hair, pulling some tendrils around her face. 'Wispy bits, suits the Victorian look.'

'It's not a date, Sal,' said Jessica, but she was rather pleased with the whole effect, and glad she'd worn smart casual pants and changed from her tennis shoes into leather ballet flats.

'Doesn't matter. You feel fabulous. That's what counts.'

*

Jessica walked through the city and up the rise to the Botanical Gardens, pausing to catch her breath and look across the Derwent River. She was trying to imagine the paddocks and fields around the Government Domain and Gardens in colonial days.

She strolled through the grand gates and followed the path that led to the Seed Conservation Centre. Dan was standing outside talking to the woman they'd met on their first visit. He waved as Jessica came towards them. 'Hi, Jess. You remember Denyse?'

'Of course. How are you?' said Jessica.

'Very well, thanks,' Denyse said. 'We're thrilled we've identified your *Thismia*. It's rare and specific to Tasmania. And it hasn't been described at all until now.'

'It could be named for Sally's grandmother,' Dan said with a grin.

'Wow, wouldn't that be something,' said Jessica.

'Are there other paintings, sketches of it?' asked Denyse.

'I'm not sure, although there are lots of Stella's sketches and paintings at Sally's place.'

'We'd like to take a look at them, if you find any. My colleagues and I are keen to go and see the site, too. Does the flower still grow there? Has it appeared again?'

'I have no idea. I'm not sure anyone has bothered to observe it,' said Jessica.

'And even if it was there, it might have been disturbed or destroyed when the fungi were stolen, I guess,' Dan said.

'Yes,' said Jessica despondently.

'Speaking of the fungi,' he continued, 'I think they could be the same ones that are being used at Seawinds.'

'What makes you think that?'

'Do you remember I mentioned I'd snuck a sample when I was poking around at Seawinds? And we found that tiny sample of a mushroom under a tree in the forest at Arcadia? Well, I asked Denyse to test them.'

Jessica nodded, recalling their walk in the forest.

'It's generated quite some interest,' said Denyse. 'From the sample it looks like the mushrooms they're cultivating have possible medicinal properties, as well as other really interesting uses.'

'What do you mean by *interesting uses*?' asked Jessica.

'Pesticides, deadly poisons,' Dan said. 'But like Sean told us, their potential to mop up and absorb toxic chemicals and clean up industrial waste is a whole new field. As is the use of mushrooms for medicinal purposes to treat serious diseases.'

'There's probably a lot of secret research under way,' said Denyse. 'Once the properties are isolated and can be reproduced on a mass scale, you've got a big business proposition to sell.' She glanced at her watch. 'Anyway, I'd better get back to work. Good to see you again, Jessica.'

'You too, and thanks for all your work on the painting and the sample,' Jessica said.

Denyse waved as she headed back into the building.

'Let's go and have lunch,' said Dan. 'Is eating here okay with you? Sitting out on the restaurant's verandah is great when it's sunny like this.'

*

Dan and Jessica lingered over lunch and talked of many things, from great concerts they'd seen and places they'd been, to others they wanted to see as well as favourite movies, and politics.

Jessica was relieved they were on the same page over current issues in the news, and when she asked about sports, Dan wrinkled his nose. 'I was on the rowing team at uni, and as I think I told you, I'm a sailor. Love it. But that's as far as my sporting career ever went, I'm afraid. Now you're going to tell me you were a star netball player, aren't you?'

Jessica laughed. 'Nope. Swimming team, but I gave it away when I was sixteen. I couldn't hack all the training sessions before and after school.'

'Did you go to school here or in Sydney?' Dan asked.

'Both. My family moved to the mainland when I was fourteen. I missed Sal, I missed the life here. I got over it, but I never lost contact with Sally and it has been so lovely reconnecting with her, and with Tassie.'

'There are some people you meet who stay friends for life,' said Dan.

'Yes. Sally never judges me, has my back no matter what. She's the one I can call at 2 am and she's right there for me.'

'As you are for her, I'm sure,' said Dan. He lifted his

319

coffee cup, his eyes fixed on her. 'You look stunning today, Jess. Like a vintage cameo brooch.'

'Thanks, Dan.' She laughed. 'It must be my new blouse. Sally insisted I buy it this morning.'

'It's beautiful. Now, I want you to meet a special fellow here.'

They paid the bill and headed out onto the lawn.

'I have to get a taxi back to meet Sally and Toby at their hotel as we're heading back to Arcadia. Toby wants to be there before dark,' said Jessica.

'Okay. Let's go up to the main gates now,' said Dan. 'He's meeting us there. Then I'll drop you at the hotel.'

As they reached the entrance and the information booth, Jessica spotted the older man she and Sally had met on their first visit. 'Oh, there's Terry. He took us to the Seed Conservation Centre the other day. He was so helpful. Lovely man.'

'Well, there you go. That's who I want to introduce you to. I'd like to bring Terry to Arcadia. I'll speak to Sally first, of course.'

'Why would he want to go there?' Jessica was puzzled.

Before Dan could answer, Terry saw them and waved. 'I remember you.' He shook Jessica's hand warmly. 'How are you, Dan? Here, let's sit down.' He pointed to a bench near the gate. 'Where's your friend?' he asked Jessica.

'Having a leisurely lunch with her husband,' she said, smiling. 'It's good to see you again.'

'You too.' Terry settled himself on the seat and Jessica and Dan sat on either side of him. 'So, Dan tells me you got your plant identified, eh? And it came from Arcadia, he said.'

'Yes. That's right. You know of Arcadia?' said Jessica, turning to look at him.

'I most certainly do. I grew up there. James is my surname – my parents worked there and I did for a few years, too.' He paused and, seeing Jessica's startled face, he gave a soft smile and went on, 'Such a coincidence that we met when you came to the Seed Centre.'

'I'm sorry Sally didn't recognise you,' said Jessica.

'Oh, she wouldn't know me; all before her time, really. My mother was the housekeeper at Arcadia, and Dad was the caretaker who looked after the property. My brothers and sisters and I all lived there. It was a great life; till the polio came.' He lifted a foot. 'Luckily I was the only one in the family who contracted it. And I've never let it hold me back.'

'Terry, I'm just surprised. This seems so . . . bizarre . . .' stammered Jessica. 'You said you worked there too?'

'Yes. After Dad died I managed the farm and helped my mum, as she was getting on.'

'Did you know Sally's mother, Mollie, then?' asked Jessica.

'Oh, yes indeed. I promised my mother I'd always keep an eye on her. But after Mollie and her husband moved back and took over, and Mrs H died, I felt it was my turn to travel and start my own life away from Arcadia. You know.'

'Of course,' said Jessica.

'I always kept in touch, sent Christmas cards to Mollie. Once she was back at Arcadia, I felt the circle had closed and the family was back there for the long haul. I travelled, worked in a few different jobs over the years, hiked on Macquarie Island,' he said proudly. 'That's where I met some of the scientific people and I ended up here, at the Gardens.'

'Terry, I wondered if you would like to visit Arcadia,'

321

said Dan. 'Been a while since you were back there, eh? I can ask Mollie and Sally if that's all right.'

'Oh, yes,' he said fervently. 'I'd love to see the place one more time. I'm getting on, you know.'

'I think Sally would like to ask you about some of the old history, family memories,' said Jessica gently. 'Things her mother doesn't know much about.'

'Well, certainly, if I can help . . .'

'You can meet her little girl, too. Katie. She's four,' said Jessica.

The old man's eyes looked misty. 'That's about how old Mollie was when I used to take her for walks . . . she was like my baby sister.'

*

They said goodbye to Terry and walked close, side by side, to Dan's car.

'I'm just blown away by that,' said Jessica shakily. 'Imagine how Sally is going to feel when I tell her the man we met here grew up at Arcadia.'

'Not to mention the surprise her mother will have. He's pretty good for someone in his mid-eighties, isn't he?'

'Yes, amazing. Terry probably knows more about Sally's family than any relative.'

'Often the way, I suppose. When families are scattered over the country, a long-time friend or neighbour can know all the details of the day-to-day dramas and triumphs that have happened over the years while relations haven't a clue. Perhaps you can ask Sally and Toby on the drive home if it's okay for Terry and me to visit? That's if Mollie agrees too, of course.'

'Will do. Maybe Terry holds the key to Stella's story,' said Jessica.

When they reached the boutique hotel where Sally and Toby were staying, Dan stopped the car, jumped out and held the door for Jessica.

'Well, I'll call you tonight or tomorrow, Dan,' she said as she climbed out. 'Gosh, what a day – a delicious lunch, and thanks so much for introducing me to Terry properly. My mind is spinning.'

Dan leaned over and kissed her quickly on the cheek. 'Let me know how it goes with Sally and Mollie. I'll keep investigating up here.'

Impulsively Jessica reached out and hugged him tightly. 'I can't thank you enough. It's just been so . . . magical.'

He hugged her back, and for a moment or two they clung together, sensing that not only had they shared something special, but that it was a beginning.

Dan was first to pull away, but he stood close, holding her by the shoulders and staring into her sparkling eyes. 'Magic, indeed. You're amazing.'

Jessica thought he was going to kiss her and her heart started racing, but he dropped his arms, then reached out and gently touched her cheek before turning away.

*

When they arrived back at Arcadia, Jessica pleaded tiredness and went to bed after an early dinner. Mollie was at an evening meeting in town but was due back soon, and Sally sensed that Jessica was getting out of their way to give them some time on their own. So once Katie was in bed, she and Toby settled with a nightcap, sitting close together on the sofa.

'When do you think you'll talk to your mum about this visit from Terry James?' asked Toby.

'Tonight, if she gets back from her meeting soon,

otherwise first thing tomorrow. She's off razzing up the council over some development proposal.'

'Oh, that tourism complex they want to do up on the coast? Yeah, it sounds a bit too big for this state.'

'She thinks they're trying to push through a casino licence. Anyway, good on her for fighting for it,' said Sally, then she paused and took a sip of her drink.

'Toby, how are we doing here?' She turned and looked at him. 'We've sunk everything into these new ventures, and you left your family farm to be here at Arcadia. Now I'm worried about whether we've done the right thing. Do you ever think about your family, the farm, I mean?'

Toby reached for her hand. 'Hey, what's brought this on? We talked about this years ago. Robert's running the place very well, though Dad still thinks he's in charge.'

'I feel a bit rattled with everything that's going on. Unearthing all these secrets in the family history, people stealing from us, it frightens me. And I realise that if things get bad I can't just say, okay, let's sell up. It's hit me how . . . ingrained Arcadia is in our family. I couldn't imagine living anywhere else.'

'Me either.' He leaned over and kissed her. 'But no matter what happens, wherever we're together with Katie, your mum, well, that's home. Right? Anyway, we're doing okay. We'll be fine.'

Sally sighed and felt relief flow through her. 'You're wonderful. It's weird how it's only struck me now. I've always taken this place for granted. It's all I've ever known as home. And it's where I always expected to be. I'm so lucky to have you.' She leaned her head on his shoulder. 'I just never thought of who else might have lived here. And I can't imagine anyone else ever living here but our family . . .'

'It's not surprising you're thinking about this now,

Sal. You and Jess have uncovered so much about your family that has been hidden for decades.'

'Yes, it's a bit overwhelming. The truffles being taken, the fungi disappearing, and some possible link with the strange, scary man at Seawinds, Gordon Broadbent, and his work with mushrooms. And then us meeting Terry James,' said Sally, nestling closer to Toby. Then, hearing a key turn in the front door, she straightened up. 'Is that you, Mum? We're in here.'

Mollie poked her head in the door. 'Having a nightcap? I saw the light on and just wanted to say goodnight, I won't disturb you. I'm going to have a quick cuppa and then go to bed myself.'

'Bring it in here, Mum. We were just having a chat.'

'No, you two have some alone time. I'm heading to bed. All that discussion and arguing at the council meeting has given me a headache.'

'Did you have a win, Mollie?' asked Toby.

'Not yet. But there's no way our group wants to see a mega overseas development on the coast near here. The rush for dollars and development is killing us. This plan would be a whole town, far bigger than anything anywhere else along the coast.'

'Wow, that sounds a bit extreme,' said Sally.

'A resort, an eighteen-hole golf course; a nine-hole golf course; a runway for aircraft; a 120-room sky hotel, restaurants, villas and townhouses, a spa and health retreat and finally a palliative care unit. I haven't heard about a cemetery. Yet. Plus a temple and art gallery,' said Mollie. 'We're selling our country. Thank goodness we'll never sell Arcadia.'

'Maybe we should build a wall and a moat,' said Toby with a slight smile, trying to defuse Mollie's visible anger.

'Not a bad idea. Well, that's enough from me. Good night.'

'Go Mollie,' Toby said when she'd left. 'C'mon, Sal, let's go to bed.'

*

Jessica had made morning tea when Sally came in from the farm.

'Smoko, Mum,' Sally said, calling her mother away from her computer. 'Hey, thanks, Jess.'

'Nothing fancy. I don't bake much, so it's sourdough bread from the Burridge baker, cheese and local pickles. Thought it'd be a change from biscuits and cake,' said Jessica.

'Toby'll be in soon. He's with one of the workers.' Sally washed her hands and sat down at the breakfast table.

Sipping her cup of tea, Mollie smiled at the two girls. 'So, you enjoyed your little break? When is your friend Dan coming to visit again?'

'Probably the day after tomorrow. He's wondering if he can bring a friend, if that's okay?' said Jessica.

'Of course. Who's he bringing?'

Jessica glanced at Sally. 'A friend he knows at the Botanical Gardens. As it turns out, you know him too. He used to live here,' said Jessica.

'Live here? In Burridge?'

'No, here. At Arcadia. Terry James,' Sally said.

'No!' Mollie clapped her hands. 'Dear old Terry! Oh, gosh, I feel badly, I haven't seen him in years. We rather lost touch, although we always exchange a card at Christmas. Last I remember he was travelling all over the place and he hiked around Macquarie Island. With those feet! Bless him. He must be nearly ninety.'

'In his eighties and very fit. I saw him yesterday,' explained Jessica. 'He works a few days a week at the Gardens. He'd love to see you and meet Sally and Katie, and look around at all you've done at Arcadia. I'm sure it's changed a lot from his day.'

'You didn't meet him, Sal?'

'I did, but only very briefly when Jess and I went to the Gardens the other day; that was before we knew about his connection to Arcadia. Coincidence, eh?'

'Well, I never.' Mollie shook her head. 'How lovely.'

'There's a bit more to the story,' said Sally gently. 'We're hoping you can fill in some of the gaps, Mum. It's to do with Grandmother Stella, in a way. You know the painting we love with the forest and mushrooms and the odd little lantern flower? Well, the people at the Gardens have identified the flower.'

'How exciting. What is it?'

'It's called a *Thismia*, known as a Fairy Lantern. Rare and endemic to Tassie, apparently. Grows underground and only pops up to flower for a short time then disappears. It grows on the fungi and rotting wood, tree roots and stuff.'

'It's never been named, so the Botanical Gardens staff said it could possibly be named after Stella,' said Jessica.

'Oh, my. I don't know what to say. My mother would have been so proud and delighted,' she said, sounding a little emotional.

'Mum,' Sally said tentatively, 'Jess and I have been trying to work out a connection between Arcadia and that house at Shelter Bay, Seawinds. There was a mention of it in those things of Stella's that we found. You said you hadn't heard of Seawinds or the Broadbents,' she added. 'Is that right?'

Mollie looked at her, frowning with concentration. 'Did I? Broadbent rings a bell . . . Of course! Hilda. Hilda Broadbent. Dad's first wife. She passed away long before he met my mother. Afraid I don't know anything about her, though. Why?'

Jessica and Sally exchanged a glance. 'Well, we don't know all the details yet, but we found out that Arcadia used to be owned by the Broadbents and they weren't happy when Hilda left it to Grandpa. Hilda's relations, Gordon Broadbent and an older woman, are still living at Seawinds, and it was Broadbent's four-wheel drive that followed Jess and me. It's registered in his name.'

'Oh no, Sally, that's terrible.' Mollie put her hand to her mouth. She looked concerned and puzzled. 'Hilda and my father never had children. I came along as a bit of a surprise after Dad and Mother had been married quite a while. I sometimes regretted that I didn't have siblings, as my father was not the type to take me on camping trips or things like that. I realised he was older than my friends' fathers and also a bit formal, stuffy, I suppose. But he was a good man.' She stopped and looked deep in thought.

'So you never met any of the Broadbents?' asked Sally.

'Goodness, no. I only remember the name Hilda Broadbent. Old Mr Stanthorpe, the family solicitor, would have known more. He handled the paperwork and estate matters when Dad died,' Mollie said. She stared from Sally to Jessica. 'Why are you both so interested in all this? Is it because this Gordon Broadbent seems to have cropped up in our lives?'

'Well, it's partly that but, actually, Mum, it's like I was saying to Toby last night, I've just never thought much about our history – the family, and who else has lived here. I don't know much about Grandpa's life. Like, where did his family come from before he married Hilda? Who actually built Arcadia?' She turned to Jessica. 'This is the first time I ever considered that. It's always simply been *our* place, but it turns out it wasn't really ours at all until Grandpa inherited it.'

'Mollie, you mentioned the old family paperwork. Just wondering, is it in a safe or something?' Jessica asked. 'If you needed to look at it, say.'

'Some of it's up in the attic.' Mollie sighed. 'I know I should go through it properly one day. I did put mouse bait up there and lots of camphor, so I'm sure it's all fine,' she added. 'So tell me more about the Broadbents who are living in Seawinds now, and why that man might have followed you?'

'We think they're developing a business or doing scientific research that is somehow linked with the old forest here . . .' Seeing Mollie's startled expression Jessica added, 'With the fungi. There are some rare mushrooms that grow wild in old-growth forests, including in the Far Forest.'

Mollie shook her head and looked concerned. 'So, what's led to you finding out all of this? Was it those old letters or whatever it was in the trunk, and Mother's art collection?'

'I suppose so,' said Sally quickly, with a smile. 'Why don't we wait and talk to Dan about the fungi? He knows a lot more than we do. Maybe there could be new opportunities to spin off and develop something ourselves and help raise awareness of the precious plants in the old forests.'

Mollie didn't look convinced. 'I think the truffles are enough. And there's that huge patch of turmeric you and Toby have planted. What next, for goodness sake, Sally?' she asked.

'Oh, that's to help out our dairy farmer friends. They're making kefir, a fermented yoghurt drink, and they add curcumin from turmeric. Supposed to be very good for you,' Sally said.

'I'm happy with plain billy tea, myself.' Mollie stood up rather quickly. 'Thanks for morning tea, Jess. I'd better go back to my spreadsheets.'

When Mollie had returned to her computer, Sally sighed quietly and said, 'I don't think she knows much about the family. Plus I have the feeling she is getting a bit upset about it all.'

'I think we need another visit to the attic,' said Jessica. 'See if we can find the old papers and documents Mollie stored there. Do you think that would be okay?'

'Yes, I was thinking that too. I'm sure Mum wouldn't mind if we looked for them,' said Sally. 'Also, I'm keen to go through Stella's art again to see if we can find any more paintings of the *Thismia* plant for the people at the Botanical Gardens. I'd love to see her work recognised.'

'Well, let's ask your mum if that's all right with her,' said Jessica. 'And we just might find something else about those Broadbent boys while we're at it.'

*

After dinner, as Sally, Katie and Toby were reading bedtime stories and Mollie was sitting with a drink and chatting on the phone to a friend, Jessica prowled slowly around the cluttered but quaint sitting room that had once been Stella's studio. Jessica, like Sally, felt the presence of a young Stella; the bride, the artist, the modest wife, the free spirit with a special relationship with a wild owl, and a passionate sprite of the forest who'd swum naked with her lover, made passionate love in a secret cave, and who remained unknown to them all, even her only child. Jessica thought of her own maternal grandmother, and simply couldn't picture the stolid, wholesome, practical woman doing anything so exotic as Stella had.

But then, how well did one ever know the vibrant younger life once lived by people who now sat quietly, lost in the past, in the faded shell of their old bodies? They knew their place was to not speak out, talk about the old times, how it was 'back then'. No one was really interested, nor could anyone imagine these frail, fragile people ever being wild and passionate, carefree and hilarious, brave and careless.

Somehow Stella had transcended this. Perhaps because Jessica and Sally had stumbled into her world in the Far Forest, and had been able to see her as a beautiful, talented young woman, trapped in a conventional life of that time, married to a stolid older man and living in an isolated corner at the bottom of Tasmania. Mollie knew none of this. Mothers always protect their daughters. Jessica had the feeling, however, that had Stella been alive, she would have heartily shared all with Sally, her granddaughter.

Jessica could feel Stella's pain, and had caught a glimmer of how she must have felt. Two generations later, Jessica had walked out of her unhappy marriage, freed herself, and was starting over, options that would have been difficult to the point of impossible for Stella. The cost would have been too great.

In the charming room where the perfume of flowers always lingered, Jessica stood and gazed around at what had been Stella's studio, and, she suspected, a place where she'd spent a lot of time.

On the bookcase was a framed photo of Stella at her easel. Jessica picked it up and looked at it closely, comparing it with the more gracious and spacious room today. Its 1930s décor was definitely shabby chic – there was the chintz sofa, which Mollie had re-covered, a favourite chair and a rocker with an embroidered silk shawl flung across it. There was the old chest that was now in the attic, books, art supplies, paintings stacked up and hanging on the wall, including the one of the owl in the forest, which was still hanging in the same position. While all the art paraphernalia had been removed, the room still had a distinctive look and atmosphere. As Jessica stared at the old black-and-white picture, she noticed in a dark corner a collection of frames stacked against a chinoiserie-style cabinet.

'What're you doing?' Sally joined her.

'Admiring this old photo from Stella's time. I love this Chinese cabinet here. Now where is that these days?'

'I can't recall. I hadn't really noticed it. Hope we still have it. I don't think it was in the attic.'

'No, it wasn't. In the photo it's almost completely covered by all those heavy carved frames in front of it.'

'I'll ask Mum about it. She should know where it is now. Perhaps she stored more of Stella's things in it.'

*

As it was such a still and sunny day, they set up lunch in the arbour next to the rose garden, awaiting Dan and Terry James. Sally looked at Jessica, noticing she had gone to a bit more trouble than usual with her hair and make-up, even though it was subtle and natural looking.

Dan held the car door open as Terry climbed slowly out of the passenger seat and gasped as he looked around at the neat rows of trees on the hill, the tended paddocks and the front rose garden. 'You've done so much! It looks wonderful. What would Mum and Dad think! It's even more beautiful than I remember,' he said as Mollie gave him a teary hug. 'So many memories, eh, Mollie,' he said quietly.

'Yes. Weren't we lucky to grow up here?'

Jessica hugged Dan and they held hands as Sally gave Terry a warm welcome. When she introduced Katie, Terry handed her a gift, which she shyly thanked him for and promptly sat on the ground to open.

'Here's Toby,' Mollie said, introducing the two men. 'Hello, Dan, it's good to see you again. Come on, let's all go and sit down,' she added. 'Terry, you can go and freshen up if you like, not a lot has changed indoors.'

'You relax, Mum, Jess and I will bring out the food. Toby, can you do the drinks?' said Sally.

'Mummy, Mummy, Granny . . .' Katie came running. 'Look . . .'

'Oh my gosh, what have you there?' said Mollie as Katie climbed onto her lap. Mollie looked at Terry, tears in her eyes. 'Well I never . . . where did you find it?'

'Stumbled across it at a craft market on the weekend, just after Dan asked me if I'd like to come here. So I bought it for little Katie, thinking of you and Mrs H, Mollie,' Terry said.

'It's Nyx!' cried Katie, holding up the handmade knitted owl, who wore a jacket with jaunty feathers, and had wire spectacles on his beak and alert, glass eyes sewn on his white face.

'Terry, that's wonderful! How sweet of you,' said Sally.

After lunch Toby stood up and stretched. 'I have to get a few jobs done this afternoon. Will you come and help me, Katie?' She nodded and, hugging Nyx, walked over and took her dad's hand. 'We'll be back later for more of that cake you made, Mollie,' Toby added.

Sally smiled at them. 'Good girl, Katie. You're Dad's helper,' she said, and then turned to Terry. 'Do you remember the painting my grandmother did of some fronds and a purple flower among the mushrooms in the forest?'

'I do. And now we know that it's newly described. Denyse was very thrilled about it. They're very keen to see the whole collection, in case there might be something else,' said Terry.

'It's not just that it's a newly identified plant, but they're also interested in the place where it was growing and the fungi there,' said Sally.

Terry nodded. 'That'd be right. I hear there's a lot more investigation going on with fungi. Other people are getting on to it.'

'Yes, that's true. Terry, have you ever been to a place called Seawinds?' Dan asked.

'Not personally. I just heard about it from Mum.' He paused. 'The family who lived there was a bit difficult, according to my mother. Though Doc Holland kept in touch with them. These old colonial families have histories, of course. You knew Seawinds was a smuggler's den? Not sure when the family friction came about. Could go back to convict days. Those old families hold grudges,' said Terry.

'For generations,' added Mollie. 'My father talked about families not speaking to each other over incidents that went so far back they couldn't recall why or what had happened. Silly, isn't it?'

They were quiet for a while, enjoying the sunshine, then Mollie said, 'Terry, did my father ever talk about his first wife?' She surprised Sally with her directness.

'No. He never mentioned her that I recall,' Terry said gently. 'But as you know my mother was very close to your family for so long, very much a confidante. Almost one of the family in some ways, and everyone knew she would never gossip or reveal anything she was privy to in this house.' He paused. 'Though in later years she did share things with me, when I was looking after her and managing the place.'

'So what do you remember your mother telling you about Hilda?' prodded Jessica.

'Hilda Broadbent lived here at Arcadia with her parents. From what I remember Mum telling me, her brother Joseph lived at Seawinds. When Hilda and Dr H got married Dr H moved here, and he was the one who hired my mum as the housekeeper. Mum wouldn't have known Hilda's parents very well as they passed on not long after Dr H married Hilda. Apparently Hilda was never a strong type, always rather sickly,' he said. After a pause, he added, 'There was some issue over the two houses, I know that.'

'Which houses?' asked Mollie with a frown.

'The two properties owned by the Broadbent family: Seawinds and Arcadia.'

'We found out the other day that Hilda bequeathed Arcadia to Dr Holland,' said Jessica. 'It was owned by the Broadbents before that.'

'Indeed. And that caused some friction with Hilda's family, I believe,' Terry said.

Jessica and Sally exchanged glances.

'Mollie, where did your father live before he came here?' Jess asked.

'Oh, gosh, I don't know. His family were in Melbourne and he graduated from Melbourne Uni. That's all I recall.'

'Compared with Melbourne, Burridge must have been a bit of a backwater when he moved here in the 1920s,' said Sally.

'And it still is, relatively, thank goodness,' said Mollie. 'My father did some work in Hobart as well as setting up his practice here. That was where he met my mother. Anyway, what's this got to do with anything?'

'Well, as far as I know, Joseph Broadbent owned Seawinds, and when he died, it passed down to the two boys,' said Terry. 'Mum said the older one got married and had a son,' he added, 'but no one knows what happened to the other brother. Dr Holland kept in touch with their father Joseph in a vague way. Mum said they never visited here, but the doc and Mrs H visited Seawinds once or twice. Mind you, Mum said Mrs H didn't like Seawinds at all.'

'Oh, why was that?' Mollie asked.

'I don't know, but she came back rather rattled, I think was the word Mum used.'

'I can believe that, it seemed a creepy place . . .' said Jessica.

'That snippy lady who opened the door must be the wife of one of the brothers then,' said Sally. 'It's a lot to take in.'

'What do you think that Gordon Broadbent is up to?' said Mollie.

They all looked at Dan.

Dan explained as best he could. 'We can't prove anything yet, but it seems to me the family at Seawinds, the Broadbents, might have kept a finger in the pie here, and didn't want the Hollands to know that the fungi in the forest on this property could be valuable,' he said.

'You mean they're the ones who've been stealing them?' said Mollie. 'And our truffles!'

'I'd say they've been raiding the Arcadia forest for maybe two generations,' said Dan. 'They've set up quite a sophisticated processing plant at Seawinds. Way ahead of its time. Someone studied mycology or stumbled over the fungi here and the research has been brought forward into the twenty-first century.'

'What!' exclaimed Mollie. 'And neither my father nor mother knew? Did your mother know?' Mollie turned to Terry.

'I would say not, or she would have told me,' Terry said, and rubbed his eyes.

'We have to stop them!' exclaimed Jessica. 'It's not fair!'

'Let's take a break first,' said Mollie, shaking her head. 'My head is in a tailspin. And you probably need a rest, Terry.'

'Yes, I'm feeling tired. Perhaps too much thinking and talking for an old man like me.' He smiled.

Dan glanced at Jessica. 'I'd love to see the forest again before we drive back.'

'You're not going back this afternoon, are you? Stay for dinner, stay the night. There's a spare room in the house and another in the cottage,' said Mollie. 'You can see your old room there, Terry! It's been so special catching up. I'd love to talk more later,' she added.

'Yes, do,' said Sally. 'Mum's enjoying this. We all are. And Toby has been busy this afternoon, he'd love to sit down and chat with you over dinner.'

'Sounds good to me. Thank you, Mollie. What do you think, Terry?' said Dan.

'Well, if it's no trouble. And I wouldn't mind a bit of an afternoon nap.'

After Jessica and Dan had helped Terry to get settled they walked into the rose garden and Jess sat on the wooden seat, stretched her legs out, and smiled up at Dan.

'On the drive coming down, Terry told me how much it means to him to come here again. I'm so glad Mollie asked us to stay the night,' he said, sitting down beside her, their legs touching. Jessica felt the solid strength of his leg against hers, and wanted to lean against him, put her head on his shoulder, but she remained as she was.

'I think she probably has a lot more questions, but doesn't know what exactly to ask. I feel a bit the same, with dangling ends, shadows, unformed ideas,' said Jessica. 'Sally even more so. This is the first she's heard about this family history. And given the mysterious caller and the chase down the mountain, it's all a bit scary.'

'There's probably not a lot Sally and Toby can do about the trespassing. Except add extra security, maybe.'

'The horse has bolted, I'd say. They've taken the truffles and they've got all the fungi in the forest and are making a business out of it, legal or not.'

'The fungi will grow back, Jess, although I don't know how long it will take,' Dan said. 'If the Broadbents really have been stealing it over the decades then it must have always grown back again.'

'Yes, of course, thank goodness for that,' said Jessica.

'I had a bit of a search through the Patents Office and patents pending, but I didn't see anything that I recognised,' said Dan. 'Of course, it could be under any name or a company I've never heard of, which is so frustrating.'

'It's good of you to take the time,' said Jessica, touching his arm.

Dan took her hand and curled it in his. 'Oh, I feel I have a vested interest, in a way. I really want to know what research that guy is doing as it seems to be overlapping into my field,' he said. 'Also, Carmen asked me to look after you and Sally when you were on the island and I take my responsibilities seriously,' he added, laughing.

'Thanks. But we can look after ourselves,' Jessica said, smiling. 'Like I told you, we've always supported each other. Since we were kids,' she said more seriously.

'I can see that. But isn't it time you spread your wings? Sally has nested, come home to roost. You're still . . .'

'Don't say flapping around or I'll get up and leave!'

Dan threw up his arms, shielding himself in mock defence. 'Wouldn't dare! You're not a flapper. You're a fighter. I admire that.' He took her hand again.

'Oh.' She was a bit stumped for words. 'Thanks. Well, shall we walk down to the forest?'

He squeezed her hand and helped her to her feet.

They started out holding hands, but Dan kept dropping behind her, pausing to look at plants, the view, or take a photo.

'Dan, we're not even in the forest yet, it'll be dark by the time we get there.' Jessica laughed.

'There's something interesting everywhere you look. This is my idea of heaven.' He stopped as they came to the clearing, the deepest part of the forest across the oasis of waving grass and open air. The moment they entered the green gloom of the canopy of the old forest, Dan drew a long, deep breath. 'It is just so beautiful in here,' he said quietly. 'Thank you for bringing me here again. I just love places like this.'

'Me too. That's why knowing that someone came here and stole the mushrooms is so upsetting.' She hesitated. 'I can understand how a woman could fall in love in here, feel like a different person, believe that anything is possible . . .' Jessica stopped.

'Like what?' Dan prompted gently.

'That life can be better, we can have a safer, cleaner, healthier world, that somehow the answers are here, waiting for us to find them.' She shook her head. 'Oh, I sound silly. I just get so . . . overwhelmed in here. I wish politicians, the bureaucrats, greedy corporate business-people could quietly sit in here and learn what is truly important. It might help bring about some changes.' She straightened up. 'Wishful thinking, I know . . .' Suddenly Jessica spread her arms and called out in the silent forest, 'Hey, Prime Minister, bring all those people yapping in your ear in here and let them listen to the real story. The answers are all right before our eyes . . . money, power, position, luxuries, they mean nothing if we can't breathe clean air, drink pure water, eat healthy food, care for our families, love our land . . . know what matters . . .'

She collapsed on a log, and looked up at Dan with tears in her eyes. 'I suppose you think I'm nuts. But I feel as if I've just woken up, like Sleeping Beauty, and seen what's happening, but no one believes me.'

'I think you should be on national television.'

'*Pfff*,' she snorted. 'What do we do, Dan?' Jessica glanced around at the forest. 'Some of us can see our world being destroyed, and ask ourselves, what's our future? Do we just say, bugger it, eat drink and be merry, for tomorrow we die? Who the hell is listening?'

'I am,' Dan said. He leaned down, pulled her to her feet and held her close to him, rocking and hugging her. 'I hear you, Jess. I hear you.'

He lifted her face and kissed her. And kissed her again. And again. As Jessica, still anxious and resisting at first, finally dissolved into his arms, returning his kisses, over-whelmed to be acknowledged, to be understood. They were one. And somehow together they'd find their way home.

10

Arcadia, 1985

THE ROSES WERE NO longer. Stunted, dead-looking sticks in a cold and frost-covered bare bed. A desolate sight from her windows.

Stella wondered what the tropics must be like. Strange countries of blue lagoons, everlasting sun, balmy breezes. She recalled childhood memories of Melbourne, and being taken to the beach on the Mornington Peninsula. She'd been too scared to venture out of her depth as she couldn't swim, but she'd been astonished by the rich colours, and the sensuous seeping of sun and salt water swirling around her legs as she paddled. That was another life. A time of carefree childhood days never recaptured once she ventured southwards.

But she had grown to love Tasmania. Her body had

adapted to the seasons, the air, the mists and dampness, the ocean winds, the joyous sunny days of postcard perfection, and, best of all, the shiver of shock from slipping into the crystal-clear creek on a hot day, the water tingling against bare skin.

And clinging together, the warmth of two naked bodies melding into one another.

The thought brought a smile to her face. Like hearing a favourite melody on a gramophone, she played it over again.

Stella was feeling frailer these days and couldn't contemplate venturing as far as the forest. Her studio was her world, a place where more and more she kept thinking backwards rather than forward. Her dreams were vivid; she'd awake to another time and struggle to focus on the present. Daily life was a calm routine that flowed around her as Mollie and Graham picked up the reins at Arcadia, steering the property in a new direction, while she saw it all as it had been, when she'd been its mistress, if only in name.

Until Mollie and Graham had come and established Arcadia as a working farm, Stella had considered it her oasis. Stephen would leave the house every weekday and often even on Saturdays, to work in his surgery office in Burridge, and had travelled to Hobart regularly. Other than the cottage garden around the house and the cows' small paddock, Stephen had left the property almost untouched. The cows, along with a handful of chickens and lambs, had kept the grass down and added to their food supply. In the old apple orchards, trees had stooped under their fruit, which had been left to rot apart from the basketfuls Mrs James collected for her jams and preserves.

So the activity, energy and new ideas Mollie and Graham had brought with them, as well as Graham's day job as a school principal, had led Stella to decide to step aside. Since Stephen had passed away, she'd led a solitary life, allowing first the Jameses and then Mollie to handle all practical matters. Now Stella was slowing down. These past years since the excitement of her painting being exhibited at the Art Society show had begun to blend together.

'I've made you a cup of tea.' Mollie came into the studio and put a dainty cup on the side table. 'And there's some mail for you, and the paper. Would you like a biscuit, too?' Mollie glanced at Stella's thin frame.

'Oh, no, but the tea is lovely. Thank you. Are you having one?'

'Actually, I will. Be back in a jiffy.'

As Mollie left the room, Stella thought about the baby that was on the way, and smiled. Mollie and Graham's first child and another generation to live in Arcadia. It made her so happy to think about her family continuing to enjoy life here in this beautiful place, after she'd gone.

She sat down and glanced idly at the mail: a catalogue Mollie had ordered, the latest copy of *The Australian Women's Weekly*, a circular from the Art Society, and the local newspaper.

Mollie came back in carrying a steaming mug, and mother and daughter chatted as they sipped their tea. Mollie also noticed the roses. 'They look dreadful, really butchered. I'm not sure if that the new fellow helping on the farm has much of a clue about gardening.'

'Particularly pruning roses,' said Stella.

'I'll have a word to him. Are you okay, Mother? I'd better get back to work, but would you like anything? Do you need anything?'

'No, thank you, dear. I can get anything I need and I don't want you to overdo it. It's not long now till your baby arrives. Don't worry about me; I have some little jobs to do in here.'

'Right, well if you do want anything, ring the bell by the back door. See you later, Mum.' Mollie kissed her mother on the cheek and walked outside.

Carefully, Stella replaced the Royal Albert cup in its saucer. Reaching for the paper, she unfolded it, then turned the pages, not sure why she was even bothering. There wasn't much in the news that interested her these days. On page seven her eyes lingered on a short article about the death of a local man who'd left Tasmania to further his work as a scientist. Then Stella drew in a sharp breath and her hand flew to her mouth. It was about Thomas Broadbent – Tommy – who had 'recently died peacefully at his home in London. A well-respected scientist, he leaves behind a brother, sister-in-law and nephew in Tasmania but had no children of his own.'

Stella dropped the paper, putting her face in her hands, her shoulders shaking. A feeling of heaviness washed over her. It was news she had never wanted to hear.

She felt like a sylph lost in the shadows now that Mrs James had died, years after Stephen. Terry was off travelling, and Mollie and Graham were busy running Arcadia. Everyone fulfilled some purpose, had some value, contributed in their own way, she thought, except for her. She didn't agonise over missed opportunities or those she'd never taken; she had lived in her own world. She'd had that luxury, and she knew she'd been fortunate. But now . . . times were different. Women were assertive, they had a role to play and fight for. Mollie and Graham were equal partners. Mrs James had been rather forthright, too, even if her own opportunities in life had been limited. For a moment Stella allowed herself to wonder . . . what might her life have been like if she'd run away with her clever, adoring man? Would they have had a large family, been feted in his world, travelled? She forced herself to stop thinking. Arcadia was her world. She loved her painting, her visits with her owl . . . she was never meant to lead any other life.

She'd had a good life with Stephen. While their intimate encounters had brought her little pleasure, that was just how some men were, she told herself. They demanded, and women submitted. He had loved her and had only ever wanted her to be happy and to enjoy living at Arcadia.

Eventually Stella rose and closed the door that led to the kitchen. Then she sat down at her desk and took out a sheet of paper and an envelope from a drawer.

She wrote swiftly, before she changed her mind, before the thoughts of 'what might have been' swamped her.

My darling daughter,
As you await the birth of your first child I must share with you a truth that has long haunted me . . .

When she'd finished, she folded the letter, wrote *Mollie* on the envelope and sealed it. Then she sat back, deep in thought. What had happened to Tommy in the years before his death? In her small world she'd known little of his subsequent life. However, she had read about him in the newspaper a couple of times. The Broadbent brothers had been written about for their scientific achievements. Both were extremely intelligent, though one brother, the journalist had noted, was erratic and something of a wild genius with theories yet to be substantiated. The other, Thomas, resided in England, and worked in a top-secret government laboratory. There was no mention of their

345

personal lives, although much was made of the brothers from a backwater forging brilliant careers in obscure and differing scientific fields.

Stella stood up and slowly dragged the art table away from where it blocked her old Chinese cabinet. She moved a few frames and canvases aside, opened the lacquered doors and crouched down to pull out the bottom drawer. Groping to the back, she found a large brown envelope and drew it out. Stiffly she straightened up and placed the envelope on the table among her art materials.

It had been many years since she had looked at these papers.

Her birth and marriage certificates. A few letters from her parents, the last postcard from her brother before he was killed in the war, and a birthday card painted by her best friend Mollie, who died when she was only sixteen. The girls were so close that Stella named her baby after Mollie. Slowly she fingered these documents and thought of the old tin box that held other small mementoes so precious to her. No one would ever know where her heart truly lay from those small things she treasured most: gifts from him of flowers and leaves, a couple of photos, a note or two, and some of Tommy's papers and documents. She had given him a painting, a silver eggcup with Arcadia's crest engraved on it, a beautiful owl feather, and . . . her heart.

Sighing, she slipped her letter to her daughter into the big envelope, and stuffed it back into the drawer. She did not know when Mollie would find it, but her heart was at peace now that she had written the truth.

Stella felt completely drained and decided to lie down. Rather than nap on her sofa as she usually did, she went to her bedroom, each breath a clutching pain in her chest. She felt calmer as she stretched out on the bed, glancing at the window where a green bough rustled gently, its leaves waving softly to her.

When she awoke, she felt better. As if she'd taken a long trip and had now recovered her strength. Had she slept till dark? The room was dim.

'She's stirring. Mother . . .?'

Stella felt Mollie's hand take hers and stroke it gently.

'We're here, Mum, Graham and me, even our little baby,' Mollie said, and put her hand on her belly for a moment. 'And when he or she is born I will tell this child all about you. We love you so much . . .'

Mollie's voice was distant, fading, hard to hear in a rush of sudden wind and light.

And then, with a feeling of joy, Stella realised that here she was, lying on the grass in her forest, the warm sunlight blinding her as the trees leaned over her and then . . . Stella felt herself lifted, wrapped in soft feathers and borne up and up so fast into the light . . .

*

'She's gone.'

'Stay with her, Mollie. Sit beside your mother for as long as you feel you need. I'll bring you a cup of tea,' said Graham gently. 'There's no rush. Remember all your happy times.' He touched his wife's weeping face as Mollie leaned her head on her mother's still chest, her cheek resting on Stella's fine thin hands. Hands that had caressed her, led her to magical places, had painted pictures of their stories, smoothed her hair, adjusted her wedding veil and kissed her good night.

In the stillness of the night outside, the long, sad shriek of an owl echoed far into the forest.

Dan drove back to Hobart early in the morning and called Jessica after he'd dropped Terry home.

'Hey, how was the drive?' asked Jessica as she settled back to talk.

'Fine, thanks. It didn't take long. Jess, I just checked my emails and Denyse at the Seed Centre lab has some news about what's happening at Seawinds.'

'Really! What?'

'Remember how I told you the sample I took from there had some potentially interesting qualities? Well, turns out they're trialling some medicinal products at Seawinds – made from a very specific fungus. Broadbent submitted a research paper to a scientific journal that's published in Melbourne. Denyse said in her email that it was sent to a friend of hers for peer review and he's just started to read it, so they have a good idea of what Broadbent is doing at Seawinds. And Denyse is nearly sure now that the rare fungi Broadbent's using originally came from Arcadia.'

'How can we stop them?'

'Well, this could be a good thing – a product that is very beneficial for general health and wellbeing, not a specific disease . . .'

'But Broadbent stole the main ingredient! From here!' exclaimed Jessica.

'I know. It's a shame we can't prove conclusively that he took it from Arcadia. But maybe Sally and Toby should look into taking legal steps of some kind. Mention it to them, and we might be able to get more info from Denyse and her friend.'

'Okay, I will.' Jessica thought for a moment. 'What I find strange is that everything with this Broadbent character seems to have happened at once. He started calling Sally, stole the truffles and the mushrooms and followed us, all in the space of a couple of weeks,' said Jessica.

'You're right. I wonder what triggered it? How do you think he even got Sally's mobile number?' Dan asked.

'Oh, that's easy. It's on the Arcadia Farm website; or it was. Sally and Toby have taken it down. Knowing where we were was simple too, because Sally and I were posting photos of our road trip on Facebook. In fact, Sally posted a photo at the start of our trip so Katie could see it. She mentioned where we were going and what we were doing.'

'You'd never expect someone to pick up on that and start following you,' Dan said.

'No, not at all. It was just a fun selfie. But I'm pretty sure that's what started him calling Sally and then chasing us. It's so creepy.' She paused. 'You know that cigarette butt we found? Well, I bet it *was* him who went to the cave. The timing makes sense. He probably saw that we'd been there and had rummaged around a bit, and decided he needed to keep a closer eye on what was going on at Arcadia. That might have prompted him to look up Sally's Facebook page.'

'Could be,' Dan agreed. 'And this fungi research could mean big dollars. He'd be pretty paranoid about anything that could threaten it.'

'But if there's so much at stake for him, why would he risk getting so reckless? If he's been stealing from Arcadia without anyone knowing for years, why would he suddenly steal the truffles as well?'

There was silence down the line while Dan thought about it. 'Probably for the money. You said Toby and Sally made no secret of the fact that it looked like it would be a big crop,' he said. 'Broadbent must have worked out that he could make some money on the side to fund his work. He's obviously getting greedier and willing to take bigger risks.'

'Oh, this is all really unsettling, let's talk about something else,' said Jess. 'Actually, I have some news.'

'Oh, good news, I hope. You're not going back home?' His voice sounded anxious.

'Where's home?' She laughed. 'I can't keep camping here, much as I love it. No, I think I might have a lead on a job. I saw the ad online today and I've started to do some research. I wanted to talk to you about it.'

'Sure. Where is it? Who with?'

'It's an environmental consultancy firm, gets peanuts from the government, apparently, but has huge public and philanthropic support – it's based on the model of the American Schweitzer Fellowship Program, which was inspired by Albert Schweitzer. You've heard of him?'

'Of course, not too many of his ilk around these days, but his work lives on. Sean is a fan of Dr Schweitzer and the work the Schweitzer Institute does in Africa. What would you be doing?'

'Well, according to the job description I could be working in various places depending what projects the firm takes on – tackling land clearing, studying the effects of run-off and development affecting the Great Barrier Reef, that sort of thing. I'm keen on their programs to protect old-growth forests and prove how valuable they are.'

'Very different from what you were doing at the uni in Sydney. But with your passion and training, Dr Foster, I think you'd be the ideal candidate. No more white coats, microscopes and reports in a lab, eh?'

Jess laughed. 'I hope you're right. You know, being

here has really refocused me. And meeting you, and through you so many amazing people, has been inspiring. Thanks, Dan.'

'Have you talked about it with Sally and Toby?'

'Not yet. I wanted to discuss it with you first. I won't mention it to Mum and Dad till I've applied and know something definite. They do wonder how I'm managing, and where I'm going with my life. They asked me if I wanted some money last week, which was thoughtful of them.'

'When are you coming to Hobart again? We can have lunch, or dinner.'

'Well, if I get an interview I'll be up. Now, that's enough about me. How're things with you?'

*

Over lunch, when Jessica told the others about Denyse's email and Dan's suggestion of taking legal action, Sally said immediately, 'That's not a bad idea. That man has been trespassing and stealing.'

'I'm not too clear on the whole thing,' Mollie said. 'I mean, how do we prove that Broadbent was ever here on the property? I know it's a long shot, but it's possible that someone could have found the same mushrooms in another forest.' She shrugged. 'We need extra security to keep people out. You know, motion cameras, or something. And signs along the boundaries so that trespassers – Broadbent especially – know they'd be caught on camera if they tried to get in.'

'A letter from a solicitor warning him off would be cheaper,' said Toby.

'Well, let's think about it,' said Sally. 'I've had enough of this Gordon Broadbent scaring me and apparently

351

sneaking around Arcadia. I've been feeling sick to the stomach with the stress of it all.' Sally's face was drawn and tired.

Later in the day, Sally and Jessica found a quiet place and talked the idea through.

'Sal, I didn't want to worry your mum earlier, but I took Dan to the cave when he first came here,' said Jessica, 'and we found a cigarette butt. Someone had been there recently and my guess is that it was Broadbent.'

Sally looked aggrieved. 'Right, then. That's it. I'm making an appointment with the solicitor,' she declared.

*

The next evening Jessica danced into the sitting room waving a bottle of champagne as Toby poured himself a cold beer. 'I have bubbles. French ones. Would you prefer this? Where's Sally? And Mollie?'

'Mollie is cooking and Sal is giving Katie her bath. Are you celebrating something?' His voice sounded flat.

'Is everything okay?' Jessica looked concerned.

'Sorry, Jess, I don't want to put a dampener on things. Is it about your job?'

'Sort of. I rang them this morning and spoke to the manager. We talked for ages about the position and my experience. Well, she called back just now and asked me to come in for a formal interview with the bigwigs on Wednesday. It sounds promising,' she said as she opened the champagne.

'Hey, congratulations. That's great news. They're mad if they don't hire you.'

'I think mentioning Sean Hyland's name helped,' she said. 'The manager realised then that I had a good idea of what was going on internationally as well as in Tassie.'

'Here, let me.' Toby poured her a glass of champagne and tipped his beer into a tall glass for a change. 'Good luck. I think it's great you're starting on a whole new path, Jess.' He clinked his glass against hers.

Jessica eyed him over her glass as she took a sip. 'What's up, Toby?'

'Hmm. Sally sometimes says each of us can manifest things, that as soon as you think of something, someone else does too.'

'Yep, that might be true. Has someone beaten you to a great idea?' Jessica sat down in what she'd claimed as 'her' chair.

'Not exactly. It's a bit shocking really.' As Jessica raised her eyebrows, he pulled an envelope from his pocket and put it on the table.

Seeing the letterhead, she asked, 'You've been to a solicitor already?'

'Not us. Him. Broadbent has gone on the attack first.'

'You're joking! Saying what? Does Mollie know?'

'Yes, she's very upset.'

Jessica glanced at the letter and back at Toby. 'What does it say?'

'Basically the lawyer says that his client's instructed him that Hilda Holland's will was a forgery, possibly made by Stephen Holland, and Broadbent claims he can track down the real one, which apparently has Hilda leaving everything to the oldest surviving Broadbent.'

'What does that mean?' Jessica stammered.

'If his claim is true, then Gordon Broadbent would be the legal owner of Arcadia,' Toby said, rubbing his hand over his eyes.

'What! Surely that's not possible.'

Toby waved the letter. 'Well, we don't really know what

documents he's got to prove his claims but we have to take this seriously. The solicitor is only putting in the letter what his client has instructed him to say. He says Broadbent is "willing to negotiate to avoid costly court proceedings", but that he will start formal legal proceedings if he has to.'

'If he has to?' asked Jessica.

'The lawyer wants us to make Broadbent an offer. He says Broadbent is willing to be "reasonable" – ha! – and would be willing to come to some sort of arrangement for the division of Arcadia's land. We'll have to be prepared for whatever could happen next.'

Jessica shook her head distractedly. 'But if Broadbent is right and there is another will, why didn't he get hold of it and go to his lawyer years ago?'

'We don't know. Maybe he's only recently found out about it.'

'What does Mollie know about this?'

'Nothing. She's never heard of anyone questioning the authenticity of Hilda's will; it was long before she and her mum came on the scene. Now Mollie is not only scared and upset, but angry.'

'God, I'm not surprised. I might go and check she's okay.' Jessica hurried into the kitchen, where Mollie was standing at the stove, stirring something. 'Can I help, Mollie?'

'Dinner is under control,' Mollie said tightly.

Jessica reached out and touched her arm. 'Toby just told me about the solicitor's letter. It must be frightening, and of course it's a shock. But I'm sure it can't be right.'

'If this terrible claim is true, then I could have lost Arcadia years ago. Now Sally and Toby could lose it, but I won't let that happen.' Mollie's eyes had a dangerous spark. 'I want to know why Broadbent waited so long to bring this up. Do you think he's only just found something valuable in those mushrooms and now he wants permanent access to them?'

Jessica nodded. 'It does look that way. It strikes me as convenient that all of a sudden, just when we hear of trials at Seawinds of potentially very profitable medicinal products linked to Arcadia's mushrooms, Broadbent claims he's discovered a new will that'll give him ownership of the land.'

Sally came into the kitchen, red-eyed. 'I've put on a DVD for Katie. Just for half an hour while we have dinner. I need time to think. This is all really getting me down. I feel quite exhausted.'

Jessica took her arm. 'Oh, Sal. I'm sure this will come to nothing. It has to.'

'Thanks, Jess. I really can't believe it,' Sally said. 'And just when we were about to send him a letter about trespassing!'

Sitting around the dinner table, they barely touched their food. Sally opened the letter again and read it quietly, then pushed it away.

'When he talks of dividing up the land, I bet it's the forest he wants, not this house,' said Sally.

'Well, I'm not losing our home, or any part of the land,' said Mollie firmly.

Toby looked at her. 'Sally and I are seeing our solicitor tomorrow, Mollie. I called him after the letter arrived and made an urgent appointment. Can you please go through the paperwork, see if you can find your father's will and anything else that might be relevant?'

Mollie nodded. 'Of course. My father left everything in order. All the most important documents are with the family solicitor. It's only some of my mother's things that are stored here.'

Katie appeared at the door, clutching her owl toy, looking sleepy.

Sally scooped her up. 'You're ready for bed, sweetheart. Come on, Daddy and I will come and tuck you in.' She looked at Toby, who got to his feet.

'I'll start on the washing up,' said Mollie.

'Oh no, Mollie. Let me,' said Jessica, standing up.

'No, it's all right, Jess. I need some time alone to think.'

As Jessica sat down again, her phone rang. She was relieved when she saw it was Dan.

'You sound down in the dumps,' he said.

She quickly filled him in on the devastating news from Broadbent's solicitor. 'So, after coming here and stealing the truffles and the mushrooms and following Sally and me, he's made his next move,' she explained.

'I wonder if Terry would know anything more that could be useful? Maybe you and Sally should come up and see him?' Dan said. 'I can call him and set up a time. I do have an ulterior motive to get you up to Hobart, though – I miss you.'

'Really?' Jessica felt a warm rush and smiled to herself. 'I miss you too,' she said a bit shyly. 'But as it happens you might see me soon. I got an interview for that job, so I'll be up on Wednesday.'

'I knew you would!' said Dan. 'Congratulations. I'm sure you'll be brilliant.'

'Gosh, I hope so,' Jessica replied. 'Listen, I'd better go. I'll talk to Sally about Terry. Thanks for all your help.'

'Sending you all a big hug.'

'Thanks, Dan. And one back to you.'

'I'll collect it when I see you on Wednesday.'

*

Mollie picked up the mail from the box at the front gate when she and Jasper, who was well on the way to recovering from his ordeal during the truffle theft, went for their mid-morning walk. She shuffled through the bills and the junk mail, and then stopped as she came to an envelope that was addressed in unfamiliar scrawled handwriting. There was no stamp. She paused and something made her rip it open then and there.

I know what went on in your family. Your father murdered my great-aunt Hilda, then forged her will to get Arcadia. Your family has been doing my family over for generations. Now I want that land and it's rightfully mine. And I'll get it.

Mollie started to shake with shock, then hurried indoors. She was still sitting quietly in the kitchen, her head in her hands, when Sally and Toby returned from seeing their solicitor.

'Hey, Mum, what's up?' asked Sally. 'You look like you've seen a ghost.'

Silently Mollie handed Sally the letter. 'This was in the mailbox,' she managed.

Sally read the note and sat down heavily. 'Oh my God. I'll make us a pot of tea.' She gave the letter to Toby, who read it and shook his head.

'It's horrible, just horrible,' said Mollie. 'Why would he even say that about my father? It's not true, so he can't prove anything.'

'Mum, I don't believe it either, but you weren't born then, so it's hard to know what went on in Grandad's first marriage,' said Sally gently.

'You're right, I don't know anything about their

marriage, but I knew my father. He was dedicated to *saving* lives! He would never have done what this man is suggesting. Broadbent is really scraping the bottom of the barrel with this. He must be very, very keen to grab our land,' said Mollie bitterly.

'Seems that way,' said Toby. 'He's getting desperate, and his behaviour is spiralling out of control. I think he might be a bit unhinged. In a way, this note is useful evidence of that.'

'I need some fresh air,' said Mollie. 'Don't worry about tea for me, love. I'm going out to the garden for a while.' She pushed back her chair and went out the back door.

'I wanted to tell her what the solicitor had to say,' sighed Sally.

'Let her cool down first. That's a shocking thing to read,' said Toby, pushing the note away from him.

'Oh, hello, you're back,' said Jessica as she joined them, then stopped short when she saw their faces. 'What's up?'

'Mum found this in the letterbox this morning.' Sally handed her the note and Jessica skimmed it.

'No way! This is outrageous. Really nasty. What a horrible man.' She dropped the note as though it were burning her fingers. 'Ugh. Poor Mollie. So did your solicitor have any good news?' Jessica asked.

'He took a very balanced approach,' said Sally. 'He explained that the lawyer's letter doesn't mean formal legal proceedings are underway, and that's good. He said Broadbent is probably just trying to intimidate us to force us to negotiate: court cases cost a fortune, and a lot of people choose to settle and compromise, even if they're in the right, because it's cheaper that way. Our lawyer reckons that's what Broadbent is hoping we'll do.

Informally he said that if it went further, we could consider trying to negotiate to relinquish part of the property, the forest and surrounding area, which is a big piece of land. I can't even bear the thought of that, though.' Sally paused, looking wretched. 'This whole thing is making me feel sick,' she added. 'Poor Mum.'

'She'll come out fighting, you know her. But it's a huge shock. Dan suggested we see what Terry has to say, and after reading that note, I think it's even more important that we talk to him again,' said Jessica quietly. 'He might know something. Why don't you come up with me when I go for my interview and we'll see him together? Dan can set up a meeting.'

'Yes, that's a good idea,' said Sally slowly. 'Maybe Terry knows more than he originally let on. I'll look for documents up in the attic again, too, but I don't think I'll find anything new.'

'Perhaps Stella had her own hiding place for her most important papers. She might even have something about Stephen and Hilda.'

'I'm not going back to that cave!'

'No, there's nothing left there anyway. What about the bedroom I'm using?'

'I don't think so. If there was anything in this house, I think Mum would have found it when she redecorated.'

'Why don't we have another look in Stella's studio. You never know,' suggested Jessica.

'I'm sure it's all been gone through, but I guess it won't hurt.' Sally sighed as she followed Jessica down the hall.

They stood in the doorway of the studio, which was now the comfortable sitting room.

'I'm trying to look at it through my grandmother's eyes,' said Sally. 'Mum said she spent most of her time in here.'

Jessica looked about the room. 'Did you find out where that Chinese cabinet we saw in the photo is?'

'Oh, yes. Mum said it's in the visitor's room in her place. We can go and look now,' said Sally.

They made their way over to the cottage and opened the double doors leading into the guest room.

'There it is,' Jessica said with satisfaction, and walked over to it. Sally stood next to her as Jess opened the cabinet and pulled out each of the three drawers. 'Now, what's in this bottom drawer . . . paintbrushes. A palette . . . and something back here.' Reaching right to the back, she drew out a brown envelope. 'What's in here?' Jessica sat back on her heels. 'Leaves, dried roses. A receipt from the art supply shop . . . what's this?' It was a small sealed white envelope. She handed it to Sally and stood up.

'It's addressed to Mum. I'd better give it to her to open,' Sally said, and put the smaller envelope back into the large brown one. They searched the rest of the cabinet but came up empty-handed.

'Well, that little search didn't lead to much,' Jessica said as they walked back to the main house.

'Let's hear what Terry has to say, and then our lawyer will tackle Broadbent's solicitor. I don't want to see that man Broadbent in person, he's too scary, and after that letter, I think he's unstable,' said Sally. She put the brown envelope in the farm office and the two women walked into the kitchen, where Toby was sitting at the table with his laptop.

'We didn't find anything, unfortunately,' she told him. 'Just something addressed to Mum – could be anything, though.'

Toby rubbed his eyes. 'Man, this is a nightmare. Maybe the trip to Hobart and seeing Terry will help.

I hope all this isn't distracting you too much from your interview for that job, Jess.'

'Thanks, Toby. It's not exactly like a school exam! I can only be honest and say what I think and feel,' said Jessica.

But Jessica was nonetheless nervous as she packed a small bag after considering what to wear to her interview. Toby and Sally had decided they would drive up with her so they could all meet with Terry, and Jessica was glad of the company. However she thought she should give her friends some space, so she arranged to stay with Carmen rather than at the hotel they'd booked.

Mollie insisted on remaining behind with Katie. 'I'll be fine here,' she assured them. 'The pickers are all still here working, after all, so there are plenty of people about. Ask Terry if he wants to come back with you, or come again soon with Dan,' she added. 'And good luck, Jess!'

*

Toby and Sally dropped Jessica at Carmen's house and arranged to meet her at the Botanical Gardens the next day.

Carmen embraced Jessica. 'Good to see you, and I'm so sorry to hear about Sally's problems. Dan said Sally's mother received some sort of threatening letter and a solicitor is contesting a will from generations ago. Sounds mad to me, but her mother must be distraught. Why is this man causing such trouble?'

'We're not sure. It's a long story that goes back to Sally's grandfather's day. It's terrible how things can come back to haunt you decades later.'

Carmen shook her head in concern. 'Come and sit down, take your mind off it by telling me about this job. Where would you be working?'

'Out in the field a lot; depends what issue the agency

is dealing with, whether it's ocean, land or forest. I could move anywhere, really, though I think initially the project they're working on is here in Tassie.'

'From what you told me over the phone, it sounds like a cross between the CSIRO, Greenpeace and the Department of the Environment,' said Carmen. 'Well, whether you'd be doing research or promotion of their work, your passion will shine through. I'm sure they'll see that too. Now, Sean and I have a function to attend tonight, but you're welcome to hang out here and make yourself some dinner.'

'Actually, I'm going to dinner with Dan, but thank you. Seeing him will distract me from the interview tomorrow – and this terrible business at Arcadia,' said Jessica.

*

Dan hugged her tightly after Jessica opened the door, then kissed her.

Jessica drew a breath and laughed as they pulled apart. 'Wow, anyone would think we hadn't seen each other in years!'

He smiled and took her hand. 'It feels like years.'

'Thanks for offering dinner. I don't want to make it a late night, though, my interview is first thing in the morning.'

'Grab your coat then, and let's go.'

As they stepped outside into the twilight, Dan asked, 'How are you feeling about tomorrow?'

'Well, I've got this far, so I don't know what else I can do but answer as honestly as I can. If I get this job it'll be good for me to get back into the real world and start working again.'

His grip tightened on her hand as they walked down the road towards the waterfront. 'Time out is useful sometimes.'

'You're right, and I can never thank Sally and the family enough for putting up with me. But now I feel ready to get on with my life.'

'That's good, but I was going to suggest a little more time out. Once you've finished all your business tomorrow and seen Terry, that is,' said Dan.

'Oh yes? I'm sure that can be arranged,' said Jessica, laughing.

'I was hoping to come down to Arcadia again, and wanted to ask if you'd like to travel with me.'

'Sure. Of course.' She leaned her head against his shoulder. 'So where are we having dinner? I love the waterfront.'

'Follow me, I want you to see something before it gets dark.'

They walked along the cobblestones, past the convict-built warehouses where lights from surrounding buildings were glimmering on the calm harbour waters, past jetties and moorings where rigging lights twinkled and metal stays jingled as boats bobbed on the night-time sea. Cabin lights glowed, there was an occasional burst of laughter, and the smell of food drifted across the air as the small community of seafarers settled for the evening.

Dan stopped. 'What do you think?'

'It's lovely. Such a pretty setting. So romantic.'

He leaned over and kissed her. 'Good, glad you approve of her.'

'Huh? Who?' said Jessica.

Dan pointed. 'The *Lady Jane*, over there.'

Jessica looked again, and saw that he was pointing at a tidy sloop of burnished teak and fresh white paint. Below the cockpit, portholes looked out from what appeared to be a comfortable interior.

'That sloop?'

'Uh-huh, she's an Arthur Robb thirty-five-footer, well, a bit over ten metres, a Sloop Classic Yacht, late 1960s, but in good nick,' said Dan proudly. 'Four berths, lots of space. She's raced in the Sydney to Hobart. But easy to sail solo.'

'And she's yours?' said Jessica incredulously, turning to look at Dan.

Dan grinned. 'Once I worked out I'd be spending more and more time in Hobart working on the projects here, I decided to start looking for a boat I could live on. The *Lady Jane* came up for sale and I settled last week. I thought we could sail back to Arcadia. Well, to Burridge.'

'You're joking! I mean, that's amazing. How fabulous! Of course. Oh, wow!'

Dan chuckled. 'The weather is looking good, so if we leave after lunch, when you're finished with Terry, we can moor somewhere for the night and get to Burridge in time for morning tea.'

'So we're not going out to dinner, after all? Are you sleeping on board tonight?'

'No. Much as I'd like to invite you on board this evening, she's not quite fitted out yet. But by lunchtime tomorrow she'll be all shipshape, provisioned, and ready to go. I hoped you'd agree.'

Jessica threw her arms around him and kissed him. 'That's so romantic. You know I love to sail.'

'C'mon, let's go eat. There's a great little seafood place up here.'

Holding hands, they wandered away from the water-front to a small taverna.

*

Jessica walked slowly out of the building, putting on her sunglasses in the glare of the mid-morning sun.

The past hour had gone by in a blur as she'd jumped through the hoops of the interview process in front of the panel of four charged with making a decision about her prospects. She'd dressed carefully, pulling her hair back into a neat knot, and keeping her make-up subtle. The interview had been wide-ranging, covering everything from a mock media interview to her feedback on a promotional video and her views on climate change and energy. While not canvassing her political views, she was asked penetrating questions on how to influence government bodies, where she thought changes needed to be made, how she saw the future prospects for specific environments, habitats and wildlife. Finally they'd asked her why she wanted this job.

She hoped she'd made a good impression and that they'd seen her passion and heart as she'd talked about how Tasmania had changed her.

As Jessica walked into the sunshine she had no idea how she had fared, but she thanked her lucky stars that she'd met Dan, Carmen and Sean Hyland, and that she knew good people like Toby and Mollie. Above all, she thought about how lucky she was to have Sally as her dearest friend.

Well, it was done, and she could only be patient now and wait to hear from them. It was time to move forward to the next step on her journey, she told herself.

She met Sally and Toby for a quick lunch at the

Botanical Gardens, then Dan joined them and they went to meet Terry.

He was sitting at a table in the sun, at the rear of the conservatory, his eyes closed, his white hair shining in the warm sunlight.

Dan tapped him on the shoulder. 'Visitors, mate.'

'Aha! How lovely!' Terry smiled.

'Don't get up, we'll squeeze in around you,' said Sally.

'Fine, fine. Where's your mum?'

'Holding the fort, looking after Katie. Who sends you a kiss, by the way. She loves that owl you gave her.'

'We're in town on errands, and Jess went for a job interview,' said Toby.

And as Terry gave her a questioning look and a raised thumb, Jessica replied, 'No idea yet, but fingers crossed, Terry.'

Dan leaned forward, cutting to the chase. 'Okay. I've told you about the solicitor's letter, Terry, and then the threatening note from Gordon Broadbent, and, well, we wondered if you knew anything about Stephen and Hilda Holland that could be helpful,' he said.

'So what do you think, Terry?' asked Sally anxiously. 'About my grandfather? Mum said he would never have hurt anyone. Do you know anything about that time when he was married to Hilda? Did your mother ever talk about it, or mention anything, perhaps . . .?'

Terry paused, looking down at his hands. 'Dr Holland was a good doctor. I remember him in that polio time when I was a kid. He saved a lot of lives. My parents respected him.' He paused, then looked up at them. 'In her last years, Mum and I had a lot of talks. And she sat me down and told me things she felt I should know. She told me that Hilda had always been delicate, and in the

366

end she was very sick, maybe it was cancer, they never said. But she suffered for a long time and towards the end, back in those days, there wasn't a lot that could be done for her. Mum said Doc Holland adored her and couldn't bear to see her in such awful pain. So he, well –' Terry took a deep breath '– he made it easier for her. At the very end, Mum said the first Mrs Holland's suffering was really terrible, so Dr Holland got some medicine to ease her pain and, well, help her go, if you get my drift.'

'He euthanased her?' said Toby quietly.

'He let her die in peace,' said Terry firmly. 'Mum said she passed with a smile and holding his hand.'

'Your mother was present?' asked Dan softly.

'The doc asked her to be there, apparently. Asked her to witness it, like. Only my mother and the doc knew what happened. Mum didn't tell anyone apart from me and Mrs H – Stella, that is – after the doc himself passed. It would be impossible to prove.' He paused. 'Mum told me all about it but she made me swear first that I wouldn't mention it to anyone outside of the Holland family. She wanted me to know so that one day, if someone ever told your mother, Sally, like Broadbent has done, then I could fill her in on the actual situation.'

'So, my grandfather helped the woman he loved to die. That is so sad,' said Sally.

'My mother thought about writing it all down as a record to protect Dr Holland's name, but she soon realised that could be used against him. So she told me instead,' Terry said. 'I hope it's all right that I've told you.'

Jessica took his hand as the old man fell silent. Finally he looked up and said, 'I don't believe anything about a forged will, Sally. Dr Holland didn't help his wife to die because he wanted the land.'

'Do you have any idea why Gordon Broadbent would be bringing all of this up now, after all this time?' asked Jessica.

Terry shrugged. 'Mum told me old Mr Broadbent stayed in touch with your grandfather, but that his son John always hated the Hollands, both Stella and the doc. He never stopped believing that Arcadia should have been his. I think Joseph, their old man, kept John in line while he was alive, and maybe his brother, Thomas, did too. Don't know why John's son would bring all this up now, though. He'd be in his sixties himself, I reckon. Seems very strange.'

'We believe it's because of the rare fungi and the value of the old forest on Arcadia,' said Sally. 'Gordon Broadbent's been stealing from Arcadia and manufacturing something with the rare mushrooms. He's probably been doing it for years but maybe his research is cranking up and he's ready to start manufacturing products, if he can.'

'Hmm. He's supposed to be pretty clever. His father and uncle certainly were. Mum read about them in the paper a few times.'

'You've been a huge help, Terry,' said Jessica. 'Thank you.'

'You're like part of the family,' said Sally, reaching over to squeeze his other hand. 'Mum said she'd love to see you again. Come down any time.'

'Thank you, pet,' said Terry, suddenly misty-eyed. 'Arcadia always felt like home for my brothers and sisters and me. Mum and Dad felt the same way. Your grandmother was very good to my mum, let her stay on at the cottage,' he said.

Sally smiled and Jessica added, 'Yep, they're a special

family all right. They belong at Arcadia.'

They all sat quietly for a moment, taking in everything they'd just heard, until Dan glanced at his watch. 'I think we might have to make a move. Jess and I are heading back to Arcadia.'

'Sailing back!' exclaimed Jessica, clapping her hands. 'In Dan's sloop, the *Lady Jane*.'

'What? Dan, you devil, how fabulous!' cried Sally.

'We need to reach a cove I know before it gets dark, to moor for the night. We'll lob into Burridge in time for morning tea,' Dan said, smiling.

Toby grinned. 'We'll be there to meet you, mate, as arranged.'

'So you knew all about this, Toby?' Sally said, laughing. 'Katie will be so excited. She loves boats.'

They all gathered their things and stood up. Sally gave Terry a hug. 'I can't thank you enough for sharing this,' she said.

'It's all thanks to my mum really,' Terry said. 'Tell Mollie I'll take her up on the offer to visit in a week or so. Thank you.'

*

When the four of them were heading back to the main gates of the Gardens, Sally shook her head. 'I'm still trying to process all this. The Jameses really were like family for my grandparents. It's good we've connected with Terry.'

'Hearing what Mrs James told Terry is reassuring, but it won't stop Broadbent from making trouble,' said Toby. 'He could still say that Stephen Holland killed his wife, forged a will, and he might carry through with his threat of trying to prove it. And maybe he really does have a legal document saying that Arcadia should have gone to the oldest living Broadbent, which is him.'

They walked past the coolly beautiful fernery, mist spraying onto the path from the ferns and waterfall. Jessica was deep in thought, holding Dan's hand. Then she stopped.

'Sal . . . I'm thinking. The notes we found, the photos . . . of, you know, Stella and the Adonis . . .'

'You mean, Thomas Adonis! Poor Thomas. Who was actually brilliant Thomas Broadbent?' said Sally.

'The note she left for him . . . *I have to stop seeing you* . . .'

'What are you talking about?' asked Dan.

Sally stared at Jessica, her meaning suddenly hitting her. 'My grandmother told Thomas she couldn't see him any more, and broke off their relationship. Do you remember the date on that letter? It was 1949. Mum was born in 1950. My grandpa and his first wife didn't have any children, and my grandparents were married for over fifteen years before Mum came along.'

Toby stared at them. 'You mean Mollie's father could have been Thomas Broadbent, not Dr Holland?'

'Crikey! Does Mollie have any idea?' asked Dan. 'And did Thomas know, I wonder?'

'I've only just thought of it, and we don't think Mollie knows about Stella's relationship, so I think it's pretty unlikely that anyone knows,' said Jessica.

'But if it were true, it would make Mollie the oldest living Broadbent,' exclaimed Toby. 'She's about ten years older than Gordon. A DNA test would prove it, if it came to that.' He turned to Sally. 'It would make you a Broadbent too,' he said gently.

Sally stopped in her tracks. 'Wow, of course,' she stuttered. 'It's a lot to take in.'

370

'Mrs James might have had an idea about it,' said Jessica. 'She seems to have been the family confidante.'

'Should you ask Terry?' said Dan.

'No, not today. He looked pretty exhausted and emotional after talking about his mother,' said Jessica.

'Mum certainly doesn't know,' Sally said firmly. 'She would have told me. When I was pregnant with Katie I asked her a bit about our family history,' she added.

'Are you sure about this? About Stella and Thomas?' asked Toby.

'No, I guess we can't be absolutely sure without a DNA test that shows that Mum and I are related to Gordon Broadbent,' said Sally with a shudder. 'But if we raise the issue, it might be enough to get Broadbent to back down. It might be a risk he's not willing to take,' she added. 'For me the hardest part is, how do I tell Mum?'

'Take your time, Sal, and you guys should talk it over first,' said Jessica to Sally and Toby. Then she paused. 'Hang on, what about that envelope we found addressed to your mum? Did you give it to her?'

Sally started. 'I got distracted getting ready to come to Hobart and forgot! I'll give it to her as soon as we get home. Maybe it'll contain some answers.'

'Do you know what happened to Thomas?' asked Dan.

'No. That's a story to look into another day,' said Sally. 'Finding the right moment to tell Mum about all this is more of a priority, I think. I wish I could be completely sure before I talk to her, though. She's had so many shocks this week already.'

'Like I say, you don't need to rush into it. Give it some thought.' Jessica hugged Sally. 'See you tomorrow.'

*

Jessica woke, momentarily disoriented, but then in a rush of warmth she smiled, realising where she was – wrapped in Dan's arms.

The berth was snug, and they'd fallen asleep in each other's arms, limbs entwined, their lovemaking as wonderful as Jessica had ever dreamed it could be.

In the deserted cove, sheltered by rocky cliffs, the *Lady Jane* rocked gently in the moonlight, the sea moving slowly, as if breathing.

By the time they berthed upriver at Burridge the following morning, Jessica was becoming familiar with the quirks of the *Lady Jane*, and she just knew this lovely old boat would be part of her life from now on. As would Dan.

As she stood at the wheel, a breeze lifted a strand of her hair, and Dan leaned over and kissed her neck.

'I'm glad you and *Lady Jane* get on,' he said, and smiled. 'Could you stand sharing your life with me and a boat, wherever jobs take us?'

'I'll give it a shot,' said Jessica. A great welling feeling of peace and joy and love for this man beside her brought tears to her eyes, and she couldn't speak. So she lifted her face to the breeze and looked instead to the horizon.

*

As they nudged into the dock at Burridge to secure *Lady Jane*, a small figure raced down the path to the wharf, waving to them.

'It's Katie,' said Jessica. 'With Nyx. Gosh, she loves that bird. Such a find by Terry.'

'There's Toby and Sally right behind her. Maybe a milkshake is in order.'

'For you? Or Katie?'

As Dan lifted Katie up onto his shoulders and walked ahead with Toby, Sally looked at Jessica. 'How was it? The sailing, I mean.' She gave a knowing smile.

Jessica laughed. 'Don't be wicked. Or pry. All I can say is . . . I couldn't be happier.' Her voice caught and Sally put her arm around her friend's waist and hugged her.

'Me too. I'm really happy for you, Jess. Dan's so the right man for you,' Sally said.

'Thanks, Sal. Have you talked to your mum yet?'

'Not yet. I'm going to find the right time today, and give her that envelope, too,' she said. 'Then I feel like driving up there and bashing on Seawinds' door and telling the Broadbent guy off, no matter how scary he is.'

'What a great idea. But you'd better talk to the lawyer first.'

'And to Mum, I suppose. I emailed Broadbent's letter to our solicitor, so he has a good idea of the type of person we're dealing with. And I'll have to update him with this theory about Thomas Broadbent, once I've spoken to mum.'

Atop Dan's shoulders, Katie turned around and shouted to the two friends. 'Mummy, we're going for milkshakes, come on!'

*

In the lazy light of a spring afternoon, Mollie knelt by the garden bed where she'd been weeding. Pulling off her gardening gloves she stood up and patted Jasper just as Sally came along the path from the farm office.

'Hello darling. You look tired! Shall I stop and we'll have a cuppa?'

'We had the same idea. Jess is putting on the kettle. She came with Dan in his beautiful old boat. Wait till you see it.'

'Oh, sounds very romantic. So is there something happening between those two? I hope so, Dan seems a lovely man.'

'Looks like it. Jessica is very starry-eyed. They're well suited.'

Mollie grinned. 'You've been a good friend to her, Sal.'

'You and Toby have been a big support for her too.'

'If Jess is sailing off into the sunset with Dan, we'll miss her. But she knows this is her second home,' said Mollie as they turned and headed along the white gravel path towards the kitchen, Jasper trotting at Mollie's heel.

'Mum, let's sit here a minute.' Sally pointed to the old garden seat.

Mollie gave her a look, and sat down.

'The sun is nice,' said Sally.

'So?' Mollie's eyes narrowed. 'What's up? What's happening? I know you. Tell me. Is it something you learned from Terry that you haven't told me about?'

'Yes, but first – I found this.' Sally handed her mother the white envelope with her name written on it in beautiful handwriting.

Mollie looked at her daughter, tears springing to her eyes. 'It's from Mother,' she said softly.

'I thought it might be. I'm not sure what it's about, but I have an idea. Read it while we're on our own.'

Mollie slowly opened the letter, looking curious and apprehensive all at once.

When she finished reading she was silent, her face white. She passed it to Sally while staring straight ahead.

My darling daughter,

As you await the birth of your first child I must share with you a truth that has long haunted me, and that is the circumstances of your own birth. Please don't think badly of me, for I loved the man I married . . . he was my anchor, my shelter, my rock. But understanding what real love really means is like comparing our quiet creek with a surging waterfall and an Amazonian river. Until you discover it, you don't know the worlds apart they can be. I was young and innocent, but I make no excuses for what happened; after I married Stephen I met a man I believe destiny had always intended for me. We loved each other in secret, a love we thought had never been known before by any other. When I was with Thomas I was in another world, undreamed of, unimagined, grasped moments never to be forgotten. Nor shared by any other. And then I found I was expecting you. A gift I never expected after so many childless years. Tommy, your true father, wanted you to be with us more than anything. His joy as he kissed my belly, singing to you, I will never forget.

My dearest Mollie, sometimes in life one has to make choices and decisions that are not what you wish. To Tommy, it was simple. He wanted me to leave Arcadia, and all it meant, to abandon a man who had done no wrong, and to grasp the joy of sharing our life with each other and our child. He was a brilliant man, but not a practical man, and while I would have lived in a grass hut or an igloo with him, I thought of Stephen and of you. Tommy and I might have provided a loving home for you with parents who passionately adored each other, but always there would have been the shadow . . . of punishing a man for no reason, of depriving you of your rightful heritage. Arcadia is my home, and yours, and your child's. Would you grow up and learn the truth and hate us, no matter what your circumstances? I tortured myself for years but the decision was made for me. Tommy saw and understood my dilemma . . . he wanted the very best life for you and decided he could not give it. He gave me one last chance to go with him. I had to tell him I could never see him again . . . and so I walked away.

I don't know if Stephen knew; if he ever suspected anything he didn't let on, and he loved you as much as any father has ever loved a child. It comforted me to watch the bond between you and Stephen, and in the end, I hope you accept I made the right choice.

Thomas Broadbent was a good man, he had his own difficulties with his family, but he only ever wanted the best for you, which I believe has come to pass.

Forgive me withholding this from you. It is your decision to share this with your husband and your child, or not when the time comes. Perhaps when you become a mother you may feel differently. Forgive me. You were born of love and I have loved you all my life. May your child, perhaps your daughter, love and admire you as I do, dearest Mollie mine.

Your loving mother
Stella Holland
May 5th 1985

*

Through the kitchen window Jessica watched the mother and daughter, then turned away and took five teacups down from the cupboard.

Toby and Dan came into the kitchen, followed by Katie.

'Thanks for getting the tea ready. What's happening? Where're Sal and Mollie?' asked Toby as he settled Katie at her own small table and she opened her box of coloured pencils.

Jessica nodded at the window. 'In the garden. Sally is giving her the old letter we found. Let's hope it throws some light on this whole situation.'

They all glanced outside, then Jessica poured the tea as Dan and Toby sat quietly at the table.

Sally came inside and joined them.

'How is she?' Toby took Sally's hand.

'She'll be okay. She needs a few moments. I can't quite believe it, but that letter *was* from Stella, and she said that Thomas was Mollie's father. Stella wrote in the letter that she always loved Tommy, as she must have called him, but that she loved Stephen, too, in her own way, and that Mollie should know that Stephen was a good man who loved Mollie with all his heart, and that Stella was at peace with her choice to spend her life with Stephen rather than Thomas.

'It's a shock, of course, and Mum couldn't speak for a few minutes after reading it. Such a lot to take in. She was mad at Stella at first. She can't quite cope with the idea she could be a member of the same family as her "enemies". And she feels sorry for her father. Well, for Stephen Holland.'

They sat drinking their tea as Mollie walked in, looking red-eyed, her face set in a grim expression, and sat down. Wordlessly, Jessica poured her a cup of tea and passed it to her.

'I might be needing something stronger,' said Mollie.

She straightened up. 'Okay, tell me everything you know. I don't want to have any more secrets in this family, now or from the past.'

It took a long time, but they went through every detail of what they'd found out since first finding the tin in the cave, and on their travels, and finally explained what Mrs James had told Terry about Hilda Holland's death.

Mollie dabbed at her eyes with a tissue. 'I never for one moment thought my father, my father . . .' Her voice faltered for a moment. 'That Stephen Holland would ever do anything wrong. He cared for all his patients. And Hilda was his wife . . . Of course he didn't want to see her suffer. But to use that as a threat, to accuse someone of murder, and of forging a will! I'm just hanging on to the idea that the other brother, Thomas, who took off, was a bit more decent. Mum must have seen something good in him. But there's no way that family's getting their hands on this place.'

'Mollie, based on what Terry said, Stephen loved his first wife, Hilda, and cared for her right up until her death,' said Toby. 'I don't believe that this other "real will" exists. And even if it does, surely Stella's letter confirms that you are the oldest living Broadbent, and we can prove it if we have to. Broadbent loses either way.'

Mollie was thoughtful. 'There was that terrible drawing we found in my mother's sketchbook,' she said. 'John Broadbent must have done it, trying to scare her off "his" land. They've been stealing from us, threatening us, for decades. My poor mother, carrying that secret for so long.'

'Mum, we'll show you everything we found in the cave another time,' said Sally. 'And we can find out more about Thomas Broadbent too, if you want to.'

Mollie straightened up and said firmly, 'Stephen

Holland will always be my father in my mind. From what you've said, Joseph Broadbent knew how my father had cared for his sister all those years. It sounds like his son John was greedy, mean and selfish, and so is John's son, Gordon.' Mollie dropped her face in her hands. 'This is so overwhelming.' But then she looked up. 'I wonder if Mrs James knew, about my mother and Thomas?'

'Quite possibly. But she was very loyal. Like Terry. She protected this family,' said Sally.

'She certainly sounds like a kind, decent person,' said Dan.

'She was like a mother or a granny to everyone. And she had a big family. Terry must be the only one left now. Other than his siblings' offspring.' Mollie sighed. 'Families. Funny things. I'm so glad Terry and I have made contact again. He's part of Arcadia too.'

'Arcadia is a very embracing place,' said Jessica.

'I think that's because of the forest. It's such a special world down there. Katie loves it, just as you girls did. Now that she's seen it she wants to go there all the time!' Mollie smiled.

'Who's coming to our forest?' asked Katie, looking up from her colouring book.

Sally laughed. 'Come over here, sweetie, and give Mummy a hug.'

'I know it's a lot to deal with, Mollie, but it means you don't need to worry about losing this place now,' said Jessica.

Mollie sighed. 'Thank you for helping us with this horrible mess, Jess. I might just pay a personal visit to Seawinds.' She stood up. 'Right. I'm going back to my garden. I feel like the sun is shining again.'

They watched her leave.

'She's not serious about fronting the new rellies at Seawinds, is she?' asked Jessica quietly.

Sally shrugged. 'You know my mother.'

*

The next day, Sally and Toby returned from their solicitor's office to find Mollie, Dan and Jessica sitting in the mellow afternoon light in Arcadia's garden, with Katie playing nearby. Mollie looked slightly more cheerful than she had the day before.

'Good news?' asked Jessica.

Sally smiled tentatively. 'We'd already sent him a copy of Broadbent's horrible letter to Mum, and we showed him Grandma's letter, too. He said they could make things really difficult for Broadbent, especially if we get a DNA test to prove who Mum's biological father was. He also said that everything happened so long ago it will be hard to prove, which means Broadbent's credibility could be relevant.'

'Well, you're going to love our news then!' said Jessica, nodding at Dan, who grinned and cleared his throat.

'Remember I told you about Denyse's friend, Kevin, who was asked to peer review Broadbent's research paper about mushrooms? I had a call from Denyse earlier, who told me about the review findings. Apparently while most of the research is above board and even very useful, Kevin realised that Broadbent had plagiarised another scientist's work, he stole their intellectual property. So his reputation could take a serious battering.'

'Could it mean the end of his career?' said Sally.

'It would depend on how much of the paper was plagiarised, really,' Jessica said. 'It certainly is very serious.'

'It's a small field of extremely intelligent and dedicated

scientists and mycologists and they don't take lightly to someone being unprofessional,' said Dan. 'I guess Broadbent was hoping to get this through under the radar of people like Kevin and his colleagues.'

'I'm just so pleased he got caught out,' said Mollie.

'And I'd say this just about settles things: shows we can't believe a word he says,' said Sally. 'We'll instruct our solicitor to tell Broadbent about Mollie's father, that we know about Broadbent's plagiarism, that we have absolutely no interest in negotiating with him, and we'll fight him every step of the way if he doesn't back down.'

'Too right, we will,' said Mollie, standing up with resolve in her eyes. 'The main thing is, we know that Arcadia belongs to this family, and we'll make sure it always does.'

'After all this,' said Toby, 'I'd be surprised if we ever hear from Broadbent again. He hasn't got a leg to stand on.'

'And good luck to anyone who tries to take on *this* family,' said Sally, putting an arm around Mollie's shoulder.

Mollie pulled Jessica to her other side, and the three of them embraced. 'You're part of this family, too, Jess. Thank you, girls.'

Epilogue

THEIR FOOTFALLS WERE SOFT and quiet. When someone stepped on a twig, the snap broke the reverent silence and Jessica laughed.

'Oops,' said Sally.

'Aha, is that a cue for me to speak?' Sean stopped, lifted an arm and, pulling his cloth hat from his head, said, 'We are gathered here today . . . to pay homage to . . .' He made a sweeping gesture . . . 'to this miracle of nature, which shelters and sustains all life. And brings us immense peace and joy. To the forests of the world, we salute you!'

The little group broke into applause and laughter.

'Here's to Arcadia,' said Dan, squeezing Jessica's hand.

'I really do feel myself relaxing,' Sally said as she drew

in a slow, deep breath of the crystal-clear air. 'I'm going to come here whenever I feel stressed. And I'll bring Katie here more often, too.'

'It is so special. How lucky we are that it's stayed intact,' said Mollie.

Carmen nodded. 'You can just feel and hear the trees breathing; it's utter madness to destroy places like this. Thank you so much for inviting us here, Mollie.'

'Yes, thank you, Mollie,' Sean said as he strode off towards one of the tallest trees. Then suddenly he bent down and raised his arm triumphantly. 'It's here! *Stella-Arcadiana*. It's back!'

As they clustered around the great girth of the tree where the tiny blue flower was pushing though the soil, they heard a laughing voice. Katie was skipping and running towards them, waving her arms.

'Daddy and Uncle Terry say you have to come 'cause the barbecue is ready and they're *hungry*!'

'At your command, my dear!' Sean leaned down and lifted the little girl onto his shoulders.

'First up the hill wins,' Katie called out.

Laughing, Mollie and Sally linked arms, Dan took Jessica's hand and Sean burst into song, as Carmen, fit and strong, charged ahead.

*

Dan stayed the night, and the following afternoon Sally and Jessica drove him into Burridge to sail the *Lady Jane* back to Hobart.

He held Jessica tightly. 'I'll be back in a few days, then we hit the high seas.'

Dan kissed Sally's cheek. 'Take good care of yourself, Sal. And thanks for introducing me to Arcadia.'

Sally and Jessica watched the *Lady Jane* sail down the river towards the Channel and the sea.

'Pinch me, Sal.'

'It's real. And you deserve it.'

'I'd forgotten what it feels like to be happy, gloriously, wildly, crazy happy.'

They stood there in the sunlight, the river glittering, a slight breeze ruffling its surface.

'You know what I'm thinking?' said Sally.

Jessica glanced at her. 'Let's go. Let's do it.'

They scrambled into the car and drove back the way they'd come, turning down to the river and the dock below Arcadia.

As they got out of the car, Jessica's phone rang. 'I bet it's Dan, he'll be getting out of range soon.'

'I'll go and get the key,' said Sally. She made her way to the old boatshed, lifting the key from its hook under a loose plank.

She had the electric winch going, and the *Charlotte-Ann* was sliding easily into the water as Jessica came running towards the shed.

'Hey, guess what!'

'What?'

'I got the job!'

'No way! Fantastic!' The two women hugged. 'You'd better ring Dan.'

'Yes, I will. But let's get the sails up and sorted first.'

As they'd always done, they worked in unison, finally pushing off from the little dock and nosing into the river, watching the mainsail fill and swell.

'I always think of a woman letting her hair down and shaking her head when the sails start to fill,' said Sally. 'Shall we head up past the forest? I like seeing the trees rising up the hill.'

Jessica had the tiller. 'This place is so beautiful. I couldn't be happier.'

'Me too. Jess, I've been waiting for the perfect time to tell you: I have some wonderful news. I'm pregnant! I've been feeling so tired and crook. I thought it was stress! Toby and I went to the doctor after the meeting with the solicitor.'

'Oh, wow! I'm thrilled for you,' Jessica said, hugging her friend with one arm while keeping the other hand firmly on the tiller.

Sally put her arm around Jessica's waist. 'Seems like we've lived another whole chunk of our lives together in this short time!'

'I feel like I've been around the world twice. When I look back on how bleak everything seemed when I arrived . . . I thought I'd never be truly happy again. And now your baby – a brother or sister for Katie – and meeting Dan! I don't know where it might go, but I can't think of anyone I'd rather be with, Sal. I feel so content. So safe. Thanks for putting up with me.'

'We're friends, Jess. Always will be. You'd do the same for me. End of story.'

*

Several hours later the river was turning gold, the hills darkening as they went about to head back to the dock.

Together they berthed the little boat, closed the old bleached wooden doors and hung the key back under the plank.

For a moment the girls stood in the fast-falling twilight, as those moments between sundown and night lingered, nothing moving save the shadows of the hills and trees on the smooth surface of the light-streaked river.

And as they turned and walked to the car, they heard it.

The distant warning screech of an owl, emerging from its nest in an ancient tree, to hunt in the forest it knew was home.

A suggested reading list . . .

- *Wesley the Owl* by Stacey O'Brien (2008, Simon & Schuster)

- *King of the Wilderness: The Life of Deny King* by Christobel Mattingley (2002, Text Publishing)

- *Win & Clyde* by Janet Fenton (2010, Forty South Publishing)

- *Love! Nature* and *Save Nature Now* by Dr Reese Halter (2018, both self-published)

- *Mycelium Running* by Paul Stamets (2005, Ten Speed Press)

- *Radical Mycology* by Peter McCoy (2016, Chthaeus Press)